Chapter One

Edinburgh, Scotland, Late February, 2014

Shortly before midnight the hotel fire alarm goes off, a frightful blaring noise that tears into each of the rooms, shattering sleep and creating instant panic. Polly, who had been working late on her laptop and had thrown herself fully dressed onto the bed and fallen asleep, shoots bolt upright: confused, disorientated, her heart pounding. Alarm, she thinks, alarm, shit, I have to get out, and she staggers blurrily around the room stubbing her toe painfully on the leg of the desk. She feels giddy and nauseous – shock, fear or perhaps the combination of an empty stomach and a large gin and tonic from the bar fridge before she fell asleep? Focus, she tells herself, focus: shoes, laptop, coat, handbag, passport, money, and she drags on her boots, shoves the laptop and her handbag into her backpack and heads for the door.

The passage is crowded with anxious, bleary-eyed people in various stages of dress or undress, heading like lemmings for the fire exit which is already jammed. An elderly woman, unable to push through, starts to panic, screaming and waving her arms. Alongside Polly a man wearing an army greatcoat open over cotton undershorts and a t-shirt starts shaking violently, so

1

violently that his clenched fist catches the side of her face and at the contact he begins to howl – a chilling, unearthly sound. Polly reaches out to grasp his hands and still them. His eyes rake wildly over the people pushing towards the doorway and she can see that he is elsewhere, Iraq perhaps, or Afghanistan. He looks so young, barely more than a boy, but he has known terror and seen the unspeakable. He has stopped the howling and is talking now, talking fast into the distance in a low monotone, half English, half something else, all of it incomprehensible.

'Come on,' Polly says, 'come on, you're in the hotel, it's the fire alarm, we have to get out.' But he is taller and much stronger than her, and frozen to the spot.

The panic in the passage is building, it needs only one more person to panic, to push until someone falls, or to throw a punch, and all hell will break loose. Polly tries to drag the soldier towards the fire door, but he is rigid in his traumatic state.

'Can someone help me?' she shouts, but she is shoved aside as people struggle to get to the door.

'Here,' a voice says behind her, and a man pushes his way through the crowd. 'Okay, soldier,' he says. He's taller than Polly and able to look the young man straight in the face. 'We're going to get you out of here,' he says, grabbing the soldier by the arm.

The soldier stops shaking; sweat trickles down his temples, his fixed expression seems to crack and he breaks into gut wrenching sobs, doubling over at the waist, staggering, almost knocking Polly over.

'Good,' the man says, nodding at her, 'we can move him now. We can get him down the stairs.' And awkwardly they steer him, still shaking, through the fire door. The log jam has cleared now but people are still coming down from the upper levels and they are trapped on the landing until two women in hotel bathrobes, clutching each other's arms, make a space for them to join the descent. Slowly they get the soldier down the five flights of stairs, along the passage and out into the street where the ragged mob of evacuees in pyjamas and dressing gowns waits in eerie silence by the flashing lights of two fire engines, two ambulances and three police cars. Polly and the other man lean with the soldier against the wall, while more stragglers emerge from the hotel and are steered by fire officers to join those on the opposite pavement.

It has started to snow and large flakes dance against the black sky. There is no evidence of fire, no smoke, no smell of burning, no sense of panic out here. A fire officer urges them away from the building. The soldier is calmer now, still shaking violently, but he has stifled his sobs, and is standing, Polly realises, barefoot on the icy pavement. She points down at his feet. 'Can we take him to the ambulance first, leave him there?' she asks, and the officer nods and leads them to the nearest ambulance.

'Sounds like post-traumatic stress,' says the paramedic, pulling thick white socks onto the soldier's feet. 'Good you got him out, we'll look after him now.' And he wraps a thermal blanket around the young man's shoulders.

Polly steps back and the soldier reaches out a hand. 'Thank you,' he says, tears starting again as he turns to the man who had helped them. 'Thank you, too, I'm sorry, so sorry, thank you.'

Polly takes his hand in both of hers and holds it briefly. The older man pats the soldier on his shoulder, and they turn away and cross the street to join the shivering crowd.

'Someone said it might be a false alarm,' says one of the women who had let them pass on the stairs. 'What a drama, I was really quite frightened, but my mother was positively stoic.'

Her mother, who appears to be well into her eighties, is sitting on a low wall wrapped in one of the hotel's bathrobes, sending a text on her mobile phone. 'I went through the Blitz,' she says, glancing up, 'it prepares you for emergencies. How's that poor young man?'

Polly starts to shiver and then can't stop; she stamps her feet and wraps her arms around herself as the man who helped her talks to the two women, then turns to her.

'Were you asleep with your clothes on?' he asks, looking her up and down.

She nods. 'I was. Lucky for me.'

'Indeed. I was dead to the world. Grabbed my coat and shoes and ran.'

'I grabbed my . . .' she hesitates, remembering. 'Oh shit . . . I just remembered I put my backpack down in the passage, my bag and computer are in it. Lord knows what's happened to it.'

'It'll probably just be there waiting for you when we get back in,' he says. 'You sound like an Aussie.'

Polly nods. 'And you're not a Scot.'

'No, originally from South Africa, came to London as a teenager.'

'But you're wearing an Australian coat.'

He grins. 'Well I don't think there's any law that says only Aussies can wear Drizabones. I bought it a couple of years ago in Melbourne, best coat I've ever had and very stylish over navy blue pyjamas, don't you think?' He reaches out to shake hands. 'Leo,' he says, 'Leo Croft.'

She takes his hand. 'Polly Griffin. Thanks for helping, I wouldn't have got him out on my own.'

No one seems to know what's happening, people are stamping their feet, rubbing their hands and complaining and it's another ten minutes or so before the fire chief tells them through the megaphone that this was indeed a false alarm and they can safely return to their rooms, using the stairs as the lifts are not yet reactivated.

'Come on,' Leo says, 'let's get back inside and see if we can find your backpack.'

They find it exactly where she had left it, leaning against the wall where the soldier had been standing. She sighs with relief. 'I would have been totally stuffed without this. I have a conference presentation to give tomorrow.'

He turns in surprise. 'Are you at the university?'

'Just a small conference in the arts faculty.'

'So you're an artist?'

She shakes her head, stops outside her room and pulls her

keycard out of her coat pocket. 'A writer, it's a conference on life-writing in the School of Literature and Languages. Well this is me.' She slides her card into the slot, it flashes green, and she opens the door.

He laughs. 'What a coincidence. I'm here for a symposium in the School of Social and Political Science,' he points to the door opposite hers, 'and that's my room. Look here, d'you fancy a brandy? There are a couple of miniatures in my room – good for shock and very warming.'

Polly hesitates. 'Um . . . well . . . well no thanks, I need to get some sleep, I've a big day tomorrow.'

'Not even a quick one?'

'Not even that, but thanks anyway.'

He takes a small step back. 'Ah well, I'll have to drink it all myself,' he says. 'Good night then; maybe catch you at breakfast?'

'Maybe,' she says. 'And thanks for helping with the soldier. No one else did.'

He shrugs. 'I'm glad we could do it. Good luck with your presentation.'

Inside the room Polly kicks off her boots and coat and stands in the silence, thinking. Then she goes to the bedside table and picks up the room service breakfast menu; there is still time to hang it on her door before collection time. The buffet breakfast in the dining room is excellent but the last thing she'll need in the morning is a conversation before she has to deliver her keynote. She fills out the menu, opens her door very quietly, slips it onto the handle and closes it again. Good decision. He seemed nice but right now she doesn't need any distractions.

*

Fremantle, Western Australia, Early March

Joyce, unloading the dishwasher and making breakfast at the same time, straightens up and cracks her head on the open door of the cupboard where she keeps the cups.

'Bugger!' she says, rubbing it with one hand and stirring the scrambled eggs with the other. 'It's ready,' she calls down the passage, and she piles the eggs on top of the already buttered toast and reaches for the tongs to extract tomatoes and bacon from the grill. 'Mac, c'mon, it'll get cold.'

'Coming!'

She hears the sound of his bare feet padding along the polished boards, the unmistakable rhythm of his steps, somehow entirely distinguishable from the sound of anyone else walking towards her. Soon I will have Sunday breakfasts alone for months on end, she thinks, lifting the coffee pot onto the bench top, pushing his plate and mug to the other side so that they can sit facing each other.

'Ripper!' Mac says, hitching himself onto his stool, pulling his breakfast towards him. 'I'm going to miss this.'

She nods, saying nothing, feeling suddenly crushed by the enormity of what they have agreed. Picking up her knife and fork she feels strangely revolted by the food, puts the cutlery down again, reaches for the plunger and pours their coffee.

'I've sorted out the pool pump,' Mac says. 'It's running like a dream now.'

'Good,' she nods, sipping scalding coffee and burning her mouth.

'Not eating?' he asks, pointing his fork at her plate.

'In a minute.'

'You okay?'

She nods, looking up, tries to smile but feels her face crumble, tears slide down her cheeks.

Mac swallows his food. 'Delayed reaction?'

'Yep.' She attempts to get a grip on her voice. 'It just seems such a big change, such a big thing to do.'

'It *is* a big thing to do, but it isn't something that's *undoable*,' he says. 'A year, remember, that's what we said. See how it goes for a year. It was your idea. You said it was what you wanted.'

'But you . . . you do want it too . . . don't you?'

'I do – I wouldn't have agreed otherwise.'

Joyce nods, patting her eyes on the tea towel. 'It's just that when I heard you walking along the passage I suddenly thought . . . I won't hear that . . . I won't hear his feet walking towards me for ages, months at a time. It just sort of got to me, I suppose.'

He nods, reaches across the bench top to take her hand. 'Me too. I woke up twice in a real sweat about it, nearly woke you. But we've been talking about this for ages. It's time to give it a go.'

Joyce takes a huge breath and sits up straighter. 'I know, you're right, and it's not as though we're splitting up, just that we . . .' she pauses, unable to go on.

'We're at a time in our lives when we want different things. You want to be here, I want to be down in Albany, so we're going to try it. It's just . . . well just a change in the way we live for a while.'

Joyce looks up at him, grips his hand. 'When I told you I wanted us to live apart for a while I expected a fight, I was ready for it. I suppose I didn't think you'd jump at the idea like you did . . . so now I'm wondering . . .'

Mac smiles. 'You're wondering why; but my reasons are the same as yours. Time to be alone with myself, to see how I manage living alone. We bought that place to retire to and that's what I want to do. I'm ready for it, you're not, and you said you really want to do your own thing for a bit so I'll take off and do my bloke-in-his-shed thing, and you can think about what you want to do. I can wait.'

'Suppose . . . well suppose I never want to retire there?'

He shrugs and returns to his food. 'Well let's worry about that if it happens. This is just a trial, that's all, time for both of us to do something we want, and see what happens. Just as you said.'

She looks at him. He's nearly seventy-two, six years older than me, she thinks, but he looks so much younger and fitter. How has that happened, why haven't I noticed that before?

'You're going to do something new,' he says. 'Something entirely your own.'

She smiles. 'Yes . . . well, when I work out what that is. Should we ring the kids and tell them what we've decided?'

'I think we should get Ben and Nessa round for a barbecue. Shame we can't get Lucy and Kara at the same time but I doubt they'd want to trek back from uni for this. Anyway, we'll tell Ben and Nessa and we can talk to Gemma on Skype, either before that or straight after, then they'll all hear it round about the same time.'

'Okay. How d'you think they'll take it? It might be a bit confronting for them, they might not approve.'

'Bugger that,' Mac says, laughing now. 'They've got their own lives and we have ours. But I think they'll be fine. Let's pick a date in March. Okay?'

And they stand together in front of the calendar.

'End of the month . . . I'll leave on the twenty-fifth,' Mac says.

'It's seems awfully soon. Less than three weeks.'

He puts his arm around her shoulders. 'Now that we've made the decision we need to act on it. Before either of us has too many disturbing second thoughts.'

She nods and leans against him. 'It's not about you,' she says. 'You know that, don't you?'

He hugs her to him. 'We've been through all this, it's not about you either. It's about giving each other some space to do what we want.' They stand there hugging each other for a moment. 'Will you tell Stella yet?' Mac asks.

'When she gets back from Albany next week, I think, but not anyone else, not until we've told the family. Stella will miss you.'

'She'll certainly have something to say about it.'

'She'll think we're being very grown-up! Very *modern*. I'll bet you ten bucks that's what she says. Ha, you're being very *modern*.'

Mac laughs. 'That's exactly what she'll say. I'm glad you'll have her there next door.'

'Me too. But you . . .' she stops herself from saying that he won't have anyone nearby, because somehow she knows that he doesn't need that, doesn't need someone to be there next door for him. He can do this, he can be on his own. What she doesn't know is whether she can do that too.

'And the others? Polly? Helen and Dennis?' Mac asks.

'Polly's away for a while yet. And I don't want to tell Helen and Dennis until we've told the family. They'll have far too much to say about it. I think we'll tell them last!'

Mac sips his coffee, watching her. The phone rings and he slides off his stool to answer it. 'You do know that I love you as much as ever, don't you?' he says.

'I do,' she says, calmer now.

Mac picks up the phone. 'Helen,' he says a moment later, taking the receiver away from his ear. 'Would we like to have fish and chips down at Cicerello's this evening?'

*

All the restaurants at the fishing boat harbour are packed but typically Helen had called earlier and managed to snag a cancellation. They sit now, at a table by the window, sharing a nicely chilled bottle of Semillon, four old friends very much at ease, and greet the arrival of their food with enthusiasm. They had lived next door to each other for almost three decades until a few years ago when Helen felt she needed a change – a down-size from the rambling old nineteen-thirties house in South Fremantle. She'd wanted somewhere modern, easier to manage. So they had sold up and moved to a large and elegant apart-ment in North Fremantle, overlooking the river.

'How's Stella?' Helen asks.

'Fine,' Joyce says. 'She's in Albany filming for the new series of *Cross Currents*.'

Helen rolls her eyes. 'I thought her character died in the last series.'

Joyce nods. 'She did but she's back to do a haunting.'

'I wonder why she bothers,' Helen says, 'what is she now – eighty? It's just attention-seeking. I wonder she hasn't got over that yet.'

'Stella's an actor, Helen,' Mac says, pouring the wine. 'It's been her life. Why should she give it up if they still want her?'

Helen shrugs and looks out of the window. 'Crazy if you want my opinion.'

Joyce is about to defend Stella but stops herself; she really doesn't want to get into an argument with Helen in this sort of mood. For some time now Helen has been increasingly snappy and critical, delivering her judgements or comments without a shred of sensitivity. Throughout their long friendship she has always had a foot-in-mouth problem, often apparently unaware of how hurtful she can be. And in recent years she's grown harsher.

'Do you feel that getting old gives you the right to be *so* blunt?' Joyce had asked her recently. 'Sometimes I wonder if you realise the effect you have on people.'

Helen had laughed. 'I've always been blunt, no bullshit. Tell it like it is. You know me well enough by now, Joyce,' she'd said.

And Joyce, who did indeed know her very well, had decided not to pursue it. This is who Helen is, she'd told herself, she's important to me, I know what to ignore and what to take seriously. But these days it's becoming harder for her to tolerate Helen's blundering judgements and evident thoughtlessness.

'We got a bit of good news,' Dennis says. 'Damian and Ellie and the kids are coming home for a visit at the end of March.'

Joyce has a brief flash of nostalgia for the days when Helen and Dennis lived next door, when Ben and Gemma grew up alongside Damian and Nick, went to the same school and when, for such a long time, life had seemed like an endless series of sleepovers in one house or the other. Those days when she and Helen had been so much closer and Helen had seemed so much easier to get on with.

'Lovely,' she says, 'you must be pleased. We must get yours and ours together, come round to our place and Mac can do one of his famous barbecues . . .' She stops, looks up at him, suddenly realising, 'oh . . . but you'll be gone by then.'

'Gone?' Helen says. 'Where to?'

Mac raises his eyebrows, and Joyce flushes, then shrugs. 'Um . . . well, we're sort of . . .'

Mac takes a sip of his wine, puts down his glass and clears his throat. 'We were going to wait a while to tell you, until after we'd told the family, but as . . .' he hesitates.

'As I've just blurted it out we might as well tell you now,' Joyce says, her face burning.

'Yes, we'll come clean,' Mac says and starts to explain, laying it out carefully: a year living apart, Joyce here, himself in the cottage in Albany. An experiment, see how it goes for a while . . .

'You're splitting up,' Helen says, her eyes darkening.

'No,' they say in unison.

'Just spending time apart because we want to do different things, be in different places,' Mac adds. 'But I'll pop back from time to time and Joyce will come and visit me in Albany.'

Dennis raises his eyebrows.

'Well that's how it'll end,' Helen says. 'A year and then you'll be splitting up. It's a terrible idea. You must be mad.'

This is 'angry Helen' whom they both know well, but rarely is her anger directed at them. Joyce feels Mac stiffen in response. 'We're not splitting up, Helen,' she says, 'that's not what either of us wants. Just a bit of space for a while.'

'And then what?' Dennis asks.

Mac shrugs. 'We don't know yet. One thing at a time.'

Silence.

'Space!' Helen says, in disgust. 'What do Ben and Vanessa, and Gemma think about this? I bet they're not too happy.'

'As I said, we haven't told them yet,' Joyce says. 'So if you run into Ben or Nessa, please don't say anything. We'll call Gemma the same day we tell them.'

Mac steps in. He talks about renovating the Albany cottage.

'And you?' Helen barks, looking at Joyce. 'What's your great new plan for living alone?'

Joyce is tense now, hurt, annoyed. 'Not sure yet,' she says. 'I want to do something new, different. I've thought about getting a stall in the markets, or maybe even going back to uni.'

'Oh my god, now I've heard it all. You're both having a delayed mid-life crisis. I never heard of anything so silly.'

Joyce had known the conversation, when it came, would be difficult, but she hadn't imagined this level of hostility.

Dennis puts his hand on his wife's arm as if to restrain her. 'Calm down, Helen, calm down.' He looks across at Mac. 'It does sound a bit like seventies hippie bullshit if you ask me.'

'Mate, we *didn't* ask you,' Mac says. 'We *told* you our plan; that's it. End of story. If you and Helen don't like it that's a shame, but this is what's happening.'

There is an awkward silence. Helen draws up her shoulders, glaring at Joyce, then tosses her serviette on top of the food she has barely touched. She gets to her feet and grabs her bag from the back of her chair. 'That's it, I won't be part of this conversation anymore. Come along, Dennis.'

'Well I don't think that's . . .' Dennis says pushing his chair back slightly from the table.

'Then I'll go alone,' Helen says. She leans towards Joyce. 'You'll regret this, don't say I didn't warn you,' and she turns sharply and strides out of the restaurant.

Dennis glances from her across to Mac and Joyce. 'Er . . . well it looks like we're off,' he says. And he shrugs, raises his hand in a half-wave and follows Helen out of the restaurant.

Mac turns to Joyce. 'Well that was weird.'

She sighs. 'My fault. I should have told Helen in small increments.'

'You weren't going to tell her at all just yet.'

'Mmm, opened my mouth without thinking, sorry.'

He shrugs. 'Can't be helped, they had to know sometime. They'll get over it . . . at least Dennis will. But Helen seems to have taken it as a personal insult.'

They finish their food and the wine in comparative silence

and Joyce, pushing her empty plate aside, contemplates the fact that her own anger has completely subsided and she feels nothing at all.

'You know what?' she says. 'I don't give a shit what they think.' She raises her glass. 'Here's to the year of living dangerously.'

*

Helen wakes at midnight to the sound of Dennis snoring. He has rolled onto his back and is lying there alongside her, occupying more than his share of the bed, mouth wide open, emitting a series of snorts and whistles.

'Shh-shh!' she hisses. 'Shut up, Dennis, roll over.' She nudges him in the ribs and he grunts loudly and rolls onto his side, facing away from her. She lies there waiting for silence, for him to rearrange his limbs and his breathing, knowing that even when he does she won't get back to sleep. Eventually she sits up, sighing, swings her legs out of the bed, puts on her dressing gown, pads out to the kitchen and leans on the worktop, gazing out across the moonlit river. They are high up here, on the fourth floor with gorgeous views up and down the river, and across to the tree-clad East Fremantle escarpment, dotted with elegant houses. Any time, day or night, there is always something happening – even now a couple of small boats are moving swiftly up river, and others bob around on their moorings at the jetty. A few cars creep across the traffic bridge and beyond that a train glides across the rail bridge and slips out of sight. This was what she had wanted, this spacious apartment with these views, a short walk from the centre of town, and a short drive from Emerald Street.

She had wanted an end to living in an old house which, although it had never been a thing of beauty like Joyce and Mac's place, had served them well for years. Built in the nineteen--thirties it lacked any of the attractive art deco features of some others of that period, but it was spacious and practical, and sat on a very large block of land. It had been a sound investment in the long term and they had turned it into a comfortable family home, but over the years Helen had struggled to make it look the way she wanted. Perhaps an expert with a big budget could have transformed it but Helen couldn't, and by the time the kids had left home, Dennis, who had grown accustomed to going along with what she wanted, dug in his heels.

'I'm not spending thousands on some tosser who'll turn it into a place where I can't feel at home,' he'd said.

But Helen was desperate for some sort of change. She felt trapped by the house. She had had enough of the skirtings that never quite met the floorboards, the window frames that were always slightly wonky, and the cockroaches and mice that found every crack and cranny. She was sick of the dust that the house seemed to generate, the creaks and drafts, the constant maintenance. She was sick of the endless lists of things that needed doing. She had wanted gleaming tiles, smooth white walls, pale carpets, pale fabrics, a perfect modern kitchen and two and a half bathrooms, top of the range air-conditioning and heating, lots of built-in cupboards and robes. And an end to the garden with its wobbly brick paths, overgrown natives, and ancient roses with thorns like daggers, where everything seemed to grow faster than she could cut it back. She had been so over it all she couldn't wait to escape.

It had been fun when they were younger, when Damian and Nick were kids, and when Joyce and Mac bought the house next door. Ben and Gemma were similar in age and all the children moved freely between the two homes; sometimes it seemed as though they were just one big family. But the kids grew up and left; Damian eventually married Ellie, got a high profile job in oil and gas, and they and the two children are now in Dubai. Nick, still single, is in his early forties, and seems more interested in studying bats in a cave in South Australia than thinking about a relationship. There had been a time when Helen had thought that Nick and Gemma might get together. They were always around together as teenagers and Helen loved Gemma. She had always wanted a daughter, and Gemma had filled a little of that space for her. Back then Helen and Joyce had cautiously speculated on the possibility of it being more than friendship and Helen had fondly imagined a beautiful white wedding, but it never happened. Gemma and Nick remained close friends, but that was where it stopped. Nick ended up in weird places across the country recording bat movements, and a few years later Gemma took off for a job in Geneva.

Helen sighs. Yes, she had wanted this place so much, and now, five years later, here she is in the middle of the night, gazing longingly across the river, back to the old part of the city, imagining what lies beyond her line of sight: the leafy streets, the elegant old red brick and limestone houses and weatherboard cottages of South Fremantle. The cafés and eccentric little shops, the bakeries, the Italian deli, all just minutes from the cappuccino strip, the bookshop, the banks, the markets.

'I wish you weren't going,' Joyce had said at the time. 'I'll really miss you, but if it's what you want . . .'

It had been, but she hadn't expected to feel like this – like an outsider, cut off from her best friend and her neighbours, watching those precious relationships stretch and fade away from her for lack of daily attention. She had thought it would last forever, that she and Dennis could move and that everything would otherwise stay the same, but somehow they haven't. Living next door, or close by in the same street, is so different: popping in for a coffee, borrowing or lending things, slipping through the side-gate that Dennis and Mac had made in the dividing fence, sitting on the verandah with a bottle of wine on summer evenings. She hadn't realised how she would miss all that, how impossible it would be to sustain or recapture its essence once they had left. She hadn't anticipated the boredom, the lassitude that so often settled on her for days on end. She had expected freedom but found herself trapped.

Helen opens the fridge and takes out a half-empty bottle of wine. She'd polished off the first half before she went to bed. She hesitates, glances guiltily over her shoulder, pours some into a glass, and takes bottle and glass with her to the sofa. That stupid business in the restaurant had given her a headache and she plumps up a cushion and stretches out, half sitting, half lying, wondering if she can take something for her head or whether she's already had too much wine for that. Ah well, the view, she thinks, that's one thing that's always here, the million-dollar view, from this open living area, the kitchen and their bedroom. The view and the clean lines, the minimal housework, the domestic convenience of it all, but you can only look so long at the view, and five years on it hasn't even started to feel like home. She has grown to take those things for granted now and yearns instead for some of the earthy, chaotic aspects of life in Emerald Street. She had changed their lifestyle and changed herself to suit it. Previously content with her mix of casual clothes and a few more formal pieces Helen had taken pride in the way that her height and naturally slim build enabled her to look pretty good in most things. But since casting off the trappings of that life she has been opting for a more upmarket, dressy look, paying too much for everything, especially shoes, shoes, shoes. From a perfectly adequate and well-chosen wardrobe she now has two wardrobes of expensive and fashionable clothes that she rarely wears. It was how she had envisaged the new life that she and Dennis would have here, but in reality their way of living has changed little except to be more isolated and less relaxed.

Helen knows that she'd behaved badly when Joyce and Mac explained what they were going to do. It had touched the raw nerve of her discontent, and she'd felt it as another loss. She had forced a change in her own and Dennis's lives, and it was a bad move, although she won't admit that. Now Joyce is planning a big change without discussing it, mentioning it only by mistake. What Joyce wants will simply widen the gap between them. And Joyce and Mac's decision feels deeply personal, as though it is aimed at her and her alone, as though Joyce is saying: well you're the one who moved, now wait and see what I can do. Helen had wanted to slap her tonight, and she knows she did that, not physically but with her words and the way she left the table. Maybe she was a bit over the top walking out of the restaurant like that but, really, Joyce should have discussed it with her. It came as such a shock.

Helen hears a step behind her, tucks the glass and bottle on the floor under her legs and turns. Dennis in his pyjama trousers is standing in the doorway, rubbing his balding head and yawning.

'What's up?' he asks. 'Can't sleep? Or are you sick or something?'

Sick, Helen thinks, sick of this life, sick of you.

'Can't sleep,' she says. 'Go to bed, I'll be back soon.'

Dennis yawns and shuffles to the bathroom and she hears him peeing copiously against the porcelain. Then he belches, huffs and puffs, and she waits angrily for the sound of him washing his hands, but of course he doesn't. 'Fuck off, Dennis,' she murmurs, rage rising up within her. 'I want something to change, I don't want to be in this life any longer and I can't bear to think about what the next twenty years will be like.'

Chapter Two

The trouble with Albany, Stella thinks, is that even in summer that wretched wind off the Southern Ocean can freeze your bones. Everyone goes on about the purity of the air but they fail to mention that it comes directly from the Antarctic. I'm too old for this: too old to be sitting here at five in the morning, barefoot, wearing a long white nightdress waiting for the director to decide that the light is right for him to start shooting. They'd already made a start this morning but bloody Gareth decided to take a break. It wouldn't be so bad, she thinks, if she was over there with the others, but Gareth had set her up here on this great expanse of rock called The Gap, above all this wild and churning white water, and then there'd been this hoo-ha about having to wait for the light.

'You stay here, Stella,' he'd said. 'I know you hate having to get back and forth across the rocks. One of the minions will bring you some tea.' And he'd shaken out a blanket and wrapped it around her shoulders.

Stella has spent much of her working life waiting for directors to make decisions about light or distance, background distractions or minor adjustments to costume, make-up or hair. It's the nature

19

of television and she is an old hand: costume drama, soaps, crime, and commercials for everything from dog food to cosmetics, sliced bread to car tyres and, in more recent years, retirement villages and incontinence pads. She'd learned early that physical stamina, emotional restraint, and an ability to tolerate the worst excesses of fellow actors, directors and crew were as important as learning her lines and turning up on time. It was always a waiting game: waiting for her agent, waiting for directors, waiting for yet another take, or for some fresh-faced prima donna of either sex to get over themselves, waiting for the last take and the ride back to the accommodation, waiting to get paid. After this, she thinks, it is definitely time to say no. She's already retired twice and been lured back, first by an actor turned director with whom she'd had a wild affair decades earlier, and this time by the revival of *Cross Currents,* a long running soap opera in which she'd been killed off some months before the whole series was canned.

'Yes, I know they're bringing it back, but I've already died, remember?' Stella had said when her agent called her out of the blue.

'If I understand it correctly,' Bethany had said, 'they want your old character, Cassandra, to be . . . well hang on, I'll read you part of the email. What it says is, *the presence of Cassandra in the revival series was inspired by the meaning of the character's name. She is not just the woman who died in the final weeks of the last series, but a prophet who has passed over and weaves her way through the lives of the characters, providing narrative links and flashbacks, and extracting revenge on characters whom she believes have done her wrong in the past. We will see many old scores settled here, and Stella's interpretation of Cassandra will obviously be the key to the character's authenticity.* Gareth Stokes is directing,' Bethany continued, 'and he's insisting you're the only person who can carry it off.'

'It sounds abysmal; he probably thinks I'm the only person fool enough to take it on,' Stella had replied. 'I'd heard he'd gone a bit feral with the supernatural recently. Give me twenty-four hours to think about it.'

She had put the phone down and gone next door to ask Polly what she thought. Their friendship goes back years to when they met on the set of a crime series for which Polly had written several episodes.

Polly had hooted with laughter. 'Bloody Gareth,' she'd said, getting a bottle of gin out of the fridge. 'Bloody Gareth. But of course you must do it. Honestly, Stella, it'll only work if it's you because all the old fans will be so thrilled to see you they'll be prepared to suspend their disbelief.'

'Is that supposed to be some sort of compliment?' Stella had asked.

'Well – yes of course. They loved Cassandra because of what you made of her. I bet Gareth had them write Cassandra back in and if you don't agree they'll have to drop that strand of the narrative. Go on, do it.'

'I've already retired, twice.'

'Third time lucky then! Go on, one last fling. Cheers!'

So here she is now, a blanket around her shoulders in the early morning light, waiting for bloody Gareth. It's not as though they're not looking after her properly – but this is not natural territory for the elderly. Younger members of the cast and crew nip back and forth across the rocks, agile as mountain goats, carrying clipboards or clapper boards, light meters and cameras, mikes and mufflers. But at eighty there is nothing like rough terrain, segmented with gashes where white water boils up with spray, to make one feel one's age and potential instability.

Stella sighs. 'Polly, where are you now?' she murmurs, but she knows where Polly is because she got a text from her yesterday, with a picture of her sitting on a wall in Edinburgh, the castle in the background. As Polly doesn't know anyone in Edinburgh, Stella would like to know who took that photograph, because even at her age, she can tell a selfie from a snap taken by someone else; someone who has managed to capture Polly with the smile usually reserved for her oldest friends.

Stella shivers and pulls the blanket around her. One of the young goats . . . oh dear, whatever is her name? . . . is heading towards her with a large mug in her hand, and something else.

'Oh! Tim Tams, *six* of them, darling, *thank* you. Don't tell Gareth you brought me so many, he'll sack you for blowing the budget.'

'He's not that bad,' says the young woman. 'He told me to buy in a lot as they're your favourites.'

They turn together to look at Gareth, who waves and mimes chomping on a biscuit. 'Not long now, Stella, couple of minutes,' he calls to her.

'Bloody Gareth,' she says, waving back, 'that means quarter of an hour at least, don't you think . . . um . . .'

'Trixie,' the girl supplies.

'Of course, sorry, dear . . . Trixie. My memory's getting worse.'

'Why does everyone call him Bloody Gareth?' Trixie asks. 'They say it all the time as though it's his name.'

'It's sort of become his name,' Stella explains, 'largely because he messes us all about so much, keeps everyone waiting, changes his mind a million times, does lots of unnecessary takes. He's good but bloody annoying.'

Trixie is looking at her, Stella realises, with the sort of affectionate bewilderment with which young people observe the elderly, as though they are a completely different species.

'Well he thinks the world of you,' Trixie says. 'He was telling me that you were in *Neighbours* for a while.'

'I was indeed. But that's a very long time ago.'

'Did you actually *meet* Kylie Minogue?'

'Of course, we worked together for several months, and lovely Jason too. So sweet, both of them, they weren't famous then. Jason was especially good in the part where he murdered that young girl . . .'

'Was there a murder in *Neighbours*?' Trixie asks in surprise. 'I never knew that. I thought his character, Scott – wasn't it? – I thought he was a really sweet sort of . . .'

Stella looks at Trixie in confusion as the girl continues, then she cuts across her. 'You're right, Trixie, of course you are. Silly me, I got it mixed up with something else Jason was in.' But she can't for the life of her remember what production that was. She flushes with embarrassment, she's done this quite a bit recently, muddled things, people, names. Sometimes she thinks she's actually making up things that have never happened. And she overhears herself talking like the stereotype of an old actress in a soap which, of course, is just what she is at this moment, but normally she doesn't talk like this, the little rhetorical flourishes, slightly unnatural intonations. Is she becoming one of those tedious old theatrical pains in the bum, boring everyone with their memories, big noting themselves with name-dropping and grand gestures? That's not who she is, nor what she wants to be. She wants to be herself: Stella, the old woman who lives in the house with the blue front door, Joyce and Mac on one side, Polly on the other. Stella, eaten up with arthritis, reading three or four books a week, making her way slowly down to the Italian deli in Wray Avenue for her shopping, and usually in bed by nine o'clock. Here she is an old trouper, drinks in the pub at the end of the day, joking with the make-up artist, returning calmly to take after take, and speculating with June, who's in charge of wardrobe, about who among the younger actors is sleeping with whom. But this other persona keeps creeping up on her: Stella – ageing star of stage and screen with all the stereotypical and pretentious baggage. I'm living a double life, she tells herself; what I need is to go home and lie down for a long time in a darkened room.

'So were you . . . like, really famous or something?'

'Famous or something . . . mmm . . . well how about we go for moderately well known,' Stella says. 'You know, one of those actors you see in small roles in lots of things but they're never important enough for you to actually remember their names.'

Trixie gives her a long look. 'Right,' she says, 'probably my mum would've seen you, or my nan.'

'Probably.'

'Gareth says we might have to wind up at nine 'cos there's some sort of problem, and if it doesn't get sorted we can all have the rest of the day off,' Trixie says.

Stella rolls her eyes. 'Does he indeed? Well that's a nice thought but I wouldn't start making plans, Trixie, don't ring your boyfriend or anything yet. We'll probably still be here into the afternoon if Bloody Gareth runs true to form.'

*

Edinburgh

The morning after the fire alarm Polly had eaten breakfast in her room while going through her presentation for the umpteenth time. She was not new to conferences and had, in the past, been a confident speaker. Back then, when she was young and very full of herself, she could fly through any sort of presentation by the seat of her pants and still make an impression. She'd been writing for television then, and at one time – for a very short time – she had been considered the wild child of the industry, for her gritty, often bloodthirsty dramas set in the back streets of Kings Cross, or harsh, remote locations in the outback. But in her forties she'd begun to feel she had had enough of the dark side.

'I can't face shedding any more blood or planning any more murders,' she'd told Stella at the wrap party for a short and particularly brutal series set during the gold rush. 'I want to do something nice, a love story maybe, a mild family soap perhaps.'

'But you're so good at it, darl,' Stella had said, 'you've got a reputation for blood and guts.'

'Well that's just it,' Polly had said. 'I don't think I want that sort of reputation. I'm a bit over being controversial and having to defend my penchant for brutality. I think I'll take some time off.'

The wild child period had been great financially, and she had headed for Europe, managing to pick up bits of work along the way. In Paris for three months she'd rented a cramped, rather damp room off the Boulevard St Michel, and fallen for the charms of Shakespeare and Company. There she discovered new writers and classics in both English and French, titles and authors she'd never heard of, and she would lose herself for hours among the packed shelves before finding a spot in the nearby café to dunk croissants in huge bowls of coffee, and read about everything but crime and violence. She learned a lot in those weeks, especially about the women who lived on the Left Bank in the nineteen-twenties and thirties. There were writers and artists, political activists, dancers, singers and musicians, and it was the minor characters that enthralled her. A new world of possibilities opened up for her. While she knew then that she would probably still have to make her living by writing for television, her new passion was to read and learn more about the lives of some of those women and to write about them.

Back in Australia two years later she had met up again with Stella on the set of *Neighbours*. By then she had completed a year's diploma in life-writing and had started to write a short biography of a barely known dancer. A stint on *Neighbours* helped to restore the bank balance, and when the biography was published, first in England and later in France, it was a surprising success. Two years later she followed it with another on a group of women who had formed an erotic writing club in Montmartre in the early thirties. It had been the end of television and the end of big money, but there were other, more lasting and satisfying rewards, and she began to teach some writing classes to top up her income.

When Stella had first decided to retire, almost twenty years ago, she had given up the lease on her apartment in Melbourne and moved back to her own house in Fremantle, and it was this that had brought Polly back on a visit to the west coast for the first time in many years. She had arrived there as a teenager in the early sixties with her parents and her older brother, Alistair. The whole family had been shocked by the long and relentlessly hot Perth summers. Fortunately, within a few months, their father, an engineer, landed a job in New South Wales, and the family had crossed the Nullarbor in a Kombi, and settled in Newcastle. Neither Polly nor Alistair held any affection for the west, and only returned if or when required for work reasons. But when Polly flew over to visit Stella for a long weekend, she discovered a different place from the one she remembered. That weekend she had fallen in love with Fremantle and stayed on for two weeks, leaving with a sense of regret and a longing to return to the port city, to the forests of the southwest and the sharp new sophistication of the growing capital. She started talking casually about perhaps moving west. Just over a year later Stella called to tell her that the house next door to her own was for sale, and Polly had booked a flight and made the fastest decision of her life. The house was an old limestone cottage, a neglected duplicate of Stella's, and three months later she was winding up her Melbourne life. It was 1996, she was forty-five and felt closer to her true self, the self she wanted to be, than ever before.

Within months of the move she found contract work teaching a life-writing class for three hours a week at a local university. One year later she couldn't imagine how she had ever sat down every day to create stories in which people were bashed to death, had their teeth pulled out with pliers or their fingers chopped off by villains, nor how she had coped with the volatile environment of television. She had opted for simplicity and a slower pace and she loved it. More books followed and she was developing a significant profile. But she never regained the brash self-confidence of her youth. She had chosen a fluid discipline with complex roots, a fertile battleground for would-be experts, and one that was increasingly popular and contentious, and she frequently felt like a fraud. Now, each time she delivers a lecture, a talk, or occupies a seat on a panel at a writers' festival, she has to psych herself up for the performance in ways she never needed to do in the past.

And so, that morning in Edinburgh, as she had taken the lift to the ground floor, she was focused solely on her keynote and the fact that by eleven-thirty it would be over and she could relax.

'Ah, Polly – I wondered if I might run into you again,' a voice called as she crossed the hotel lobby. 'I assume you're heading for the university? Let's walk together.'

Polly's stomach sank. He . . . this man, he was perfectly nice but she wished he would go away.

'The thing is,' she'd said, looking straight at him, 'I am anxious about my keynote. I need to keep my head focused on it so I'm not really in the mood to talk.'

'Me too,' he had said. 'Pre-performance anxiety. Should we walk in silence?'

'Can the silence be relied on?'

'Women usually accuse me of too much of it.'

She took a deep breath; there seemed to be no escape. 'Okay,' she said, 'let's give it a go.'

And together they passed through the revolving doors out into the brilliant sunlight of a bitterly cold morning, their feet crunching across the snowy pavement, and not a word passed between them until they reached the point at which their paths diverged.

Leo paused. 'Good luck,' he said. 'I hope you're a smash hit.'

Polly smiled and managed a small laugh. 'You too.'

He nodded towards a café across the road. 'Would you like to have lunch over there later?'

It was her need to stay focused, to concentrate without distraction, that had made her decline the brandy last night, and stay in hiding this morning. But he seemed genuine, he could cope with silence, and apparently he shared her professional anxiety. She suspected he also had a sense of humour.

'Twelve-thirty?'

He nodded. 'Perfect, see you then.' And he was gone, striding briskly away across the snowy campus.

Now, three days later as she puts the last of her clothes into her suitcase and walks around the room checking that she's leaving nothing behind, she realises that she's quite disappointed that this is the last time she'll see him. By chance they are booked on the same flight to London so are sharing a taxi to the airport. Yesterday she had texted Stella a photograph Leo had taken of her sitting on a low wall with the castle in the background. *Great conference, fabulous city, pleasant company,* she had written. *Leaving here tomorrow for Paris, then to Bali.* Since that first walk in the snow they had not only eaten lunch but also taken a tour of the castle, eaten two dinners and breakfasts and sat up late in the bar talking.

'Are you going straight home from Heathrow?' he had asked her last night.

Polly shook her head. 'No, I'm going to Paris, I've some research to do there, then on to Bali for a holiday on the way home.'

'Pity,' he'd said. 'I thought I might persuade you to stay on in London for a while. I've so enjoyed your company.'

'Me too,' she'd said, 'but I have commitments in Paris.' This was not really true; she was her own boss and committed only to getting into some document archives, and doing what she called her 'street level' research – quietly walking the streets where the women she's writing about had lived. It's something she must do alone, imagining herself living there among them in the twenties, in a small boarding house or apartment, choosing croissants in the bakery, walking to visit friends on wintry days, or in spring sunshine. Ordering coffee for breakfast, or buying flowers from the street stall. She could postpone it for a couple of days but her head is in the right place for all this now, she's hungry for it and knows how much she will regret it if she lets anything get in the way. Too often in the past she has put aside her work, her consuming passions, to fit in with someone else's plans, and the someone else has always been a man who seemed different, interesting, who seemed to offer a deeper connection.

Keep your safe distance, she reminds herself. But as she lugs her case down to reception she can't help wishing that they'd had a little more time in which she could have got to know him better.

Three hours later, in the chaos of Heathrow, their ways finally part, she to St Pancras to catch the Eurostar, Leo for the underground to Paddington and his nearby flat.

'It's been terrific,' he says, leaning forward to kiss her on the cheek. 'Had I been twenty, even ten, years younger I would have tried to seduce you.'

She laughs. 'I'm glad you didn't, I'm really over all that.'

'Oh, don't kid yourself,' he says, laughing, 'we never get over it – if we do we might as well be dead.'

'Speak for yourself,' she says with a grin.

'I am,' he says. 'We're not all that old, you and I, Polly, there is much to look forward to. I'll be in touch.'

And putting his hand up to her cheek, he smiles, turns and walks away.

Men, Polly thinks, are so full of shit. But he really was rather nice and the conversations were great. Outside the snow that had closed the airport for some hours the previous day is rapidly disappearing, washed away by torrential rain. Life is full of interesting encounters, that's all it was, and she packs it away in her memory, and turns her mind to Paris, and then to Bali, to the house on the edge of the forest, to peaceful days, and equally good company.

Chapter Three

South Fremantle, Western Australia, March

The stillness of the house is eerie. It's odd really because Mac is not a noisy person, he doesn't raise his voice or stomp around the place banging doors; he walks quietly, and his voice is well modulated. True he has an irritating humming habit, soft but entirely tuneless. Joyce feels that the house is in a state of uneasy stillness, as though it's waiting for him to come back to breathe life into it.

It's only two weeks since he left and already she feels like a fraud. She'd wanted space to sort herself out. Now that she's got all this space and silence she doesn't know what to do with it. There is a certain pleasure in the tidiness, in not having to think about shopping, in being able to ignore mealtimes and snack when it suits her, but this sense of liminality, of being on the threshold of something without knowing what it is, is far from comfortable. The ideas she has toyed with for months, years even, seem pointless, silly, or just too hard. It's as though the day that Mac drove away, the ute packed with his clothes, books, tools and god knows what else, the change became not only real, but challenging; her motivation disappeared, almost as though Mac had packed that as well. She hasn't told him that of course, she hasn't told anyone.

'Gracious me, how exciting,' Stella had said when they had told her about their plan over dinner on the evening after she got back from Albany. 'How very modern!'

And Joyce and Mac had laughed. 'We guessed you'd say that,' Mac said, 'we would have put a bet on it had there been anyone to bet against us.'

If they had done something like this years ago, Joyce thinks, Helen would have been the first person she'd have told; in fact she'd probably have talked to Helen about it before she and Mac decided anything. They would have sat together with mugs of coffee on the back verandah of one of the two houses, and talked about it. Helen would have been supportive, encouraging, a little too brisk but nonetheless understanding. But Helen has changed, and Joyce is still trying to work out quite how and why. Helen and Dennis had been living in the house next door for a couple of years before Joyce and Mac moved into theirs. Mac had seen it first and Joyce had been sceptical of his enthusiasm until he took her there.

'It needs a lot doing to it,' she'd said, 'but I adore it. Can we afford it?'

That was before the America's Cup came to Fremantle and prices shot through the roof. A few years later and they couldn't have dreamed of affording it. It was a lovely old federation home, which had been sadly neglected, and she knew it would need heaps of work. But she fell for it that first day and it has been a wonderful house for children and later for grand-children. Ben had been ten and Gemma just eight when they moved here. Ben and Vanessa had met and married young, and their two daughters, Kara and Lucy, have both left home: Kara to study journalism in Sydney and Lucy, health sciences in Newcastle. Gemma, still single, is a research scientist, and has been working for the past seven years with a private foundation that's affiliated to the World Health Organisation, in Geneva. Mac and Joyce have been over there several times for visits, but Gemma has been home only once. Sometimes Joyce wonders if her daughter has gone for good; Gemma loves the job and she has a full and interesting life in Europe.

When Helen had announced that she and Dennis were selling and the estate agent's sign would go up the following day, Joyce had imagined all that shared history of being next-door neighbours disappearing. The lives of their two families had leaked into each other in such an enriching way and she'd felt sick with despair at the prospect of the change.

'What about Damian and Ellie, and the baby, and didn't you say that they want another one quite soon? Wouldn't they want to be near you? I mean I know both Damian and Ellie are younger than Ben and Nessa, but they can't leave it too long if they want a second child,' she'd said. 'And Nick? If he ever gets fed up with counting bats in caves he might get married and have children.'

Helen had laughed then. 'What woman would put up with Batman? When he's not in a cave with them he's examining their dead bodies or their eating habits in the lab at uni. Remember when we thought he and Gemma might get together? Well that went nowhere. And Damian's applied for a transfer to Sydney, he reckons it's the next step towards a promotion overseas. If he gets that then he and Ellie reckon it'll set them up for life.'

'But wouldn't it be somewhere in the Middle East?' Joyce had asked.

'That's what they want,' Helen had said. 'They want to do several years out there. The lifestyle with those big companies is quite privileged: big money, big rent-free homes, swimming pools, heaps of perks.'

Helen had been adamant that the move was what she wanted, and Joyce had felt selfish for minding that her friend could do this without even a dash of regret. Her sense of an ending was so acute that she had asked Mac to close off the gate in the fence. Something important was changing; something they'd never get back.

'Besides,' Helen had said, 'you'll still have Stella and Polly, and some other lovely family might move in next door.'

Now Joyce believes that while she had always known that something would be lost in the process, Helen had assumed that nothing would change. With the closing of one gate she looks to the other side of the property, to the gate they'd created to Stella's garden, and beyond that to Polly's.

Helen and Dennis had sold their house to a local architect, who had knocked it down, subdivided the block and built a large and elegant place for himself on one, and a small but charming house, referencing art deco style and incorporating recycled doors, and leadlight windows, on the block adjacent to Joyce and Mac's home. This he kept as an investment property and since it was completed three years ago there has been a series of short term tenants, the latest of whom – both flight attendants – were pleasant, but so frequently absent they might as well not have been there at all. Since they moved out a couple of months ago the house has been empty.

Joyce sighs and returns to the list of possibilities written on the blackboard that Mac had fixed to the kitchen wall when the children were teenagers. Some of the things she'd had in mind have now been crossed off: leasing a stall in the market, selling sarongs and scarves, maybe other clothes. That had been top of her list for a long time until she had actually looked into it and discovered the crippling rents for stalls, and the complexities of finding a source and importing stock. Getting a job at the Arts Centre, or a bookshop, was still up there, but taking a course in massage or jewellery making had for some reason lost their appeal. Enrolling at university is still a possibility, but what would she study? She has no particular strengths.

'But you'd be going there to *find and develop* your strength or strengths,' Mac had said when she'd mentioned this. 'You love books and reading, maybe you should pick literature, or writing.'

'Definitely not writing,' Joyce had said, 'I could never do what Polly does.'

'You don't have to, you could do something very different, and you were always good at history.'

So uni is still on the list, as is joining the local refugee support and action group. Joyce stares critically at her reflection in the bedroom mirror. She feels as though she is on the threshold of something: a new way of life, a new way of being herself, but she has no idea how to step into that. Would changing her appearance help?, she wonders. She has watched Helen's metamorphosis from economical and conservative dresser to a conventionally upmarket, well dressed older woman style which must be costing her a fortune. It's not a change that Joyce thinks she could make; hers is a more neutral, casual look and she rates comfort far too highly to return to short fitted skirts and heels. I've been stuck in a rut at home for so long, in the same job for so long, that I don't even know a way to be different, she tells herself.

A familiar voice calls out from the garden and she walks through to the kitchen window and sees Stella, closing the connecting gate. Thank goodness, someone to talk to, someone sensible who won't pull any punches. Although these days her judgement is not what it once was, and she is increasingly forgetful, she is always distinctively Stella, warm, generous, funny, frequently infuriating and with her own style developed from her love of op shops. She puts together things that on anyone else would look preposterous or simply messy, but which somehow work on her. Her spare bedroom is full of clothes from which she has cut the sleeves in order to attach them to something else, skirts that are being shortened or lengthened by the addition of a wide strip of fabric cut from another garment, jackets appliqued with a motif from something else, all delightfully unique.

'I am a sartorial disaster,' Stella had said once when Joyce had commented on something she was wearing. 'A walking patchwork, it comes from working in the theatre for years, earning practically nothing and cutting up other people's cast-offs. Now it seems to be a habit I can't break.'

'Come on in. Coffee?' Joyce says as Stella makes her way up the steps onto the back verandah.

'Definitely,' Stella says. 'Do you by any chance have . . .?'

'Yes,' Joyce cuts in, 'a whole new packet.' And she props open the screen door and gets the Tim Tams out of the pantry.

'You're not doing anything that can't be interrupted then?'

'I never do anything that can't be interrupted these days,' Joyce says. 'I am the most interruptible woman in Fremantle, possibly in the whole of Western Australia. I haven't even cooked a proper meal since Mac left.'

'How *is* Mac?'

'Fine, happy as the proverbial sand boy, sawing, chiselling, sanding, staining, and enjoying listening uninterrupted to Radio National. He's trying not to sound as though he's having too good a time without me but I'm not fooled.'

Stella laughs and hitches herself up on a stool at the bench top. 'Bet he misses you though.'

'Maybe,' Joyce says, pouring the water onto the coffee. 'But he's fine without me.'

'And you?'

Joyce grimaces. 'Still working on it.'

Stella looks across at the blackboard. 'Mmm. Not much progress there. Why don't you just go along to the refugee support group, see what it's like. I bet you could do as much or as little as you want, depending on what else you decide to take on.'

It sounds so simple, so easy, perhaps Stella is right, perhaps this is exactly what she needs – a cautious first step. She smiles. 'Maybe I will. I just assumed that once Mac had left everything would become clear as crystal, but it hasn't.'

'And it doesn't have to,' Stella says. 'Give yourself time. It's only a few weeks. You'll work it out, I know you will.'

Joyce puts their coffee onto a tray with the biscuits, and they go out onto the back verandah. 'Have you heard from Polly, is she still in Bali?'

'She is,' Stella says, 'she's having a wonderful time, resting, reading, flopping in and out of the pool. Decided to add on a bit of extra time there, she'll be back on Friday.'

'How's Alistair?'

'Not too bad, apparently, quite perky. He's got some new medication that seems to be better for him. But that's not what I've come for.'

Joyce raises her eyebrows. 'I thought you'd come for a coffee.'

'Naturally that, but I just saw the sign next door.'

'Next door?'

'For goodness sake, haven't you noticed, there's a "For Sale" sign on the verge. So we'll be getting new neighbours, hopefully interesting ones who'll stay a long time.'

*

Ubud, Bali, Early April

Stretched out on a sunbed in the shade by the pool Polly is pretending to be asleep, eyes closed, still as a lizard on a rock, listening to the gentle splashing of the water, the low voices, the occasional laughter. What does it take, she wonders, to spend every waking hour with someone who is dying very, very slowly? To get them up in the mornings, prepare their meals, help them move around, make sure they take their medication, fetch and carry . . . everything. Surely love alone is not enough to activate the sort of selfless devotion required to do this without resentment or irritation, and Alistair can be really irritating. As a younger man he'd had remarkable skills in pissing people off: relatives, friends, lovers, colleagues. But he also had that winning way of letting people know they mattered to him and so they always came back. The magic had not worked so easily on Polly; irritation was probably a fact of life between older brother and younger sister, and she knows there have been times that she has driven him to distraction. Having an older brother who is generally recognised as being a brilliant mind was always going to be something of a problem. She's always loved him though, and probably more now than ever, now that age and illness have slowed and softened him, shaved off the sharp corners, enabled them to connect more deeply than they had before, to speak more honestly. As she lies there, listening, the weight of her love for him is disturbing. She will be bereft without him and yet she knows that she could never do what Steve is doing, never give herself – her life – over to someone else in the way that he has done.

Alistair and Steve have been together for more than thirty years – it's inconceivable to Polly that people can live so intimately together for so long. They are like Joyce and Mac – so closely attuned to each other that you can't imagine one without the other. Polly believes she lacks that capacity, that if she ever did have it she has squandered it in her unerring ability to fall for the wrong men – men with whom she is unable to be herself, men she has tried to rescue from themselves, until she has had to escape from them in order to rescue herself. She opens her eyes, watching now, as Steve steers Alistair towards the shallow steps at the end of the pool and pushes him gently down to sit there, waist high in the water, leaning against an inflatable cushion, encouraging him to gently move his legs as though he were still floating.

Polly sits up slowly, gets to her feet and strolls over to sit beside them, dangling her legs in the water.

Steve smiles. 'Ah, sleeping beauty wakes. Could you stay with Al for a while, Polly? I've got some stuff to do indoors, just make sure he doesn't drown.'

'Christ,' Alistair says, 'don't leave me here with the Red Queen, she'll have my head underwater the minute your back's turned!'

Polly laughs, swings her foot and splashes him. 'Too right,' she says, 'I've been waiting for an opportunity like this since I was about twelve.' She slides off the pool side into the water to sit beside him on the steps.

'Were you asleep?'

'Dozing, and listening to you two,' she says. 'I was eaves-dropping on love.'

He smiles. 'I'm so lucky, all these years, and he's still here and still loves me. God knows why; anyone else would have left me before I got sick, let alone sticking with me from diagnosis until almost death.'

She grasps his hand under the water. 'I hate it when you talk about death.'

'I know, but I have to. It has to become part of the life that's left. It has to feel like the most normal thing in the world, which of course it is. Pretending it's not happening makes it harder.'

'Yes, but you've been a pain in the arse most of your life and now you've become cuddly big brother and you're going to leave me.'

'Yep, life sucks. You could come and stay with us more, you know. I don't mean just because of me dying . . . but for you, for yourself. This place is good for the soul – or at least it's been good for mine.' He pauses, looking at her, narrows his eyes. 'But it's not what you want, is it? You want libraries and bookshops, the cappuccino strip, the university, grotty film sets, all that crap.'

'I do,' she laughs, leaning against him. 'Just not the crappy film sets these days. I love coming here, being with you guys, but it's not my sort of life. Besides, it's too hot and humid, and I have the wrong sort of hair for Bali. How come you got Mum's lovely tanned skin and thick straight hair and I got Dad's pale English skin and this gingery frizz?'

'Well at least you haven't gone bald like Dad,' Alistair says, 'but I suppose there's still time for that. I've always liked your hair.'

Polly rolls her eyes. 'That's because you're not stuck with it.'

'Maybe. But seriously, I know you'd go raving mad here, as I would have done had this not happened to me. I watched so many friends die in the eighties and nineties I thought I was somehow immune. But, there you go, things change.'

'Do you never miss your old life?' Polly asks, remembering the time when they were both living in Sydney, when they couldn't walk down Oxford Street, or sit in the café by the El Alamein fountain, without him constantly being greeted by people he knew. He was always busy in those days, always on the go, in demand for social or cultural commentary for some newspaper or radio station, invited to all the best parties.

'Never,' he says now, 'not for one moment. I don't know why I ever thought I enjoyed it, why I even thought it mattered. I suppose I needed to feel *I* mattered, to be recognised and occasionally deferred to.'

'Only occasionally?' she says, nudging him with her elbow.

'Well, fair enough, it does go to one's head a bit. Being treated as an expert, having a *profile* . . .' He lifts his hands out of the water, enclosing the word in quotes with his fingers. 'It's addictive. You have to keep at it, keep building and feeding it for fear of being overlooked. And then one day you open an envelope from the STD clinic and your heart stops beating, your throat closes off, your head spins . . .' Alistair inhales deeply, looks down into the water. 'Oh well . . . you remember how it was . . . bits of me fell away, and I ran away, *we* ran away. There are still only half a dozen people from that life who know we're here, who call or visit from time to time. Now I wonder why I wasted so much time thinking I was so important.'

'You *are* important,' she says, 'to me, to Steve, to your friends here, to those people from that life. You were just a different sort of important then.'

'An important, arrogant bastard,' he laughs. 'I thought that being in demand – publicly and professionally – was what life was all about. Anyway, Poll, what about you? Ever since you got here I've felt you were on the edge of telling us something but then deciding not to.'

'I'm acclimatising.'

'Bullshit. You're procrastinating. C'mon, spit it out.'

Polly sighs. 'Oh well, it's just that . . . well I was wondering whether, in your important days, you ever came across someone called Leo Croft?'

Alistair closes his eyes, tilts his face up to the sun. 'Croft,' he says, 'Leo Croft, it sounds familiar . . . should I know him, what does he do?'

'Well I thought you might know him because of the time you spent in London. He used to work for the BBC, first as a political reporter and then he hosted a current affairs program called . . . er . . . *Roundup* . . .'

'Hah, yes, I know who you mean. I think he left the BBC and worked at Channel Four for a while. He was . . . probably still is . . . quite busy on the speaking circuit . . .' he pauses, 'I think he might have reinvented himself as a sort of minor celebrity atheist.'

Polly nods. 'That's him.'

'Okay, well I've seen him in action on television, years ago of course, and I've read some of his stuff in the past, but not since he became a supposed expert on the non-existence of the Almighty.'

'Supposed?'

He laughs. 'Well it's all *supposed* really, isn't it? We smart bastards suppose ourselves to be experts, we write something controversial on a topic, publish, make the right noises to the right people, they suppose we're right, or at least interestingly and entertainingly wrong, and hey presto everyone else believes we know what we're talking about. That's how it works. Yes, I know who you mean.'

'So d'you think he's okay?'

'Okay in what sense?' he asks, turning towards her. 'I mean, as far as I can remember his stuff was pretty good, and he can probably do the show pony thing quite well. Is that what . . .?' He stops, peering into her face. 'Oh I seeeee. You've met him, haven't you, in London?'

'Edinburgh, just briefly.'

'Brief encounter?'

'Not in the way you mean it. We met by chance, talked, had lunch, that sort of thing.'

'And now?'

'Well . . . I did like him. And I like him more now I've had time to think about it.'

'And since Edinburgh?'

'We've been emailing . . .' Polly hesitates. 'It's sort of changing, the email conversations, I mean, they're becoming . . .'

'Pornographic?'

'Don't be ridiculous, Al. I need you to help me with this.'

'Sorry, darling. What are they becoming, these emails?'

'Um . . . affectionate, almost intimate, not sexually, intellectually, which is, of course, quite sexy if you know what I mean.'

'I do know what you mean. And you think I can help you with this?'

'Well you've never held back about my other relationships.'

'So it *is* a relationship.'

'No . . . I . . . no . . .'

'But you think it *could* be?'

She sighs. 'Possibly. I suppose that's it. I suppose I think it could be.'

Alistair swishes his arm through the water, shifts his position. 'Well I don't know anything bad about him, not much about him at all. I suppose you've gone through the checklist of risk factors from your previous disastrous involvements: already married, drinks too much, drugs – recreational and medicinal – hates his mother, hates his father, pulls the wings off flies . . .'

'Of course, and I couldn't see any sign of any of that, except perhaps he . . . well . . . the mother thing, no love lost there, that's for sure.'

'Well one risk factor is probably okay. He'll have an ego the size of the British Museum, of course. Worse even than mine because his profile is, in a small way, international. We should go inside and Google him.'

'I already have.'

'Of course you have, but *I* haven't, and I'm much better at that than you.'

*

It's several hours later, while they are sitting around the table after dinner, that Alistair, reaching down into the canvas bag attached to the side of his wheelchair, pulls out his iPad.

'Okay, let's check out the godless Mr Croft.'

Steve looks across the table at Polly. 'Are you sure you want him to do this, Polly?' he asks. 'You know what a bastard he can be.'

'It's for her own good,' Alistair says, playfully. 'I'm sort of responsible for her, after all . . .'

Polly splutters with laughter and looks at Steve, who rolls his eyes. 'Don't say I didn't warn you,' he says.

Alistair handles the iPad cautiously, standing it upright in its case which opens up into a keyboard, with a slot stand for the screen. Polly watches, uncomfortable at the time it takes him to get it ready, the difficulty he has in getting his fingers to work on the keyboard. She reaches out to him. 'Here, let me . . .'

'I am perfectly able to use an iPad, thank you, Polly,' he says, looking hard at her, putting a shaking hand firmly on top of hers and pushing it away from the keyboard.

She exchanges a glance with Steve, who smiles reassuringly. She has known him for years, since before he and Alistair met, when he and Polly had been working on the set of a crime series. Steve was a psychologist who specialised in profiling and had been brought in as an advisor. Alistair had turned up to meet Polly for lunch one day; Steve and a couple of others had tagged along and now here they are all these years later, two old men still together.

'How strange it is that we're so old,' she says suddenly. 'It's as though it's snuck up on us.'

'We're only sixty-seven, Poll,' Steve says, 'and you're what – sixty-three now? It's not really old these days.'

'No, but think of our parents at this age. We thought they were old then. It doesn't seem possible that we're now the over-sixties. Isn't it odd that inside yourself you know you're the same person but suddenly you see yourself in a mirror or reflected in a shop window and think – who is that old person that looks a bit like me?'

Alistair looks up at her over the top of his glasses. 'Are you saying you're too old for something in particular, Polly?' he asks. 'Like a relationship, or even a brief encounter?'

'No I . . . oh I don't know what I'm saying. Haven't you found him yet?'

'I have indeed found him, *Croft, Leonard George, born Johannesburg, South Africa 1947, joined BBC radio as a news reporter in 1969* blah, blah, blah.' He pushes the iPad towards Steve, who draws it towards him, studies the screen for a moment then looks up at her, smiling, raising his eyebrows.

'Mmm, Polly – silver fox! Now how old do you *really* feel?'

'Oh stop it, you two. I wish I'd never told you.'

'Is there more you want to tell us?' Alistair says, teasingly. 'More about what happened in Edinburgh?'

'Nothing happened in Edinburgh. Nothing like what you're thinking anyway. It was just a chance meeting that turned into a really interesting . . . well, an interesting connection.'

'And since Edinburgh?' Steve persists. 'The emails? These days whole relationships begin online without the people having even met.'

Polly looks away, then down at her hands resting on the table, clasps them, unclasps them. 'I don't know what's happening, but whatever it is he started it. I only got friendly with him because of how we met – you know, I told you about the soldier. I liked the way he treated that young man, he was the only person that stopped thinking of himself to help a stranger.'

'The only one except you.'

'Well yes. And then I had lunch with him and found we had things in common . . .' she hesitates, 'and we laughed a lot. When we said goodbye at the airport I wished I'd taken another day or two to stay in London like he'd suggested. It was a pleasant interlude but now it seems to be changing, becoming more than that.'

'So what's wrong with that?' Steve asks.

'Well at our age . . .' she stops, unsure where she is going.

'At our age what?'

She hesitates again, shrugs. 'Oh I don't know, I don't know what to think. Shouldn't we be past . . . well past . . .?'

'Past what?' Alistair demands. 'Past love, or romance, or sex? Heaven forbid, Polly, you're both still alive, aren't you?'

Silence again.

'He said something like that, that first night,' she says. 'When you're past that you might as well be dead, I think it was.'

'Quite right,' Alistair says. 'D'you want to know what I think, 'cos I'm going to tell you anyway. I think you feel you can't bear to put yourself into the whole relationship thing again, risk getting hurt again, and I can understand that. Your entire approach to this man is constantly discoloured by the past and what you see as your own errors of judgement. But what you need to think about is who he actually is, and most importantly, how he made you feel when you were with him.'

She stares at him for what seems ages, trying to name it, holding her breath as she tries to pin down how she had felt, sitting across the table from Leo, throwing a snowball at him in the park, when he put his hand to her cheek at the airport.

She opens her mouth to speak, starts, then stops, then begins again. 'When I was with him,' she says, 'he made me feel that he could see me, the real me, not the surface and not what he might want to see, but the person I really am. That's how he made me feel.'

Chapter Four

North Fremantle, Western Australia, Early April

*I*t's eleven in the morning and Helen is still in her dressing gown, standing in the kitchen, pouring herself a glass of wine, when the doorbell rings. At first she thinks she won't bother answering it, it's probably the Mormons again, or that awful woman with the beauty products catalogue. But then she remembers that the handbag she'd ordered online at the end of last week is due to be delivered round about now; it cost an arm and a leg and is coming by courier. She takes a sip of her wine and hurries through to the front door remembering, just in time, to put her glass down on the hall table.

'Helen!' Stella says when she opens the door. 'I was just passing . . . but are you okay? You're not sick, are you?'

Helen tightens the sash of her dressing gown. 'Stella, what a lovely surprise. No of course I'm not sick, just . . . didn't sleep very well and so I went back to bed after Dennis left. Just got up again.'

It's clear that this does not convince Stella. She hesitates in the doorway looking puzzled. 'Well look, I won't disturb you then,' she says, 'if you're sure you're okay. I was just driving past and I thought I'd drop off these books that you lent me ages ago. But I can see . . .'

'Why don't you come in,' Helen says, desperate to sound normal. 'I'll make some coffee.' The last thing she wants is coffee and chat but although Stella has been losing it a bit recently she is still a wily old bird, and you can't be sure things will slip past her, so Helen needs to look as natural and relaxed as possible. 'Come on through and I'll put the kettle on.' And she opens the door wider and leads the way, hoping to get the wine bottle off the worktop before Stella makes it through to the kitchen.

'Shall I leave the books out here?' Stella calls after her. 'I'm sorry I've had them so long, I've been driving around with them in the car for ages, meaning to return them.'

'Lovely, thanks, on the table would be good . . .' Helen calls back, whisking the wine bottle into the fridge just as she realises that Stella is putting the books down alongside her wineglass. Ah well, not much she can do about it now. With any luck Stella will think the glass is left over from the previous evening.

'I do love your view,' Stella says, walking through to the kitchen at last, 'it always takes my breath away when I come in here.'

There is something artificial about her tone, Helen thinks. She's trying to make conversation; they were never close, and now Stella sounds forced and awkward.

'So,' Stella continues, 'you really are okay?'

'Oh, you mean the dressing gown,' Helen says, taking a jar of instant coffee from the cupboard. 'Of course I'm fine, just – well as I said, I went back to bed for a while and haven't got around to having a shower yet.'

'And Dennis?'

'He's fine; off to his Men's Shed thing – you know, all the old blokes get together and play sheds. They're making wheelchairs for kids in Africa now, I think. Something like that.'

Stella nods. 'I heard something about that on the radio. It's a great idea, they seem to be getting the chairs to children who really need them.'

'I suppose so. He's off there almost every day, goes about eight-thirty and comes back about two. And what about you, Stella, how was Albany?'

Stella perches on a stool at the bench top. 'Oh, pretty tiring, and sometimes tedious, but a lot of fun as well.'

'I don't know how you stand it,' Helen says. 'All that waiting around, and doing things over and over again. I'd go raving mad.'

'It's not all like that. Sometimes it moves along quite fast, and we always have a lot of laughs. They're a nice crowd.'

'Do you really have to keep doing it?' Helen says, getting two mugs from the cupboard. 'At your age I'd have thought you'd want to give it up.'

There is a silence and Helen, sensing this was a misstep, pours the boiling water into the mugs, and stirs them furiously.

'Well, Helen,' Stella says, slowly, 'at my age I think I'm lucky to still be doing it, to still be *invited* to do it. And it's not as though I have superannuation or much in the way of savings. Acting has always been financially hazardous unless one makes it to the big time, so I'm glad of the extra money to pay the bills. Sometimes it does all seem a bit much but I'd rather that than being stuck at home doing nothing all day.'

Helen feels herself flush, feels the heat creeping up her neck to her face. 'Oh well, yes, well of course. I'd certainly be lost without . . .' Without what? What can she say? The doorbell saves her. 'Goodness I'm popular this morning! Sorry, Stella, I'll just get that.'

It is the courier with her handbag, and Helen takes her time signing his delivery sheet, keeping up a pleasant banter with him as she does so.

'Online shopping,' she says, returning to the living room. 'Don't you just love it?'

'I do buy books online,' Stella says, 'but not really anything else.'

Helen knows she has misfired again. Of course Stella would not be buying bags or jewellery or designer gear or anything else online, she has only ever been interested in ferreting through op shops for some imagined bargain that she can convert into something weird and inappropriate. And she has always been close to the line where money was concerned, hanging out to know that her pay had been deposited in the bank.

'I suppose I might have enjoyed it when I was younger,' Stella continues, and Helen realises that she is trying; she's making an effort to ease the way for both of them. She must try harder herself.

'So how's everyone?' Helen asks brightly. 'Polly back yet?'

'Couple of days,' Stella says. 'I'll be so glad to have her back. I hear Damian and Ellie were home recently. That must have been lovely for you.'

Helen grasps this lifeline. 'It was,' she says, 'it was so good to have them here . . .' and she launches into a description of their visit, how well they both were, how much the children had grown, what a wonderful time they'd all spent together, and how she and Dennis are thinking of going over to Dubai in the middle of the year. She talks so much she almost exhausts herself, and then stops abruptly, leaving that awkward silence once again.

'Well that's lovely,' Stella says, 'you'll enjoy that. I was expecting to see you at Mac's little farewell.'

'Ah yes. So sorry to have missed that.' Helen feels the flush rising again. 'Just didn't feel too good that day, I thought I might have a bug and didn't want to pass it on to anyone else.' She wonders how long this can possibly go on, how long she and Stella can keep pretending that things are like they used to be. And of course things were never really easy between the two of them. Helen has always thought Stella eccentric, has always been slightly ill at ease in her presence. Both Stella and Polly, while always pleasant company, were never important to her in the way that Joyce was. They had existed for her as amiable neighbours, adjuncts to that really important friendship. She has never needed either of them because there was always Joyce and Mac and the whole rowdy, unmanageable, chaotic mix of their various children and, later, Joyce and Mac's grandchildren; always there, always in and out. But now . . .

Eventually Stella stands up and makes noises about having to get going.

'And I must get in the shower and get on too,' Helen says. 'So much to do.'

They exchange pecks on the cheek and Helen closes the door behind Stella, and leans back against it in relief, eyes closed, arms folded across her chest. She stands there for a moment, then hurries back to the kitchen window from where she can see Stella's red Honda edging out of the parking space below and into the street.

The last half-hour or however long it was seems like a nightmare. She wonders what she said, what she did, how it will all sound when Stella relates it to Joyce, as she surely will. Could Joyce have sent Stella here, to check up on her? Check up on what exactly? Everything probably, because they haven't seen each other since the night at Cicerello's. It was Mac who had called to invite them round for supper and drinks before he left: 'There'll just be a few of us,' he'd told Dennis, who'd answered the phone, and Dennis had accepted for both of them without consulting her.

'Well I won't be going,' she'd said sharply. 'You can do as you like.'

'I think you've gone over the top about this, Helen, I really do,' Dennis had said. 'They're our oldest friends, and they've a right to do just as they want about their living arrangements.'

'That may be so,' she'd said, 'but as Joyce's oldest friend I think I have a right to tell it how it is. It's a ridiculous thing to be doing at their age. And it's not just about them – what about us? Like you said, they're our oldest friends, but they weren't even going to tell us yet, and they're breaking everything up, as though all those years mean nothing.'

Dennis, who had been standing with his back to her looking out of the window, had turned around then. 'We're the ones who broke it up,' he'd said. 'We did that when we moved away, nothing's been the same since then. And we did that because it was what you wanted. I warned you what it would mean, that what we had there, in Emerald Street, would just fade away, but you wouldn't have it. Wouldn't listen. You wanted all this so badly that you couldn't talk about anything else. So now you've got what you wanted, your river view, your fittings and furnishings, it's cost us a fortune, and *you* don't like it and *I* never wanted it anyway. And now you don't like Joyce and Mac trying something new? Well you can just stop whingeing about things not being the same because I'm sick of hearing it. Find yourself something else to do, like I have. I'm off to the Shed now, and I'll be going to say goodbye to Mac on Wednesday and you can do what you sodding well like.' And he had picked up his car keys, stalked off out the door and disappeared for the rest of the day.

Helen stares at the hall table, the three novels Stella has returned, the full glass of wine. She presses her hands to her temples feeling a headache coming on. The rawness of Stella's visit, the awkwardness, her own stupidity, crowd in on her, but at the heart of it all is the emptiness. The emptiness of her life, the yawning gap in herself that she's always known was there, but which for so many years had been softened and then filled by everything about their life in Emerald Street. Every day since they moved here that gap has been reopening little by little, the edges eroding, slipping elusively away like soft sand leaving this black hole growing slowly bigger. Helen looks at the glass on the hall table, reaches out, picks it up and sips the wine. Sips it again. She walks back to the kitchen and takes another sip, then tosses back the remainder in one gulp, stares at the bottom of the glass, turns to the fridge, takes out the bottle, and refills it.

*

Stella pulls out into the street and drives back towards the bridge as though she is running from the scene of some crime. The shock of seeing Helen in her dressing gown, of smelling the drink on her breath, the wine in the hallway, the forced smile and awkward pleasantries, had left her feeling as though some evil fairy had scattered her with a cloying dust of unreality. She forces herself to concentrate on driving, tells herself to wait until she gets home when she can make herself a restorative cup of tea. It wasn't only the instant coffee, like paint stripper, that had left a bad taste in her mouth, but Helen and instant coffee? That in itself was an unbelievable combination. By the time she has crossed the bridge Stella is wondering whether it was all her fault. Had she behaved badly, had she unwittingly done something to upset Helen? Her memory is so dodgy these days maybe she trampled on some touchy topic without realising. But it had started the moment Helen had opened the door.

By the time she gets home, Stella is sure that her part in the debacle was in calling in on the off chance. Helen could always be touchy, take offence, feel slighted by something you didn't even know you'd done, and she wouldn't have liked being caught in her dressing gown, unwashed, hair all over the place, swigging wine at eleven o'clock in the morning. Stella pauses, kettle in hand. Should she say something to Joyce, or wait until Friday and talk to Polly when she gets back? Then, still contemplating action, she makes the tea, stirs in a large teaspoonful of honey, searches in every room for her glasses and, eventually finding them on her head, settles into her favourite chair on the back verandah. Maybe I'd just be telling tales, she thinks, but on the other hand . . . . oh well, Polly will know what to do.

She picks up her script and starts to read, not aloud, not silently, but in a very soft whisper to herself, which is the way she's always found it best to learn her lines. Since Albany they've been given a longish break to allow a couple of the cast to finish off other commitments. It all starts again in . . . well she can't remember when exactly, and this time they'll be filming in Perth and Fremantle, so no more sitting around on the rocks in her nightdress. This script, she thinks, is crap. Polly would have a word or two to say if she read it. And she's never had so many problems getting to grips with her lines and the character. She'd played Cassandra for so many years but this time Stella feels like she's losing her grip. I should retire, she thinks for the umpteenth time, and this time I should mean it.

She'd started to talk to Joyce and Mac about it when she'd got back from Albany.

'But why?' Joyce had asked. 'You're so good, and so many people love you. What about that article in *The West Australian* – the one about you being brought back for another series of *Cross Currents*? They said you were a television icon . . .'

'Much loved,' Mac had interrupted. '*A much loved icon of Australian television*, I think it said. I've got a copy of it somewhere. Anyway, you retired before and you've been asked to come back, twice, just like Frank Sinatra. This is the third time so that must tell you something.'

And whatever Stella had said about it being time, about *knowing* it was time, they kept brushing it aside. She'd loved them for their belief in her, for their support, their offers of anything they could do to make it easier for her to keep going, but she had wanted them to engage seriously with her about it, to let her talk it all through. It's best to go while I'm ahead, she thinks as she rests the script down on her lap and half closes her eyes.

The thing is, she tells herself, that when it's time to go you really do know it, and that's the difference this time. This time I'm sure. Third time lucky.

Through the filter of her lashes she sees the glorious greens of the garden that she has both tended and neglected over the years, the sparkle of the water feature that Mac installed for her a couple of years ago. I could sit here day after day, no scripts to learn, no bags to pack, no director's foibles to accommodate, she tells herself. She has a house full of books still to read, when will she do that if she doesn't start soon? And suddenly she longs for a sense of uninterrupted time to do exactly what she wants even if that means nothing at all. She feels the script slip to the floor but she doesn't move to retrieve it, just sits there until her eyes close.

*

South Fremantle, April

Polly pays the cab driver, grabs the handle of her suitcase and wheels it in through the front gate, stopping only to glance up and down the street, which is bathed in midday somnolence. There is no sign of life at Joyce's place or Stella's, but outside the property next to Joyce and Mac's there is a 'For Sale' sign. Hmm, she thinks, that'll be interesting. And she lets herself in to the glorious, cool stillness of her own home, leaves her case inside the front door and wanders through to the back, sniffing the scent of the lemon oil that she always uses on her mother's old dining table. In the kitchen she opens the back door and then, wandering into the lounge, throws open the French windows to freshen the air. Home at last, the joy of it never fails her. Wherever she goes, she knows she will always return to this, her own little piece of the world. On the kitchen table there is the stack of mail that Stella and Joyce between them have rescued from the mailbox – bills, circulars, letters, postcards – but she is not really interested in these right now. The first thing she wants is a shower and to change into some old jeans and a t-shirt, and then to see Stella, whose car is out there standing on the driveway in the sun.

Half an hour later, revived after her shower, Polly goes down the back steps, across the lawn and opens the side-gate.

'Stella,' she calls softly. 'Stella, are you there?'

She steps in, closing the gate behind her, turns to walk up to the house and stops abruptly. Stella is sitting uncannily still in her cane chair, eyes closed, a cup beside her, some papers at her feet, and Polly's heart pounds . . . is she . . .? Could she have . . .? She reels backwards, turning her ankle as her foot sinks into the soft earth of the rose bed, then straightens up and looks again.

Stella shifts her position very slightly and Polly relaxes, takes several deep breaths and walks softly up the verandah steps to stand beside her and pauses for a moment. How old Stella looks, sleeping like this. The eccentricity of her appearance evaporates without the vibrance of her personality to carry it. Polly stares sadly at the folds of skin barely apparent when Stella is awake: the way her mouth droops, the greying eyebrows, the silvery hair once thick and lustrous which is thinning now, and her hands mottled with age spots, raised veins and thickening knuckles. She wonders if Stella herself sees all this, if she is immune to changes in her appearance, or struggles to live with the uncomfortable reality of it all. What will I feel, she wonders, when I'm Stella's age? Will I mind these obvious signs of ageing, the sense of dilapidation, or will I slowly learn to live with it?

'Stella,' she says again, this time putting her hand gently on Stella's arm.

'Oh!' Stella opens her eyes and sits up straight. 'Oh, I . . . Polly, oh Polly, I was asleep.' She blinks, puts a hand to her face. 'What are you doing here, you're not due back until Friday, or did I forget? Is everything all right?'

'Everything's fine,' Polly says, leaning forward to kiss her, then pulling the other chair closer to sit down. 'I always planned to come back today.'

'But I thought Friday . . .'

'It is Friday,' Polly says.

'Is it really? Are you sure? I thought today was Wednesday . . . I was going to get you some shopping, goodness what a mess, I must have mixed up . . .'

'Don't get up,' Polly says, gripping her arm to stop her. 'It's fine, I can pop out later. Besides, you shouldn't be running around after me.'

Stella flops back in her chair. 'But I like doing that. Anyway, it's lovely to see you, what a wonderful surprise. And you look so good. Did it all go well, the conference, the research, and Alistair? Would you like some tea, or a cold drink?'

Polly senses that Stella's delight is also tinged with relief. This friendship has sustained them both over so many years and she knows that her friend has come to rely on her presence. Now, as age closes in on Stella, Polly thinks, her own unusually long absence has stirred something in her; a sense of herself as vulnerable, a foreshadowing of the loss of autonomy, a fear of dependence.

'You know what?' Polly says, taking her hand. 'I've had a shower, changed my clothes, and all I need to do is sit here quietly with you and catch up on all the news.'

*

'It was weird, it really was,' Stella says later that evening. 'The drinking, not being dressed, the tension . . . I didn't know what to make of it while I was there but now I think it was unhappiness – Helen's unhappiness – that I felt. And an awful brooding sort of anger.'

'That anger has been smouldering for a while,' Joyce says, stirring the risotto with one hand and reaching out with the other to take the glass of wine Polly is holding out to her. 'But the night we went to Cicerello's was when I realised how bad it is. Helen's never found it easy to apologise for anything but I hoped she might make some sort of mute apology by turning up to say goodbye to Mac. But she didn't, and she hasn't returned my calls.' She pulls the pan off the heat and carries it to them at the table. 'I think you're right, Stella, she is very unhappy but she can't admit it.'

Polly watches in silence as Joyce serves the risotto. This meal was a spur of the moment decision made when Joyce had turned up at Stella's place this afternoon and found them sitting on the verandah.

'Dinner, my place at seven,' she had said. 'I'll throw something together.'

'I gave up trying to work Helen out years ago,' Polly says now. 'And what you and Mac decide to do is entirely up to the two of you. It's no one else's business.'

'Except ours,' Stella says, laughing. 'Polly and I, as your best friends, expect everything to be run past us first, don't we, Poll?'

'Of course,' Polly laughs. 'But seriously, I really admire you both for having a go at this, giving each other the freedom. It must be a challenge after all these years.'

'Mmm. Well I have to admit that I haven't quite got a grip on the challenge yet but I think I might be getting there,' Joyce says. 'I went to the refugee support group yesterday evening. It was all a bit vague – people wanting to do something useful but not sure what or how. But one thing they badly need is people to teach English. I thought I might talk to Ben about the course he did before he trekked off to Europe after he graduated.'

Stella nods. 'You'd be good at that.'

'You would,' Polly adds. 'By the way, you have to tell me what's going on next door.'

Joyce looks puzzled. 'Oh, you mean the "For Sale" sign? It went up a couple of weeks ago, that's all we know. Let's hope we get some nice, interesting neighbours. A quiet older couple or a single woman would be good.'

'Or a quiet older man, for Polly,' Stella says, winking at Joyce. 'But it may be too late. I have a feeling she's already met someone.'

*

Perhaps it's jet-lag, or simply the readjustment to being home, but whatever it is Polly's restlessness will not let her sleep. One moment she's determined to keep her distance from Leo, the next she is feverishly re-reading his emails, measuring each word for its exact meaning, studying the way the correspondence has escalated from friendly and light-hearted to something deeper. They haven't spoken since they parted company at Heathrow, but Polly feels she is learning to know him better than might have been possible on the phone. She wishes now that she had followed her instincts when, at St Pancras, she had hesitated and considered texting him to say she had decided to

stay on in London for a couple of days. But the Eurostar depar-
ture announcement had cut across her thoughts, and she'd
taken a deep breath and walked straight through the gate and
onto the train. Now she feels herself being drawn into a sort
of intimacy, not sexual but certainly very personal, cultural
and intellectual, and each day she vacillates between wanting
more and wanting to turn away before she invests too much
in whatever this is or might become. Men make life so complicated, or is it just her response to them that complicates things?
There is nothing in her past that gives her confidence that she
might make the right choice or the right moves. Her relationships have always begun on a high and veered steadily, often
rapidly, into decline until she has escaped back into her single
life and the sense of congruence it gives her. But sometimes she
gets a treacherous feeling that it must be possible for her to have
at least one functional relationship after so many disasters. The
odds must be in her favour, mustn't they?

'Don't sell yourself short, Poll,' Alistair had said, hugging
her as she left. 'Be open to the possibilities. This could be the
time you really get it right.' But even as she remembers this she
shrinks back again into all the old fears harvested from a lifetime of disappointments.

Chapter Five

*M*ac plunges into the water off Middleton beach and starts to swim out against the incoming tide. He's been doing this every morning since he arrived, a swim, then a walk to the café for coffee, then home to cook some breakfast. He swims vigorously this morning, pushing himself against the current and then turning onto his back to look up at the clear, early morning sky. He loves being down here on the south coast, loves the strong cold wind off the Southern Ocean, the air that seems so pure you can feel it doing you good. And he loves the way he spends his days. He's supposed to be renovating the cottage but he hasn't touched it yet because he has this burning desire to do something he's been thinking of for ages – make a rocking chair for Joyce. Years had passed since he'd promised he would do this, so hopefully it will be a nice surprise.

But this morning he's got an important meeting, too important even to stop for his usual coffee. He has a meeting with a dog.

'A dog?' Joyce had said when he'd asked her on the phone whether she minded if he got one. 'Of course I don't mind.'

'Even if you decided to move down here, you wouldn't mind living with a dog?'

'I love dogs,' she'd said. 'You know I do, it's always been me who wanted one and you said it was too much trouble.'

'I know,' he'd said sheepishly. 'Being down here alone is great but I think it would be nicer with a dog to talk to.'

'A dog that doesn't argue with you or remind you to put out the rubbish?' she'd laughed. 'Of course you should get a dog if that's what you want, and you know what we agreed – we don't have to ask each other's permission to do what we want.'

'I know, but a dog lasts more than a year,' Mac had said. 'So whatever we decide at the end of the year the dog will be a part of that.'

'It's okay, Mac, just do it,' Joyce had said. 'Why not get a rescue dog? There's a lot of places on the Internet. And, by the way, I'm going for an interview next week, at the language school, for the same course as Ben did. Remember?'

Mac remembered; he remembered the month Ben was on the course, it is engraved on his memory: Ben, then twenty-two, confidently enrolling in the intensive one-month course, setting off enthusiastically, and returning each day utterly exhausted, saying his brain hurt and disappearing into his room to spend several more hours preparing for the following day. He remembers the start of the third week: Ben looking pale and drawn, tearful even as he staggered off to classes, and how he and Joyce had told each other that it was good that Ben was so committed but he did seem to be making a meal of it. They'd agreed that the pressure would toughen him up – he needed to be pushed. At the end of the course Ben had done well and they had celebrated by taking the whole family out for a special dinner.

'That is the hardest thing I've ever done,' Ben had said as they drank to his health. And later that night Joyce and Mac had shared their amusement that a fit young man could be so knocked over by the pressure of a four-week course.

'Are you sure?' Mac had said when Joyce told him about the interview. 'Remember how Ben was? Can't you do it over a longer period?'

'I'll be fine,' Joyce had said, irritably. 'He was young, he wasn't used to pressure. I'd rather do the intensive one, assuming I get in at all.'

'He still says the course was the hardest thing he's ever done,' Mac reminded her. 'And he's forty-four now and apart from the teaching he did after that, he's done a lot of other very difficult and challenging things. Remember when he . . .'

'Mac, stop!' Joyce had interrupted. 'Ben remembers it that way and I am sure it *was* tough on him, but I'm a grown woman, a mother and a grandmother, and I'm used to hard work and long hours. I am perfectly capable of doing this.'

So he backed off. Okay, he thought, suit yourself, I was only trying to help. And he'd got straight onto the computer and started dog hunting. It was the eyes that were important, he thought, as he scrolled through the images of dogs needing homes. The look in the eyes was what mattered, that, and it had to be a sensible sized dog, nothing small or fine boned, a strong dog, a man's dog, and he made a mental note not to describe it that way to Joyce.

There were lots of different sites, but not many dogs needing homes in this area. You could adopt one from another state or region and it could be flown to you, but Mac wanted to meet the dog face to face before deciding. He'd considered a German Shepherd called Gloria, but wasn't too sure about the eyes, although that could have been the fault of the camera. He lingered over a Staffy but the eyes, he thought, looked slightly demented. And then, on another site, he'd spotted Charlie, a chocolate brown Labrador cross. Crossed with what?, Mac had wondered. Something pretty big, by the look of it, maybe too big? But when he enlarged the picture he could see the eyes and the eyes said 'come and get me and I'll love you forever'. So he'd emailed that night and the following morning a woman named Carol had called.

'He's adorable,' she'd said, 'he's been quite well trained. I've been fostering him for a couple of weeks and no nasty surprises. I can bring him to you if you like, to see if the two of you get along.'

Back home now Mac has a quick shower and feels a sudden compulsion to tidy the house before Carol arrives. Joyce's training, he thinks, she'd be proud of me. And he goes around the cottage gathering up an empty cup, a glass, his jacket, two pairs of shoes and some books and papers and odd tools that he has left scattered across the living room. As he is washing his breakfast things in the kitchen Mac hears the sound of a car and he crosses to the front windows where he sees a small, yellow, four-wheel drive turn in at the gate. A woman with untidy, greying hair piled on top of her head climbs out of the driver's seat. There is something vaguely familiar about her, but also something that seems totally at odds with the familiarity. He dries his hands and goes to the door.

'Carol?' he says.

'That's me,' she says, and her smile is familiar too. 'Okay if I let Charlie out of the car?'

'Sure thing,' he says. 'Thanks for bringing him over.'

'My pleasure. We really want to find a home for him soon, he's such a lovely dog. He might just ignore you at first and run straight into the house – is that okay?'

'That's fine; let him out. If he ends up staying here he'll have the run of the house anyway.'

The dog leaps out of the back seat wagging his tail, sniffing the air. 'He's big, bigger than I expected,' Mac says. 'Hey, Charlie, come here.'

'Does that matter?' Carol asks. 'The size, I mean. We think he has a touch of some other breed, not sure what, but something bigger than a Labrador.'

'A horse maybe?' Mac says, laughing. 'But no, it doesn't matter. He's beautiful.'

Charlie sniffs around Mac's ute, cocks a leg on one of the tyres and bounds over to him and he takes the dog's head in his hands, fondling his ears. Charlie looks up at him, then pokes his head forward in an attempt to lick his face.

'Crikey, that was quick,' Carol says. 'He's taken an instant liking to you. I've not seen him do that before.'

Mac straightens up and Charlie bounds away from him and into the house. 'Come inside and tell me more about him. Would you like a coffee?' Close up now he has the same feeling of familiarity and disjunction that he'd had at the window.

'I'd love one,' she says. 'I went for a swim and then didn't have time for coffee.'

'Do you swim at Middleton?'

She nods. 'Most mornings.'

'Me too.'

Inside the house Charlie is making a tour of the premises, sniffing chair legs, cupboard doors, Mac's boots, and the sofa. 'He's not destructive and he won't pee on your boots,' Carol says. 'You know it's odd but I have this strange feeling that we've met before. Are you from around here?'

'No. We've been living in Fremantle for years, my wife's still there.' He crosses the room to get the coffee from the pantry. 'Strong okay?'

'Strong is good,' Carol says. 'Anyway, about Charlie, he's a bit of a one-person dog. Not very interested in other dogs, likes people, but if you and he get together he'll follow you everywhere. If you decide you want a trial with him I can leave him with you for two weeks.'

Mac puts the coffee into the plunger, and walks around the bench top to where Charlie is checking out the sofa. 'What d'you think, mate?' he says, looking into the dog's eyes again. 'Want to give it a go?' Charlie jumps onto the sofa, turns around a couple of times, rearranging the cushions, then lies down. 'I guess that's a yes,' Mac says. 'We'll give it a go. Want to show me the paperwork you'll need if I keep him?'

Carol sits on a stool at the bench top and takes some forms from her bag. 'Sure,' she says, taking out her pen. 'You said your name was Mac, is that . . .?'

'Short for Mackenzie, Robert Mackenzie.'

She starts to write, then stops, looks across at him as he switches off the kettle. 'Rob Mackenzie . . . I've got it. Chemistry, UWA, late sixties?'

He stares at her. 'Yes, but I don't remember . . .'

'You were a couple of years ahead of me, Carol Fisher.'

Mac stares at her. 'Carol Fisher, of course,' he says at last, and for the first time in years, possibly in decades, he feels himself blush. 'Yes, yes of course I remember.' And indeed he does remember Carol Fisher: lithe and tough, all black leather and jeans, spikey hair and attitude. And yes, he can just see her in this interesting looking woman in her sixties in her mid-calf length cotton caftan and leather sandals. She is attractive still, but in a very different way, a few sizes larger, and with unruly hair that escapes in strands each time she moves her head. As if she can read his mind she reaches up now, pulls it out of the scrunched up thing that holds it, drags it back into position and anchors it again. He laughs. 'Good lord, it must be forty years.'

'More,' she says, smiling. 'What did you do with your PhD?'

'Research chemist. And you?'

'I only got as far as Honours and then dropped out,' she says. 'Fell in love, got pregnant and had to get married in a hurry – well, you can imagine the rest.'

He nods. 'That's a shame, you were doing well, weren't you?'

'I was, but once you drop out it's hard to get back, especially in the sciences where the research moves on so fast. Anyway, I'll get on with this paperwork while you make the coffee.'

They work through the forms, and Carol slips them into a folder with information on Charlie's diet and habits. They face each other across the bench, recalling memories of their time at uni, eccentric staff, and fellow students. Eventually Carol gets up to leave and goes to the couch where Charlie has fallen asleep. He makes no attempt to move when she strokes him.

'I've been abandoned,' she says, as Mac walks her out to the car. 'Still, it's a good sign, I hope you enjoy him. Give me a call if you have any problems. If I don't hear from you I'll get back to you in a couple of weeks.'

'Thanks,' he says. 'And thanks for bringing him over. Nice to see you after all this time.'

'You too,' she says, slipping into the driving seat. 'Remember that night we went crabbing in Mandurah?'

'I do,' he says, awkward now. What is he supposed to say? It was, after all, just a one-night stand. 'Probably best forgotten,' he says, his face blazing with embarrassment.

She smiles. 'Well I wouldn't say that. But they were good times and . . .' she pauses, 'I was going to say it feels like a lifetime ago, but of course it is. Well I'd best get on.' And she starts the engine and reverses back down the unmade drive to the gate.

Mac stands there watching her turn out of the drive and onto the road. Idiot, he thinks, why the fuck did I say that . . . *best forgotten*? Was she offended? Hopefully she took it as it was – a throwaway line delivered in a moment of embarrassment. The car disappears from sight and he wanders back to the house, and drops down beside Charlie on the sofa. 'I always did have a winning way with women,' he says grimly, rubbing the dog's tummy. 'Foot in mouth again – story of my life.'

*

The senior teacher's office is stuffed with books and papers, and framed certificates bearing his name crowd the walls. Ewan Heathcote, nice, Joyce thinks, a name suitable for a romantic hero, and the rather rakish good looks to go with it.

'Well this all looks fine, Mrs . . . er . . . Joyce,' he says, shuffling through her application and evidence of her unfinished degree in English literature. 'We do have a few places left on the intensive course starting the week after next. But are you sure you wouldn't rather do the easier version? The intensive is – well, it is *very* intensive.'

Joyce studies his face; he is in his mid-forties and has, she thinks, a rather gentlemanly demeanour slightly at odds with his appearance.

'You see,' he continues, 'the intensive course is really designed for people who are trying to gain the qualification in their annual leave from other jobs. From what you've told me you're free to do it at a more measured pace.'

Joyce likes him, she likes the place, she likes the whole idea of intensive learning. She leans forward. 'Mr Heathcote . . .'

'Ewan, please,' he says.

'Well, Ewan, I want to be pushed, I want to be immersed in it. I think I'll learn better that way,' she says.

He smiles. 'Well in that case we'll be happy to have you. Provided of course that you pass the test.'

'The test?'

'The English and grammar test; it's outlined in the leaflet I sent you. Very straightforward, I don't think you'll have any problems with it.'

A wave of nausea sweeps over her. How did she let that slip past her? 'So when would I have to do that?' She has always been useless at exams.

'Well, now, preferably, today, or you can come back later . . .'

'Now,' she says, sounding more confident than she feels. 'Best get it done now. How long will it take?'

'Forty-five minutes,' he says. 'We just pop you in a quiet room on your own with the test paper, and someone will come and tell you when the time is up. If you finish earlier you can just give your paper to the receptionist on your way out and I'll get back to you in the next couple of days.'

Joyce takes a deep breath. 'Fine,' she says. 'Just one more thing. The people on the course, will they all be young? I mean – just out of university?'

'We do have a lot of recent graduates,' Ewan says, 'but we also have a lot of older people. People from their forties to their seventies. I think you'll find at least a few others about your age.'

A few minutes later Joyce settles herself at the desk in the little office, closes her eyes, takes a deep breath, opens them, puts on her glasses and starts to read the test paper. There are questions about the use of pronouns and adverbs, verb tenses, modifiers, conditionals, the appropriate uses of colons and semi-colons, Oxford commas, gerunds and everything else she's forgotten, if she ever knew it. Then there are long paragraphs with no punctuation and others with incorrect punctuation, all of which have to be corrected. Finally there is a long list of words and phrases to which grammatical form must be ascribed. Joyce closes her eyes again and tries to force down another wave of nausea. Whatever made her think she could possibly teach English? She sits in silence in the cell-like room where the only sound is that of muffled footsteps moving back and forth along the carpeted corridor, wondering how she can escape without detection. Run away and never come back.

She pushes the paper away from her across the desk, and leans back in her chair and stares up at the clock on the wall, watching the minute hand jerk slowly forward. How hopeless I am, she tells herself, all those years at home, and in the same job on and off, and now I'm fit for nothing. 'But I want this,' she whispers into the silence. 'I really want this. What will everyone say? Mac and Stella, and Polly, and Gemma, and what about Vanessa and Ben, especially Ben, he'd be ashamed of me. I have to do it. I have to try.' And she grabs some tissues from her bag, wipes her eyes, puts her glasses back on and starts to read the test paper again.

Chapter Six

South Fremantle, May

There is a sort of magic in the silence, Polly thinks, as she checks her emails once again. No message so far this morning but it will come, Leo hasn't missed a day yet, and against her own better judgement she waits for his messages, the certainty of their arrival constantly distracting her from her work. She is torn between wanting to keep the silence, and actually wanting to hear his voice. Email is safe of course, and for two people who spend their lives working with words this is a very comfortable way of getting to know each other. They have both written about what had seemed, at first, an unspoken agreement, to communicate only in this way. They are getting to know each other in the safe and silent world of cyberspace.

'It sounds a bit weird,' Stella had said, when Polly told her about it. 'A bit impersonal.'

'Far from it,' Polly said. 'It feels quite intimate, sharing things about our lives, what we believe in, what we value, what makes us laugh and what drives us right up the wall. Books, music, politics, writing, all sorts of things.' Only to herself will she admit that she really wants to hear his voice, that she tries to conjure it in her mind, the resonance, the hint of an almost unidentifiable accent.

'Have you told him about Alistair?'

Polly nods. 'I have and he told me about his sister, Judith. It's really sad, she's in her late fifties and has Multiple Sclerosis. They own a cottage in Cornwall which belonged to their parents, and she lives there with a carer. He goes down there a lot, it's hard on him of course, but he's totally committed to her, really makes sure she has everything she needs.'

Stella raises her eyebrows. 'He told you that?'

'Mmm. It was quite touching really. And it's something else we share, although of course I don't have to do anything for Al because he has Steve.'

Stella nods. 'How sad, that poor woman. And you, Polly – you're feeling there's more, yet you seem to be holding everything off at a distance. I don't understand how you can – it'd drive me crazy.'

'That's because you're a very *out there* sort of person, Stella,' Polly had said. 'I'm an introvert. And there's something else: I feel, and I suspect he does too, that we're both enjoying this so much that neither of us wants to risk damaging it.'

'But you could go on like this forever,' Stella says, 'and I might die before I know what happens!'

Polly smiles as she thinks of it now. Stella was joking, but there is also a serious undercurrent to her impatience. Stella, fiercely independent as she is, fears what is to come, and having Polly close by tempers her sense of vulnerability; similarly, Stella is Polly's foundation stone and her sounding board. Neither has spoken of it but Polly knows that any radical change in her own life could have implications for Stella's. She checks the email again but there is still no message and she reminds herself that Leo is in Hong Kong now, at a conference, and perhaps won't get a chance to email for a while.

Standing by the sink, staring out across the back garden, her mind ranges again through the weeks of emails, what's been said and what left unsaid, what it all might mean, but she's jerked suddenly out of this by a fierce hammering on the front door.

'Polly,' Stella calls through the letterbox. 'Polly, are you there?'

It's only a few hours since Stella left for work, expecting to be there until at least early evening. Polly hurries along the passage and opens the door, and Stella almost falls through, tears running down her cheeks.

'Oh you're here, thank god,' Stella says, as Polly grabs hold of her. 'It was awful, I can't tell you how awful it was.'

'Whatever's happened?' Polly asks, leading her through to the sofa. 'Here, sit down, do you need something? A glass of water, should I call a doctor?'

'No, no,' Stella says, shaking her head. 'No, nothing like that. Oh, Polly, it was mortifying. You know how I've been struggling with my lines. Well last night I had today's scenes down pat. And then in the car this morning I went through them carefully and I was feeling quite confident – all the time I was in make-up I was running through them too. But when I went out on the set I started saying something different. It had all disappeared, just like that, the whole scene had disappeared and I didn't even realise it. Gone, just like that, everything stopped and they were all looking at me as though I'd gone mad.'

She stops briefly, taking a couple of deep breaths. 'Anyway,' she says, 'then Gareth says, "You're on the wrong page, Stella, we're shooting the scene in the bedroom. So let's go for another take". So off we went again and I came in on cue with what I thought was next, and everything stopped again. And Gareth told everyone to take a break, and he came and sat next to me. I knew it was serious because he was speaking so quietly, and he said, "Stella, you're starring in the wrong movie. What you just gave me came from something else. Maybe that film you made about the World War I nurses, but it sure wasn't from *Cross Currents*, so let's just talk through the lines together". He was so kind to me but I couldn't do it, Polly, I had no idea what

I was supposed to do and I still don't, it was all just gone. All I had were lines from that film – remember? That's years ago. I kept trying but it was as though that was all that I had in my head. I didn't even know I still knew that stuff . . . I . . . oh, Polly, you can imagine . . .'

Polly puts an arm around Stella's shoulders. 'Yes I can imagine how that felt. But these things happen, it's probably just a glitch . . .'

'They cancelled the whole day's filming; we lost a whole day because of me and you know what a disaster that is.'

Polly does know, but she also needs to wind Stella down. 'But it happens, Stella; everyone has a day like this sometime and you're a real trouper. You have such a good reputation, and decades of good will and admiration to lean on. What did Gareth say?'

'Bloody Gareth, he was lovely. Well you know what he can be like, but he was so patient. That was the thing, you see, it was all very low key, no shouting or swearing, everyone was so kind. Normally they'd all be effing and blinding, *especially* Gareth. So I could see I was some sort of special case, they all know I'm past it, losing my marbles. The shame of it, Polly, the awful shame.'

*

Later that afternoon, when Stella is back in her own house, Polly returns to her desk but the drama of the morning's events has destroyed her concentration. How bad is it really? How much of Stella's memory problem and her confusion can be attributed to age and how much to something more sinister? She and Stella had often joked with Mac and Joyce about forgetfulness and the tendency to do weirdly unpredictable things as they got older. They related instances of locking themselves out of the car or the house, losing their keys or their glasses, forgetting names and appointments; sharing it normalised it as not just old age, but part of contemporary life. Too much information, too many things to remember from pin numbers to passwords to tasks that need to be done. But last week Stella had let a saucepan of potatoes burn out on the stove, and not even the smell of burning had alerted her to seek out the source. Fortunately, Joyce, who was watering her garden, had smelled it and nipped through the side-gate and into the house, and found Stella sifting through a box of old scripts, seemingly unaware that she had even put the potatoes on to boil, or indeed why.

'We need to watch out for her,' Joyce had said to Polly later. 'This was more than forgetfulness. We all forget stuff all the time, but that loss of insight could be a sign of something more serious.'

Today's incident *was* more serious but not dangerous, at least she has some insight into what happened. And that, Polly reassures herself, is significant. Stella understands what happened, and her sense of shame comes from being able to understand the disruption for the rest of the cast and crew, and the implications for Gareth's schedule and budget. Polly fills the kettle to make herself some tea, wondering whether she should encourage Stella to get some medical advice or if even the mention of this could make a delicate situation worse. Maybe she'll discuss it with Joyce first. Leaving the tea to draw she goes back to her desk hoping for a message to lift her spirits.

Nothing. Polly's chest tightens with tension and she sits there, staring at the screen, hating her own vulnerability. This is ridiculous, she tells herself, he's only an acquaintance and we barely know each other. But even as she thinks this she feels that she *does* know him, and that he knows her; that something special has developed between them, something she doesn't want to lose. Shit, she says aloud, the last thing I need is a man distracting me from what's really important. Still swearing, only silently now, she returns to the kitchen to pour her tea and carries it out to the verandah to sit in the fading light, staring out at the garden but not really seeing it.

It's almost six years now since, at the end of her last disastrous relationship, she had vowed never to get involved with a man again. This time she had confronted her own innate tendency to adjust to someone else's expectations at the expense of her own sense of herself, and then later to resent it. Never again, she had said, and she had believed it, but now . . . Polly sighs; but you're *not in* a relationship, she reminds herself, it's just a long, ongoing conversation, stimulating, amusing, energising, it doesn't have to have anything else attached to it. But she *has* attached more to it and so too, she thinks, has Leo.

Inside the house her mobile rings and, sighing again, she sets down her cup and goes to answer it.

'Polly darling, how are you?' Gareth says.

Polly's heart sinks; had she stopped to think about it she could have predicted that he'd call her. It's a couple of years since they were last in touch and they talk pleasantries briefly, but she has no doubt about where they are heading.

'I'm wondering if you've seen Stella and whether she's told you what happened today.'

'She has, she came here straight from the set, very distressed, but she's back home now and I think she's gone to bed.'

'Poor love,' Gareth says, 'she completely lost it and it really shocked her.'

'What actually happened? Did she just go blank?'

'Oh no.' He gives a short sharp laugh. 'She had lines, plenty of them, from all sorts of things. Some of them I remember from working with her – there were a few snippets from *Neighbours* in there, and then a chunk of stuff from that World War I movie. The thing is, Polly . . .'

'Would you be able to give her a break?' Polly cuts in. 'I know it's a pain, the schedule and everything, but . . .'

'Well that's what I was going to suggest,' he says. 'I've been looking at the schedule and I could actually give her a week, *or* I could re-do the schedule. Ted Schmidt hasn't been well and needs to have surgery within the next few weeks. If I re-work the schedule to accommodate him I could do it so that we also leave Stella's scenes until later.' He hesitates and Polly holds her breath. 'It means I wouldn't need her again until the end of June, possibly early July. It's difficult, you know what it's like, the time and money issues, other people with other commitments. But I *can* do it. But the thing is . . . did Stella tell you about Albany?'

'What about Albany?'

'Oh, you don't know. I thought you might not because I don't think she knows either.'

'Knows what?'

'Well a similar thing happened a couple of times while we were there. She lost it completely, came up with all sorts of weird old dialogue from years ago and she didn't seem to know she'd done it. Everyone sort of froze, it was a nightmare. I didn't say anything, just asked her to do the take again, and the next time she got it right. But later it happened again, very early one morning out on the rocks, and again she'd clearly no idea that anything was wrong. I called a tea break, said I wanted to wait for better light, and I got one of the girls to take her tea and Tim Tams, but then it happened again and I chickened out again and decided to send her home. The next day she didn't seem to know anything about it. Just turned up as usual and did a good job.'

Polly closes her eyes, here it is then, the lack of insight that is so chilling. She imagines the confusion on the faces of the cast and crew, the highly charged silence as they waited for Gareth to do something, the tension and frustration of the delays. 'She didn't tell me that. I think she would have done if she remembered,' she said.

'Mmm. Well today she *did* know, and it was awful to see her so upset and embarrassed. So, of course, I'm worried about this, worried for Stella. I thought it might be just the disruption in Albany; it was a bit rugged. But now I just don't know . . . and I have to think of the production. I mean, today she couldn't get it back at all. I had to send everyone home and you know what it means to lose a day's shooting . . .' his voice trails away.

Polly grips the receiver. 'Yes,' she says, 'yes of course. It's a nightmare for you but a long break may be just what she needs.

I'll keep an eye on her and we'll do the lines together. I could even bring her along myself when you start shooting again, hang around the set if you didn't mind. That might help. And imagine trying to replace her now, Gareth, you'd have to reshoot everything she's done so far, including the Albany footage.'

'God forbid – besides, there's been a lot of media interest in her comeback. What with Stella and Ted the dollar signs and ratings are disappearing down the drain before my eyes, closely followed by fearsome producers and network execs with hatchets baying for my blood. It was me who insisted on getting her back for this, so . . . okay, let's give her a break. It's Stella, we all love her to bits, no one wants this to happen but at the same time . . . well, everyone's getting a bit jittery. Will you tell her?'

'Definitely not,' Polly says. 'You have to talk to her yourself. Say you think she needs a rest and you have Ted to consider as well. She's sure to tell me and then I can offer to help her with the lines and so on. I just hope . . .'

'Me too,' he cuts in. 'Okay, I'll call her first thing in the morning. Thanks, Polly. Let me know how she goes, will you?'

Polly puts down the phone and stands there in the darkened study thinking over the conversation. She needs to talk to someone, someone who will help her work out how to deal with all this. Times like this are when being confidently single and independent is not such a great way to be. Times like this are when you need someone close to work things through with. Someone to hold you in the middle of the night, someone whose sleeping breath is a reassurance of understanding and support. She wonders whether Leo would be any good at this. How can you tell until a person is tested; and by then you might have made the wrong decision. You know nothing about him, she tells herself now. You don't know how his life works, the pace and pattern of his days. He has given her a vision of himself as frequently in demand and on the move. Tedious really, he insists, how nice it would be to stop, draw breath, not always be so much in demand; but Polly is not sure she believes this.

He doesn't ever seem to decline the invitations; she wonders if it is like a drug to him, this sense that others are always seeking him out, waving business class tickets and five star hotels before his eyes. She knows his views on the state of the world, on politics, art and literature, on the British and even the Australian governments and, of course, on faith and God, but she doesn't know how he likes his tea, whether he snores or has acceptable bathroom habits, or if he can, as he claims, make a mean osso bucco. I am such a fool, she thinks, I've let myself get hung up on him and here I am again waiting for a man whom I barely know to send me an email. And she abandons her mobile and goes through to the kitchen. The landline rings immediately. Joyce, she thinks, or Stella; they're the only people who use the landline these days. And she crosses to the other side of the kitchen and picks it up.

'Polly,' a voice says, 'Polly, is that you? It's an awful line, I can hardly hear you. It's me, Leo . . . Polly, are you there?'

And as she struggles to find her voice she knows that the long email conversation is over and something else is about to begin.

Chapter Seven

North Fremantle, May

elen takes a last look at herself in the hall mirror and smooths her hair. She thinks she looks pretty good, considering. Considering what?, some treacherous voice inside her asks. 'Well,' she says aloud, 'considering how hard it's been to make myself do this when it should be Joyce taking the first step.' She smiles into the mirror, liking what she sees, the well-cut straight skirt in a deep claret with its coordinating cream shirt patterned with claret coloured roses. She likes this more tailored look these days. Dennis thinks it's all 'a bit done up', 'a bit not really Fremantle', but what does Dennis know? Nothing about women's clothes or fashion, that's for sure. And she walks out of the front door, down to the car and heads off to the main road, across the bridge and up to the Arts Centre to meet Joyce for lunch.

Helen is pleased with herself for organising this; it hadn't been easy. All her instincts told her that it was up to Joyce to try to forge some sort of reunion – after all, it was she and Mac who had caused the trouble in the first place. Admittedly Joyce had left a couple of messages on her phone and Helen hadn't called back, thinking she'd let Joyce wait and that she would certainly call again. But she hadn't. And so, after considerable pressure from Dennis, Helen had texted Joyce and suggested lunch at the Arts Centre and Joyce had texted back, *OK, Tuesday 12.30*. This had annoyed Helen, who had planned to set the day and time herself, so she'd sent an equally blunt message in agreement.

It's a bright day but the wind is surprisingly cool and as she locks the car Helen wishes she'd added the jacket that matches her skirt. She's a bit edgy because she's got another headache; she's had a quite a few recently – tension perhaps? Anyway, it'll be nice to get this sorted, she thinks as she crosses the road and walks towards the courtyard café. I've done the right thing, created an opportunity for Joyce to apologise without embarrassment. And she feels a pleasant glow of self-righteousness. She glances around the courtyard and as she spots Joyce sitting at a table in the shade, she feels a stab of nostalgic pleasure at the sight of her. Joyce, she notices, looks the same as ever, no change there: jeans, white shirt, with a navy sweater draped over her shoulders. Helen waves. Joyce does not wave back, just smiles in a restrained sort of way, slips the book she was reading into her handbag and takes off her glasses. She's embarrassed, Helen thinks: a few weeks with Mac away and she probably realises now how ridiculous it all is. And reminding herself to be firm but gracious, Helen weaves her way between the tables and sits down.

It's awkward at first and she'd expected that, but somehow they get through the first five minutes by consulting the menu. A waiter appears and takes their order, then gathers up the menus and leaves and they are alone again, facing each other across the table.

'Well,' Helen says brightly, 'this is nice, and long overdue.'

'Sure is,' Joyce says. 'I wondered how long it would take you to come around, but I never imagined it would be this long.'

Helen is completely taken aback. She jerks upright in her chair, her mouth drops open and she struggles to catch her breath. 'Well, really . . .'

'Oh come on, Helen,' Joyce says, 'we've known each other for donkey's years. I know you can do a good sulk, but this one's been epic.'

Helen feels her mouth tighten. 'I wasn't sulking, Joyce, I was hurt, very hurt. How could you make such a big decision without discussing it with me? In fact why didn't you and Mac discuss it with both of us?'

Joyce tosses her head, clearly unmoved. 'You mean like when you decided to move out of Emerald Street without mentioning it until the day before the estate agent's board went up?'

Helen blushes, immediately wrong-footed, remembering the shock and dismay on Joyce's face when she had broken the news to her. But backing down is not one of her finer qualities. She tilts her chin. 'I see, so it was tit for tat, was it?'

Joyce sighs. 'Mac and I made our plan just as you and Dennis made yours. I was stunned when you told me you were going to sell and move away, but I did understand why you had to sort things out for yourselves first. And forgive me if I've forgotten, but I don't think I was openly rude, hostile or aggressive about it at the time. And I didn't walk out on you.'

Helen flushes. 'Well,' she begins, 'you know me. I like to be honest, I have to tell it like it is.'

'No you don't,' Joyce interrupts. 'I've seen you do this so often; you say "I have to tell it like it is", well actually you *don't*, especially not when it is none of your business. If you don't like the idea you can at least treat your friends with respect. There is no virtue in thrusting your opinion down other people's throats so that they choke on it. It's rude and hurtful.'

The waiter arrives with a carafe of water, glasses and some cutlery and Helen takes a deep breath and draws herself up waiting for him to leave, struggling to mask her embarrassment with confidence.

'Well if I'm such a horrible person I can't imagine why you bothered to come along today,' she says, hating the petty, self-righteous tone in her own voice. Joyce seems different, more assertive; she's always been one to back down easily for the sake of a quiet life. She does it with everyone. Now, Helen thinks, she is behaving like a terrier.

'I came because you're my oldest friend,' Joyce says. 'We have a lot of history. I was devastated when you moved but it was what you wanted so I had to respect that. I knew something would be lost, and it was, but I never dreamed we'd end up like this. So I'm here to see what we can salvage, for the sake of the past and both our families, because it's been precious to me, to all of us.'

Helen feels herself deflating, as though Joyce has suddenly loosened the pressure valve and all the steam that has been building up for weeks is hissing steadily out. She won't risk saying anything, not yet, and they sit in silence, ostensibly watching the customers at other tables chatting, tucking into their salads, or soup, buttering their rolls, sipping their coffee. What did I want from this? Helen wonders. What did I really think would happen? What have I been doing all this time? To her dismay she, a woman who has never shed a tear in public since the age of thirteen, feels as though she might cry. She clears her throat and looks away, gazing down to the end of the courtyard and the open gate that leads back out through the garden to the street where the safety of her car awaits her. Helen tightens her lips, picks up her bag and starts to get to her feet.

'No!' Joyce says, and leaning forward she whisks the bag from Helen's hand and puts it out of reach just inside the garden bed on the far side of her own chair. 'Sit down, for goodness sake, Helen. I am not letting you leave here without sorting this out. Where would you go anyway? Back to that soulless apartment to open another bottle of wine?'

Helen freezes, caught between her chair and the table, stares at Joyce and sits down abruptly, rocking the table as she does so, making the water splash out of the glasses, and sending cutlery flying to the ground.

Joyce steadies the table. 'Good decision,' she says as the waiter appears beside her. 'So sorry about that,' she says, 'my friend tripped. Could you mop this up for us, please?' And they wait again, in silence, while he blots up the water, gathers the cutlery from the paving stones and disappears to fetch more.

Joyce leans forward and puts her hand on Helen's arm. 'We're friends, Helen. At least we were. I want that back, that's why I'm here. I'm sorry for what I just said about the apartment, but I don't think you're happy there, you haven't been for ages, so our decision has just made it harder for you.' She leans back again, moving her hand to allow the waiter to put Helen's cutlery down and then her own. 'Let's nip this in the bud now, before it gets worse. Before it goes beyond the point of no return.'

Helen is silent. She feels her body unwinding, the tension of past months, years maybe, unravelling and the threat that she may well unravel along with it. Around her other women and a few men are talking and laughing, tasting each other's meals, ordering wine. Such an ordinary scene with her at the centre of it, her life falling apart, and Joyce . . . who seems to be looking straight inside her.

'Do you really think it's soulless?'

'Sorry, that was rude, it's . . . look, it's a beautiful apartment with amazing views but it's so . . . so different, so *not* the life of Emerald Street which you loved. I don't . . .'

'It is,' Helen says. 'Soulless. That's just what it is. I wanted it so much, wanted to escape from the house that seemed to be weighing me down, but I hate it. I feel like a tenant, living in someone else's home with their things. So I keep buying more things to make it feel like home but it doesn't make any difference.'

Joyce nods. 'I thought it might be like that.'

'But you never said anything.'

Joyce raises her eyebrows. 'And get my head bitten off?'

Helen sighs. 'I've made a terrible mistake, Joyce, and I haven't been able to face telling Dennis. He hates it, he's said so, and he never wanted to move in the first place. It feels so bleak, and all the time I'm there I'm lonely. There's nothing to do. At least before there was always something that needed repairing or pruning or cleaning. I miss Emerald Street, you and Mac and the others, the whole feel of the place – the neighbourhood.'

The waiter returns with their orders. 'Anything else, ladies?'

'No thanks, we're fine,' Joyce says and he fades away to clear other tables. 'And you haven't said anything to Dennis?'

Helen shakes her head. 'I can't, I couldn't make myself admit it, but he knows. I'm sure he knows. But what can we do? The move cost us heaps, new furniture, practically everything new and the prices in South Fremantle have shot up recently. If we wanted to find a place and move back we'd really have to scale down.'

'And would that be so bad?' Joyce asks. 'We've talked about scaling down. Since the kids left we've rattled about in that great big house like the last two sardines in a tin. We're still thinking about what we'll do after this year, but it might be a move to something smaller, if not down to Albany.'

'So *you* might go away?'

'Maybe, or nearby but just to something smaller.'

Helen is silent for a moment, picking at her salad with a fork. 'Did you decide what you wanted to do this year?'

Joyce smiles. 'I want to do the intensive English language teaching course, like Ben did. I'm just waiting to find out if I've passed the entrance test. Then I'll try to help out teaching English to refugees.'

Helen nods. 'Maybe I need to do something. Not that, obviously, but something interesting or useful.'

'Better than sitting miserably at home swigging wine in the mornings,' Joyce says with a smile.

Helen feels herself blush. 'Stella told you?'

She nods. 'You must have known she would. She was concerned. You know what we need?'

'What?'

'We need to eat our lunch, go back to Emerald Street and do what we used to do. Spend a couple of hours out on the back verandah with . . . well, I was going to say a bottle of wine but a pot of tea might be better, patching things up, and chewing the fat about the future. I want that back, Helen, what we used to have, and we might just come up with something useful.'

*

Hong Kong, May

Leo opens the door of the bar fridge and stands drumming his fingers on the top of the door, trying to decide what to choose from the array of miniatures lined up neatly on the shelves, and emits a huge sigh. Why the fuck does she need time to think about it? Why couldn't she just have done what he expected and said, 'Oh yes, Leo, it'd be wonderful to see you. I'm packing my bag right now.' Picking up the hotel phone to call Polly had been a big decision because he'd wanted her to be the one to initiate the move from email to meeting again. But he'd become impatient, and then an odd collision of circumstances had left him in Hong Kong with a few days up his sleeve before he needed to be back in London.

'I really want to see you again,' he'd said. 'I'll be finished here in Hong Kong the day after tomorrow and I wondered if you'd like to come up and join me. We can spend a few days together.'

It was odd talking to her after the months of emails, and he'd been anticipating a gasp of pleasure, so her awkward pause had thrown him off balance.

'Oh . . . I'd love to . . . I just need to think about this . . . my friend Stella's not too good at the moment and I . . . '

'Well, I don't want to disrupt your schedule of course . . . I wanted to see you but if you have other things . . .' He'd recognised then that he was sounding not cool but sulky or petulant or something else he didn't want to sound.

'No, no! It is a great chance and I really want to see you. I can sort things out here. Look, I'll call you back in the morning and let you know when I can get there.'

'Okay,' he'd said, 'good, come soon.'

'I will,' she'd said, her voice more confident now. 'I really want to see you. First thing in the morning, I promise. I'll email, unless you've moved into the twenty-first century and got yourself a mobile.'

An email would be fine, he'd told her, but he also gave her the number of the hotel. Calm down, he warns himself now, have a drink, she's just being cautious. He chooses a bottle of claret and a glass from the shelves above the bar fridge, draws the cork and carries both glass and bottle across to the sofa that faces the glass doors that open onto the balcony. He drops down onto the sofa, sets the bottle on the coffee table and, glass in hand, leans back, kicks off his shoes and puts his feet up alongside the claret. Women, he thinks, make everything so complicated. Strong minded, intelligent women are all very well but they are at their best when they are agreeing with him or conceding an argument to him. When he'd spotted Polly in the hotel corridor with the young soldier, he'd seen an opening for someone to play the good guy. But he'd also liked her immediately and been disappointed when she'd refused a drink later. But the silent walk through the snow had soothed him, and when they met again over lunch, he felt a sense of connection – political, cultural, emotional all meshed together.

In the shared taxi to the airport three days later he'd thought she was going to relent and stay on in London, but she'd headed off to St Pancras and Leo had recognised that he'd have to work harder if he wanted this to go further. He'd looked her up on Google and was convinced that she'd be worth the effort. He's always liked being with women who have a certain cachet as long as it doesn't surpass his own. He realised he needed to give it time, and that's what he's done.

Leo is not a man who really likes email for anything other than urgent or essential messages about work, appointments, interviews and so on, but it has proved useful with Polly. He has stubbornly resisted the constant state of availability that a mobile phone would create; the possibility that anyone can get hold of him at any time is horrifying. Distance, both physical and emotional, is important to him and personal involvement needs to be carefully managed. He'd come to this conclusion some years ago when Judith was first diagnosed. Preaching the gospel according to Croft gets complicated when it touches on the personal dimensions of one's life. He has also been caught out recently by his own confusion about getting old. Having long been outspoken on the importance of positive attitudes to ageing, he now finds that his commentary is frequently at odds with the way he feels.

'You're hopeless,' Judith had told him once she had got a grip on what was happening for him. 'All mouth and no trousers.' And he'd gone away and sulked for a long time. 'Well,' she'd asked, 'sorted yourself out yet?'

'I'm working on it,' he'd said. And she had just rolled her eyes and said nothing. But then she'd gone on at him about getting a mobile phone.

'It would make me feel safer,' she'd said. 'I'd know I could always find you in an emergency.'

And this, though he'll admit it only to himself, is another reason for his resistance – he would rather be unavailable, he hates emergencies, especially medical or care-related ones. But he can see now that if this thing with Polly develops further he may have to submit to the tyranny of technology after all.

Chapter Eight

Mac has chopped up some chuck steak, an onion, carrots and potatoes and is dicing some celery when his mobile starts to ring and he jumps and cuts himself. He swears loudly, grabs the tea towel, wraps it around his bloody thumb, and picks up the phone.

'Hi,' he says. 'I was so excited to see it was you calling I cut my thumb.'

'I'm flattered,' Joyce says. 'Does it hurt?'

'Yes, quite a lot. I've wrapped it in a tea towel.'

'Sounds sensible.'

'You're not very sympathetic.'

'Oh I am, but there's not much I can do when I'm five hours' drive away. Run it under the cold tap and wrap it in a clean tea towel while you find a plaster.'

He sighs. 'Okay, I'm clearly not getting any sympathy from you.'

'Don't be a wuss,' Joyce says. 'You'll survive. I'm ringing to tell you I passed the test and I start the course the week after next.'

Mac feels a sudden mix of pride and emotion that brings him up in goosebumps, and bounces his thumb down into second place. 'Well done, darling, congratulations, that's terrific,' he says.

'I got ninety-two per cent,' she says. 'They called me just now – honestly, I'm over the moon, I thought I'd scrape through at best. And guess what? I had lunch with Helen the other day, and it's just as we thought, she hates that place, is desperately unhappy and doesn't know what to do.' She tells him more about their conversation. 'But she's not ready to say anything to Dennis yet.'

'From what Dennis has told me he'd be more than happy to get out of there, even if they lose money in the process,' Mac says. 'He hates it too, but doesn't want to start some sort of drama with Helen.'

'Oh well, they'll sort it out eventually, I guess. Have you sorted things out for Charlie?'

'I have, Carol came back . . .'

'Carol?'

'Remember, I told you, we were at uni together?'

'Oh yes, sorry, so she came back?'

'Yes, and we signed all the papers and he's mine, well ours, now. Anyway, love, I'm standing here talking to you and bleeding to death. I need to go and clean up my hand.'

Mac stands at the basin in the bathroom holding his thumb under the cold tap while he reaches into the bathroom cabinet with the other for Betadine and a plaster.

He thinks he should have mentioned to Joyce that when he went for his swim this morning he'd bumped into Carol at the beach, and they'd ended up having breakfast together in the café. But Joyce seemed to be in an unusually brisk mood, and his thumb was giving him the shits. It had been weird sitting across the table from her after all these years. They'd hung around in the same crowd in their uni days, and Mac had liked her, but he'd just met Joyce at the time and it was getting serious. But Carol, as she was then, was smart and confident, edgy – and he liked that. And somehow they had ended up together that one hot January night in Mandurah, when everyone was either drunk or stoned, and crawling in and out of each other's tents. He remembers now that the sensual memory of that night had haunted him for some time: the sound of shallow waves, the moonlight and the sweaty heat inside the tent had all seemed exotic after a couple of joints had done the rounds. He'd been sitting beside Carol, watching the way she held the joint to her lips and drew deeply on it, not just taking little pretend puffs like some girls did. It's all a bit of a blur in his memory now, the shifting shadows on the sloping canvas above them, their bodies moving together, slippery with sweat. Was that really me?, he'd asked himself this morning, as he'd watched her eating scrambled eggs, and listened as she'd told him about her life since uni, her marriage, and how it ended. She's improved with age, he thought, still confident but not needing to shove it in your face. And she'd worn well.

'This was fun,' she'd said eventually, getting up from the table.

'It was,' he'd said, 'just like old times.' Except of course that it wasn't; she's in her sixties, he's nearly seventy-two, whole lives have been lived, and he couldn't recall any occasion on which they had ever talked over a meal, just the two of them. But it had felt good, had transported him back to his youth, made him start to rethink himself, rethink the distance from then to now.

Mac turns off the tap and wraps a clean towel around his hand. It's still bleeding but he manages to get the plaster on it and then two more on top at different angles to cushion it a bit. Charlie appears in the bathroom doorway with an expectant look on his face. Mac scratches the top of the dog's head with his free hand. 'Hello trouble,' he says, 'what's that face for? You've already had a walk.' Charlie follows him out of the bathroom into the lounge and leaps up onto the sofa. 'I should've told her, mate. Should've told Joyce, but she was all excited about her test. Next time, I'll tell her next time.' Charlie gives him a very long look. 'I will,' Mac says. 'I promise I will, I'll tell her next time.'

*

'Shall I park and come in with you?' Joyce asks once the airport is in sight.

Polly shakes her head. 'No need, thanks. I've only the one bag. It was lovely of you to drive me.'

Joyce takes the drop-off lane where the traffic crawls along as passengers drag their bags from cars and say their goodbyes. 'We have so much in common, but our lives are so different, aren't they?' she says suddenly. 'You dashing off to Hong Kong to meet your lover, me doing the same old thing still.'

Polly turns to her. 'No you're not, you got through the entry test with ninety-two per cent. And he's not my lover – at least not yet!'

'It's pretty romantic, all those emails and then suddenly this. Are you sure it's what you want, Poll?'

Polly blushes. 'Honestly, I don't know. Past experience suggests – actually yells at me – that I'm a poor judge of character when it comes to men. It also yells that I'm always at my best when *not* in a relationship. But I need to know more about Leo, and about what we're like together. I keep telling myself that I know him really well from the emails, but of course I don't. I only know what he's chosen to tell me.'

Joyce nods. 'Well going there, spending time with him, doesn't have to have any strings attached if you have doubts.' She pulls into the kerb, switches off the engine and flicks the switch to open the boot. 'Just go and have a great time and see what happens. And don't worry about Stella, we'll keep an eye on her and when you get back we can work out what to do.'

They get the bag from the boot, and Polly turns away to the automatic doors into the terminal. Joyce slips back into the driving seat, watching as the doors close behind her and she disappears into the building. A driver waiting to discharge his passenger hoots at her, and she starts the engine and pulls away, out along the slip road onto the highway and back towards home. How weird, she thinks, to fly away at forty-eight hours' notice, to spend five days in Hong Kong with a man you barely know.

She has often envied Polly her freedom to decide things on the spur of the moment, without having to fit in with other people. They are just two years apart in age and from similar, rather conservative middle class families. But Polly's Hong Kong adventure reminds Joyce of the profound difference between her own life, defined by decades of marriage and family, and Polly's, defined by the rejection of these and the passionate pursuit of her career. She has been a risk taker in her professional and emotional life, has been battered by both and bounced back, always shaping up to start again. 'And I've always played safe,' Joyce says aloud, 'living up to everyone's expectations, or at least trying to.' She had known in her teens that what she most wanted was a husband and children, and what she wanted to *be* was a good wife and mother. When she and Mac had met he was still doing his PhD and she was part way through her Literature degree and hating every moment. She actually felt it was interfering with her love of reading and, much to her parents' disappointment, she abandoned it and enrolled in a secretarial course at the local business college. Later she'd got a job as junior secretary in the laboratory of a big chemical company and, once he had his PhD, Mac joined the company as a research chemist. The following year they were married and when Ben and, later, Gemma came along, Joyce stayed home. But she often returned to the lab to cover holiday or sick leave. And when the kids left school she had gone back part time. She knew the work like the back of her hand and loved it. By then Mac had progressed to the top of the scientific arm of the business while she was still doing what she had always done. She had liked that sameness: it made her feel competent and valued at home and at work. She and Mac had retired at the same time and he had found all sorts of things he wanted to do: projects around the house, regular fishing trips on a friend's boat, some serious bushwalking with a former colleague.

They had bought the cottage in Albany for their retirement years earlier, used it for holidays, loaned it to friends. Several times when they were all at uni, Helen's boys had gone there with Ben and Gemma, sometimes with various girlfriends. It was only in the last couple of years, when Mac had hinted that it was time to make a move there, that Joyce had begun to feel increasingly restless. She had a sense of time running out, and Albany, much as she loved it, really implied retiring from one sort of life to another.

'We'd really be doing much the same there as we do here,' Mac had said.

But to Joyce it didn't feel that way; there were things she needed to do, she just didn't know what those things were.

Time to yourself now, a friend had written in her sixty-third birthday card two years ago. *Strike a blow for freedom!*

It was a joke of course but it had resonated just the same.

As she turns onto the highway Joyce thinks of Polly, checking in her bag and browsing the airport bookshop before taking off into the unknown. I've been so predictable, she tells herself, when did I ever take a risk or try something different? Only Gemma really seems to understand how important passing the test is to her. She is desperate to succeed now and to make something valuable from what she has learned.

'That's really brilliant, Mum, honestly,' Gemma had said when Joyce had Skyped to tell her. 'I think it's a really big achievement, and it's a whole new start for you, if that's what you want.'

'I do, I do want that,' Joyce had said, moved by Gemma's enthusiasm and the questions she'd asked. 'I want to prove that I can do something really well, and to make a contribution in some way.'

Gemma had grinned. 'Well you do being a mother really well, and a grandmother too, but this is different; it's about who you want to be now.'

Gemma was right. For Joyce, signing the letter of acceptance and sending it back seemed enormous, a step into the unknown, a chance to prove herself in a new and different way.

Now, as she turns in to Emerald Street, she is looking forward to spending the whole afternoon preparing for the course, getting through the pre-reading, organising herself for four weeks of hard and demanding work. I'd better check on Stella first, though, she tells herself, I'll start after that. But as she rounds the bend she sees that there, outside the house, is Helen's car, and Helen herself is walking disconsolately away from the front door.

Joyce's heart sinks. The stand-off with Helen had been horrible, but since their lunch Helen has called and turned up at the door several times, needing to talk things through. Now as she spots Joyce's car the look of relief on her face is obvious. Joyce sighs, switches off the engine, and glances quickly at the text message that has just beeped to announce its arrival on her mobile: *Tried calling but you're not answering. Call me back – I think my thumb might be going septic.* So now there's Stella *and* Helen to deal with, and Mac and his stupid thumb. 'You and your thumb will have to wait,' she says aloud into the silence of the car. And tossing the phone back into her bag, she opens the car door, steps out and leads Helen into the house.

Chapter Nine

*O*nce they're airborne Polly slackens her seatbelt and tries to relax. 'I wonder if I'm doing the right thing,' she'd said to Stella this morning. 'It's all so sudden.'

'Yes, but what've you got to lose?' Stella had said. 'A few days and an airfare, just do it. It's an adventure. Enjoy it, don't make any commitments, but don't hold back either.'

Polly had laughed. 'Okay, that's totally confusing. Which is it – maintain my distance or jump headlong in?'

'Both of course,' Stella had said, 'whatever seems right at the time. You're grown up, you've handled much bigger things than this. Take photos, and remember everything because I'll be interrogating you when you get back.'

'You are a rock, Stella,' Polly had said, hugging her.

'A rapidly eroding one, but I'll still be standing when you get back.'

The seatbelt sign flicks off and Polly lowers the back of her seat and looks out onto a great white bed of cloud below. Since the first time she flew as a child she has loved that sight and as she stares at it now she remembers another flight, fifteen years ago, when, flushed with menopausal lust, she had gazed from another aircraft window on a flight from Paris to Cannes, imagining herself in a king-sized bed, with white linen and soft down pillows, with a man she'd met a few weeks earlier. She'd been aching with desire then, and once on the ground could barely contain herself until they got to the hotel. And, like her few previous relationships, some painfully brief, a couple lasting even more painfully a few years, it had begun with sizzling sex that, once burnt out, left little worth salvaging among the charred remains.

'Well it's a good thing you got it out of your system,' Stella had said when Polly had told her later. 'We all have to have a crazy encounter or two like that in our lives.'

And Joyce, listening in amazement, had flushed. 'I never have. I've only ever slept with Mac.'

And Helen, who was making frittata for lunch, had tightened her lips, and asked if someone could please shift themselves and lay the table.

Leo's call, a couple of nights ago, had taken her completely by surprise. The sense of possibility in the email relationship had been intoxicating. She could toy with ideas about where it might lead but now she wonders if she has been playing some sort of game and whether Leo has been playing it too. Well, even if he has he has now raised the stakes. She'd put down the phone feeling both excited and confused.

'I hope you said yes,' Alistair had said when she called him half an hour later. 'Have fun, take a risk. You can't live in that email bubble forever.'

Polly closes her eyes against the white cloud. No lust this time; the possibility of desire but a different and more significant sense of connection. It was, as she had said to Alistair, a feeling that Leo had seen who she really was, rather than someone he wanted her to be. Perhaps, she allows herself to think now, perhaps this is actually the start of something really grown up and lasting.

*

Leo arrives at the airport uncharacteristically early. He orders a coffee and perches on a stool to drink it. Does he really want this – whatever it is – a friendship, a love affair, a romantic adventure? Does it really matter? He would like to tell himself it does not, that he could take it or leave it, but in fact he knows that he wants it a lot. Not just wants it but needs it. Needs the confirmation of himself as a man whom women still find attractive. At his age, he thinks, men do not look good with much younger women hanging on their arms. But to have a good looking, intelligent woman of a similar age or a little younger adds a certain cachet. Without a partner one could possibly look like a bit of a loser. And anyway, sixty-seven is not an age to be without love, but love is a bit of a puzzle. He remembers Prince Charles, who when asked if he was in love with Diana had said 'of course, whatever that means'. A man after my own heart, Leo had thought at the time, and he has subsequently drawn comfort from the knowledge that he and HRH are as one on this subject. It's all very complicated in his experience so distance may prove to deliver all the benefits and none of the disadvantages. He weighs all this up, just as he weighs up his professional life – it's like a balance sheet. He's always imagined himself ageing in style while doing just the same things he's been doing for years: working to a greater or lesser degree, being in demand, constantly refreshing his tool kit of commentary with new ideas and arguments, all the time acquiring increasing gravitas. But there have been times lately when he has felt he could be losing his grip. A couple of significant public forums in which he's long been included have passed him by this year. People no longer respond to his emails with quite the same enthusiasm as they once did. He is plagued by the fear of becoming irrelevant, and concerned about his ability to grow old alone.

Finishing his coffee he strolls towards the arrivals area and waits, leaning on the metal guard rail, shifting his weight from one foot to another, wondering what he looks like to the rest of the crowd waiting for their loved ones or business contacts to stride out pushing their trolleys. But no one is looking at him, no one is remotely interested in him, no one gives a fuck about him. A cold bolt of fear punches him in the stomach and he straightens up and breathes deeply to calm himself. And it's then that he knows that he really needs this thing with Polly, this Relationship Thing, to work, to anchor him without intruding on the rest of his life.

Polly doesn't have a trolley, just a bag slung over her shoulder and a small suitcase on wheels, and the sight of this delights Leo. He has loathed travelling with women's luggage: loathed the way they never know whether or not they've packed what they need, and in which case, loathed lugging huge suitcases into taxis and stepping over them on the floors of hotel bedrooms. But Polly has only come for a few days, so perhaps this is not a reliable indication of seriously efficient packing.

She smiles at him and he remembers Edinburgh, the hotel passage, the walk in the snow, and he forces himself upwards and outwards towards the man he knows he can be, confident, articulate, charming, a lot smarter than most, and he steps forward to meet her. As they walk towards the taxi rank Polly slips her arm through his. It's a good sign, but insufficient to liberate either of them from the suddenly paralysing awkward-ness of being together. Their history of emails now seems like an encumbrance; there is almost too much information in this shift from the keyboard to being face to face.

'This all feels very strange,' Polly says later, as the cab inches its way through dense traffic and yellowish fog.

'I know,' Leo says, still unnerved by the reality of being with her. He's accustomed to shining, to wielding an upper hand, to knowing that his charm will carry him through. Panic tightens his chest, and in that moment he wants to back off, undo the last forty-eight hours, and calmly reinstate the original plan in which he would, shortly, be landing at Heathrow and heading for home. Sweat prickles his skin.

He turns to look at Polly. Her face is pale, her mouth tightly set. She loosens the scarf around her neck, closes her eyes and he leans across her to flick the window button.

'Do you need some air?'

She nods as fog floats in to the cab and they both splutter and cough.

'Window, no window,' the driver shouts over his shoulder. 'Very bad, no window.'

And thankfully they both laugh and Leo flicks the window back up and puts an arm around her shoulders.

'Nearly there now.'

'I feel ridiculous,' Polly says suddenly. 'I don't know what to do, how to be. I don't know what you expect – and worse still, I don't even know what *I* expect.'

'Me neither,' he says, 'I only know what I hope for.' And he starts to laugh. 'Let's just take it slowly, have a drink and some dinner somewhere, a walk maybe . . . let's just try to be normal. One step at a time.'

She looks at him for a long moment as the taxi pulls up outside the hotel. 'I'm glad I came,' she says, 'I'm glad to be here with you even though it feels so weird.'

*

Hours later Polly wakes and knows instantly that she is not at home. At home the shifting shadows of the peppermint tree against the night sky dance between the slats of the wooden blind and scatter themselves across her bedroom ceiling. But here it's different; here the city lights fill the darkness with a pale, rosy glow that sneaks between the half-open curtains. Polly lies perfectly still in the big white bed and listens to the sound of Leo's breathing. The evidence so far is that he is a sound sleeper, albeit a bit of a doona hog, but of course it's really too early to make judgements. It's strange to be sharing a bed again; she's grown accustomed to sleeping alone and it took her a long time to get to sleep tonight. Now, a couple of hours later, she is awake again, acutely aware of him, transported back to exhausting, disturbed nights when the presence of another person determined how well and how long she slept.

What am I doing here? She wonders. Why am I doing what I swore I'd never do again? Both Stella and Joyce had thought-fully avoided reminding her of this vow, but she knows they remember it – they had to because she'd said it so often, and despite their restraint she'd seen it in their faces.

Earlier she had discovered that it is still possible to feel desire, but that her attention span for sex is considerably shorter than it used to be. In one way it was a relief that Leo too appeared to be struggling. A few weeks ago in an email he had described how he wanted to make love to her slowly and tenderly, and this he had done, satisfying her but unable to take himself through the last lap.

'I'm tired,' he'd said eventually. 'Not just physically tired but I've had a lot to cope with recently – work, my sister's condition . . .'

'Don't worry about it,' she'd told him. And she had gone on to talk of how affection and tenderness are far more important to her at this time of life. 'Intimacy has never had to include sex for me,' she explained. 'It's about physical, intellectual and emotional closeness.'

Polly leans up on one elbow now, rests her head on her hand, and looks at Leo, studying the shape of his head, the bristle of his silvery number two haircut, the line of his jaw. With two fingers she traces the curve of his chin, then stops as he twitches and shifts his position. In a few days' time, she thinks, I will be on a flight home, back to the people I love, back in my little house, my writing and the lives of women long dead. I can leave this place, this adventure behind as a delightful interlude or take it with me as the start of something important.

'I love you, Polly,' Leo had said earlier. She thinks he meant it although his tone lacked conviction or intensity, as though he was not particularly at ease with either the words or perhaps the sentiment. Can she bear to do this again, to risk letting into her life someone who may ride through it scattering everything that matters to her in his wake?

'I wouldn't ask you to change anything,' he had said later. 'I don't expect you to give up your life. We can have a future together in separate countries, moving back and forth, sometimes together, sometimes apart.'

'We're at an age when most people are planning to settle down, not to career back and forth across continents several times a year,' she'd said. 'Besides, I can't really afford that.'

'I can afford it for both of us,' he'd said. 'It would still have permanence, commitment, but also the independence which we both value.'

But who are you?, Polly wonders now. How can I know? And she sees that she wants an assurance of risk free perfection, an assurance that what he offers is free of the pitfalls of previous relationships. She has not always been so risk averse, but time and experience have changed her. What risks can she eliminate? Drugs probably, alcohol apparently, emotional neediness – no evidence so far; poor hygiene – absolutely not; sexual incontinence – who knows? Humongous ego – quite possibly. And if he passes all those tests there is still the question of learning to be with him, and of trying to know who he really is and who she is with him. As she lines up the points in his favour she is back in that moment in the Edinburgh hotel when he appeared alongside her, the only person in that crowded passage with the compassion to help the terrified soldier. Polly flops back onto her pillows, thinking of it, of the look on his face, the way he spoke to the younger man, the calm but firm way he reached out to him and also to Polly herself. 'That's who you are,' she whispers, as her eyes begin to close at last, 'you looked at that soldier, saw a boy paralysed by fear, and your heart went out to him. That man is who you are.'

Chapter Ten

North Fremantle, June

From the kitchen window Helen watches as Dennis pulls in to one of their parking bays and disappears into the ground floor of the building. She boils the kettle, gets out two mugs and opens the jar of Anzac cookies.

Dennis's keys clatter as he drops them on the hall table. 'Just going to change my clothes.'

'Come and have a cup of tea first,' she calls.

There is a pause, and she thinks she detects a sigh as he changes direction and heads towards the kitchen.

'Mmm!' He sniffs the air and spots the cookie jar. 'Stone the crows, Anzacs, you haven't made those for ages.' He takes one from the jar and bites into it. 'I suppose you're softening me up for something.'

'Maybe,' Helen says, 'but something I think you'll like.' She pushes a couple of computer printouts onto the worktop along-side the cookies. 'I bought these.'

Dennis, still munching, picks up the papers. 'Perth–Dubai–Perth,' he reads aloud. 'Departing . . . this Sunday?'

Helen wonders if her anxiety shows in her face. She is smiling, but is it that awkward rigor-mortis smile that sometimes betrays her? 'It's a surprise, I thought you'd be pleased.'

'It's certainly a surprise,' Dennis says, still staring at the paperwork.

'I spoke to Damian and Ellie before I made the booking,' she says. 'It's fine with them, wonderful, Damian said.'

Dennis starts on a second cookie, and crumbs drop onto the front of his shirt. 'Bit sudden, isn't it? Bloody hell – business class.'

'A special treat – I paid for them from my own account,' Helen says. 'I treated *us*. It's our anniversary next Wednesday, I thought we'd celebrate it in Dubai.'

Dennis nods slowly, still staring down at the e-tickets. 'I see,' he says without looking up. 'It's just . . .' he hesitates.

'Just what?' Helen's heart leaps a beat. She has thought this out so carefully. It will all be easier over there with the family. On their anniversary she'll raise the subject of selling the apartment, admit that it's all her fault and suggest they find something back in South Fremantle, even if it has to be something modest. She takes a deep breath. 'Just what?' she repeats.

'I was thinking,' Dennis says, brushing crumbs off his shirt, 'that we should have a chat.'

'About what?'

He drops the tickets onto the worktop, walks away from her towards the window and stands there, looking out over the river, his back turned to her.

'A chat about what?' Helen repeats, irritated now. She had expected enthusiasm and she's uneasy about what might be coming in its place.

'About the future,' Dennis says. He pauses, then turns to face her. 'I want us to sell this place and . . .'

'Sell it?' Helen cuts in, relief flooding through her. 'Sell it, but that's what I want too. I was going to tell you in Dubai on our anniversary . . . that's why I booked,' the words tumble out in a torrent. 'Oh what a relief, I mean we can still go to Dubai of course, and put it on the market when we come back. Thank god we both feel the same about it. I thought we could sell and find . . .' she trails off as Dennis holds up his hand to stop her.

'We *don't* feel the same,' he says, 'not anymore. *I* don't feel the same.'

And Helen thinks he has a weird look on his face, stony, that's what it is, a stony look.

'But you just said . . .'

'I said I wanted to sell,' Dennis continues. 'I can't do this anymore, Helen, I can't live . . .'

'I know, you said it. You can't live here, well neither can I.'

'I can't live here, and I can't live with you.'

Helen freezes; silence pounds in her ears, a hard lump seems to form in her throat. 'Can't live with me? What's that supposed to mean?'

'Exactly what I said, I can't . . . I don't want to live with you anymore. Not here, not anywhere. These last few years have been a bloody misery, whatever I do is wrong, you're always complaining, you put me down in front of other people, you treat me like I'm an idiot. You've behaved appallingly to our oldest friends. You've destroyed all the feelings that I ever had for you. I've already called the real estate agent to come and assess this place. We can split the proceeds and I'm off. I won't be around to annoy you, nor to be your punching bag, you can live where and how you choose. We can get a divorce if you want, or just separate. But all this . . .' he stretches out his hands indicating the apartment, '. . . all this is over. Go to Dubai if you want but I won't be going with you.'

*

Stella drags the ladder out of the shed, across the lawn and into the house. Time was, she thinks, when I could carry this with ease, and when it felt perfectly safe to go right to the top. She juggles it awkwardly up the steps into the kitchen, then walks it down the passage to her bedroom, opens it up and knocks the safety latches into place with the heel of her shoe. 'Now then, here we go,' she says aloud and, brushing the dust from her hands, she climbs up the first five steps, which seem steeper than in the past, until she can see into the top cupboard of the wardrobe, and she stands there wondering what she was looking for. Winter clothes perhaps? No. Her suitcase? Not that either. Bugger! She feels around with one hand, steadying herself with the other. What could it have been? Her hand settles on something hard, a box perhaps? She pulls it towards her. It's a black box made of tough cardboard, patterned with pink and gold roses. She tries to lift the lid but can't and so contemplates going up one step higher, but amazingly, now, one more step feels risky. She glances guiltily over her shoulder – if Polly or Mac or Joyce see her she'll be in trouble.

'Don't you go up this, Stella,' Mac had said when he'd put the ladder in her garage. 'It's simply silly at your age, an unnecessary risk. Suppose you were on your own in the house and fell, you could lie there for hours, possibly days, before any of us found you. Promise me? Please?'

And she'd promised, reluctantly, because although it made sense it felt like a little chip in her ego. But this morning it seemed imperative that she should get up here to the cupboard, to get . . . whatever it was . . . this box perhaps? Stella reaches in further and grasps the box, dragging it closer until she can use both hands to lift it out. Then, cautiously, she makes her way back down the steps, and reaches ground zero with a sense of triumph. 'So – one to me, Mac,' she says aloud. 'Maybe I'll take up rock climbing.' And she turns quickly, catches her foot on the leg of the ladder and as she crashes to the carpet, the box flies up in the air, and then down on top of her, scattering its contents of old photographs around the bedroom.

'Bugger,' Stella says aloud again, and she lies there for a moment, wondering what damage she might have done. Nothing actually hurts, only her pride. She hoists herself up on one elbow and surveys her reflection in the mirrored door of the wardrobe. I could be a bizarre still life, or portrait, she says to her reflection, Old Woman with Ladder and Photographs. Slowly she sits up straight, moves her upper body around without pain and then grasps the second tread of the ladder and hauls herself up from the floor, scattering photographs everywhere, and sits down on the edge of the bed.

Was it these photos she was looking for? No, she says out loud, it was the album I wanted; the one with the red leather cover. And she shakes her head in frustration and begins to gather up the scattered photographs, dumping them in an untidy heap on the bed. Finally she drags the ladder back out to the shed, heads back to the bedroom and lies down alongside the pile of photos shifting them around, looking for one of Annie, her oldest friend from her early days in the theatre. But she's tired now, her eyes want to close and she sinks back against the pillows.

*

'Stella?' The voice seems close. 'Stella, are you okay?'

Stella opens her eyes to see Joyce leaning over her.

'I'm fine,' she says, pushing herself up. 'Just having a little sleep.' She sits up straight, leaning back against the bedhead, and sees that she must have been asleep for a couple of hours. She yawns, rubs her eyes and looks down at the photographs scattered across the bed. 'I was just going through the old photographs,' she says.

'So I see. You don't usually sleep in the morning, do you?'

Stella thinks that concern is a wonderful thing but there are times when it can seem quite intrusive. But this is Joyce, whose intentions are always without question.

'No, but I don't think there's a law against it.'

Joyce laughs. 'Sorry, I was just worried when I got to the back door, found it wide open but you weren't answering. Were you looking for something in particular?'

Stella frowns. What *had* she been looking for? She hasn't a clue but there is a photograph in her hand. 'Oh, an album,' she remembers. 'I was looking for an old photo album with a red cover, but I found a box instead. My godmother, Nancy,' she says, holding the photograph out to Joyce. 'She lived here. I was twenty-five when she died and she left me this house.'

Joyce takes the photograph and studies it. 'I've seen this picture before, she's lovely, isn't she? I know you were very fond of her.'

Stella nods, feeling a lump in her throat.

'Wasn't she a relative as well as your godmother?'

Stella nods. 'She was my great-aunt. Mum's only relative here, and the reason Mum came to Australia herself. She came here to visit Nancy and never went back to England, that's how she met Dad.' She clears her throat. The photograph seems suddenly incredibly precious.

Joyce hands it back. 'Well I just popped in because I'm going into town and wondered if you needed anything.'

'Please,' Stella says, sliding her legs off the bed. 'I need my blood pressure tablets, I've only got one day's dose left.' She stands up, her legs feel fine, secure as ever. 'I'll get the prescription.'

Joyce gets to her feet too and glances around the room. 'What's this doing on the floor?' she asks, indicating the upturned box and its lid.

Stella glances back. 'Oh the photographs were in it.'

'The last time I saw this box was just after Christmas when you asked me to put it up in the top cupboard.'

'Really?' Stella is unconcerned, heading to the kitchen for her prescription.

'Really. So how did you get it out of the cupboard, Stella?'

'Oh I just got the ladder and . . .' she stops, but it's too late.

'Did you get that ladder out of the shed, climb up there, and then take it back again?'

'I did,' Stella says, pleased with herself; Joyce seems impressed.

'For goodness sake, Stella, that's so risky, you could have fallen.'

'Well I didn't,' Stella says. It's only half a lie as she didn't actually fall *off* the ladder. 'And if I had, you would have walked in and found me.'

'But suppose I *hadn't* walked in? And you did promise you wouldn't . . .'

Stella stops and turns around, she takes Joyce's hand in hers. 'Dearest Joyce, you and Mac and Polly are so good to me and I really am grateful. But none of you is old enough yet to understand the sheer frustration of not being able to do some apparently minor everyday things when you want to do them. It's not that I don't appreciate your concern, I really do, but I can't totally eliminate all risk from my life. I can't bear to feel dependent. Sometimes I do need to take the odd domestic risk or two.'

Joyce blushes. 'I'm sorry. I shouldn't have interfered, but we love you, Stella, we're trying to preserve you as much for our own sakes as for yours.'

'Like a snail in aspic?' Stella laughs.

'Okay, just yell at me next time and I promise to back off. Give me the prescription and I'll get going.'

And Stella watches as Joyce puts the script in her pocket, and goes out down the back steps, across the garden and back through the gate in the fence. Then she turns away from the window relieved that she has got this gripe off her chest and trying to remember what she was doing before Joyce arrived.

Chapter Eleven

Hong Kong

*I*t's cool and dull as the ferry ploughs across the harbour at the mercy of the wind and choppy waves. Polly turns up the collar of her coat, tightens her grip on the rail, and watches their progress towards the city. I don't have to make a decision now, she thinks, I could go home and then tell him what I feel when I'm back there. But in her heart she knows she's made her decision, and there is little point in keeping it to herself.

'I could do with some caffeine,' Leo says. 'How about we try that little place we saw last night?'

'Fine,' she nods, unsure how to say what she has to say. Should she do it here, or in the café, or back at the hotel over dinner? Their last dinner because tomorrow morning they will be saying goodbye at the airport and she really doesn't want to do it then.

'You okay?'

'I'm fine,' she says, still watching the city. 'Just thinking about tomorrow, about the airport and saying goodbye.' She looks up at him now. 'It's been so lovely.'

'It has,' he says. 'I'm not looking forward to the goodbyes.'

'Leo,' she hesitates. 'I . . . well . . . I wasn't sure and now I am.' She sees his expression change, his eyes narrow. 'I do love you,

I do feel we belong together – even if we are going to be apart for a lot of the time.'

His expression lightens, and he pulls her towards him.

'I think I was sure when we got here, maybe I was even sure when I almost called you and turned back at St Pancras. I've just been fighting it because . . . because of not wanting to be hurt again.'

'I know,' Leo says. 'I understand completely. I won't let you down. I'll be there to catch you if you fall.'

She looks into his face and sees a future. She loves his confidence and his competence, the way he strides through the world. She loves the excitement of being with someone so smart, with whom each conversation seems to open up new knowledge and ideas. Brilliance is so seductive, she thinks, like a drug, and she is always wanting more of it. And she knows that he really means it when he says he will always be there for her; that if she needs him he will come from wherever he is, that he is watching her back. It's a cliché, she knows that, but the power of the cliché is that it is true, ordinary, reliable and assured. This really is what I want, she tells herself. I'm sixty-three, and I have this last chance at love, a last chance to get it right.

'I do love you,' he says.

'I know,' she says. 'I wouldn't be standing here now if I didn't believe that.'

*

Mac is in the shed, working on Joyce's rocking chair, with Charlie stretched out on a roll of hessian beside him. The dog's legs are twitching, and he makes soft yelping noises in his sleep. Mac looks down at him, smiling, and stoops to pat him. 'You go get 'em, mate,' he murmurs.

He's loving his time here; the solitude, the freedom to do what he wants when he wants, his only domestic responsibilities those of his own making. He's learned that he can happily go for days chatting only to Charlie, eating when he feels like it.

But he's also enjoyed catching up with Carol. They often bump into each other on the beach, although it's mostly too cold to swim, but they walk there sometimes, early in the morning, with Charlie bounding alongside them, plunging in and out of the waves in pursuit of his ball. I must mention it to Joyce, he says aloud to the dog, who promptly leaps to his feet and bounds off towards the gate, barking. Mac looks through the shed window and can just see a man leaning over the gate talking to Charlie. He puts down the sander and goes to the shed door and sees, to his amazement, that it is Dennis.

'Bloody hell, mate,' Dennis calls, 'he frightened the life out of me.'

'He's all noise,' Mac says, striding towards him. 'He's an absolute wuss. This is a surprise, what brings you here?'

'Just thought it was time we caught up,' Dennis says.

'It is indeed,' Mac says, 'come on in.' He opens the big gate and Dennis gets back into his car, drives in, gets out again, and stands looking around.

'Must be ten years since we were last here,' he says.

'More, probably,' Mac says. 'At least fifteen since you and Helen and Joyce and I had a break together down here. Is this a flying visit or are you staying?'

'Thought I might stay a couple of nights if that's okay,' Dennis says. 'If it's a problem I can always get a berth somewhere in town.'

'No way,' Mac says, slapping him on the shoulder as they walk down to the house. 'You'll stay here. Helen kick you out, did she?'

Dennis stops in his tracks. 'You haven't heard then?'

'Heard what?' Mac leads the way into the house, opens the fridge and takes out a couple of beers.

Dennis clears his throat. 'I've left her.'

Mac laughs. 'Well obviously, I realise she's not with you or she'd be first in the door, checking up on the standard of my housework!' He gets a bottle opener from the kitchen drawer, flips the tops off the bottles and hands one to Dennis. 'Here's looking at you,' he says, swigging from his beer. 'Come and sit down. Have you had anything to eat, can I make you a sandwich?'

Dennis shakes his head as he follows Mac across the room, and flops down on the sofa where Charlie immediately joins him. Dennis puts his beer on the coffee table and strokes Charlie's head and the dog looks up adoringly. 'He really is a wuss, isn't he? I'm fine, thanks, I got a pie and a coffee in Mount Barker,' he says.

'He's a cracker,' Mac says, putting his feet up on the coffee table. 'So come on, to what do I owe the . . .?'

'Like I said, I've left her,' Dennis cuts in. 'Left Helen. I told her on Thursday. We're selling that bloody awful place and splitting the proceeds. Didn't Joyce tell you?'

Mac takes his feet off the table and sits up straight. 'No. Does Joyce know?'

Dennis shrugs. 'Not sure. Helen asked me not to say anything to anyone yet, but I thought she'd probably have gone running to Joyce, even if she didn't tell anyone else. But maybe not. She's on her way to Dubai right now.'

'So what happened?'

'Nothing really. I mean nothing new or different. I just got to the end of my tether. I never wanted that move, you know that. I hate the place, seems Helen hates it too. But something changed when we moved there, or maybe it was before that, and it was the reason we moved.'

'I'm so sorry, Dennis,' Mac says. 'I'd no idea. And she's gone to Dubai for how long?'

'I don't know. I got home from the wheelchair workshop on Thursday and she'd organised this surprise,' he takes a swig of his beer, 'a trip to Dubai business class for our forty-second anniversary on Wednesday. And I looked at the tickets and knew I couldn't do it. So I just told her I couldn't live with her, and that we should sell the apartment.'

Mac nods and leans forward, hands clasped, elbows on his knees. He thinks that Helen is not the only one who's changed. Dennis himself looks different, sad certainly, and obviously cautious about how he, Mac, is taking the news, but also somehow lighter.

'Helen's never been the easiest person to get on with but soon after we got in there, she sort of turned on me. Everything that happened was my bloody fault. Even when there was that big storm and her car got damaged by the hail, that was my fault. Well, I said to her, I'm not bleedin' god, y'know, Helen, I don't control the fucking weather . . .' He stops, looks down at his feet, then turns to stroke Charlie's ears.

Mac waits for him to go on.

'And it just got worse from then on,' Dennis says, 'day by torturous day. Everything I do is wrong. A few months ago she threw a saucepan at me.'

Mac's jaw drops. 'Really?' And a memory of Dennis appearing at the door one morning to borrow some tools floods back. He was looking a bit sheepish and had a large plaster on his forehead. 'Helen hit me with a frying pan,' he'd said, laughing, when Mac asked him what had happened. But of course he hadn't taken it seriously and Dennis clearly hadn't intended that he would.

'Look, mate,' Dennis goes on, 'I'm probably a boring old git, and Helen's younger than me, but we've jogged along together pretty well over the years. But recently she seems dedicated to pulling me to pieces. And the thing is now, well, I just can't be around her. Don't want to be in the same room, not even in the same house with her. So when she came up with these tickets and the plan for our anniversary, I couldn't go along with that. Know what I mean?'

Mac nods slowly. 'I do know. I'm sorry. I'd no idea, you should have said something before.'

'Wouldn't have been fair to her to do that.'

'I suppose not. How did she take it?'

Dennis shrugs. 'She went very quiet, didn't say anything at first, just stared at me. Then she just said – "Are you sure about that?" Yep, I said – nothing to discuss – and she just went and got a bottle of wine out of the fridge, poured two glasses, gave one to me and took the other off into the bedroom.'

'She said nothing? That doesn't sound like Helen.'

'I know but there you go. Bit later we had a chat about selling the place and she said she was still going to see Damian and Ellie and that I should get going with putting the place on the market. So she's gone off to Dubai and I was wondering, driving down here, if maybe it was a relief to her too. Maybe I did something she couldn't bring herself to do.'

They sit in silence for a moment. Mac studies the pattern on the rug at his feet. He feels an enormous sadness for Dennis and for Helen too. She has, he thinks, always been somewhat unpredictable and abrasive, but once he'd grown accustomed to that he'd become fond of her, admired her forthrightness, even when it wasn't all that comfortable to be around. And he had always had a deep affection for Dennis. Their friendship as couples goes so far back and it had been a huge wrench when Helen and Dennis had moved away.

'What will you do when the apartment's sold?'

'Not sure yet,' Dennis says, shaking his head. 'I wouldn't mind moving nearer to the workshop. I've made friends there, it's satisfying, knowing those little kids can get about in their chairs, and they wouldn't have them without us. It's kept me sane the last few years. The other blokes are all pretty good, and so are the women who come in to do the lunches and the morning tea. Everyone's friendly, we have a laugh together. I feel so much better there than I do at home. I don't want to spend the rest of my life being Helen's punching bag.'

'No, I understand that,' Mac says. 'And you think you'll be all right on your own?'

'I'll be bloody marvellous. I can ask the other guys around whenever I want. Helen won't have them in the house.'

'Why not?'

'Lord knows, there's nothing wrong with them and if there was she wouldn't know, because she's never met them.' Dennis leans back on the sofa. 'Sorry to land on you like this, mate, but I needed to talk to someone, and I didn't want to take it all into the workshop with me. It'll only be a couple of days, but as I said, I can find somewhere else to stay.'

'Absolutely not,' Mac says, getting to his feet. 'You're staying here until you're ready to go. You can help me with the fences, they need patching up.' He walks over to Dennis's side and puts a hand on his shoulder. 'I'm so very sorry, mate . . .' he says again. But he sees that Dennis's eyes are closed and it's as though he tries to open them and can't. Mac takes the beer bottle from his hand, puts it on the table and fetches the doona from the spare bedroom. Then he pushes Charlie gently off the sofa, lifts Dennis's feet onto it and half lifts him by the shoulders so that he is lying down. He can tell by the weight of him that Dennis is so exhausted that he has suddenly let go and fallen instantly and soundly asleep. Mac puts the doona over him, and stands looking down at him for a moment. Dennis looks so old, so tired; his face seems to have crumbled, and Mac feels an awful sadness for him and for Helen. Who could imagine that people of their age would split up, the whole edifice of more than forty years suddenly dismantled? Is Dennis right? Had Helen also wanted this? And how will she cope with being alone? Mac sighs, pats Dennis's shoulder again, then picks up his phone and goes quietly out of the door to call Joyce.

Chapter Twelve

*H*elen tucks her travel bag into the rack and settles into her window seat. Business class is such a luxury, she feels quite sorry for Dennis missing out on it; he's always been such a stickler for travelling economy. She takes her mobile out of her bag for a final check before switching it off. Still no message from Joyce – maybe she should have called rather than texting earlier. She'd been up at four and at the airport while Dennis was still sound asleep in the spare room, and she'd texted Joyce just before the flight boarded. The last time they'd spoken was when Helen had called to tell her she'd booked the flights.

'I've organised it all,' she'd said. 'We're booked to travel on Sunday, I'm going to tell him this afternoon.'

'Goodness, so soon?' Joyce had said. 'Only two clear days – you'd better get packing.'

'I'm onto it,' Helen had said. 'I'll text you when we're on our way.' She'd been impatient for Dennis to get home that afternoon, knowing how much he loved spending time with Damian and Ellie and the grandchildren. So she'd been surprised when he didn't perk up immediately he saw the tickets. And then out it all came: he didn't want to live with her, wanted to sell the place, live on his own. She'd been shocked at first, so shocked she was lost for words. Fired by years of resentment she took a breath to speak, then stopped suddenly, closing her eyes.

'If you go to Dubai I won't be going with you,' Dennis said.

And in the silence that followed Helen saw herself boarding the flight alone, she caught glimpses of herself there, and here at home – a single woman after all this time – and her heart began to race as all the responsibilities of a lifetime of marriage, everything that had weighed her down, suddenly lifted. Her head started to spin and she put both hands down on the worktop to steady herself.

There had been a number of times in their marriage when Helen had considered leaving Dennis. The first time was five years into it when she found she was pregnant, it wasn't planned and she'd realised that this was her moment of choice. She could try to end her pregnancy and then her marriage, but if she went ahead she would have to stay. Dennis was a good man, a good husband, and she was fond of him but the spark had gone out, and Helen felt their marriage was fizzling slowly like a damp squib. Police work, especially CID, was demanding and unpredictable and Dennis was devoted to it. Helen knew that the higher he rose in the force, the greater the toll it would take on him and thereby on her. Should she bring it all to an end there and then, or stay and give it another chance? A baby could make all the difference, she told herself, relight the spark, make them into a family. And so she had stayed.

The spark didn't return but Nick's birth did bring her a deeper sense of connection to Dennis, and a greater level of satisfaction in their life together. Dennis proved to be a loving and attentive father and Helen realised that although she frequently felt bored and short-changed by marriage she was lucky compared to some. She wasn't in love, but perhaps that's how life was at this stage, and the alternatives seemed impossible. She sank into a dull but fairly pleasant routine that lasted until Damian arrived four years later. After that Helen forgot to think about whether or not she was happy, she was just too busy. Sometimes she felt that being the mother of two might be easier alone, especially when the boys were in their teens. She and Dennis had different ideas about raising boys and she rebelled against his, which often caused conflict between all four of them. But although she considered leaving she knew it was not really an option. What she wanted was a different life altogether, but she was trapped now.

Things grew more complicated when Dennis's mother died and his father needed regular help and that responsibility landed in Helen's lap. Every week she cleaned his house, got his shopping, took him to appointments with the doctor and hospital, collected his medication, bought his clothes, trimmed his hair and toenails, and called in on him alternate days for more than five years. And as her father-in-law was laid to rest her own mother, widowed many years earlier and suffering from severe arthritis, also started to show the first signs of dementia. Before long she was living with them and Helen once again became a carer. What kept Helen going and reasonably sane all that time was the gate in the fence that led to Joyce and Mac's place. Stepping through that gate, sitting in Joyce's kitchen or out on the verandah with a cup of tea or a glass of wine, Helen felt restored to her own sense of herself. There she ceased, however briefly, to be the automaton she felt like at home. There she could turn the frustrations into funny or endearing anecdotes, laugh, curse and generally let off steam.

As she struggled on through her fifties Helen was so sick of looking after other people that she could have started every day with a scream. Even as a child, she had helped her mother care for her two younger brothers. Once her mother had died and Nick and Damian had left home, Helen had felt her restlessness growing. She wondered what life would have been like now had one of her children been a girl. She loved her boys but sometimes she dreamed of going shopping with a daughter, sitting at a pavement café with her, laughing, sharing disparaging but loving jokes about husbands. But although she couldn't really fault Ellie she never quite took to her either, and she would think longingly of Gemma and what she had hoped for. She was turning sixty and feeling she had nothing to show for it. She wanted something new, but felt incapable of finding it, and believed that she had left it all too late. All that caring was forgotten by everyone except her, something she'd seen happen with other women: the lives of carers gobbled up until sickness or old age brought it to an end. The carer was then apparently 'free', but free for what? Her emotional resources had been devoured by the needs of others. She was hungry for something now, but for what?

The one thing she knew for sure was that she was sick of the house in Emerald Street, which was not only high maintenance, but freighted with the history of responsibilities. But without the gate that immediately took her into Joyce's life she felt cut off, walking or driving back there had a distant, formal feel to it. Things were never the same again. Dennis might hate the apartment but he loved that wretched wheelchair workshop. He had made friends there and the time he spent away from the apartment steadily grew. She had time now, endless time, but how was she to spend it?

As she'd stood there clutching the worktop last Thursday afternoon, reeling at Dennis's words, Helen had felt a weight lift off her. She felt that she could be different, life could be different. And in that moment she felt herself straighten up, lift her head, stand tall.

Helen drew in her breath. 'So is that your final decision?' she'd asked.

And Dennis had turned to face her again. 'It is,' he said.

Part of her had wanted to punish him for being the one to make it happen as easily as this, when it suited him. Something she had struggled with over so many years he had managed to do quite suddenly. But, pragmatic as ever, she simply grasped what he handed her. How would she manage alone? Well, if she didn't find out now she never would.

'Then I agree we work out how to do it all, sell this place, find new homes, divide things up,' she said. 'But nothing is going to stop me getting onto that plane on Sunday morning.'

How extraordinary, Helen thinks, as the seatbelt light goes out and passengers shift their positions, lower the backs of their seats, and settle in for the long flight. All those years, decades, ended just like that.

It had been a strange and whirlwind couple of days, packing, buying gifts for the children and grandchildren, seeing estate agents, and last night Dennis had surprised her by saying that he was going to leave this morning and drive down to see Mac. 'I'm going early, but not as early as you'll be leaving,' he'd said.

'Boys' chat in the shed?' she'd asked.

'That's it,' he'd said. 'Good old chinwag with me mate.'

And Helen had noticed then that he looked really tired, quite drawn really. He is older than her, seventy-six last birthday, and for the very first time she wondered how much of a toll the last few years had taken on him, how much the hurt and the anger he had clearly felt had eaten away at him to the point that he had reached on Thursday. She felt a lump in her throat.

'Maybe we'll be better friends than partners,' she said. 'I'm sorry you feel I've been so hard on you.'

And he had looked at her in astonishment, and she'd realised then that she couldn't remember apologising to him for anything for years. Attack had come to define her because each time she had looked at him she had seen the cause of all her discontent, her sense of wasted time. He had epitomised the limitations of her life and that was all she had been able to see.

So there it was, over! A marriage dissolved, just like that – or had it actually dissolved years ago?

'Excuse me, madam,' says a voice close to her, 'would you like some breakfast?'

Helen's eyes fly open and she realises that she has been dozing since soon after take-off.

'I'd love some,' Helen says automatically, sitting up straight as the flight attendant flicks a white cloth onto her tray table. And as she sips an orange juice and waits for the food to arrive, she glances at her watch and realises that Dennis is well on his way to Albany by now. Before long he and Mac will be chewing the fat over a beer in the cottage. As for me, Helen thinks, I'm a single woman, more or less, and she looks around at the other passengers, wondering who they see when they look at her, or if they see her at all. The first day of the rest of my life, she thinks. It's a throwaway line that she's always despised for its triteness, but now seems a perfect fit. The rest of my life; she pauses, pushing back at the sudden wave of panic that threatens this new sense of herself. That could be quite a long time.

Chapter Thirteen

June

It's good to have Polly back but Stella wishes she could remember where she's been. Normally she'd ask about this trip, wherever it was, she'd take an interest. She rummages in a drawer to hide her embarrassment. 'You've been away for ages,' she says.

'Not really, just five days,' Polly says.

'Hmm. Well it felt longer.' She takes a punt: 'Alistair okay?'

'He was when I last spoke to him a couple of weeks ago,' Polly says.

This doesn't help; it simply eliminates the possibility of Polly having been in Bali.

'What are you looking for?' Polly asks. 'Can I can help?'

'A black and gold box . . .' Stella says, then hesitates. 'No, no, not that, I got that down recently. It's a red photograph album I'm looking for, it belonged to Nancy.'

'What about the spare room?' Polly says. 'Shall I have a look in there?'

'Good idea.' Stella shivers, the evenings are getting cold now, and she goes to a lower drawer where she spots the faded, king-fisher blue shawl that Annie crocheted for her more years ago than she can remember. Holding the soft wool to her face Stella breathes in the familiar scent. Somehow, irrespective of how long it lies in the drawer or how frequently she washes it, the scent seems unchanged. It is the scent of the past, not a tired, musty smell, but the scent of memories, as though somehow her dearest friend had worked their memories into the shawl by magic. Stella holds it up to her face and, as always, the past enfolds her, a past that only she can recall because everyone who was a part of it is now gone. She breathes in again, holding the memories.

'It's not here,' Polly calls from the spare bedroom.

And Stella hears the cupboard door close, opens her eyes and spots the corner of the photo box jutting out from under the bed. 'It's here,' she calls. 'I've found it,' and she pulls out the box and carries it through to the sitting room.

'Weren't we looking for an album?' Polly asks.

'An album? Yes, a red one, did you find it?'

Polly shakes her head. 'No sign of it, but I remember that box. Didn't one of your numerous old lovers send you something lovely in it?'

Stella laughs. 'There weren't *that* many lovers! But yes, a rather dashing man called Harry turned up outside the theatre in Melbourne in a chauffeur driven car, whisked me off to his suite at The Windsor and gave me this box. In it was a silk nightdress and kimono, swathed in masses of tissue paper. It all seemed very glamorous. Those were the days!'

Polly smiles. 'What photo did you want to find?'

Stella's mind has gone blank. 'Er ... well I ...'

'Maybe one of Annie? You mentioned her earlier.'

'Ah yes, well there might be one in the box.' And she lifts a handful of photographs from the box with a strange feeling that she has seen them quite recently but can't remember when. 'When I first met Annie I felt that she knew who I was, who I really was. That doesn't happen often, does it? Mostly people see what they're looking for, what they want to see, but Annie knew who I was from the very first day. It was like when we met, d'you remember?'

Polly nods. 'I do, you were standing in that converted hangar we used for the second series of *Blood Ties*, up the end where they'd set up the canteen. I could smell sausage rolls and I saw you there, a cup of tea in one hand and a sausage roll in the other.'

'That's it, and you said, "If that's the last sausage roll, Miss Lamont, I will have to kill you off in the next episode" . . .'

'And you choked laughing and spat bits of pastry all over the place.'

'And we both laughed our heads off and somehow I knew you knew who I really was, I knew we could be great friends.' Stella sighs with pleasure at the memory.

'I think we should keep that anecdote to ourselves when someone writes your biography,' Polly says. 'We should find something a little more dignified and appropriate to your status on the silver screen.'

'Rubbish,' Stella says. 'I like it. We laughed and in that moment we knew each other. It hasn't happened to me for a long time, not you either probably.'

'Well it did actually happen recently, with Leo.'

'Who?'

'Leo, I've just been to see him in Hong Kong, remember?'

Stella closes her eyes then shakes her head, embarrassed, and confused.

'I met him in Edinburgh,' Polly says.

'I thought you said Hong Kong . . .'

'Yes but . . .' Polly pauses, 'oh look, it doesn't matter. But what you said about being recognised for who you are – you're right, it's really important.'

Stella nods. 'It's a first eye contact thing. You can always tell. It happened to me once with a man. I felt immediately that he saw me for myself.'

'And?'

'And what?'

'Well did he . . . see who you were?'

'Sadly he saw the part of me that was vulnerable to successful older men. It was a disaster. I don't think it works with men.'

'Oh I think it does, at least I hope it does.'

'Well don't rely on it.'

They both sit in silence now and it is Polly who finally breaks it.

'Stella,' she says, 'do you think it would be a good idea to make an appointment to see Derek?'

Stella looks up. 'Derek the doctor? Whatever for, are you sick?'

Polly shakes her head. 'No, no, I meant for you.'

'Why? There's nothing wrong with me.'

'Well just before I went away we were a bit concerned about your memory . . . you were having trouble with your lines . . .'

'Was I? Well I learned them while you were away and you said you'd help. Now you're back you can start drilling me. I'm a bit forgetful but if I can still remember the day *we* met, *and* when Annie and I met, which is even longer ago, there can't be much wrong with my memory.'

*

By the Friday morning of her first week on the course Joyce is feeling the strain. She is unbearably tired; it's only her determination not to be defeated by it, and her recognition that every one of the other seventeen people on the course is equally tired, that is keeping her going. Before the first session this morning, she had joined some of her fellow students in the queue for coffee in the café next door, and they had exchanged greetings with weary nods, shuffling along in silence as the line moved forward.

'We look like prisoners going back to our cells,' Jacqui had whispered, appearing beside her. 'Still three weeks more of our sentence to serve.'

'Bring on the weekend,' Joyce had said.

'Yeah, but we'll have homework. You can't believe that they'll let us have two days without homework. I might need quite a lot of red wine to get me through that.'

'I hit the gin last night,' Joyce admitted. 'I had two large G and Ts and fell asleep almost instantly without finishing my homework.'

The prospect of homework hadn't crossed Joyce's mind when she signed up. She'd anticipated hard, intensive work but the first real indication of what was in store had come at the end of the first day. Ewan Heathcote had come into the classroom just as the teacher wound up the class.

'Starting tomorrow,' he'd said, 'you'll learn a particular aspect of teaching each morning and be required to teach it to a class on the afternoon of the following day.'

'Teach real fee-paying students?' someone had asked.

'Real students, but not fee-paying ones,' Ewan explained. 'We provide free classes to non-English speakers who can't afford private fees. We let our own students teach those, supervised by a qualified teacher of course. It's great practice for you guys, but it does mean that you learn something in the morning, go home and prepare a lesson and some teaching materials, then come back the following day, ready to go. You'll learn something new again in the morning then teach the previous day's learning that afternoon. So almost immediately you're putting into practice what you've learned and reinforcing it. You have the chance to find out what works and what doesn't.'

'So is that teaching assessed for our final marks?' someone else asked.

Ewan nodded. 'It is indeed. In fact everything that you do here is assessed and contributes to your final results. Most people find that after the first few days they start to enjoy it, but I warn you, we call it intensive and it is. You *must* do the homework – if you don't it all starts to fall apart. So if you're struggling come and talk to me before you fall off your perch.'

It was then that Joyce had decided that there was no way she was going to fall off *her* perch. She was certainly the oldest person there, although there is a man who could be in his mid-fifties, and Jacqui who, as she now knows, is forty-five. The rest seem to be in their twenties. The younger they are, Joyce has noticed, the more confident they are of being able to handle the pace. And as they'd chatted over lunch the first day a couple of them had asked her if she thought she'd be able to keep up. Irritated by their arrogance she'd been tempted to tell them to piss off and annoy someone else. But she simply smiled and said, 'Well we'll see, won't we? I'll be taking it one day at a time.'

'Let's get up to the classroom and grab those good seats by the window again,' Jacqui whispers now as they leave the queue with their coffees.

'So you've made it,' Ewan says once they are all in their seats. 'The last day of your first week; well done for sticking with it so far. I need to tell you that a couple of people have already withdrawn, so if anyone else here is feeling wobbly and wants to come and have a chat with me about it at lunch time . . .?' He looks expectantly around the classroom but there are no signs of movement. 'Good, well done, hang in there. If you can get past the tiredness barrier and make it through to the middle of next week it means you'll probably make it through to the end of the course.'

*

'Ben told you what it was like,' Mac says when Joyce calls him later that afternoon. 'He told you about the pressure.'

'I know,' Joyce says. 'I was warned, and it *is* really hard, the work is relentless, but I'm loving it. I'm just going to have something to eat and then I'll start on my homework.'

'Can't you have an evening off?' Mac asks. They haven't spoken since the end of her first day, and he's feeling cut off. Dennis has now been here for a week and despite Mac's fondness for him he could do with a break. He is longing to get back to the silence and the freedom of setting his own pace and planning his days to suit himself. And he's almost finished Joyce's chair and can't wait to give it to her.

He can hear the combination of exhaustion and elation in her voice, and remembers that feeling that came after long intense stretches in the lab, working all hours, attempting to solve some infuriating problem; there'd be a breakthrough, the elation and then the slow creep of exhaustion. It's a good few years since he felt that and he realises, quite suddenly, that he's unlikely to ever know that feeling again.

'I'm encouraging Dennis to stay on here for a while,' he says now, in an effort to change the subject. 'He's really knocked up and needs a rest. He offered to go to a hotel but I think it's best if he stays here.' As he says this he realises that he's hoping for a specific reaction from Joyce, approval of this thoughtfulness, brownie points for being a good bloke. 'But he can stay on here while I'm away, I'm going to come home next weekend.'

'Oh, I'd rather you didn't,' she says wearily.

Mac catches his breath.

'I *would* love to see you,' Joyce says, 'but I'd prefer to wait until the course is over.'

'But that's another three weeks.'

'Yes, but I'm going to be planning lessons every evening and weekend, and it's going to be the same right through. I need to be able to focus on this. I've banned Ben and Nessa and it'd be best if you stay away too, until it's finished.'

Mac takes a deep breath. 'You must be careful not to overdo it,' he says, trying to sound unfazed by the fact that she doesn't want to see him.

'I'm not overdoing it but I am trying to stay focused. I knew it would be tough. You said that yourself.'

'Well yes, but for Ben . . . well he had a lot hanging on it. You don't need to take it all so seriously. It's not as though it's essential. You're doing this for fun; you don't *have* to pass the course, or even finish, if you find it's too much you can always drop out.'

There is a deadly silence at the other end of the line.

'Joyce,' he says, 'Joyce, are you still there? I said it doesn't really matter, does it? Have a break. I'll drive up next Friday, we'll go out for a nice dinner somewhere . . .' The quality of her silence has changed and his own voice fades away.

'I'm not doing this for *fun*, Mac,' she says. 'I'm serious. I'm also exhausted and likely to be this way for another three weeks. This isn't some flash in the pan thing. It's serious, I'm serious, and I don't need any distractions. I can't do this and cope with anyone else around me. And I *won't* be dropping out. Please don't come home until the course is over.'

There's a click on the line and Mac's heart misses a beat. She has hung up on him. For the first time in forty-odd years she has hung up on him. He stares at the phone in disbelief.

Chapter Fourteen

Mid-June

*L*eo, back in London, is restless and irritable. A bit of jet-lag perhaps, but it's more than that; things are just not moving along the way he assumed they would. The Relationship Thing is proving slippery. He thinks of it in capital letters as he does any major work in progress – The Book, The Channel Four Documentary, The Lecture Tour, The Symposium and now The Relationship Thing. Sitting here at his desk in the study of his Paddington apartment he should be concentrating on either The Book or The Lecture, but instead he is gazing out of the window to the street where the rain has stopped at last, leaving the pavements glistening as the sunlight slips through the branches of the trees.

Leo loves the spring when a young man's thoughts turn to . . . well . . . turn to all the things they've been thinking of all winter, most of them involving sex. But of course it's summer now and he is no longer a young man. And the practical difficulties of having a relationship with someone on the other side of the world have crystallised somewhat. Leo has always lived his life in a compartmentalised way and distance certainly makes that easier. It eliminates the risk of things – arrangements, people, commitments – leaking into each other; the boundaries are clear and well defined, and comfortably geographic. And he likes the idea of meeting in different places; it fits with his idea of the cosmopolitan lifestyle – having a home elsewhere in which he is involved but where he has no real responsibilities. It is the perfect solution to having someone in his life but not having to be with her all the time.

Things usually fall neatly into place for Leo; his professional life has developed very satisfactorily. One trip, one symposium, one residency, one op ed piece all slip neatly into another and come together on the huge wall planner in his study. He is the master of the laptop and many USBs, of the efficiently packed suitcase, the wardrobe of very expensive designer suits and shirts defines him and equips him for all climates and occasions. But as he stares up at his wall planner this morning he sees that things are thinning out, especially in the last quarter of the year.

Before leaving Hong Kong he and Polly had failed to come up with a plan to meet again. She is obviously efficient in many ways, and very good at what she does, but she works alone most of the time, her deadlines are for drafts or manuscripts and only occasionally involve travel. The fact that she had turned up in Hong Kong without her diary had shocked him.

'But isn't there one on your mobile phone?' he'd asked.

'I don't use it,' she'd said. 'I prefer to have a desk diary – appointments and deadlines don't seem real to me unless they're in that.'

'What's the point of a mobile then?'

She'd laughed outright then. 'The point of it,' she'd said, 'is that it is a phone I can take anywhere. I use it for communication, and sometimes for listening to music or podcasts, not as a diary. But as a person who doesn't use a mobile at all you're hardly in a position to complain! Get a phone and then we'll argue about diaries.'

She would, she had promised, look at her commitments and her work in progress as soon as she got home. 'We can compare diaries on Skype,' she'd said. 'Does that help? I do have to go back to France. I have another return airfare in my grant that I need to use before next April. Would you like to meet there? Then we could go back to your place together.'

'Okay,' he'd said, 'I'd like that, but first I'd like to spend time with you in Australia.'

'Sounds lovely,' she'd said. 'We'll talk when I get home, make a plan.'

But she's been back home for more than a week now and she hasn't yet done it. Leo wants it nailed down, slotted into his wall planner. He is accustomed to women who make him a priority, who respond quickly to his needs; prompt attention, albeit not always compliance, has always reassured him of his relevance. Polly, he thinks resentfully, seems to have a lot of unnecessary responsibilities to her friends in Australia.

He gets up and paces the room for a while then drops down onto the sofa and lies there, gazing up at the ceiling, trying to pin down what it is that he actually wants: comfort, reassurance for the future now that age seems to be pressing down on him. He wants someone who will admire and, if necessary, care for him, who will put him first. Prince Charles seems to have got things sorted but does *he* really know what being in love is now, with Camilla there, always by his side? Or is he, too, still reticent, slightly puzzled, looking for solutions?

*

Polly, sitting up in bed in her white towelling dressing gown, her laptop perched on a pillow in front of her, is re-reading the chapter she finished earlier today. She scrolls slowly to the bottom of the final page; it's been a particularly troublesome section of the book but now, she thinks, it's reading quite well. Thankfully she closes the file, rests her head against the bedhead and shuts her eyes. It's only just after nine but she's been working all day and most of the evening and is ready for sleep. But a sudden beep from the computer interrupts her thoughts and the Skype icon with Leo's face in it appears on her screen. As she clicks on the image to accept the call she feels the same little twitch of pleasure she felt as a teenager when she got a call from a boyfriend. Leo is there, looking at her face on the screen, rather than into her eyes through the camera lens.

'Oh, you're in bed,' he says. 'Did I wake you? What time is it there?'

'You didn't wake me,' she says. 'I've been working on my laptop in bed. It's almost nine o'clock. Look at me, Leo.'

'I am,' he says. 'You look lovely in that white towelling thing, very cuddly.'

'No, look into my eyes,' she says. 'I told you, remember, the little green light at the top of the screen? That's how you make eye contact.' He raises his eyes and meets hers. 'That's better,' she says.

'But I can't *see* you,' he protests. 'I want to see your face, not just look at the green light.'

She laughs. 'It's off-putting to have a conversation with someone who's not making eye contact,' she says.

'It looks fine to me,' he says.

'That's because I'm looking at the camera not the screen,' she says. 'Have you really never used Skype before this week?'

'Never,' he says, 'and I can't say that my life has been any less rich for the lack of it. However, now that you've got me on it I very much like looking at you.'

Polly rolls her eyes. 'For someone so engaged with every-thing that's happening and so attuned to the Zeitgeist, you are actually something of a dinosaur,' she says.

He tilts his head to one side, grinning, looking back again at the screen. 'But dinosaurs are interesting and loveable, aren't they?'

She dissolves into laughter. 'I suppose they are.'

He raises his eyes to look into hers. 'Polly,' he says firmly, 'you promised to look at your diary.'

'I did,' she says, reaching out for the desk diary which is on the bedside table. 'I did, but I just had to work out when I can afford to take a break. I don't want to be working the whole time you're here. Anyway, I sorted that out today.' She flips through the pages. 'The last week in September,' she says.

'Okay! Three weeks?'

'Three weeks it is.'

'Write it down,' he says. 'Pick up your pen and write it down. I have to plan around it, and I need to know you're not going to change your mind.'

'I am not going to change my mind,' she says, touched by his insistence. 'Look, I'm writing it now.' And she picks up her pen and draws a series of lines through the dates, writes LEO in big letters across the pages and holds it up for him to see.

'Good,' he says, looking into her eyes at last. 'It will be wonderful, I'll book the flights. You're allowed to go to sleep now.'

'Thank you,' she says. 'I love you.'

'Yes, good,' he says, and the screen goes blank.

Polly stares at the laptop and shakes her head. 'Hopeless,' she says aloud to the blank screen, 'sometimes you are really hopeless.' If she didn't have that wonderful trail of warm and affectionate emails she would probably be really distressed by what are, apparently, black holes in his emotional intelligence. Is this characteristic of very smart, very successful men?, she wonders. Do the women in their lives constantly have to make allowances for their emotional shortcomings? Sighing, she puts the computer on the bedside table, wriggles out of her dressing gown, chucks it down to the end of the bed and snuggles under the duvet enjoying the warmth and the feeling of being really tired. Closing her eyes she thinks of Leo, imagines him here beside her in her own bed, the two of them curled together like spoons as they had been in the hotel. She wants to talk to Stella about it in the way she would have done in the past, but Stella seems to have forgotten that she'd even been to Hong Kong, let alone why. The threatened grilling hasn't happened and Polly's not sure whether she is hurt by this, or relieved at having escaped it. Stella's concentration is now focused on forays into the past through her photographs, old correspondence and her collection of theatre programs.

She closes her eyes thinking again of Leo, his confusion about the position of the camera, the way he drops his eyes constantly back to the screen. She is on the verge of sleep when she is shaken from it by her phone. She reaches automatically for it in the dark and struggles quickly into an upright position when the caller identifies himself as Constable Tony Welch at Fremantle Police Station.

Polly snaps the light back on. 'Is something wrong?' she asks, her heart pounding.

'Well, Miss Griffin,' the officer says, 'I have a lady here – a Miss Barwell, Essie Barwell – who has given us your name as her next of kin, and she wants to report a missing person. I'm sorry if this sounds rather muddled, madam, but Miss Barwell does seem a little confused and . . .'

'It's okay, officer,' Polly says, swinging her legs out of the bed, 'I understand, I'm her de facto next of kin . . . is she all right?'

'Apart from being rather confused she seems fine,' the officer says. 'She's sitting having a cup of tea with us, and is eating her way through our supply of Tim Tams.'

'That's her,' Polly says, 'the Tim Tam queen, and what's this about a missing person?'

'Ah . . . a lady called Annie. Says she's been looking for her for a long time. Do you know about this?'

'I do. Annie is an old friend who died some time ago. Look, I'll come and pick her up, I can be there in ten minutes, fifteen at the most.'

'Thank you, madam, and you're sure the lady's name is Essie Barwell? It's just that both my sergeant and I think she might be Stella Lamont, the actress who used to be in *Cross Currents* and a . . .'

'You're absolutely right,' Polly cuts in. 'She is legally Stella Lamont but she was born Estelle Barwell, Essie. It was changed for the theatre. She's been having a few problems with her memory. So could you tell her I'm on my way?'

And she hangs up, gets out of bed, throws off her pyjamas, fumbles for underwear, pulls on her tracksuit and hurries through to the bathroom. Slow down, she tells herself as she drags a brush through her hair. And she stops and stands there, staring at herself in the bathroom mirror, wondering how Stella got to the police station. Did she drive? Surely she didn't walk all that way in the dark? 'Oh dear,' she says aloud, 'poor dear Stella,' and with a horrible sinking feeling in the pit of her stomach Polly picks up her keys and goes out to her car.

*

'I was worried about Annie,' Stella says as she fastens her seat-belt in the front seat of Polly's car. 'I went to the house over the road, and someone else came to the door. A tall thin man with a beard, and he said I'd gone to the wrong house. And the thing was, Polly, he knew my name, and he said, "I don't know who you mean, Stella, but I'm Bill, Jennifer's husband, and you know there's just the two of us live here." So you see, Polly, this Bill and Jennifer have moved into Annie's house and . . .'

Polly switches on the engine and reaches out a hand to take Stella's. 'Stella, it's all right. You went to the wrong house; Annie never lived there. You went to Bill and Jennifer's place, further up the street on the other side.'

Stella shakes her head. 'No, I've never seen that man before. I'm worried about Annie.'

Polly takes a deep breath. 'Annie died a long time ago, Stella,' she says, 'about fifteen years ago.'

Stella turns to her in surprise. 'Died? Nobody told me that. Why didn't they tell me?'

'I think you must have had a little blank spot, Stella. You and I went to Annie's funeral at the cemetery, and there were so many flowers. Do you remember? You made a lovely speech about her and about your friendship.'

Stella is silent, then, 'I remember that. Annie's dead. I miss her, Polly, I miss her very much.'

Polly leans across and pats her hand. 'I know you do. But at least you know now that she's safe.'

'So do you remember Bill and Jennifer, our neighbours across the road?'

Stella shakes her head. 'I've never seen that man before.'

'Okay, but do you remember what you did when you left that house, Stella?'

Stella is silent for a moment, as Polly backs out of the car park and turns into the street. 'Well I went to the police. I walked quite a long way, I knew where the police station was but couldn't quite remember how to get there. But I kept walking and then I saw Hungry Jacks and I went in and got a double cheeseburger with fries. I do love a burger, although they give me terrible indigestion. And I had such a nice chat with a young man in there, he bought me a cup of tea because I spent all I had on the cheeseburger. He offered to drive me home and then I remembered that I was supposed to go to the police station, and tell them about Annie, and the man in her house. So he said he'd walk there with me so I wouldn't get lost. Wasn't that kind? So we walked down past the Sail and Anchor and the car park near the markets, and there we were. And I realised I knew the way after all.'

Almost an hour later, when she is sure Stella is asleep, Polly goes next door and turns off the lights and the heater in her own house, locks the doors and goes back to Stella's spare bedroom. She kicks off her shoes and, still in her tracksuit, wraps herself in the duvet on the spare bed and lies there, wondering what to do: wondering what Stella will remember in the morning.

*

It's just after seven-thirty when Polly wakes, daylight is beginning to creep between the blinds and she gets up, straightens the pillows and the duvet and tiptoes through to Stella's room to find her still fast asleep. She pulls on her shoes and slips quietly out, down the steps and through the gate back to her own house and straight into the shower. Adjusting the hot water so that it is just short of scalding, she stands there trying to decide what to do. Really she should take Stella to the doctor, but it seems important to get her through to the last few days of her work on *Cross Currents*, so that she can retire with dignity. Once that's done she'll have to get her to the doctor. Out in the kitchen she makes toast and coffee and sits at the table listening to the news. Suddenly everything seems too hard – the responsibility of Stella, the steps she's taking with Leo, juggling it all with work, and she pushes her chair back from the desk and picks up the phone.

'I'm still in bed,' Alistair says, 'just lying here looking out at the frangipanis by the pool waiting for Steve to come back from the market.'

Polly wishes she were there, floating in the pool, knowing that he was nearby. She wants him to hug her and hold her quietly, just for a while, to feel his love which, despite their many arguments and tantrums over the years, she knows is absolutely solid.

'I've rung for a hug,' she says. 'A psychic hug and a bit of advice.'

Alistair laughs. 'I'm sending the hug right now,' he says and he makes a humming noise. 'Can you hear it? It's humming to you across land and sea.'

'I can hear it,' she says, 'and I can feel it.'

'Is it your love life, Poll?'

'Yes.'

'So what's happened to the sisterhood?' Alistair asks. 'Stella and Joyce and what's-her-name – oh Helen – no, perhaps not Helen, but the other two?'

'Well, Joyce is incommunicado on an intensive language course and Stella . . . well I'll tell you more about that another time.'

'So is Mr Croft proving difficult?'

'Not exactly difficult,' Polly says, pausing for a moment, 'but he can be hard work, he sometimes seems quite remote emotionally, sort of clueless.'

Alistair clears his throat. 'I had another look at him on Google images the other night,' he says. 'His eyes seem a bit cold, a bit . . . well, as you say, remote. But that could just be the camera.'

She sighs. 'His emails are really warm,' she says, 'short but warm, just like at the beginning. Oh, maybe it's just me, wrong sort of expectations. Perhaps I'm expecting the whole romantic thing and that's probably not how it is at our age.'

'I think it *can* be that way,' Alistair says. 'But that may not be his thing.'

'I suppose I want it all to be easy and risk free,' she says. 'I've made myself a life that's safe and predictable, that protects me emotionally.'

'And you're scared of risking that?'

'Exactly.'

'Well you've come to the right person, I am a mine of useless information and advice on things I know nothing about, but I do know this. Growing old alone is unlikely to be loads of fun, well at least it wouldn't be for me.'

'You say that in the light of your own situation, you and Steve, and how he cares for you.'

'True, but I never wanted to be alone, never liked it when I was.'

'So the difference is that I have never minded it,' she says. 'And then someone comes along and makes waves and I don't know what I want anymore. And whether I'll end up with a broken heart.'

'Perhaps you have to hold back a little bit of your heart as insurance,' Alistair says.

Polly is silent.

'Polly,' he says, 'do you really want to spend the rest of your life, twenty years, maybe more, avoiding getting hurt, or are you going to have a rich and rewarding old age that involves a few risks? I know what my choice would be, but then I don't have as long as you do.'

Half an hour later Polly slips through the side-gate and taps on Stella's back door.

'Polly,' Stella says, glancing up at the kitchen clock. 'I thought you must have got caught up in something. Weren't we supposed to start at eight-thirty?'

'We were, so sorry, I was chatting with Alistair and I forgot about the time.'

'No worries, I was late waking up anyway,' Stella says, and she gestures to Polly to come inside. 'I slept so well, and I had this weird dream about walking down to Hungry Jacks, goodness I can almost taste it now. But of course I don't eat them these days, they give me terrible indigestion and I can't get to sleep.'

Polly stands just inside the kitchen, watching as Stella puts the kettle on to boil.

'Shall we stay in here?' Stella continues. 'It's such a chilly morning and it's warmer in the kitchen. I've gone through the lines again while I was eating my breakfast so I'm all ready to go. Coffee or tea?'

'Coffee please,' Polly says, and she watches as Stella spoons coffee into the plunger.

'And before we start,' Stella continues, 'I need to hear about Hong Kong. I can't believe a whole week has gone by and I haven't grilled you about Leo yet.' She pushes a plate towards her. 'Sit down, have a Tim Tam or four and tell me all about it. You're allowed to talk with your mouth full.'

Chapter Fifteen

*T*he sun is extraordinarily hot, hotter even, Helen thinks, than at the height of a Perth summer. Nine o'clock in the morning and it's already thirty-eight degrees and expected to climb to the mid-forties during the morning. For Helen, who has always considered herself a sun lover, the oppressiveness of the heat has come as a shock and that, combined with the headaches which seem to be getting worse, is making her irritable. She's restless too, unable to settle to anything for long before her energy pushes her out of her chair to do something physical. Right now she is lying on a recliner in the shade by the pool, with some iced tea, and her restlessness is apparent to her in the way she keeps tapping one of her feet on the end slat of the recliner. She has her Kindle open in front of her but can't concentrate on what she's reading, can't even concentrate on trying to hear what's going on inside the house. She's been here almost two weeks and although she and Damian had got off to an awkward start they are, she thinks, over it now.

By the time she'd arrived here Dennis had, as they'd agreed, talked to Damian and explained what was happening. And when he met her at the airport it was clear to Helen that he was pretty upset and for him, as for his father, upset meant a brooding or surly reticence. The drive back to the house was tense and awkward.

'So, you've talked to Dad and now you've heard my side of it,' Helen had said, having tried to ameliorate the silence by explaining things her own way. 'Are you going to tell me how you feel about all this?'

'I don't really think you want to know,' Damian replied, slowing down to drive in through the automatic gates of the complex where they lived.

'Of course I want to know,' Helen said. 'We're family, it affects all of us, we need to be honest with each other.'

'Have you talked to Nick?'

'Yes, we both have.'

'And what does he have to say about it?'

Helen sighs. 'Well, you know Nick, he's not super talkative but he seemed okay with it. He said of course it was up to us and he wouldn't take sides, and I told him there are no sides to take, we've agreed this between us. There's no unpleasantness, no hard feelings, we've come to the end of the road, that's all.'

By now they were in the car park underneath the house and Damian had switched off the engine, and turned to look at her. 'That is utter bullshit, Mum. Dad is leaving you because you've made his life a misery. So to say there's no unpleasantness is just a lie.'

Helen had been shocked speechless. She and Dennis had parted amicably the night before she left, and since the moment he had told her he was leaving and she had recognised that it left her free to decide what she wanted, she hadn't given any thought to the reasons behind his decision. They had got through the remaining few days by keeping a comfortable distance from each other, talking calmly about arrangements for selling the apartment, agreeing to a fifty-fifty split of their assets to be put in writing by their solicitor, who was an old friend. Neither of them thought it necessary to divorce. It had been polite and businesslike, and Helen felt that her sense of relief matched Dennis's. It simply hadn't occurred to her that he might say to Damian what he had said to her.

'It's what we both wanted,' Helen said to Damian, blushing deeply as she got out of the car. 'And if you want to start making it into something else then I'll tell you now that there have been many occasions in the past when I have considered leaving your father, but I always stayed because of you and Nick.'

'Well thanks a million for telling me that,' Damian had said, his face red with anger or distress or both, as he pulled her suit-case from the boot of the car. 'It might've been better if you'd done just that, because by the age of eleven I was sick to death of hearing you nagging and criticising Dad.'

It had all got very messy after that, so messy in fact that Helen now can't really remember what else they said to each other in the car park. What she did remember though was that Damian had finally said, 'Look, I'm sorry if you think I've been unfair, Mum. It's just that I spent a lot of my childhood on tenterhooks, listening for the next row, or another bout of you attacking Dad. I wanted to defend him but at the same time I was terrified that you were going to split up. Anyway, now you *are* splitting up, he's made his decision and you're okay with it. But I'm concerned for him. Dad's a good bit older than you and I think it's too late for him to start living alone.'

'And what about me?' Helen had asked, affronted.

'You're sixty-eight, Dad's almost eight years older. It's a big difference.'

She could see then that this was really bothering him, and she reached out and gripped the hand that was clutching her suitcase. 'Damian, one of us was always going to have to face living alone in our old age. One of us would have to die before the other. As it is I'll be there for Dad if he needs anything, we'll look out for each other.' She and Dennis had not discussed this, but in view of their very civilised parting it seemed a perfectly natural assumption.

Damian had shrugged, closed the boot of the car and steered her in through the side door and up the steps into the house. 'Well you're obviously raring to go,' he'd said as they reached the door. 'And I think you are rationalising everything into your own version of events.'

The next couple of days had been awkward. Helen had never been keen on Ellie; she thought her demanding and bossy with Damian and the children, although she was always polite and welcoming to Helen herself. This was the first time that Helen had actually stayed with them without Dennis, but she and Ellie had seemed to rub along all right. She was happy to be useful to her daughter-in-law and to put her right about a few things. She had reorganised the kitchen drawers while Ellie was out one day, so they were now much more logical, and had insisted on showing her how to make a flourless cake. Ellie seemed quieter than usual, and a bit tight-lipped from time to time. But it was great to be with the children, Toby who'll be six in October and Molly just turned four. Helen adores both of them but thinks that they could both do with a bit more discipline, she's had to correct them quite a bit, especially at the table and when it comes to putting their toys away before bed.

'You need to take a firmer line with them, Ellie,' she'd said, having reprimanded both children for their table manners. 'They seem to be ruling the roost.'

'Well, Helen, I think they're pretty good really. All kids try things on from time to time, it's how they learn.'

Helen had been a bit put out about that; Ellie sounded as though she was correcting her and she had decided to find the right moment to speak to her about it when neither Damian nor the children were around. Then, a couple of nights ago, there had been a bit of a drama when Molly couldn't find the revolting old crocheted cot blanket that she dragged everywhere.

'It's gone, Molly,' Helen had said. 'I put it in the bin.'

Ellie hadn't been too pleased about that, but as Helen had pointed out, the child had to part with it sometime and she'd soon be over it. Later that evening, as Helen took Molly upstairs for her bath, Molly started demanding her blanket again.

'Don't be a big silly,' Helen had said as she lifted Molly into the bath. 'You're a big girl now, you're not a baby anymore.'

'I want it,' Molly insisted crossly, a tear rolling down her cheek. 'Want my blanket, Toby's got his. I want mine.' And she started stamping her feet and splashing water, soaking Helen's white linen shirt.

'Stop that at once,' Helen had said, slapping Molly's leg, and Molly had screamed so loudly that Damian had rushed up the stairs, lifted her out of the bath and told Helen to go away.

This all seems to have been resolved now, although Ellie is a bit tight-lipped still and Helen knows she will have to speak to both her and Damian about this latest thing with Molly, explain how wrong it was for Damian to have swept the child up and cuddled her like that when she was being so wilful. Worse still, she discovered earlier this morning that the wretched blanket had been retrieved from the bin, washed and put through the drier, and Molly is trailing it around again. She also needs to keep an eye on Damian, who is still clearly not happy about her and Dennis separating. Well, he needs to get over it, Helen tells herself, both she and Dennis still love him even if they don't love each other. The fact that they choose to live apart in their old age can't make that much difference to Damian. Helen knows she has done the right thing coming here; Damian might have got more upset were she not here to talk to. She wonders if she should consider extending her stay to make sure he gets himself together.

Helen, deciding now that it is just too hot to stay outside, picks up her things and goes inside, up to her room. The house is surprisingly quiet; Toby is at school, Molly at playgroup and for some reason Damian didn't go in to work today. Helen thinks he and Ellie must be in their bedroom as there is no sign of life. There is a beep from her iPad – it's an email from Dennis about the apartment. Good news, he says, he's signed an agreement with the agent they'd agreed on, who said that the apartment is a highly desirable property, and has priced it higher than

Dennis had expected in view of the currently depressed state of the real estate market. He has attached the assessment and the marketing plan, which also lists the agent's fees and other fees and charges. The agent has also detailed the final sum to be divided between them, assuming they sell at the asking price. Helen, who is sitting on the edge of her bed, straightens up, takes a deep breath and opens the attachments. Carefully she reads the agent's assessment of the property and scrolls down to the recommended sale price, and then she stops breathing.

They have lived in the place for five years and it's in immaculate condition – how can it be worth so much less than she expected? When they had put the house in Emerald Street up for sale, the real estate market was at an all-time low due to the global financial crisis, but things had improved since then. The assessment is a full one hundred thousand dollars lower than she had expected, and by the time she has scrolled to the bottom of the document through the various deductions for fees and charges, the figure with which they will each be left is way short of the price of the sort of places she'd been looking at for herself online.

Helen sets the iPad down alongside her on the bed, leans back and tries to calm herself by thinking it all through again. She feels another headache looming, rubs her eyes and wonders whether she should get them tested when she gets home. This is all quite ridiculous, the agent is a complete moron. She feels a sense of rage building within her. Clearly she can't trust Dennis to do anything right. She dials the apartment but it rings out. She glances at her watch: it's midday so four in the afternoon in Western Australia. Dennis is usually home from his wheelchair place by now. She dials again and it rings out again. Is it possible he's still in Albany? A couple of days, he'd said. Helen tries his mobile and he answers almost immediately.

'What *is* this stuff you've sent me, Dennis?' she demands without even saying hello. 'Is the agent completely mad?'

'Can't hear you properly,' Dennis says. 'I'm outside repairing the fences with Mac, and it's very windy. Hang on and I'll go into the house.'

'Don't avoid the issue by pretending you can't hear,' Helen shouts into the phone. 'This is ridiculous. I suppose you just grabbed the first agent you could get to assess it. Well it's not good enough, Dennis . . . Dennis? Dennis, are you still there?'

There is silence at the other end of the line. Furiously she dials again and the line is busy, and it's still busy the second time she tries. She's now incandescent with rage.

Ellie pops her head around the open bedroom door. 'Are you okay, Helen?' she asks. 'I thought I heard you call out, is something wrong?'

Helen's phone starts to ring and she waves her hand irritably at Ellie. 'Go away, I'm trying to talk to Dennis.'

'Okay, I'm inside now,' Dennis says. 'What was it you were saying?'

Helen closes her eyes and takes a deep breath to calm herself. 'This stuff from the agent,' she says, 'it's ridiculous. For a start the property assessment is way below market value. You should've got three assessments and . . .'

'Whoa, stop there,' Dennis says. 'We got three agents in to look it over on the Saturday before we both left, you were there for two of them. When the assessments arrived I contacted this one who was recommending the highest asking price and whose fee is point four per cent lower than the others. You told me to go ahead when I found the right agent so I signed up with her. I don't know what you thought the place was worth, maybe you overestimated . . .'

Helen's image of an elegant little townhouse back in South Fremantle, only a couple of minutes' walk from Emerald Street, is disappearing before her eyes. 'I was a fool to leave you to deal with it,' she shouts. 'Don't you dare do anything until I get back . . . no, you *can* do *something*. You can find another agent who understands what it's worth.'

She hears Dennis sigh at the end of the line, imagines him standing there in the kitchen of the house in Albany where they have, in the past, spent many happy holidays with Joyce and Mac. She imagines him shaking his head in frustration and she wants to grab him by the shoulders and shake him until his teeth rattle. All the anger and resentment that she has stored up over the years is coursing through her body and it is as much as she can do to contain herself.

'So what, in your opinion, *is* the right price?' Dennis asks.

'At least a hundred thousand more than this.'

Dennis laughs. 'Helen, you really don't have a clue about the market . . . you are way over the top and I . . .'

'Shut up, Dennis, just shut the fuck up,' she shouts. 'You just get back up to Fremantle today and get this sorted and ring me tomorrow and tell me what you've done.'

'Helen,' he says, in that tone he uses when he's trying to end an argument, a measured 'let's-get-back-on-an-even-keel' tone that drives her crazy. 'We have a contract with this agent and we are bound by that. If you don't like what I've done then you'll have to wait until this agreement expires and find another one yourself, because I'm not going through all this again.'

The line goes silent. 'Hello?' Helen says, then raises her voice. 'Dennis, don't you dare hang up on me . . . Dennis?' She takes the phone away from her ear and looks at the screen; Dennis has hung up. 'Bastard!' she shouts at the blank screen. 'You stupid, incompetent bastard.' And she hurls the phone across the room. It hits the wardrobe door and drops with a soft thud onto the carpet. Helen leaps to her feet, picks it up and starts to dial again.

'Don't do that, Mum,' says a voice from the doorway.

And Helen looks up to see Damian standing there. He has a strange expression on his face.

'No more phone calls, just put the phone down.'

Helen blinks several times. There is something commanding in his voice but his eyes are red, as though he's been crying.

'You won't believe what your father's done,' she begins.

'Don't start,' Damian says, holding his hand up to stop her. 'No more phone calls, no more screaming or swearing, no more mouthing off about Dad. Once you leave this house you can do whatever you want, but not here, I won't have it. You've barely stopped since you got here, bitching about Dad, telling Ellie how to manage the house, upsetting the children. Constantly finding fault and insisting we do things your way. Well I won't put up with this anymore. You're going home this evening, Mum, there's a flight back to Perth that leaves at seven. I've called Emirates and changed your reservation and paid the change fee. I'll drive you to the airport, but you are not staying in this house one more night. I suggest you start packing.'

*

'So, she'll be back tomorrow morning,' Dennis says, finally putting down the phone some hours later. 'Damian dropped her at the airport half an hour ago.'

Mac whistles through his teeth. 'Crikey,' he says, 'this really *is* serious. So apart from yelling and swearing at you down the phone, what else has Helen been up to?'

Dennis shakes his head. 'A whole lot of stuff, bossing Ellie around, telling them both what they're doing wrong with the kids. Completely reorganised all the kitchen cupboards while Ellie was out. Then she chucked out Molly's little cuddle blanket and smacked her leg when she had a tantrum about it. There's more, but I think all that yelling on the phone this afternoon was just the final straw.' He uncaps the beer, takes a swig and sits on the edge of the sofa, leaning forward, arms on his knees staring at the floor.

'Has she ever been like this before?' Mac asks, dropping down into the chair facing him.

Dennis shakes his head. 'Well, not really. I mean, there's always been a bit of it . . . flying off the handle over small things, periods when the boys and I couldn't do anything right and she'd be very prickly. Like I said to you the other day, what you see is what you get with Helen. That side of her is there, but suddenly there's more of it, it seems to have taken over. Maybe I should have done something about it but in many ways she was so good, and . . .' he blushes, 'and, well . . . I loved her, always have until . . . until she made it impossible to love her anymore.' He stops again, and covers his face with his hands.

Mac waits to give him time but also because he has no idea what else to do.

'So,' Dennis says eventually, clearing his throat. 'D'you think I should go back there tomorrow?'

Mac shakes his head. 'No, absolutely not. You should stay here. Let her come back and harass the agent if she wants to. You stay put and see what happens.'

'She might just decide to drive down here.'

Mac sighs. 'Well, if she does, we'll deal with it. My guess is that she'll start racing around like a mad thing until she realises that she just had no idea of the market at the moment.'

Dennis nods. 'I suppose so. Maybe I should just have done it years ago.'

'Done what?'

'Ended it.'

'You think?'

'Damian said ever since he was a kid he would listen to us arguing, or Helen having a go at me, and he'd be expecting us to break up. He said that always hung over him.'

Mac can see that there are tears in Dennis's eyes and his hands are shaking. It's a really cold evening and he gets to his feet to put a couple more logs on the wood burning stove.

'Look, I don't think you should beat yourself up about this,' he says, turning back to Dennis. 'The past is the past. We do what we can, what seems right at the time. You've made a decision and now you need to stay here until we know what's happening with Helen. Didn't you say that Damian offered to come over and help you find a new place when the apartment's sold?'

Dennis nods. 'He did.'

'Then let him, he wants to help. He probably needs to have some time with you.'

They sit in silence, watching the fire, and Charlie slips furtively up onto the sofa and stretches out, his head on Dennis's knee.

'D'you think Joyce might have a word with her?' Dennis asks eventually.

Mac draws in his breath. 'I don't think we'll go there at the moment,' he says. 'Last time I spoke to Joyce she hung up on me. And frankly if Helen expects to draw her into this, I think she'll get a shock. Joyce is dealing with her own stuff at the moment. Let's just sit tight, and see what happens.'

Chapter Sixteen

Late June

'Stella, darling, that was brilliant,' Gareth calls, walking across the set to where she is sitting in her canvas chair. 'Really a touch of the old Stella there,' and he leans over and kisses her on the cheek.

'I *am* the old Stella,' she says, patting his arm. 'I think you mean a touch of the young one.'

'Whatever! It was brilliant. Five perfect days, you are a warrior woman. I wish I thought I'd be half as tough and professional as you when I'm your age. So, we're all done now, we don't need you back until the wrap party, but we certainly want you here for that. You too, Polly, if you feel like it,' he says, glancing up at her. 'Maybe you could bring Stella along and stay for the party?'

'Of course,' Polly says, 'if that's what Stella wants.'

Stella looks from one to the other, not quite sure what's going on.

'So we're done for now? But when will we shoot the other scenes?' she asks.

Gareth looks surprised. 'The other scenes?'

'Yes, you know, when I'm a nurse. Goodness, I thought my

memory was bad but yours is worse, Gareth, and you're a lot younger than me.'

Gareth opens his mouth but nothing comes out. Stella feels quite sorry for him – perhaps he's having trouble coping; it has, after all, been very tiring.

'Ah! Well I don't think . . .' Gareth begins.

'We can talk about that later,' Polly cuts in. 'We should get a move on now, Stella, it's been a long day, it's getting late and Gareth still has more to do.' She slips her hand under Stella's arm.

'Oh yes, of course,' Stella says. 'Well just let me know when you want me back for that, my time's my own.'

Gareth stands up and hugs her, then turns away slightly to face the cast and crew. 'Ladies and gentlemen, your attention please,' he calls in a faux authoritative tone. 'Miss Stella Lamont is leaving the building!'

There is applause, and someone calls for three cheers.

'What's all the fuss about?' Stella whispers to Polly.

'It's a tribute, Stella,' she says. 'A tribute to you for your wonderful work on *Cross Currents*.'

'But it's not over yet,' Stella says, 'the nursing part . . .'

'Just enjoy it,' Polly says reassuringly, although Stella thinks she looks a bit awkward as she says it.

'Really? Oh well, you know best. Good gracious, flowers! Trixie, thank you, darling.'

'They're from Gareth and all of us,' Trixie says, 'to say how we all loved working with you.'

Stella is overwhelmed, it is reminiscent of the days of live theatre, and she shivers with delight at the memory of the smell of greasepaint, the view from the wings, the swish of the curtains, and the thrilling sight of the audience packing the red velvet seats. Inspired, she executes a perfect curtsey, and blows kisses with her free hand. She is still waving as Polly drapes her coat over her shoulders.

'What about my make-up?' Stella asks. 'I like to get it off as soon as possible.'

'Why not take it off at home?' Polly says. 'You should walk out of here looking like the star that you are.'

'Yes, you're quite right, I should.' She turns to the cast and crew. 'Got to go,' she calls out, waving again. 'See you soon.'

Escorted by Gareth and Trixie they make their way outside onto the street where Stan, the driver, is sitting waiting in the car.

Trixie, blushing, takes something out from behind her back and hands it to Stella. It's a packet of Tim Tams tied with a silver bow.

'These are from me,' she says. 'It was wonderful to meet you, my first job in television and I got to work with a famous star!'

Stella feels the prick of tears, she has grown quite fond of Trixie at the last few shoots. 'Trixie, how lovely of you; but we'll be working together again soon, on the nursing scenes.' She sees Trixie look questioningly at Polly, then back again.

'Of course,' Trixie says. 'I'll stock up on the Tim Tams nearer the time.'

It all seems a bit confusing; the cheers, the flowers, everyone hugging or kissing her, the escort to the door – just like when someone's leaving the series – but her energy is flagging now, it's been a long day, and she's glad when Polly helps her into the car and turns back to speak quietly to Gareth.

'All done, Miss Lamont?' Stan says, twisting round in his seat.

'All done, Stan, but since when did you start calling me Miss Lamont?'

'Ah well, special day today, isn't it? End of an era.'

'Yes indeed,' Polly says, slipping into the back seat beside Stella. She seems to be glaring at Stan.

'End of an era?' Stella says, wracking her brains. 'What era?'

'I heard you were retir . . .'

'End of an era, Stella,' Polly interrupts, 'is the name of the episode you've been working on. Can we get moving now please, Stan, Stella's had a long day.'

'End of an era,' Stella says, twisting around to wave back at Gareth and Trixie as Stan pulls away up the street. 'That's a nice name for an episode, but it sounds a bit like the end of someone's career really, doesn't it? End of an era? Are you all right, Stan? The back of your neck has gone very red.'

Stan clears his throat. 'Must be my hot flushes, Stella,' he says, smiling at her in the rear-view mirror. 'So here we go, driving Miss Stella – how's that for a title?'

Stella rolls her eyes at him. 'It's Driving Miss Daisy,' she says. 'Try to keep up, Stan, or they'll be putting you out to pasture.'

Beside her Polly has leaned back and closed her eyes.

'It was lovely of you to help me with my lines, and to come along with me this week,' Stella says. 'I do feel I'm back on track now and I'll be all right whenever Gareth wants me back. Something I kept meaning to ask you though: why does everyone call him Bloody Gareth? Have I missed something?'

*

Polly pours herself a large glass of red wine and sits down at Stella's kitchen table. Her relief that the work on *Cross Currents* has finished, and finished on a high for Stella, is matched by her sadness that her friend's career is over and her future uncertain. She's faced with the dilemma of whether to let Stella continue believing that there are still more scenes to film, or confront her with the reality that she will never work again. Isn't it her right to be allowed to face the truth? After all, so much of what she does is perfectly okay. How is it possible to weigh that against these random lapses? But if the night walk into Fremantle that ended at the police station is anything to go by, the random lapses could be increasingly serious, dangerous even.

Not too much reality, Alistair had suggested when she'd talked to him about it, and Polly understands why he said that, but it seems disrespectful not to try to set Stella straight about what's happening. At any other time Polly knows she would be talking to Joyce right now but they'd spoken briefly yesterday morning when she'd been coming back from her early walk as Joyce was backing out of her drive. She'd thought Joyce looked wiped out.

'I'm half dead, but loving it at the same time,' Joyce had said. 'Sounds ridiculous but it's the truth. We'll catch up when it's over but I can't think about anything else until then. Did I tell you Dennis has left Helen? He's down in Albany with Mac, and she went off to Dubai to stay with Damian and Ellie, but she behaved so badly that Damian packed her off home early.'

'Crikey,' Polly had said. 'So is she back here?'

Joyce had shrugged. 'Should be by now according to Mac. He and I are still on stand-off, by the way.'

'Still on . . . I didn't know there was a stand-off.'

'Oh no, of course not. Well I hung up on him. He wasn't taking me seriously.'

'*You* hung up on Mac!' Polly had said. 'My god, the world has gone mad. Dennis and Helen split up, you and Mac . . .'

'And you fall in love in Hong Kong!' Joyce cut in. 'Gotta go. I want to hear about Stella going rogue, and about Hong Kong and Leo, so when we do catch up it'll need to be a long one.'

It's almost seven-thirty and she wonders whether or not Stella, who had gone for a rest when they got back from the studio, is still asleep. She walks through to the bedroom, taps on the door, and opens it slightly. 'Stella,' she says, softly, 'Stella, are you awake?' Crossing to the edge of the bed she can hear from Stella's breathing that she is sound asleep. Not much likelihood of her waking up and wanting a full meal, Polly thinks. If she does wake now all she'll want is a cup of tea. Polly stands there in the silence studying her, trying to match this aged face, slack with sleep, to the woman she has known through the years.

Back in the kitchen she covers the food, puts it in the fridge and picks up her glass but the prospect of the wine hitting her stomach makes her feel sick, and she tips it away down the sink. She wishes she could talk to someone, but Joyce is out of bounds, Mac is probably busy counselling Dennis, and Alistair has already told her what he thinks, which was exactly what Stella herself would have said. She could call Leo, but how would she talk to him about this? He doesn't even know Stella, and his attention span for a conversation like the one she needs is likely to be pitifully short.

Polly sighs. Stella, she knows, is exhausted from the filming. Maybe I'll give it a couple of weeks and see how she goes now it's over, she tells herself. If things don't improve, or if they get worse, I'll call straight away, make an appointment and get her there somehow. It's a relief to have made a decision, even if it is just a decision to do nothing yet. She fills the kettle, makes tea and toast and settles down at the kitchen table, thumbing through the unopened copy of *The West Australian*. At nine o'clock Stella is still sleeping and Polly decides that it might be best if she stays the night again. She goes next door to her own house, picks up her toothbrush, nightdress and her book, and slips back through the side-gate to Stella's. Once again she opens the bedroom door, walks over to the bed and stands beside her sleeping friend. It's right to give her a bit more time, she thinks, two weeks, maybe even three, because once I make that call, once I take her to the doctor, everything will change. Stella's life will have to change in ways that she'll hate, ways that will break her spirit, and my own heart. And she walks out, across the passage into the spare room, and a few minutes later she is sitting up in bed, her book open in front of her. Her eyes slide wearily across sentences and paragraphs, but the words mean nothing, nothing registers and eventually she closes the book, lies down and turns off the light. In her head the same questions and answers churn back and forth – what to do, when to do it, act now, wait a few weeks . . . and slowly her eyes close and she feels the blissful calming moment that releases her into sleep.

Chapter Seventeen

*A*t lunch time, while everyone is out in search of coffee, food, fresh air or all three, Joyce rolls up her coat, sets it down on the floor behind the rows of chairs, and lies down resting her head on it. She has somewhere between forty-five and fifty minutes before people start to drift back in for the afternoon session and if she doesn't grab a few minutes' sleep, she knows she won't last the afternoon. Relief floods through her as she closes her eyes and feels the tension ebbing away, her mind stops struggling to hang on, her thoughts begin to drift. One more week to go and that feels like liberation, but at the same time she doesn't want it to be over, the intensity of it, the small but regular satisfactions of learning something new and putting it into practice. But what will she do when it's over? All she knows is that she will be different, that these last few weeks have changed her.

'I wish I'd done it years ago,' she'd told Ewan that morning, 'but at the same time I'm so happy to be doing it now, when I really need it, when it really matters.' She'd wanted to say that she has the feeling of her life opening up to all sorts of possibilities, that getting old no longer feels as though it will be a slow and steady process of diminishment and loss. But nice as Ewan is she fears sounding pathetic. She has studied the job advertisements on the noticeboard; there are opportunities for people who want to teach everywhere from Japan to Germany, the Middle East to Mexico. It seems that if you can get up and go then you'll always find work teaching English somewhere, including here in Perth.

'Would you do that?' Jacqui had asked her this morning. 'Would you just take off somewhere and give it a go?'

'I don't know,' Joyce had said. 'My head's too full of stuff to be able to work that out right now. But knowing that I can, that it's a possibility – that's what makes it exciting. I always thought I wanted to travel as I got older, not just for a holiday, but to stay somewhere for a few months at a time.'

There is a slight noise by the door and Joyce tenses again, imagining one of her fellow students returning, spotting her flat out on the floor, asking if she's okay or needs help. 'Just leave me alone,' she murmurs into the silence, 'please just leave me alone.' But there is no one there.

She has made a determined effort to avoid distractions, and apart from a brief chat with Polly she has managed that. Mac had called her to let her know that Helen was back in Fremantle having fallen out with Damian. 'So she's back in the apartment, and apparently terrorising estate agents,' he'd said. 'Have you heard anything from her?'

'Not a word since she sent me that text the day she left,' Joyce had said.

'Well Dennis reckons you should expect a visit,' Mac said. 'He doesn't think she'll last long bouncing around on her own, and he's going to lie low here for a while.'

'So how are you going?' Joyce had asked.

'Not too bad,' he'd said, but she could hear the reservation in his voice. Mac was very fond of Dennis, but she was sure that by now, he would be itching to have the place to himself again. 'He needed a break and he's been helping me with the fences, and other things. We've done quite a bit of work.'

His tone was a bit strained and Joyce realised he was still

smarting over her hanging up on him. Perhaps he was waiting for her to apologise; if so he was in for a long wait. He'd treated what she was doing as something trivial, probably because he was unused to her having some other focus in her life. Well, he'd just have to get used to it, he'd always had other things going on, things that took him away for weekends, or fishing trips, and when he was working his attention was almost always elsewhere. Now she has other things too. Mac, she thinks, has taken a lot for granted and she has let him. Things will have to change when he comes back, and in the meantime, if there is to be an apology it will not come from her.

Joyce shifts her position slightly; the floor is very hard, especially on her lower back. She thinks of Helen being turfed out of Damian and Ellie's place and sent home, imagines her alone in the apartment calling agents, and harassing Dennis over the phone. Years ago she would have been worrying about Helen, calling her, offering help and consolation, but now, for the first time, she admits that it's a long time since she really enjoyed Helen's company. Helen had become obsessed with what she saw as the unfairness of her life and had constantly recycled angry, resentful monologues full of complaints, unanswerable questions, and calls for Joyce to support her. So despite Joyce's shock and disappointment when Helen had announced that they were moving, it hadn't taken her long to realise that it would, in some ways, free her from being Helen's listening post. Since then Joyce has felt herself being sucked into the black hole of Helen's anger or discontent. It had been the same when they had met up again at the Arts Centre. She'd hoped that by encouraging Helen back to their old spot on the verandah afterwards, they might recapture something of their past friendship, but it was the same old saga of complaints with none of the warmth and humour of the past. No more, she thinks now, and she knows that something in her has changed in the last few weeks. She feels different, so different that her response to Helen will be profoundly different too.

It's Jacqui who wakes her, eventually, with a beaker of coffee and a sandwich from the café, and as Joyce blinks and rubs her eyes she sees that there are four other people curled up on the floor nearby.

'You're a trendsetter,' Jacqui says, giving her a hand to get to her feet. 'Did you actually sleep?'

'Blissfully,' Joyce says, yawning. 'I may just make it through the afternoon now. I'm a trendsetter and you're a saint.' And she settles back at her desk with ten minutes left to eat, drink and get her head back into gear.

Later, at home, she warms up some soup, and sits on a stool at the bench top to eat it, listening to the sound of heavy rain on the roof. Then, pushing aside her bowl and spoon, she flops down into the old armchair in the corner of the dining area of the kitchen, and puts her feet up on the sagging ottoman, to study. Since the course began the kitchen has become both living and study space. She eats her meals at the bench, and her laptop, books and papers are spread the length of the kitchen table. It's warm in here, cosy, and the light is good. The chair is old, shabby and comfortable, the pile of the fabric on the arms worn thin with years of use. One day she'll replace it with a rocking chair but she has no time for that now. No time for anything except this extremely complex book chapter on the interference factor of native languages for students learning English. It's as she is struggling with a particularly complicated section that the front doorbell rings and her heart sinks. Knowing that any sort of conversation will destroy her concentration she ignores it. Ben and Vanessa are away, Stella or Polly would call out, or walk around to the back door. She turns the page and reads on, and hears the bell again. Joyce looks up, waiting for whoever it is to go away. There is a third ring and then the sound of a key turning in the front door. Joyce gets to her feet and walks out to the passage to discover Helen closing the front door behind her. Helen! She had completely forgotten about her.

'There you are,' Helen says, turning around, looking slightly affronted. 'I knew you were in but I kept ringing and you didn't answer. It's pouring out there.'

Joyce watches in amazement as Helen leans her umbrella in the corner and runs her hands through her hair. 'I didn't answer because I didn't want to be disturbed,' she says, her voice deliberately cold. 'And I really resent your letting yourself in. I didn't realise you still had a key. I'll have it back please.'

Helen is unconcerned. 'We've always gone in and out of each other's houses,' she says. 'Done it for years.'

'We haven't done it since you moved,' Joyce says. 'Which is now several years ago, and I don't even *have* a key to your home any longer so I'd like mine back.'

Helen shrugs. 'Oh well, if you're going to be like that . . .' she begins, twisting the key free of the key ring. 'But I'm hardly an intruder. You were obviously in and I thought you might not have heard or even perhaps be ill or something.'

Joyce takes the key and puts it in her pocket. 'Did you want something, Helen?'

'I came to tell you what's been happening.' She starts to unbutton her coat. 'I had to come home earlier than I planned because Dennis made such a mess of the arrangements for selling the apartment and I . . .'

Joyce holds up a hand to stop her. 'I know what's happened, Helen. Dennis told Mac and he told me. Anyway, I'm sure you'll be able to sort things out now you're back. But I need you to go. I'm very tired and still have a lot of study to do for an exam. Even Mac and the kids are banned at the moment.' She walks past Helen to the front door and opens it, taking great care to stay cool and distant. 'I hope you manage to fix everything up and get a good price, it's a lovely apartment.' And she stands there, holding the door open, waiting.

'I brought a bottle of wine,' Helen says, as though she hasn't heard a word of it. And she starts to walk away from Joyce towards the kitchen. 'I thought we could get into this and order a pizza, or a curry.'

Joyce says nothing. She is struggling to stay and look calm standing there by the door, but inside she is boiling with resentment not just at what's happening now but at all the things that have happened in the past few years, that have hurt or angered her and which, in her effort to manage the friendship and keep the peace, she has never mentioned.

They face each other in icy silence and it is Helen who breaks it.

'Oh well, if that's how you want it I'll take my wine and go home,' she says, and she walks briskly down the passage and back out through the open door. 'So much for friendship, a lifetime of friendship,' she says, grabbing her umbrella on the way, and Joyce watches as she runs down the path through the rain back to her car.

Joyce closes the door and leans back against it. She has a pain like indigestion in her chest, and is close to tears. The relief of the closed door is enormous, but it is matched by the sense of loss. It is, she knows, the end of a connection that was once very special, but which has been a long time dying. The lives of their two families had hung together largely on her friendship with Helen, a friendship now so soured that it taints the memories of the good times. She stands there, still leaning on the door, listening to the sound of Helen starting her car and accelerating away up the street, and as the sound fades she locks the door, puts on the chain, and walks back to her chair in the kitchen. She remembers a time some years ago, not long after Helen and Dennis had moved, when she and Helen had gone to an event at the Perth Festival, and then walked across the grounds of the university where it was held, in the midday heat.

'I know you're angry about a lot of things, Helen,' she'd said. 'Perhaps these are things you should have dealt with a long time ago but they all sound to me very much like the usual things that happen in a marriage, situations change, people change, some of it's you, some of it Dennis, some unavoidable circumstances. But within all that you had the chance to be happy, to make what you could of it or do something different. You were never entirely powerless, and I think you have often chosen resentment over looking for ways to change things. I mean, it seems to me that there have been times when you have chosen to be unhappy rather than looking for solutions.'

Helen had stopped walking and looked at her in amazement. 'I can't think what you mean,' she'd said. 'But it seems unfair, after all I've done . . .' and off she'd gone into one of those terrible monologues and Joyce had felt the black hole of negativity opening up in front of her again. Helen had changed so much from the days when for both of them a coffee, a glass of wine, the chance to let off steam and end up doubled up with laughter had been how they had solved their problems.

Perhaps, Joyce thinks, life is simply like that, people change. I've changed. Helen has changed. We've simply outgrown our friendship. Whatever the causes, something that was once very precious has juddered to a halt and restarting it is out of the question.

*

Despite the fact that he would like the house to himself again, Mac has enjoyed Dennis's company, as well as the feeling that he's been able to do something for his friend. They've spent more time together these last couple of weeks than ever before and it's surprised him to discover how much at ease they've become. Now as he stands on a ladder painting the ceiling in the laundry Mac pauses for a moment, thinking that without Dennis around to talk to he might have found it harder to cope with the change in Joyce. Not that he'd mentioned that to Dennis, of course, but listening to him talk, learning more about how things between him and Helen have been over the years, has helped Mac to get this in proportion. Has Joyce actually changed? The more he's thought about this the more he feels that there's something about her tone, her manner, that's different. She's abrupt, distracted, and it seems to Mac that it's always him calling her, rather than the other way around. He's still smarting over the way she'd told him not to come home, and hung up on him. At his lowest he feels she's abandoned him in favour of this new interest, and while deep down he realises that might be a bit pathetic it continues to niggle at him. But he's determined not to say anything, not to make waves, although who knows how far out a wave might be building? Dennis and I are alike, he thinks; we prefer to avoid trouble, particularly trouble at home. However did he cope all those years?

A couple of times Mac has considered calling Carol, suggesting that the three of them meet for a meal, or that Dennis goes with him on his morning walk at the beach, but something has held him back. How would he explain this to Dennis, when he has no idea how to explain it to Joyce? And because he can't answer that he decides to leave things as they are. He takes Charlie to the beach in the mornings, and Dennis, who is not by choice an early riser, takes him out along the bush path in the afternoons.

'Two old codgers doing their own thing,' Dennis had said the other day. And it had jarred with Mac, because he's not yet ready to be an old codger. In fact, as he sets out in the morning, to swim or walk or both, knowing Carol will most likely be there, Mac feels younger than he's felt in a while. There is something about being with Carol that reminds him of who he used to be; not at the time when they had met, but later, much later, the time in his fifties when he was at the top of his profession: confident, competent, respected; in control of the entire research facility, making decisions that would have serious and far-reaching consequences. The time of his life when he'd felt he'd finally grown into the man he was supposed to be. How strange that somehow that had evaporated without his even noticing it. And he lays the paint roller in the tray and stands there at the top of the ladder, wondering how to hold on to that; how to be old and at the same time hold on to that same sense of himself.

Chapter Eighteen

Early July

Stella sits in front of her computer waiting for the call. She's a bit early and as she waits she drums her fingers impatiently on the desk. She's early because she no longer trusts herself to remember how things work and sits, waiting impatiently for this call to happen like magic. She and Gemma haven't spoken for months, not since before Stella started work on *Cross Currents*, but yesterday she'd got a text from Gemma suggesting they should talk today, she set a time and said she would call then unless Stella told her not to.

It's odd, Stella thinks now, how easily you get out of the habit of catching up with someone; you miss a couple of weeks or a month and somehow the habit is broken. She's loved Gemma since the day she first saw her – a rosy cheeked, dark haired little angel, clutching her mother's hand as she watched the removalists unload their furniture from the truck. In those days Stella lived in Melbourne, but she often returned to Fremantle for a break, always staying in the house that she had inherited from Nancy. She'd been there on the day the people who'd bought the big house next door moved in, and she'd wandered out into her garden to get a glimpse of her new neighbours.

A woman was standing with her back to her holding a small girl by the hand, while nearby her husband chatted to the removalists, and a boy, older than the little girl, stood by impatiently kicking some stones at the side of the road.

Stella had just decided to go across and speak to them when the little girl turned around and saw her.

'Who are you?' the child said, tugging at the same time on her mother's arm.

'I'm Stella, I live in this house,' Stella said, and the mother turned and smiled and walked over to shake hands.

The day she first met Joyce and Gemma, and later Mac and Ben, has never faded from Stella's memory. It had been the beginning of much more than a friendship, so much more that she often feels as though Joyce and Mac, Ben and Gemma are her de facto family. Some years later, when Polly bought the place on the other side, Stella had counted herself lucky that the people she had grown to love most in the world were ideally located on either side of her. The one thing that would have made it perfect would have been to have Annie there too. But by then Annie was married and living in Queensland, and although they wrote and talked on the phone they met only occasionally.

Annie, Stella thinks now. I wish she'd hurry up with this call, I'm dying to talk to her, it seems like ages, years since we met. Now that I've finished *Cross Currents* I should fly up there for a visit, yes, that's what I'll do, we'll make a date and I'll book a ticket today . . .

The computer makes a chiming sound and an icon appears in the middle of the screen; of course that's it, that's how Skype works. Ignoring her glasses, which are resting on the table beside the keyboard, Stella clicks the icon and the screen opens up.

'Annie,' she cries in delight. 'You're late calling, I thought you might have forgotten.'

'It's Gemma, Stella,' the person on the screen says. 'Sorry I'm late, I just couldn't get the connection to work.'

Stella stares at the face on the screen, knowing that this is not Annie, but knowing too that the woman is familiar. 'I'm sorry . . .' she begins, and then the little dark haired angel slips into place. 'Gemma, of course, so sorry, I was thinking of Annie and . . .'

'It's okay,' Gemma says, smiling at her all the way from Switzerland. 'How are you, it's ages since we Skyped, you look really well. Mum says you've finished *Cross Currents* now. Did it all go well?'

Back on track again Stella eases herself into the conversation, enchanted as always by watching Gemma on the screen, and awed by the technology that makes it possible for them to talk face to face like this. They chat for a while, about Gemma's work, Joyce's course, and Mac's sojourn in Albany. 'And now Dennis is there with him.'

Stella says, 'Did you know that he and Helen split up?'

Gemma nods. 'I did, Nick let me know. It seems such a weird thing to happen at their age, doesn't it?'

'The weirdest thing to me,' Stella says, 'is that it didn't happen years ago.'

Gemma laughs. 'I guess. Aunty Helen isn't the easiest person to get on with, but she was always lovely to me. She made me feel very special.'

'We all think you're very special, Gemma,' Stella says.

'Ha! That's the advantage of being the youngest and the only girl among three boys. But you mentioned Annie . . .'

'Just me and my ancient brain,' Stella says, feeling her face flush with embarrassment. 'I was thinking about her while I was waiting for you to call, and . . . oh well . . . I had a very senior moment.'

'I never met Annie,' Gemma says. 'I wish I had.'

'I wish you had too, she was wonderful,' and a lump rising in her throat takes her by surprise.

'How did you two meet, was it in the theatre?'

Stella shakes her head. 'Not originally,' she says. 'We met

in the lingerie department of Boans; do you remember, the big department store in the city?'

Gemma nods. 'I remember it. Mum used to take us there when we were little.'

'Well my first job was in the old Boans store, and Annie used to get some casual work there. She was a bit older than me, and she was an actor and in between things she'd always pick up a few days' work in Boans. It was Annie that got me into the theatre, but I must have told you this before.'

Gemma shakes her head. 'No, never. I never knew how you got started.'

'Oh well, Annie was always telling me that I should audition for something. She thought I'd be good because I could mimic people and could dance and sing. Then one day she persuaded me to go with her to an audition. "Come on, Ess," she said, "give it a go. What've you got to lose?" So eventually I gave in and went with her one Saturday morning and . . .' Stella stops abruptly, rummaging in her memory, which seems to be deserting her.

'Go on,' Gemma says.

'I was just trying to remember what the production was – I can see it all so clearly but can't remember the title,' Stella says. 'Anyway, there were quite a few girls my age and four of us were called out of this long line of hopefuls to read for the part of a French maid. Awful cliché, isn't it, but that's what it was. After we four had each read the part the director picked one and the other three of us trouped off all disappointed, but then he called me back. "You with the red hair, Essie, is it?" he said. "We want you to read for something else." And he gave me a passage from one of the bigger parts, the heroine's younger sister. So I read it, and they didn't say anything. The director and his assistant and some other man with them just looked at each other and sort of shrugged and then nodded, and the director said, "Okay, love, you've got it." And he stuck a copy of the script in my hands and said, "Be here ten o'clock Monday week, be on time and make sure you know your lines." And I said, "Well I can't do that because I have to go to work." And he just looked at me and rolled his eyes and said, "Do you want this job or not?" And of course I said yes. So I went home and told Nancy. I thought she might be annoyed with me but she was really excited. She'd always loved the theatre and had wanted to be a dancer. So I gave my notice on the Monday and worked my last week at Boans and Annie and I learned our lines together in the evenings. That's how I got my start in acting.'

'So it happened almost by chance,' Gemma says. 'What a lovely story, and is that when you changed your name?'

Stella nods. 'Yes, when I turned up for the first rehearsal the director couldn't remember my name, so I reminded him. "It's Essie," I said, "Estelle Barwell." And he just looked me up and down. "Not anymore," he said. "Dull, far too dull and infinitely forgettable. Estelle, eh? How about Stella? And Barwell's a shocker. Lamont! That's it – from now on you're Stella Lamont." And so that's who I became.'

Later, when she and Gemma have hung up, Stella strolls out into the garden with the secateurs, snips the dead heads off the roses and then sits for a moment on the back step thinking back on their conversation. Did I really do that?, she asks herself. Did I really forget even just for an instant that Annie is dead? If I can forget that then I could forget anything; important things, how to do things, how to look after myself. The idea of it turns her cold with fear, and she gets to her feet and paces across the lawn and back again. I could do anything, something really crazy. I could hurt myself, or even someone else. She reaches the open door at the back of the garage, sees her red Honda and stops suddenly. I might cause an accident, she thinks, might crash or run someone over. Should I be driving? I might get lost, not be able to find my way home. She slams the door shut, her head reeling. The enormity of what this means is overwhelming: her whole life is changing before her eyes, her independence sliding away. But if it was really bad someone would have told me, Polly or Joyce, or Gareth – he'd certainly have told me . . . and then she remembers something. Polly a while ago, looking at photographs . . . saying something about forgetfulness, about seeing a doctor . . .

Stella drops the secateurs on the back steps and opens the side-gate into Polly's garden. Polly will help me, she tells herself, Polly will know what to do.

*

When Stella calls out to her from the back door Polly is talking to Alistair on her laptop.

'Hang on,' she says, 'it's Stella at the back door, I'll bring her in so you can say hello.'

Stella is standing in the kitchen looking as though she's seen a ghost. 'Thank goodness, Polly,' she says. 'I had to come straight away, I had to see you,' and then suddenly her expression changes from anxiety to a sort of puzzlement. 'I had to come . . . it was important . . . but now I don't know what it was . . .'

'Okay,' Polly says, 'don't worry, it'll probably come back to you. I was just talking to Alistair on Skype, do you want to come and say hello?'

Stella's face clears, she breaks into a smile. 'I'd love to. I haven't seen Alistair for ages. I was talking to someone earlier . . . someone . . . oh yes, Gemma, I was talking to Gemma. I love Skype, it seems quite magical to be able to see the person you're talking to, so much better than the phone.'

She is relaxed now, caught up in a moment of pleasure, and Polly urges her through into the study, where Alistair is waving to them, and she pulls another chair over to the desk and drops into it.

'Stella, my darling, how lovely to see you,' Alistair says. 'And you look simply marvellous. Younger than ever.'

'And you are as full of bullshit,' Stella says, laughing, 'but the very best kind of bullshit, it's lovely to see you too.'

Polly watches them for a moment. Clearly Stella has forgotten why she came, but it looked serious. Two minutes, she mimes to Alistair out of Stella's sight and he nods and she knows she can trust him to keep her talking. Quickly she slips out of the room, out of the house, through the side-gate and in through Stella's back door. Everything seems absolutely normal, there is no water running, no gas hissing, no forgotten pot burning on the stove, the iron is not plugged in, the front door is safely locked from the inside. Polly shrugs. Whatever upset Stella, and she was seriously upset, is not something in the house. She has seemed better since the stint on *Cross Currents* finished. Perhaps, with a bit more rest, a quiet life, there will be real improvement.

And with a big sigh of relief Polly goes back through the gate to her own house, and rejoins the conversation at the computer.

Chapter Nineteen

July

It's the final day of the language course and Joyce is trying to balance relief with sadness that it is coming to an end. It has been a month of her life in which she has done nothing except study, learn, teach, eat and sleep, and it's been amazingly satisfying and now, suddenly, it's all over.

'We're all going to the pub when we finish,' Jacqui says.

It's four-thirty and they are waiting in the classroom for Ewan to arrive for what the school secretary has told them is a small informal closing ceremony. There is champagne, nibbles and their certificates will be presented. Interim certificates with their marks. The formal certificates will be sent in the mail during the following week.

'We're going to walk down to the Brass Monkey, you'll come, won't you?'

'Wouldn't miss it,' Joyce says, 'but I may not stay long. I need to go home and lie down for a long time in a darkened room.'

Of the original group who began the course six have dropped out and Joyce is proud of the fact that she's stuck it out to the end. Barry, a former builder in his fifties, is still there too, and apart from him, Jacqui and herself, everyone else is very much younger.

Ewan's speech is brief and amusing. He names each of them, noting something amusing or endearing about everyone that he has observed in their four weeks together. Someone's insistence on washing and reusing the cardboard beakers from the coffee shop, Barry nipping out for a fag when things get too much, young Sophie's constant doodles of snails, Joyce as the instigator of the lunchtime kip on the classroom floor. He is, Joyce thinks, the perfect man for his job, a leader who has kept them going, intervened when necessary, been generous with praise when it's deserved. They fidget in their seats awaiting their results.

'As usual most people got a B,' Ewan says. 'It's an excellent mark and the standard that is accepted everywhere that you may want to teach. So – let's go through these alphabetically. When I read out your name come up and get your certificate.'

Joyce leans back, waiting for her turn, and as each person gets their certificate the group applauds. When her turn comes she crosses the room to collect her certificate.

'Joyce, congratulations,' Ewan says. 'You're our only A student in this course, it's a terrific achievement.'

There's a moment in which she actually thinks he's joking, and then the whoops and cheers kick in. Ewan leans forward and kisses her on the cheek, and with a smile so wide it could split her face, she walks back to her seat.

'Well done, you swat!' Jacquie says, hugging her. 'I thought you might manage that!'

Later they celebrate at the pub, with the drinks flowing fast. Joyce orders a glass of wine, and takes only a couple of sips before realising she is just too tired to drink, and she pushes it aside and opts for water. Now that the pressure is off the collective relief and exhaustion mean that emotions are running high. There are more drinks and then they all begin to flag at about the same time. There are hugs and promises, email addresses and phone numbers are exchanged, they will be friends forever, wherever they are. There will be a reunion, every year.

'Is it always like this?' Joyce asks Ewan, who is sitting beside her.

'Mostly,' he says. 'Once the tension is gone it gets very emotional. And then when everyone has recovered it usually just fades away. You'll be a great teacher, Joyce. Have you decided what you'll do now?'

'I'm not sure yet,' she says. 'I decided to do it because the refugee support group said they needed people who could teach English, but I also needed to do something new for myself. And now it's given me the urge to travel. China maybe, or Japan. But first I'm going to have a rest. My husband's been down in Albany for a few months, and I told him he couldn't come home until this was over. He wasn't too happy about it but he gave in and now he's driving back on Sunday.'

'So how will he feel if you decide to travel for a while?' Ewan asks.

Joyce grimaces. 'Really, I haven't a clue. But maybe he'll just have to get used to the idea that things are different now. Anyway, I think I'll cross that bridge when I come to it.'

*

Helen is unstoppable; she feels it herself, the huge reserve of energy that was building when she was in Dubai has carried her home and driven her through every day since she arrived. She's tried, unsuccessfully, to sack the existing agent but is legally stuck with her for the remainder of the contract. Meanwhile she has been searching for a replacement agent and viewing properties, and is living on Nurofen for the headaches which she's sure will ease up when she has managed to sort things out. Dennis has said he will be home sometime soon – whether he is or not no longer bothers her. I'm dealing with this now, she tells herself, so he can just stay out of my way.

As for Joyce, Helen is still smarting over her rudeness, but she's felt for some time that their friendship was cooling, even before Joyce and Mac had decided to embark on this ridiculous year of living apart. Although of course that doesn't seem so ridiculous to Helen now, not since she's started to relish the pleasure of freedom. 'Hard luck, Joyce,' Helen says out loud to the empty apartment, 'I don't have to put up with your tantrums.' As she says this aloud she is crawling backwards on her knees extracting herself from the cupboard under the sink, which she has tackled as part of her effort to sort and clean out everything in readiness for a move. 'Get over it, Joyce,' she says again, straightening up, but as she attempts to get to her feet she is hit over the head by an iron bar and she reels backwards and slides onto her side on the floor in a black cloud shot through with daggers of dazzling pain. For a moment Helen lies there paralysed. Who has done this to her? How did someone get into the flat? She wants to get to her feet but is too dizzy and she turns her head cautiously from side to side, and realises that she is still alone, no one is there, and nothing, at least nothing external, has hit her.

Helen sits up slowly and, not yet game to try standing, she crawls towards the wall and leans against it. Drawing up her knees then resting her elbows on them, she drops her head forward, pressing the palms of her hands into her eyes, which feel tight and swollen, as if pressure inside her head is about to burst out through them. When she opens them again everything is as it was. The bolt that hit her seemed so colossal that it's impossible to believe it hasn't created any damage. The tiles should be smashed, shattered crockery scattered across the floor, the contents of the fridge disgorging itself, but nothing, not a thing is out of place except the sponge and the brush she had been holding when it hit.

Still dizzy, Helen attempts to get to her feet; the daggers are down to pinpricks now. I might lie on the bed, she thinks, but she slides back down as her head begins to spin faster and she begins to vomit, knowing that she is losing consciousness, feeling herself swirling downward into darkness.

When she comes to, she's not sure how much later, she is lying in her own vomit. Dragging herself upright she is revolted by the soiling of her clothes, the vomit spattered across the floor, she even feels it clogged in her hair. Still giddy but repulsed by her condition she knows she must get cleaned up as soon as she can. Helen hates any sort of human soiling; dirty nappies, babies' vomit, blood and guts have always revolted her and the realities of motherhood and caring for the elderly have not diluted that disgust. She stands up cautiously, peels off her clothes and stuffs them in a bin bag. Then, dragging reams of paper towel from its roll, she mops up the worst of the mess, then fills a bucket with water, disinfectant and floor cleaner and proceeds, stark naked, to mop it. It's unusually difficult because she can't seem to make the mop work, she can't coordinate her movements, and she trips against the bucket and realises she could slip and fall on the wet tiles, but she has to do it. She can think of nothing else until it is done. Finally she dumps the bucket and mop and the bag of clothes into the laundry and closes the door. Then, very cautiously, keeping one hand on the wall all the time, she makes her way out of the kitchen across the passage and into the ensuite bathroom where she steps into the shower and turns on the taps. The hot water feels wonderful coursing over her head and down her body and she stands there, one hand against the wall to steady herself, the other pouring shampoo onto her hair, wishing she had agreed to have the safety handles fitted in the shower as Dennis had suggested. For a two-minute shower woman she stands there for a very long time, waiting for the remaining pain and nausea to subside, and for the water to wash any dregs of vomit down the drain.

Maybe I need to slow down a bit, she tells herself, find time to see the doctor about the headaches. Eventually, out of the shower, dry and wrapped in her towelling dressing gown, she makes herself a cup of tea. But despite the utter exhaustion and weakness that has overtaken her she feels her fingers drumming on the worktop, and can't stop her right foot tapping. Helen takes some long, calming breaths, carries her mug into the bedroom and slides wearily into bed. It's ten-thirty on Sunday morning and she's been up since five. Her body is exhausted but her head is still spinning with images of Dennis standing with his back to her on the day he told her he was leaving, obdurate estate agents shaking their heads at her, Damian's face as he told her to pack her bags, endless open homes, and spreadsheets and Nick – where is Nick? In some cave full of bats under the Nullarbor probably, and Joyce standing by the open door waiting for her to leave. She gropes for the image she had of herself as she flew out to Dubai: a single woman, a free woman, with a single life of substance, a future; a confident woman, happy to be alone.

*

It's almost ten o'clock on Sunday morning when Mac pulls in to the roadhouse; he's been driving for well over two hours and is about halfway home and desperate for coffee. He and Dennis had left the cottage at the same time, him to drive straight home to Fremantle, Dennis stopping off to call in on a former colleague in Mount Barker. They had locked everything securely and stood facing each other, both wondering if they'd forgotten anything.

'Well thanks for all your help, mate,' Mac had said. 'I'd never have got those fences finished without you, nor the laundry painted.'

'My pleasure,' Dennis said. 'It was the least I could do. Thank *you* for putting up with me, listening to me whingeing on for hours. I came for a couple of nights and stayed for a month. Any other bloke would have kicked me out weeks ago.' He bent down to take Charlie's head in his hands, rubbing his ears affectionately. 'And thank you, old mate, for making me walk more, my knees feel a whole lot better for the exercise.'

Mac strolls across the forecourt towards the café and the irresistible smell of sausages frying and, throwing gastronomic caution to the wind, he orders sausages, eggs and fries and lets Charlie out to stretch his legs while he waits for his food. It's strange to be driving back home and he can't help wondering what might have changed; he realises suddenly that it really matters to him that things are just the same as when he left. It matters that everything in the house is the same, but more than that it matters that he and Joyce are the same, and that this sense of disruption dissolves when they are back together again.

The waitress, whose expression is remarkably sullen, pushes open the swing doors and dumps his meal unceremoniously on the table.

'That all?'

'No, I ordered a long black coffee as well,' Mac says.

And with a huge sigh she turns back into the café.

As he sits there now, tucking into his food, passing on little bits of sausage to Charlie, Mac's stomach churns, and it's nothing to do with the food. Sometime this weekend he will have to tell Joyce about Carol.

'I thought you said you'd told her when we met,' Carol had said when they'd walked on the beach yesterday morning.

'I did. But I never got around to telling her that we'd been having coffee or breakfast or walking together, several times a week.'

Carol had raised her eyebrows. 'Why ever not?'

He'd shrugged. 'Joyce has had a lot on with the course, and then there's our neighbour who's in her eighties; she's really part of the family and she seems to be losing it a bit . . . dementia . . . maybe Alzheimer's, although none of us actually says that word.'

'Well, you should tell Joyce,' Carol had said. 'After all, we're not doing anything wrong. But the fact that you haven't mentioned it doesn't look too good. I wouldn't be happy about it in her position.'

'I know, but frankly, things were a bit awkward, tense really, while Joyce was on the course.'

'One big reason why you should have been open about it,' Carol had said. 'Anyway, I'm sure you'll work it out.'

'Yes,' he'd said. 'Yes, I'm sure it'll be fine.'

But as he sits here now, offering a chip to Charlie, Mac is not convinced that fine is what it will be when he tries to explain it to Joyce.

*

Joyce is sitting with her legs draped over one arm of the big chair in the kitchen, reading the weekend papers that arrived yesterday but she didn't open until today. Yesterday, glorious lazy Saturday, she slept late and then wandered through the gate in the fence for lunch with Stella and Polly. Polly had made chicken and vegetable soup and they had sat around her table to eat it, tearing lumps off a fresh baguette. To Joyce it had felt like a joyful return to normal life, but a life inevitably changed by the past four weeks. She needed to find a way to make this experience, and what it has taught her about herself, part of her normal life, not just have it as something that she once did for a few weeks before she returned to life as it had been before. And at lunch she'd felt Helen's absence, although to some extent Helen had always been an outsider, and that largely seemed to be of her own making. She preferred to spend time just with Joyce, or with her, Mac and Dennis.

'It's different when it's just women,' she'd once said. 'Not as important, not quite the real thing.'

Joyce had thought of this often, because those friendships were so precious to her, so much a part of the way she chose to live her life, she couldn't understand how Helen could feel that way. Now she chucks the weekend magazines on the floor and picks up her book. A novel, at last! No more books on language interference or verb tenses, no pressure to compose lessons and try to come up with new and interesting visual aids for a class just a day away. She closes her eyes for a moment.

It will be weird to have Mac back, weird but good. This is the longest they have ever been apart and now that the pressure is off she knows how much she's missed him. Missed his wonderfully reassuring presence, his sense of humour, the special quality of Mac-ness that he brings to the house, and she realises that she is also quite nervous about how it will be. Will he expect her to slip back into her domesticated self? Because she's not sure she can. In fact she knows she doesn't want that anymore, that routine of thinking what to buy and what to cook, the expectations about who will do what and when. When they'd embarked on their year of living dangerously they had never discussed where it might take them. She has changed in their time apart. What if he expects her to be the same?

She hears the sound of a car on the driveway and swings her legs off the chair arm and gets to her feet. How will we be different?, she wonders as she pauses at the front door. Have we unravelled something that can't be reassembled?

Mac, seeing her at the door, waves and leans across to open the passenger door. Charlie, who seems larger in life than in photographs, bounds from the front seat, stopping only to pee on the roses before heading for Joyce and screeching to a halt in front of her, head tilted to one side, tail wagging furiously.

'Hello, Charlie,' she says, bending down to take his face in her hands, 'aren't you just gorgeous!' He licks her hand in agreement and heads past her into the house, his legs splaying out at angles as his paws slide over the polished floor.

'He's a little short on manners,' Mac says, coming up the steps, 'but he's big on charm.'

'So I see,' she says. 'He's even bigger than I imagined.'

They stand in the doorway hugging each other, neither of them ready to let go, as though, Joyce thinks, they're recharging each other's batteries. And then they walk slowly into the house, and she sees Mac looking around him as if to check that nothing has changed. He seems uncertain, a little awkward perhaps, and this makes her uncertain too.

Charlie, having checked out the kitchen, has made his way out into the back yard and is discovering amazing new smells, and taking a serious interest in the swimming pool.

'Wait there,' Mac says, 'close your eyes and don't open them until I say so.'

Joyce stands there, in the middle of the room, eyes closed, and hears him go back out through the front door to the ute, and return more slowly and put something heavy down on the floor.

'Not yet,' he warns, shifting whatever it is in the direction of the old fireplace, which they had long ago converted to a wood-burning stove. 'Okay.'

Joyce turns in his direction and opens her eyes. Alongside the stove is a rocking chair and Mac has grabbed the patchwork cushion that Stella made for her birthday years ago, and dropped it at an angle on the gorgeously polished wooden seat.

'Oh Mac, it's beautiful, beautiful, just what I always wanted.' She walks over to the chair and around it, strokes the curved arms, the top of the railed back, and finally sits down in it, leaning back, feeling the perfect balance, the ideal shape and angle of the seat. 'It's gorgeous, absolutely gorgeous, a work of art. I've wanted one like this for so long. Wherever did you find it?'

'Find it?' he laughs. 'I made it, Joyce, I made it for you, just as I always promised.'

*

It has been the best of times, this bright and breezy Sunday, Mac thinks. He is high on the pleasure of being home with his family. Ben and Nessa had arrived soon after with Lucy and Kara, both home for a couple of weeks in the mid-year break. They had opted for lunch at the big table in the yard, protected from the breeze, and tucked into a ham cooked by Nessa, cheeses, bread that Ben had baked, olives, salad, and some excellent wine. There are changes of course, Mac keeps spotting them: small things in the house have been moved, some new plants are in the pots, a slight shift in the lounge room furniture, but only one change that unnerved him. A magnificent oil painting of Fremantle Harbour, on the big wall near the wood stove.

'I went to an exhibition at the Arts Centre,' Joyce had said, 'and I loved it so much I had to buy it. You do like it, don't you?'

'I love it,' he'd said, 'and we always said we wanted something sensational there. It's perfect, who's the artist?'

She'd told him about the artist, showed him the certificate of provenance, and as she talked about the painting, Mac felt a growing tension in his gut. This was so unlike Joyce, to buy a painting, an expensive painting, without conferring with him, without even mentioning it. He loves it, he's fine about the money, it's the fear of what this uncharacteristic behaviour might mean that bugs him.

Later, before the family leave, they gather around the computer to Skype Gemma, and have a rambling and hilarious conversation in which everyone talks over each other, and ancient jokes and family anecdotes are unearthed and replayed.

'You all sound drunk,' says Gemma, for whom it's early in the morning. 'My whole family is plastered, even my nieces. And it's not even breakfast time yet.'

'Come home, Gem,' Ben calls, 'we miss you.'

She shakes her head, grinning. 'Next year,' she says. 'Next year, I promise.'

It's almost six o'clock when they have the house to themselves again, and Joyce sinks into her new chair and leans back, closing her eyes.

'What a great day,' she says. 'It's so lovely to have you back, darling.'

Mac takes a deep breath; the longer he leaves it to tell her about Carol the more difficult it will get.

'Look, darl,' he says, sitting down on the squishy old chair by the stove. 'There's something I need to tell you,' and he feels like a naughty child owning up to the headmistress about some misdemeanour.

'Mmm, okay,' Joyce says without opening her eyes.

'Well, remember I told you about Carol?'

'Yes, she brought Charlie.'

'Yes, and she and I . . . well, we had a . . .'

'A hot sweaty night in a tent in Mandurah years ago.'

Mac opens his mouth to speak, closes it. 'How did you know that?'

'Oh, someone told me, years ago; that scrawny blonde that your friend Tony used to go out with. She told me quite soon after we got married that you'd had a hot and steamy night – her words - in Mandurah with a girl in your tent. She was always trying to stir up trouble somewhere.'

'You never said anything.'

'No, because at the time I chose not to believe it. Then when you told me that you'd met her again I remembered the name. And of course you've just confirmed it!' She opens her eyes and grins at him. 'It's an awfully long time ago, don't worry about it. I think it was that time I had German measles and couldn't go crabbing.'

'You weren't upset at the time?'

She shrugs. 'As I said, I didn't believe it, but I *did* believe in you.'

'And now?'

Joyce laughs again. 'It's history, I still believe in you.'

Mac's embarrassment seems to be setting fire to his face. 'It was only once, Joyce. There's never been anyone else . . .'

She rolls her eyes. 'Duuh! I never thought there was. Relax.' Joyce leans her head back again and closes her eyes.

'Okay, well that's a relief, but the reason I mentioned her is that, as you know, she brought Charlie around and then . . . well, since then we've been seeing a bit of each other.'

Joyce opens her eyes. 'A bit?'

'Yes, well, you know, walking, swimming, breakfast, coffee sometimes, lunch a couple of times . . .' Mac's newfound relief is beginning to fade.

'Walking, swimming, breakfast, lunch, anything else?'

'No,' he says firmly, 'absolutely not. She's nice, you'd like her . . . we talk about a lot of interesting . . . look, there's nothing in it, Joyce, don't think that, nothing at all . . .'

Joyce narrows her eyes. 'How long?'

'Well . . . well . . . a couple of days after I got Charlie we met at the beach . . . so . . . well, since then.'

There is a brief excruciating silence.

'You've been meeting this woman, several times a week for weeks, no, months, and you never thought to mention it?'

Put like this it sounds appalling and Mac's face catches fire again. He clears his throat, twists his hands together, sighs.

'Why?' Joyce asks. Her tone is low and unusually harsh. Is she angry or wounded or both? Her eyes are dark, unreadable.

Mac is lost for words, words that can make this right, can fix what's happening. 'I kept trying to find the right time, you were busy and then you were pissed off and hung up on me . . .'

'This is not my fault, Mac. I can't believe you would do this, have this relationship . . .'

'It's not a relationship,' he cuts in. 'It's just . . . well it was . . . we started talking about the past and she's really easy to talk to . . .'

Joyce rolls her eyes. 'So what else is there that I don't know, that you haven't told me? I thought you were supposed to be toughing it out on your own. Solitude, you said, time to think about the future and at the first opportunity you get involved with this woman . . .'

'We're not involved,' Mac says, 'just . . .'

Joyce gets up, turns, looks at the rocking chair, then back at him. 'So what's this Mac? This chair; is it your guilty conscience, a peace offering, just what exactly is it?'

Charlie, lying on the floor between them, lets out a big sigh and drops his head gloomily onto his front paws.

'I was making the chair before I even met Carol, I promised you years ago that I would. Honestly Joyce we just started talking and I just never found the right moment to . . .'

The phone rings suddenly and Charlie, not yet fully accustomed to the noises of the house, leaps to his feet and starts barking wildly at it.

'Shut up, Charlie,' Joyce says. 'Answer it, for god's sake, Mac.'

He gets to his feet and picks up the receiver with one hand, patting Charlie to calm him with the other.

'Mac,' Dennis says, 'Mac, I . . .'

'Dennis, can I call you back? I . . .'

'No, no. Mac, don't hang up . . .' Dennis's voice is strange, shaky.

Mac feels a prick of fear at the back of his neck. 'Is something wrong, mate? Where are you?'

'Home,' Dennis says. 'I'm home. I just got home. It's Helen . . . she's . . . she's dead, Mac. Helen's dead.'

Chapter Twenty

At the end of the first week in October, Polly wakes early, slips out of bed and pads out to the kitchen to make some tea. She loves the early mornings; the silence and stillness in which she does some of her most effective reading, or thinking. Sometimes she walks on the beach or into town for an early coffee, focused on what she's writing, trying to get inside the heads of the women whose lives she is working on. This morning, though, she is thinking, yet again, of Leo and the fact that he is quite high maintenance, both emotionally in time spent worrying about him and whether he is okay about being here, and practically in all sorts of small ways, she seems to be spending an inordinate amount of time and energy trying to accommodate him and adjust to his presence. She wonders, too, whether he has given any thought at all to what sort of experience this might be for her. She suspects not. She is constantly running up against small challenges to the way she lives her life; challenges so small that it seems petty to mention them. And so she keeps reminding herself that this is new, and special, and that it is unreasonable to expect things to be otherwise.

Eventually, mug of tea in hand, she walks back to the bedroom and pauses by the open door watching him sleep; curled protectively into himself, he lies perfectly still, undisturbed by the fact that she has quit the bed. Indeed, he appears not to notice that she frequently moves out during the night because she seems to have lost the art of sleeping in occupied territory. She turns away from the bedroom and wanders outside to sit on the back steps contemplating the fact that Leo is, in many ways, an intrusive presence. In her thirties or forties much of what Leo does would not have bothered her, just having a lover or partner staying with her, even living with her, had never seemed so disruptive. Perhaps then she was too caught up in the belief that the mere presence of the man in her home, in her bed, meant he loved her and wanted to be with her.

Leo seems to be trying to organising things to suit himself, and she wonders if this is just a male thing. With former lovers she has given ground on far too many small things that mattered to her, has been too ready to concede or compromise in the name of love, and ended up feeling exploited, and resenting it. She wants to believe that she has now moved beyond this, that there are certain things she will concede, but others that are not negotiable. At the same time she knows that she is set in her ways, accustomed to everything being where she wants it, okay with any mess of her own creation, uneasy with anyone else's. Leo, she suspects, is much the same. He is used to owning his own space, and in the six days he's been here he's been making adjustments, some of them not particularly subtle. So this morning Polly is considering the rules of engagement – how to establish them, how to respond to irritations without being petty and nagging – before they become entrenched and lie between them like little bombs waiting to explode.

Stella thinks the long distance factor is eccentric and rather romantic, 'in theory', she had added. 'It *sounds* ideal, although it might be hard to make it work. But if you both want it badly enough you'll both do the work. Just make sure you're not the only one making the adjustments, Polly.'

Leo has considerable intellectual arrogance, a tendency to talk over her, an uncompromising position on some issues on which her own boundaries are more porous, and an infuriating habit of explaining things that she already understands or about which she actually knows more than he does. While it's easy to write off some of this by ascribing it purely to gender, Polly suspects there are some tough conversations to come. But what she is sure of is that he is a good person who wants to do the right thing but frequently doesn't hit the spot. She relishes the constant ebb and flow of their conversations, which are wide ranging and robust, threaded with argument, discovery and humour. Except, that is, if Leo ventures into the subject of faith. A belief in any sort of higher power is, according to him, naïve, simple minded, rooted in the superstitions of ignorant peasants. In their early days in Edinburgh she had told him that her faith was important to her, but he has either forgotten, or chosen to ignore it. Polly has vowed to herself not to engage with him on this. She is comfortable with and confident about her own beliefs and feels no need to defend this nor desire to discuss it with someone who simply wants to dismantle it. The air is still and in the cool morning sunlight the only disturbance comes from a flock of parrots in the top branches of the peppermint tree in Joyce and Mac's garden. Joyce and Mac, she thinks, really are the couple who made the right choice decades ago and have worked to keep it that way. But Helen's death has hit them hard, Joyce riven with guilt and obsessed with having failed her old friend, Mac shocked, bewildered, fiercely concerned for Joyce. Both seem unsure what to do next, their year of living dangerously is disrupted and they are both committed to supporting Dennis. It's almost three months now but they are still trying to work out how to pick up the threads of the new sort of life they had been trying to create.

'I just hope Joyce won't let herself be derailed by this,' Stella had said a few weeks ago. 'She'd begun so well with her course, she was talking about teaching the asylum seekers, or even going away somewhere. Now here she is, back doing what she's always done, looking after other people.'

Just as she thinks of Stella, Polly hears a rattle at the side-gate and Stella herself sticks her head around it.

'Is it okay to come in?' she says in a loud whisper.

'Of course,' Polly says, beckoning her.

'Leo won't mind?'

'Leo is still asleep and probably will be for a couple of hours.'

'So,' says Stella, settling alongside Polly on the steps and lowering her voice, 'how's it all going?'

'It's going really well,' says a voice behind them, and the two women swing around in unison. Leo is standing in the kitchen doorway in jeans and a long sleeved black t-shirt, rubbing his chin. 'Are you checking up on me, Stella?'

'Of course I am,' she says, laughing. 'Polly is like a daughter to me, which means I'm sort of your de facto mother-in-law. I'm looking after her interests.'

'I thought that was my responsibility,' Leo says with an edge to his voice.

'I am perfectly capable of looking after my own interests, thank you,' Polly says, 'so you two can stop sizing each other up for fisticuffs over my supervision.'

They had both generated hostility since the moment they met at dinner at Mac and Joyce's place the night after Leo arrived.

'Everyone will be checking you out, of course,' she'd warned him.

'I'm sure I can handle it,' Leo had said.

But although the evening had passed without incident, it was awkward at times, and Leo seemed ill at ease. Jet-lag, she'd thought, he'll soon adjust.

'You're up very early,' Polly says now.

'Mmm. Thought I'd join you for a walk, Polly. What's the tea situation?'

'Um . . . well, the kettle is recently boiled and the tea bags are in the canister,' Polly says, smiling and holding her mug up to him. 'And yes, thanks, I'll have another one.'

Leo looks slightly affronted and then seems to decide not to be. Had he really expected her to jump to her feet just because he'd chosen to join them?

He took her mug. 'Stella, tea?'

'No thanks, Leo,' she says, getting to her feet. 'I'll leave you to it.'

'You only just got here,' Polly says.

'Yes, I needed your advice on something,' Stella says, grasping the handrail and descending the two remaining steps. 'But we can do that another time. Should be beautiful at the beach this morning.' And she sets off down the garden and turns at the gate to wave. 'Have a lovely day.'

'Stella doesn't like me,' Leo says when he returns with the tea. 'I can tell.'

Polly sighs and takes her mug from him. 'And you don't like her, *I* can tell.'

'It's not that I don't like her, it's just . . . well, perhaps I haven't quite got her measure yet.'

Polly suppresses a grin. 'She's eighty, Leo, and she doesn't give a toss how smart or important you are, just whether or not you're going to be good for me. She's my oldest, dearest friend and yes, she *is* like a mother to me, but she's *not* my mother. That's Stella, so just get over it.'

The silence is freighted now with mutual resentment.

Leo clears his throat. 'It's pretty early in the morning to turn up on the doorstep.'

'In your world maybe, but not in mine,' Polly says, 'and right now, Leo, you're in my world. Live with it for a while before you start trying to adjust it to your own liking.'

'I didn't like finding her here so early.'

'And she didn't like you walking into our conversation. Look, I usually see Stella almost every day, but she has stayed away since you arrived, until this morning. So – as I said, get over it.'

Leo is silent. They sit sipping their tea.

He shrugs. 'Sorry,' he says. 'It all feels strange, different here, from Edinburgh or Hong Kong.'

Polly sighs. 'Of course it does, we barely knew each other in Edinburgh, the circumstances were entirely different. No expectations. In Hong Kong I was in your space, your room, it felt weird for me to move into that so I know this must seem strange to you. But Stella is family to me, she, Alistair and Steve *are* my family, Joyce and Mac too.'

'I liked them.'

'Good, I hope you'll like Alistair and Steve too. Sometime when you're here we'll go over to Bali together.' The tension has evaporated now, it feels like a natural, useful conversation.

He hesitates. 'Maybe,' he says. 'I've never been to Bali.'

'Look,' Polly says, 'we're teething. We both like our own way; we both like not having to consult anyone else about what we do. But if we're going to stick with this we're both going to have to adjust. You'll get used to Stella and she to you. Just as I'll have to get used to your family.'

'There'll be no need for that,' he says quickly. 'My brother lives in Texas, we have very little in common and I haven't seen him for years. Judith is happy down there in Cornwall and Rosemary, who looks after her, is an old school friend who was widowed in her forties, and is happy to be a live-in carer.'

Polly nods. 'Sounds like a good arrangement, but I still want to get to know them.'

Leo says nothing. They sit in comfortable silence for a while, drinking their tea, watching the parrots doing their housekeeping.

'The thing about Stella,' Leo says eventually, 'is that she somehow reminds me of my mother.'

'Oh for god's sake,' Polly says, 'I'm not getting into this. I'll put some clothes on and we can go for a walk,' and she gets to her feet, tips the remains of her tea onto the flower bed and walks back into the house to get dressed.

*

Every morning Joyce wakes up feeling normal and within seconds a grey blanket of sadness settles on her, shutting out the light, leaving her struggling to escape its suffocating effect. She knows that she is now the only one who has been unable to move on from the horror of Helen's death. The moment when she walked into the apartment that Sunday afternoon and saw Dennis, his head in his hands, a young policewoman at his side, and Helen's body being lifted onto a stretcher, still grips her in its legacy of grief and guilt. Until recently Dennis too was trapped, but a month ago he had decided it was time for him to move out from their spare room where he had been living since Helen's death. Mac has, to some extent, Joyce thinks, dealt with it best of the three of them, but of course while he was fond of Helen he was never really close to her.

Joyce is paralysed by all the things she could or should have done: if only I'd known, if only I'd thought about the headaches, urged her to see a doctor, if only I'd made more effort, hadn't turned her out that last night, if only . . . if only . . . Dennis had his 'if onlys' too and each has tried to comfort the other, but in the end they were both stuck with the horror of what happened, not just that Helen had suddenly and tragically died, but the way it happened, and the feeling that they should have seen it coming. A brain tumour, something that had been affecting her for some time, and the questions were devastating. Did she mention headaches, perhaps increasing in intensity and frequency? Yes. Do you know if she vomited from time to time? Yes, she mentioned it but put it down to the fact that she needed to cut down on her drinking. Any behavioural changes? Yes: the increased drinking, more volatile, quicker to anger and the anger more fierce, illogical and sometimes, according to Dennis, way out of control, less ability to compromise or see another side of an argument, more controlling. Energy? Well, she was always energetic but recently seemed a bit manic. And then the question they asked themselves – why didn't we spot it? Why didn't we do something about it?

But over and above all of this there was the way it happened, the chaos of her last minutes or hours written across the walls in the kitchen, the bathroom, the bedroom, the passage and the lounge, in blood and vomit. It seemed, from the plastic bag of soiled clothes in the laundry, that Helen had already had an attack of vomiting and possibly a fall, and cleaned up. That she had had a shower, then made herself a cup of tea and gone to lie down wearing just her kimono. But something – the pain in her head, or nausea – had got her out of bed again. Was she dizzy or desperate or both? She had staggered from room to room, vomiting, had fallen once at least, hit her head on the corner of the glass coffee table and drawn blood. Then it appeared that she tried to get back to the bathroom, crashing into furniture and walls leaving traces of vomit, bloody hand prints, and at some point the sash of her kimono had unravelled and dropped away. At the bathroom door she had stopped, bloodied hand prints were on both door jambs, and there she had finally collapsed, face down on the white floor tiles. How long all this had taken was not clear but a neighbour had seen her park her car and take the elevator up to the top floor at midday on Saturday, and she had been dead for approximately eight hours when Dennis let himself into the apartment on Sunday, dropped his keys on the hall table, and knew instantly that something was terribly wrong.

It is the horror of those last hours that Joyce can't lay to rest. Did Helen know what was happening? Was she frightened? Was she in terrible pain? Why didn't she try to call for help?

Joyce and Mac had taken Dennis home with them and Nick had emerged from the bat cave and flown home to Perth, also staying with Joyce and Mac. Damian, Ellie and the children had arrived from Dubai and stayed with Ellie's family in Cottesloe. No one wanted to go near the apartment and Mac had organised professional cleaners. Finally Joyce, Mac, Damian and Nick went together, packed Dennis's clothes and the few other things he wanted. He couldn't bring himself to set foot in the apartment again. They also packed Helen's things, deciding to store them for a while until Dennis could decide what he wanted done with them. The apartment sold quickly, to a couple who had just returned from living overseas and were happy to buy it furnished. Dennis had signed the contract within days.

Now Dennis has found a temporary home. A friend from the wheelchair workshop was looking for a house and dog sitter for a few months and Dennis had volunteered. It's a comfortable little house with a small garden, only ten minutes' walk from the workshop.

'You've put up with me long enough,' he'd said to Mac and Joyce the afternoon he'd told them he'd found a place to stay. 'I have to get a life and find a place of my own. I don't know how I'd have got through this without you.'

And he and Joyce had clung on to each other shaking with silent sobs. 'We're here for you always, Dennis,' she told him.

'Always, mate,' Mac had nodded in agreement. 'You come back whenever you need it.'

But Joyce knows that he won't be back, at least not to stay. Moving out was, for Dennis, a step towards moving on. What's not clear to Joyce, though, is how she too can step out from beneath the torpor of her own grief and guilt, and find a way forward.

As she sits quietly in her rocking chair with the newspaper on this sunny morning in October, watching the way the light falls in a shaft of rainbow-tinged light through the window, Joyce thinks wearily about the way things have changed since she and Mac sat here in the kitchen, making their plan for the year. Helen has gone and Dennis's life has been turned upside down. Stella ricochets between her old stable, rational self and the increasingly obvious signs of dementia. Polly is in this relationship with Leo.

'What did you think of him?' Joyce had asked Mac after they'd met him earlier this week.

Mac had shrugged. 'Not sure,' he'd said. 'Bit opinionated, isn't he?'

'He is,' Joyce had said. 'I decided to give him the benefit of the doubt on that though – I thought he might be feeling a bit insecure, you know, early days with Polly and then having to cope with us and Stella.'

'Mmm, maybe,' Mac had said. 'I can't say I took to him though. But Polly looks happy enough and that's what matters.'

Joyce gets to her feet with a sigh of despair. It's not simply these big changes, she thinks, but she can't get past that unfinished conversation that was interrupted by Dennis's phone call. What happened next, and then in the days and weeks that followed, had consigned everything else to insignificance. Even so it remains unresolved. On the one hand it seems to Joyce like pure male stupidity; she understands that it is perfectly okay for Mac to have a friendship with this woman. But she feels displaced by it, and wounded by his secrecy. It's up to him to make an effort to put things right. But his head seems buried in the sand, as though he thinks that if he ignores it it will eventually go away. And this is just one more thing to struggle with every day, one more thing on top of the burden of guilt Joyce feels for failing her oldest friend.

Out in the back yard Mac is cutting back the bougainvillea, which is surprisingly early this year. She watches as he grasps the recalcitrant branches, clips them with the secateurs and tosses the straggly prunings into the wheelbarrow. He has been back to Albany once for a few days since Helen's death, and she knows he's longing to get back there, to reinstate their plan, or at least live it out for a little longer. But he won't go, he can't let himself go until this is sorted out between them, and he won't go until she manages to throw off some of the burden of grief and guilt.

Mac grasps the handles of the wheelbarrow, backs it out of the corner and wheels it to the bulging garden bag at the back of the garage. Stray purple blossoms float up in the wind and scatter themselves in random patterns across the paving. Joyce sighs, it would be easier just to settle it, she could do it in a moment, let go, snap the tension and toss it away. But that's what she always does, and she always ends up resentful about it. This time is different, she is different. This time he has to make the first move because he created the problem, and she will wait for him to fix it however long it takes. Her mobile rings and she turns away from the window to answer it.

'Joyce, hello, it's Ewan, Ewan Heathcote, how are you?'

'Oh Ewan!' Joyce says, struggling to focus on something and someone who slipped through the cracks of her mind weeks ago. 'Sorry – I was totally elsewhere. I'm okay, and you?'

'Good,' he says. 'I was wondering if I'd be able to get hold of you, thought you might have headed off somewhere exotic by now.'

Joyce takes a deep breath. 'Er . . . no, not . . . well not yet,' she says, feeling foolish, fumbling, totally disconnected from the woman who collected her certificate and sat in a pub talking about going to China or Japan. 'It's been a bit difficult . . . since the course, I mean. A dear friend died, it's been upsetting for all of us.'

'Oh . . .' Ewan pauses. 'Look, I'm so sorry, I shouldn't be bothering you . . .'

'It's all right, I'm over it now,' she lies, trying to inject some energy into her voice. 'You're not bothering me, it's lovely to hear from you.'

'Well, if you're sure . . .'

'I'm sure.'

'I was calling to see if you might be able to help us out for a few weeks.'

'Help you out?'

'Yes, do you remember Sandi, one of our teachers? Well she's had an accident, fell off her bike, broke her leg and a wrist, cut her head, so she's a bit of a mess, poor thing. And we've got another teacher on maternity leave and our usual fill-in teacher is covering that, so I'm looking for someone to do some teaching for us for the next few weeks. I thought you might be interested and available to help us out . . .'

Joyce stands there looking out into the back yard, from which Mac has now disappeared. A sudden breeze toys with the bougainvillea blossoms sending them dancing into the air, allowing some to settle on the surface of the pool, the movement making her blink.

'What do you mean by help you out?'

'We need someone to teach the two level one classes every day for at least the next four weeks,' he says.

'And you're asking me to do that? To work for you, to teach your fee-paying students . . .?'

'That's right, nine 'til eleven and one 'til three. Of course we'll pay you the standard rate and we pay a small bonus for someone stepping in at the last minute.'

Joyce feels like choking, her stomach churns, the world of the language school seems so alien and distant, she feels she has lived several lives since then. 'Oh I don't know, Ewan, I don't think I . . .'

'I'm asking you because you were obviously such a good teacher. We keep a list, you see, and when we need some temporary help we call our graduates. You're top of our list because you did so outstandingly well.'

He stops and the silence tells her she should say something, but what?

'We need someone who can start the day after tomorrow. I'm not desperate, I do have a list of other possible people, but I came to you first because we all really want *you*.'

Joyce opens her mouth but nothing comes out, then, 'I'm not sure I could . . . I mean, teaching in your school . . .'

'Take it,' says a voice behind her, and she turns to see Mac standing in the kitchen doorway. 'If he's offering you some work you should take it,' he says. 'Take it, Joyce, please take it, set yourself free.'

Chapter Twenty-one

'I need a bigger screwdriver, Stella,' Mac says, descending two steps on the ladder and holding a small screwdriver out to her. 'Could you see if you can find one in my toolbox, please? A Phillips, d'you know what that looks like?'

Stella rolls her eyes and bends down to rummage in the toolbox. 'I'm eighty Mac,' she says. 'Of course I know a Phillips screwdriver when I see one.' And she picks up two that are larger than the one he handed her, and holds them up to him.

'Of course you do, sorry,' he says, smothering a smile and taking them. 'Ah, one of these will do,' and he goes back up the two steps of the ladder to finish fitting her new extractor fan.

'So how was Joyce's first day at work?' Stella asks.

'Good. She was a bit jittery in the morning, but came back really confident. What a bit of luck that came up. I was wondering if she was ever going to emerge from all that guilt about Helen.'

'Joyce had nothing to feel guilty about,' Stella says, 'but I guess we all felt it to some extent, felt we had let Helen down, or should have made more of an effort for her.'

'Mmm, well from what the doctor said this had been brewing a long time, and no one could have known,' Mac says. 'And of course Helen was never the easiest person to get on with, especially in the last few years – well, more than a few really.'

'And how's Dennis?' Stella asks.

Mac pauses, carefully locating the last screw and tightening it. 'All done,' he says, handing the tools down to Stella. 'Dennis is doing all right, enjoying the house and dog sitting, and looking for a place of his own. He's sold the four-wheel drive. He was going to keep Helen's Mazda but he's changed his mind, too many reminders. So he's looking around for a decent second-hand car – just something small for himself.'

'Coffee?' Stella asks, and Mac glances at his watch.

'Please, that'd be good, then I'll be off.' He packs up his tools, closes the box, and sits down at the kitchen table, watching as Stella spoons coffee into the plunger and gets out the milk.

'What did you think of Leo?' he asks.

'I'm trying not to make any judgements yet,' she says. 'What about you?'

Mac shakes his head. 'Well I didn't take to him much. Did you notice how he never really looks you in the eye?'

'I did,' Stella says. 'I found that quite unnerving – the way he just looks past you. Odd, isn't it?'

'Odd and rather off-putting,' Mac says. 'That and the way he talks about himself.'

'Exactly.' Stella pulls out her tin of Tim Tams, opens it and puts it on the table. 'Help yourself, Mac. I do worry about Polly; she seems very taken with him. I just hope she doesn't end up getting hurt.'

Mac helps himself to a biscuit. 'Yes, she has been through the mill with relationships. Anyway, how are you, Stella?'

She smiles. 'Pretty good. I did the right thing retiring again, the last week on *Cross Currents* is all a bit of a blur . . .' she pauses. 'Mac, do you think Dennis would be interested in buying my car?'

'Your car?' The thought of Stella without wheels comes as a shock.

'Yes, I think it's time for me to stop driving.'

'But if you're feeling better . . .'

'Well I do *feel* better,' she says, carrying the coffee pot and cups to the table. 'And that's the problem, because I don't think I have a very good sense of what I can and can't do anymore.' She sits down opposite him. 'I haven't told anyone else this but last week I went to the Fremantle cemetery.'

Mac nodded. 'You lost your way to the cemetery?'

'Oh no, it seems I found my way there.'

'Okay, why the cemetery?'

'I have no idea. And I've no memory of driving there but I found myself wandering around among the graves. I didn't know why I was there, or even *where* I was. I mean, I could have been in a cemetery anywhere.'

Mac takes a deep breath, remembering the first time his father disappeared one afternoon and no one had any idea where he was until they got a call from the manager of a restaurant in North Perth, where he'd ordered and eaten a meal and then refused to pay the bill. When Mac had driven up to collect him his dad had no memory of how he had got there and wondered what all the fuss was about. Now he has a sinking feeling in his stomach, just like he'd had that day, a feeling that everything will be sliding steadily downhill from now on. He musters an encouraging tone that is at odds with all his instincts. 'But you *did* get home?'

'I did. I asked for help in the reception area, and a very pleasant young woman told me where I was and offered to call me a taxi. I think she must have thought I was left over from some funeral earlier in the day. So I came home in the taxi feeling very relieved, and the next morning I went out to the garage to drive into town and the car wasn't there.'

Stella pauses, and Mac can see that she is struggling with the telling.

'It was in the cemetery car park?' he asks.

'Of course.'

'You worked that out though?'

There is a long pause. 'No, no I didn't. I didn't even know that I'd been at the cemetery. I thought the car had been stolen and I rang the police and spoke to a very nice constable whose name was Tony. He said he knew me, that I had been at that station one night not long ago, having a cup of tea with him and the sergeant, and he hoped I was well. And when I told him about the car and gave him the number, he said he'd not long had a call from the cemetery reporting that a car with that registration was found there that morning in a no parking area and they believed it had been left there the day before. He was just about to check his computer to trace the owner.'

Stella's hands are shaking as she sets down her coffee mug. Mac reaches out and takes them in his own. 'But you remember it all now?'

'I remember what I've been told about it. I don't remember going to the cemetery. I have no idea why I would do that. I don't remember being in the police station, and having to be collected by a friend. The friend I assume must have been Polly. Do you know anything about that?'

Mac shakes his head. 'I don't, Stella, but I do remember Joyce saying some time ago, before . . . well, before Helen, that Polly was worried because you'd gone walkabout one night.'

Stella nods. 'That sounds right. Polly didn't tell me . . . or maybe she did and I've forgotten.'

'Have you told her about this business with the car and the cemetery?'

'No,' she shakes her head. 'Not now, not while Leo's there. I'll wait until he's gone. I know I need to do something, see a doctor, whatever. This is not something that's going to stop or get better, Mac. And you do see, don't you, that I can't keep driving?'

'I do,' Mac says. He is silent a moment, then grasps her hands more firmly. 'I think you're right, Stella, and I'll talk to Dennis about the car this afternoon. Can I tell Joyce?'

She nods. 'Yes, but I don't want Polly to know yet. I don't want Polly to worry about it while Leo's here.'

They sit there for a moment in silence.

'Well there's one more thing, Stella,' Mac says. 'I will definitely talk to Dennis, maybe bring him back here later today to look at the car, but . . .' he hesitates, hating this moment, hating what he's about to say but knowing he has to say it. 'In view of what you've just told me, I think that you should probably give me your car keys now.'

Stella is silent for a long moment, staring straight at him, stony faced, and he thinks she might be going to refuse. Then she clears her throat and nods. 'Of course I should,' she says, 'of course that's the right thing to do.' And she gets to her feet, crosses the kitchen, takes two sets of car keys down from the key rack and stands there looking down at them in her hands. Then she turns back to the table and gives them to him with a huge sigh.

'That's it then,' she says with a crack in her voice. 'That's the first step in losing my independence . . . just one moment of handing over some keys and it's gone. So what's next, Mac? What's the next stage of diminishment, I wonder?'

*

It's Sunday morning and Leo has set up his laptop in Polly's spare bedroom. Like her he is unable to leave his work completely alone even when on holiday. This pleasant little room has a window that looks out over the greenery of the front garden onto the street, and under it is a desk perfectly placed to catch the light. He's felt more at home since he's grabbed this room for himself. It's a bolthole and although he doesn't really want to bolt, the room with his things in it feels like a zone of safety to which he can repair when necessary. This need must have been obvious to Polly as it was she who suggested it.

'You could use it as a study,' she'd said, 'spread your stuff out, go and do your work in there.'

Maybe she's thinking that this is what she would want; what a bind if he has to organise something when she comes to his place. Leo doesn't like people staying with him, though he can see that it's part of the deal, so to speak, but it makes everything so complicated. In some ways the long distance thing is ideal, in others it's difficult. Ideally Polly would have her own place in London, just a few minutes' walk from his. Then they wouldn't actually have to live together. Perhaps he could persuade her into this; a short walk is infinitely more manageable than the other side of the world. He wonders briefly whether she really would mind moving – after all, who would not rather live in London than here, miles and oceans away from anywhere?

He thinks longingly of London, his place in the world, the world he has built for himself in which he moves in comfort and with confidence. In that world he manages the way that others see him: from his physical appearance and his clothes to the way he presents his work, that is the real world, that is what matters. He clings to what he knows, or professes to know, and sometimes says, about himself: I try to be a good person, I'm open-minded, smarter than most people, I like strong, feisty women, I have my principles, I don't lie, I just say something that is as close as possible to the truth. It's his personal state-ment to himself, one that can be, and often has been, delivered, in full or in part, to others as required.

More recently, though, he's struggled to respond to his own questions about how he might craft his life in old age. How shall I live? What will I do with my time? Who will care for me if I need it? Do I want to be alone? The questions circle him, waiting for answers, but he has none. He's considered developing a posi-tion on this as a new area of expertise and commentary, but he doesn't know what that position would be – so far he has failed to learn much about getting old, and can think of nothing to say about it. Is it because he's a man? Women, as he understands it, are far better at being alone in old age than men. They do all sorts of new things, sometimes get into relationships with other women having previously only loved men, they socialise, travel, get new hobbies, even new jobs in their sixties. Men, apparently, fade away, live in a mess, forget to wash their clothes and themselves, spit on the pavement and wander about farting, miserable and depressed. Well no, he's exaggerating here, but the outlook for men alone in old age is not pleasant. Could this happen to him?

Leo's life has been one of short and disappointing relationships. Now he wonders if he could have learned more from these experiences, but he's never really had time to think about that sort of thing. There have always been other, more pressing matters on his mind and in his view. He has, for example, never thought much about love, although when younger he thought a lot about sex. But surely, hopefully, if you have love, a woman who loves you, then you will always be relevant, as well as cared for. So love has now appeared on his agenda at a time of uncertainty, something he may have to incorporate into his life to stop him crashing over the cliff edge into decline. Does he love Polly? Does Charles love Camilla? HRH is not providing much help these days; just wandering around smiling and waving, like an ageing squire. Sometimes Leo wishes he had an old love tucked away somewhere, ready to leap out in front of him like the Easter Bunny and take charge of him. Except of course that if that actually happened he'd hate it: hate to have a Camilla hovering, smothering him by her mere existence. Relationships seem to require tiresome adjustments, Polly's friends and neighbours have to be factored into the whole thing. Leo has little to do with his neighbours; there are mutual agreements about holding keys and keeping an eye on each other's places while they are away, joint action on problems with the local authority or failures of services, but friendship is not a part of it. He knows lots of people and it's pleasant, this knowing and being known, not infrequently being recognised by people who have read and admired his work; this fuels his belief in who he is and what he does. So although he speaks about his many friends he is coming to understand that friendship means different things to different people.

'You just don't understand, Leo,' Judith had said to him some years ago. 'Friends are not just people that you know. Friendship involves connection and commitment, support, loyalty, give and take. You have to work at it, cultivate it, give it some loving attention. It's more than just having a list of people who know you and whom you occasionally bump into somewhere in the world.'

And so now he throws an occasional dinner party for a few people to whom he owes hospitality. He cooks one of his 'signature dishes', as he refers to them – osso buco, a curry or perhaps a fish stir fry – opens some good wine, and hopes the guests will turn up with cheese or fruit, even a cake for dessert, and they usually do.

'That,' Judith has told him, 'does not constitute friendship. You have to be there for your friends, reach out, stand by them and help out when things are hard.'

'I'm not good at that,' he had said. 'It's not my thing.'

And she had laughed out loud. 'Well you're right about *that*, you can't even do it for me. You just don't have a clue, do you!' It was a statement not a question.

But the dinner parties fit with his liking for a compartmentalised life; guests are selected from the same compartment so that they don't cross-fertilise and become confused with those from other compartments. And he makes it known that he is always very busy, always in demand, so they feel that being invited is an indication of their value to him – at least until they discover his limitations.

So this life of Polly's, this interconnectedness in which the neighbours are also close friends who know your business and can drop in and out when they choose, in which they seem to feel a strong sense of responsibility to one another, is alien to him. It's the same when he goes down to Cornwall: Judith and Rosemary thrive on all this cosy friends-and-neighbours-as-extended-family stuff, while he feels smothered by it. When he turns his mind to the future Leo realises that he is going to have to get to grips with a bit of this blurring of boundaries if the Relationship Thing is going to work.

On his first day Polly had suggested they walk to Fremantle for a late breakfast. Leo had felt totally out of place. Fremantle is too small, a parochial version of a small Californian coastal town, albeit more prosaic, lacking, in his opinion, any sense of cool.

'The light is beautiful here,' he'd said awkwardly, trying to find something to say to counter his discomfort at the feeling of being in a place where the tools of his real life seem useless. 'It would be wonderful for artists. I used to paint a bit myself, years ago.'

'Fremantle is seething with artists,' Polly had said. 'You might want to take up painting again when you come for longer stays.'

'Mmm, maybe,' Leo had said, but the prospect horrified him. He has no desire to dabble in anything amateur. While he can see that the place does have its charms, he feels exiled from the real world of European cities, central London, or buzzing regional centres steeped in centuries of history. The prospect of hanging out here for long periods of time among amateur artists is not in the least attractive to him. Polly, he thinks, will have to be encouraged to spend most of their time together in his world, and he'll have to work out how to fit her into the rest of his life. Tomorrow they are heading off even further from civilisation for a few days, to the southwest where, from the map, it looks as though there is nothing but . . . well . . . nothing but scenery.

Leo opens his email and begins to check his messages. A few days ago he had emailed Kurt, a friend in Berlin, asking for information on the next international conference on atheism. It's an event held each year in different European cities, and at which he has, for more years than he can remember, been an invited speaker. He has usually heard from Kurt by now as the conference is in January. He scrolls quickly through the list of emails and sees that Kurt has responded from the convenor's email address. He opens it, reaching at the same time for his diary so he can enter the dates. The message, he sees instantly, is not from Kurt but from someone whose name is Andreas, who tells him that Kurt retired earlier in the year and that he is now the convenor. There have been some changes in the structure of the organising body, Andreas writes, as well as in the approach to conference streams: *While the organising committee has very much appreciated your contributions in the past, we will not be extending an invitation to you to address us this year, although of course we will be delighted to see you if you choose to join us. I attach a document which outlines details of the registration fees, and suggested conference hotels.*

Leo re-reads the email several times. A fluttery, nauseous feeling stirs in his stomach and he takes several deep breaths and opens the attachment. The four topics are all areas on which he has spoken and written, although admittedly the questions posed have a more contemporary and specific focus. Leo looks at the program, and the names of the speakers – Dawkins is there of course, and Grayling, but the rest of them are new and young, only vaguely familiar. He checks the names of the new organising committee and finds not even one friend or acquaintance on it. The old guard, his old guard, has gone, phased out presumably, put out to grass. Déjà vu. Just before he left for Perth he had received a similar email from people in Canada with whom he had worked regularly for the last five years. He sighs and checks the fees and hotel costs, and is jolted unceremoniously into the world of the uninvited participants – it's a shock. He is used to being provided with business class travel, free five star accommodation, complimentary registration, free wi-fi, goodie bags and often a healthy fee.

The nausea becomes a hard knot of anger, and he knocks out an immediate and deeply offended response. Fortunately he holds back from sending it for when he reads it over he can see that it sounds petulant, too much like what it is – the outrage of a man who suddenly finds he has become superfluous. Leo gets up, walks around the room, takes lots of deep breaths, then returns to the computer and deletes the draft message. But the anger still burns, and surging up behind it is panic: irrelevance is snapping at his heels. For several long and painful minutes Leo is paralysed, and when he does break through the paralysis it is into self-preservation. It's their loss, they always were a bunch of tossers. So what? Fewer responsibilities, more time to do what he wants. And he does not allow himself to venture towards the reality that what he wants is to keep doing what he has always done, in just the way he has always done it.

'Leo?'

He breathes deeply, trying to bring himself back to where he is this minute, this day, in Fremantle with Polly. Judith's words about connection and commitment flash like subtitles across the image of Polly standing in the doorway.

'Leo? Did you hear what I said? Joyce and Mac are walking into town for lunch at Gino's, they wondered if we'd like to join them.'

Leo clears his throat, smiles, pushes back his chair and gets to his feet. 'That sounds great,' he says but he can hear the artificiality of his own voice.

Chapter Twenty-two

Stella is sitting on the bed in the spare room surrounded by papers. She's been promising herself for ages that she will sort out all the papers that, for the last few years, she has dumped into shoe boxes. The other day when Mac came in to fix the new fan, he'd kindly got the boxes down from the top of the cupboard. She's quite proud of the fact that she's actually made a start: it's important, she thinks, because if something happens to her then Polly, who has her power of attorney, will need to find things. But now that she's looking at them she's finding it hard to work out what Polly *would* need. She wishes she'd asked Mac about it, he'd been so helpful with fitting the fan and the following day he'd brought Dennis over to have a look at the car and drive it.

'It's in lovely nick, Stella,' Dennis had said. 'I've always liked the Civic and this will do me very nicely.'

So they had sat at the kitchen table and done the paperwork together, and Dennis had given her a cheque, which Mac later took to the bank for her, and came back with the receipt.

It had been horrible watching Dennis drive away in the car which now, in its absence, seems to represent so much more than just a handy way to get around. She had stood at the open front door, Mac alongside her with his arm around her shoulders, watching with a sense of despair as Dennis backed out of her drive and headed off up the street.

'You okay?' Mac had asked.

'Not really, but I think I've done the right thing.'

'You have, Stella,' he'd said. 'And it was good to do it straight away. You told Polly, didn't you?'

She'd nodded. 'I did, but I didn't tell her about . . . well, about the cemetery. I'll tell her that later, when they come back from their trip, when Leo's gone. I'd be embarrassed . . .'

Mac squeezed her shoulders. 'There is nothing to be embarrassed about,' he'd said. 'This sort of thing can happen to any of us at any time as we get older. You've dealt with it very responsibly.'

It was then that she'd asked him to get the ladder and lift down the boxes, and now here they are lined up neatly on the spare room bed, ready for the big cull. But she should have asked him to help her with that too because now none of the contents make sense to her. Stella closes her eyes, her confusion and rising panic makes her head spin and prickles her skin. Could she just throw it all out, dump everything in the recycling bin? But no, because Polly might need something. Stella sighs, she can no longer sit here with all this stuff around her, and she gets up, and rapidly stuffs everything back into boxes at random, and stacks the boxes into the narrow space between the bed and the window. There is just one box, filled with theatre programs, and this she carries through to the kitchen, this alone makes sense to her. Then she goes back to the spare room, looks with satisfaction at the neat stack of boxes and closes the door on it with a sigh of relief.

*

'Wow, that's some beach!' Leo says, raising his hand to shade his eyes, looking along the seemingly endless curve of coastline. 'So long and so flat.'

Polly laughs and punches his upper arm. 'Well I'm glad it

inspires such poetic language. So long and so flat! Really, Leo, is that the best you can do?'

'Well,' he says, 'well . . . I didn't know this was a test of creativity or I'd have tried harder, but it *is* very long and very flat. And it's breathtaking, is that better?'

'Not much,' she says, 'but I'll let you off the hook. This is one of my favourite places, certainly my favourite beach.'

'How long *is* it?'

'Honestly I've no idea, it's just . . . well, like you said, it's *long*. But I do know that the Busselton jetty is two kilometres long, which makes it the longest wooden jetty in the southern hemisphere.'

'It is beautiful here,' he says. 'Shall we walk out on it?'

She nods, happy to have found something that pleases him. The natural world is not really his thing; he would rather be hoofing it along city streets, browsing an art gallery or an ancient cathedral, all things that she also loves, but not to the exclusion of the natural landscape.

He'd arrived tense and jittery, obviously pleased to see her but distracted, so that when she had kissed him at the airport he had ignored it and said simply, 'Let's get out of here.' Although she sensed this was not about her it had still hurt, especially as all around them people were hugging and kissing, and squealing in delight at the sight of each other.

'It's just turned out to be a difficult time,' he'd said later when she'd asked what was wrong. 'Things building up, other things changing.'

But it was clear that he didn't want to talk about these 'things' that were bothering him.

'Later,' he'd said, 'when I've got my head around it.'

Polly's initial impressions of Leo, first in Edinburgh and then in Hong Kong, were of someone supremely confident who, dumped anywhere, would instantly find a way to feel at home. But Australia seems to have challenged him. He had been to Melbourne a couple of years ago, he'd told her, and loved it, but the thing he had loved about Melbourne was that it felt something like a European city. Several times he has mentioned that Perth and Fremantle are fragile settlements clinging to a remote coastline. Polly suspects some sophistry here; it sounds to her like something he has read in a guide book or travel magazine, and she suspects that what he really feels is that he's a long way from everywhere and everything that is safe and familiar to him, and of course he is.

And it is not only concerns about his work and the location that have spooked him; he is having trouble adjusting to her friends. The night they'd had dinner with Joyce and Mac he seemed to be trying to establish himself as he might do in a professional situation. Here, though, it simply made him sound pretentious and opinionated. He'd talked a lot about himself, had virtually ignored Dennis, seemed most at ease with Mac, flattered Joyce in a rather patronising way on her cooking, and generally looked uncomfortable for most of the time. But it was Stella who had really spooked him. So it's a good thing, Polly thinks, that they have come away to be on their own – away from those threads of her life that seem to bother him. But even as she thinks this she knows that this is something that can't just be shelved indefinitely, it has to be sorted at some stage, because her friends, her home and her work constitute the life that she has chosen and which she loves, and Leo will have to accept this, just as she knows she will have to accept his.

Together they stroll out onto the jetty above the clear, sparkling depth of the water. A light breeze ruffles the surface and gulls swoop and rise alongside them, their calls raucous in the silence. To Polly this is like a meditation, a walk she always takes in Busselton, a walk that calms and refreshes her.

Finally, at the entrance to the observatory, she leads the way down to the glass-walled space that always takes her breath away. It's quiet today, almost closing time, and only a few people remain, staring transfixed, like Polly, by the sensation of being submerged and surrounded by water. Dazzling shoals of vividly coloured fish drift past, weaving in and out of rocky outcrops and waving clumps of seaweed. Nearby several crabs crouch under the rocks, and sea anemones close over their prey. Polly puts her hands flat against the glass, overwhelmed as always by a longing to be actually swimming there, gliding silently through the water, weaving her own way between the rocks.

'Isn't it just magic?' she says eventually, turning back to Leo.

He is standing behind her, alarmingly pale; sweat has broken out on his forehead, he is breathing fast and seems unable to speak.

'Are you okay, Leo?' she asks. He seems fixed to the spot and when she puts her hand on his arm she feels him trembling. In that instant she is catapulted back to Edinburgh, the hotel passage, the frozen, terrified soldier. 'Leo,' she says, 'come on, take my arm, we're going back up right now.' And she slips her arm through his, grasping his hand, nudges him hard and steers him slowly back up the steps, out into the afternoon sunlight, and pushes him down onto a nearby seat. He closes his eyes and leans forward, burying his face in his hands. Polly wedges herself against him fearing he might fall forward. His shirt is damp with sweat. 'It's okay,' she says, stroking his hunched back, 'it's okay, we're out now,' and with her other hand she reaches into the bag slung across her chest and pulls out a bottle of water.

'Come on,' she says. 'Come on, Leo, sit up and breathe properly.'

He straightens up slowly, obviously dizzy. 'Here,' she says, unscrewing the water bottle, 'drink some of this.'

He takes the bottle, gulps down some water, takes several deep breaths, then leans back against the seat. The trembling has stopped now, the colour is returning to his face. 'I'm sorry,' he says, shaking his head. 'So sorry.'

'Don't,' she says. 'Please don't apologise. Are you feeling a bit better?'

He nods. 'Yes, I just need to sit here a little longer. I shouldn't have gone in there . . .'

'I should have warned you,' she says. 'I love it so much I didn't think . . . but I've seen that happen to other people – if you suffer from claustrophobia . . .'

'I do,' he says. 'But I thought because it was water, because I would be able to look out for some distance, it might be okay.'

They sit there alone, above the water.

'If you're finding all of this very hard, Leo,' she says softly, 'that's really okay. Actually I'm finding it quite hard too and I'm on my own turf. Despite all those months of emails we're still getting to know each other. It's a big step for both of us, and we're not young anymore so it seems there is more at stake.'

As she says it she knows that it is only in this moment of his vulnerability that she is able to say this to him, able to acknowledge not only his fear and uncertainty but also her own; that until now she too has been ill at ease, hyper-alert for the things that aren't working, instead of clinging to those that are.

'It's just the claustrophobia,' he says. 'And a bit of other stuff about work.'

'Perhaps it's time for both of us to think about how we do things. How we use our work to avoid other aspects of life. We're both getting old. I'm trying to see it as just another stage of life.' She stops for a moment, pulls back slightly to look him in the face. 'Both you and I have friends who haven't made it this far so I want to make the most of it. Work, a public life, is not necessarily a good fit with getting old.'

And as she turns to look at him she sees that his expression has changed from vulnerability to something else entirely – something like fear.

He shakes his head, gets to his feet. 'Come on, let's get going, I'm fine now.'

*

Joyce glances up at the clock at the front of the classroom.

'Who can tell me what time it is?' she asks.

A young woman in the front row raises her hand. 'It is four

o'clock so we can go home now?' she says, smiling, her inflection rising at the end of the sentence.

'You may,' Joyce says, and she smiles as they gather up their books, and prepare to leave. There are several Chinese students in this class, a few Japanese, two from Korea and six from Indonesia. They are courteous and conscientious, thanking her, smiling, some give her a little bow which she returns. They jostle out of the room, down the passage and out into the late afternoon sunlight. No one had told her how good it would feel to stand at the front of a classroom as a qualified teacher, to get to know a group of students, mostly in their very late teens or early twenties, from different backgrounds, to be in charge of that classroom, and to see, even after just three weeks, the rapidity with which their command of the language improved.

'It's powerful,' she'd said to Mac at the end of the first week. 'I know that sounds weird, but honestly it's a great feeling.'

'So I don't need to worry about how you're coping then?' he'd said. 'No need for rugged husbandly support?'

She had hesitated at this, had been on the verge of challenging him, taking him back to their unfinished conversation, but her conviction that it had to be he who made the first move remained strong. 'I'm fine,' she'd said. 'You should go back to Albany for a while.'

'End of next week,' he'd said. 'Polly will be back then, meanwhile I'll do my share of Stella-watch. And when I do go I don't want it to be so long this time.'

The awkward silence again, everything unspoken hanging in the air, and she had turned away and got on with folding the laundry. And so Mac had stayed another week. Polly and Leo had come home on Saturday, and they'd invited everyone over for dinner on Sunday evening. Mac had left the following day and Polly had driven Leo to the airport a couple of days after that. Life is, in some ways, returning to normal.

Joyce puts her books and the students' assignments into her bag, closes the zip, then picks up the cloth to clean the whiteboard.

227

'Ah! I hoped I might catch you,' Ewan says, appearing in the doorway. 'Do you have a moment?'

'Of course,' she says. 'Is there a problem?'

'Far from it,' he says. 'You're doing such a good job that we don't want to let you go.'

Joyce blinks. 'You want me to stay on? How long for?'

'Well, we'd like to offer you a permanent full-time job starting next year, but I suspect you wouldn't want that.'

She shakes her head. 'No, Ewan, I'd love to work here but not just yet, and not full time.'

He nods. 'I thought so, but maybe we could talk about what would work for you. We could fill that position with two part-timers.'

'I'll need to think about it,' she says cautiously. 'You see, the reason I took the course was because I wanted to teach English to refugees. I want to run a small class, free, in my own home.'

It has been bubbling gently away in the back of her mind since her first visit to the support group. But passing the course had initially made her want more – to travel and live for a while in another country. Then Helen's death had derailed her. 'I've been going to the support group regularly,' she says, 'getting to know people, helping a bit, learning more about what's needed. Now I think it's time to do something.'

'Well, if you need any help with organising that just let me know. But think about it for a while. I don't need a decision now. We're very flexible.'

The next day Joyce starts to shift the furniture in what was once Ben's bedroom. All his personal things were gone years ago of course, but the basic furnishings are still there, grand-children had stayed from time to time and, more recently, Dennis had occupied it in the weeks following Helen's death. She strips the linen off the bed and covers it with a big colourful quilt that Gemma had bought in India. Then she clears the desk of the books and magazines she had put in there for Dennis, and takes from the cupboard some of Mac's unused file boxes, filing trays, a box of pens and markers. She hangs Ben's old whiteboard back on its original fixings, and turns the desk so that it sits under the window, looking out across the back yard. So, she thinks, standing back to admire her handiwork, I have an office, and she takes her treasured certificate in its frame and fixes it to the wall. Now all I have to do is figure out how to do it. And she sits down at her new desk to start work.

Chapter Twenty-three

London, Late October

*L*eo lets himself into his apartment, puts down his suit-case and walks straight through to the kitchen. He takes a glass from the cupboard, ice cubes from the fridge and pours himself a double scotch. Then, leaning back against the sink, he takes a large swig and sighs with the relief of being back again in civilisation. Everything in the apart-ment is immaculately clean and tidy, there is fresh milk, cheese, a packet of smoked salmon, a carton of salad, and two ready meals from Marks and Spencer in the fridge, rye bread in the appropriate container, and a selection of his favourite fruit in the bowl in the middle of the table. The super efficient and hide-ously expensive housekeeping service that he's used for years has triumphed once again. He is restored to life.

The flight home was appalling, but not as bad as it had been on the way out. In a sudden and uncharacteristic mood of prudence he had decided that as he was paying for this trip himself he would risk economy. Bad decision. His hips and back protested at the confines of the seating, the food was terrible. The small child in the seat behind him seemed to be practising goal kicks against the back of his seat and his personal screen failed, dropping him out of movies several times. And that was just in the short leg of the journey to Dubai. He'd tried to upgrade for the second leg to Perth but there was nothing available in business and so for more than eleven hours he had to tolerate the large sweaty man in the adjacent seat, sniffing, coughing, belching and completely commandeering the shared armrest.

'It was torturous,' he'd told Polly when she met him at the arrivals gate.

'Welcome to the world of travel as I know it,' she'd laughed. No sympathy there.

The first thing he'd done when he switched on his laptop the next morning was to upgrade his flight home. Now he relishes the feeling of sinking back into his own comfortable, well ordered life. 'Fuck you, Australia!' he says, raising his glass and swallowing the remains of his whisky. 'Never again!'

Since his visit to Melbourne a few years ago he'd had high hopes of Australia, and when he met Polly the prospect of dividing his life between two sides of the world seemed inviting and timely; and he'd thought it would add a certain cachet to his profile in all those mini-biogs one had to provide for conferences and other events. *'Leo Croft divides his time between London and Western Australia,'* he liked the sound of that. So he had assumed he would cruise into this new environment and adjust with ease, find his level there as he has elsewhere. But within the first few days he knew that there was nothing there that he wanted, except Polly of course. He is always discombobulated away from his public life, but in Fremantle, with the desert in one direction and the ocean in the other, he had felt unknown, adrift and, worst of all, ordinary. Leo abhors ordinariness. That was what had first appealed to him about Polly, she was far from ordinary, and somehow he had felt that her lifestyle would be similar to his own. But while Polly is, in her own way, as professional and involved in her work as he is in his own, her life is cluttered with friends and neighbours, responsibilities and attachments. She is an exceptional woman, but her life is so suburban, so ordinary. He felt stifled by it. It had all come to a head for him in the underwater observatory, the claustrophobic effect of that enclosed space symbolising the same sort of feeling that he'd felt in her house in Fremantle. Trapped in there he realised he was also trapped outside, suffocated by all those vast open spaces. The endless deserts, the dense forests, the ocean. He'd told Polly about that when they had been walking back down the jetty, and she had been amazed.

'But you haven't been to the desert, or any vast open spaces yet,' she'd said. 'The mid-west, or the northwest, or the Nullarbor – those are the vast open spaces.'

She didn't seem to understand that he didn't have to visit them to feel trapped by them, just looking at a map was enough. And he hadn't mentioned the suburban feel of her life, her overbearing involvement with people who really didn't interest him. The whole experience was one of too much of nothing that he could relate to.

Despite his relief at being home now, the difficulties of this are nagging at him. Wild horses won't get him back there, so what to do? And at the same time life here is changing. His friends and acquaintances are either falling off their perches or withdrawing from the things that matter to him. They are retiring to their places in the sun, to live happily with the spouses who have waited patiently for them, and who will help them learn to live different lives. The prospect of domestic bliss in retirement has always appalled Leo, but now, faced with the black hole that seems about to swallow him, he is aware that he is entirely unprepared for old age and unwilling to change any aspect of his life to accommodate it. He had thought that Polly could solve this for him in a variety of ways, but now he wonders . . . And there is always the threat of Cornwall. Judith and Rosemary are always telling him he should go down there more frequently. Rosemary in particular had reprimanded him recently for his neglect of Judith, and urged him to visit more often, take more responsibility for her.

'Who's going to look after her if something happens to me?' she'd asked. 'You can't ask her to accept a stranger moving into the house at this stage of life. You're perfectly capable of looking after her. And really, Leo, it wouldn't be that hard for you to pop her in the car or on the train sometimes and take her to London to stay with you. It would be a change of scene for her. There's a lift in your building, she just needs help getting in and out of the chair, dressing, putting on shoes and so on. You should get some practice in now.'

But Leo has never been able to cope with close proximity to Judith's condition for more than a day or two at a time, the tasks of a carer are often unpleasant, tedious and demanding, it is a very burdensome life and far too ordinary for him.

No, his life is here in London, in close proximity to Europe. Others may retire but he doesn't have to, he just needs to reinvent himself a bit, get a new edge on some of his earlier work, emerge in shiny new colours. And as for Polly, well, they will just have to renegotiate things. Once she's been here, experienced his life, she will doubtless see that this is a far better way to live. She can sell that poky cottage and get a nice place, somewhere not too near and not too far away.

So, Leo, he tells himself, plan of action: two problems to deal with here. Number one, hanging on to the professional relevance – it *is* possible but you just have to work out how, come up with something new. Number two, organising something with Polly in a way that doesn't mess up other arrangements. This is the more complex problem

*

Since Leo left Polly has devoted all her energy to gathering information on possible long term solutions for Stella's future, and the first step is an assessment by an aged care team. For this she needs to get Stella to the doctor. It is the first step on her list of awful things she'll have to do. One more thing to occupy her mind and fuel her anxiety, the other being Leo.

His obvious unease outside his own environment is entirely at odds with her first impressions of him in Edinburgh. But it's helped her to understand him better. On top of his public commitments he does, he'd explained, have significant family responsibilities, so he is always under pressure. But she has also discovered how inflexible he is. His sense of himself seems to depend entirely on maintaining the status quo of his public, professional life. The only change he's interested in is making her a part of that, but he can't explain how this will work from different sides of the world.

'We'll sort it out,' he'd said airily. 'Don't worry about it, we'll get there.'

But Polly wonders how, at what cost and to whom.

And she had so hoped that Stella would like him – that the two of them would like each other. But Stella's total silence on the subject has been remarkable. Has Stella simply forgotten that Leo was here at all?

As she sips the remains of a cup of tea Polly longs for the voice of the old Stella. Listen to yourself, Polly, she'd have said, you're growing old too, *you* have a brother whose condition is as bad or worse as Leo's sister's, you too have unreliable sources of work and have lived with that for years. And frankly, you are far less prepared financially for old age than he is. Work out what you want and need for yourself, and hold to that. Don't try to find solutions for Leo at your own expense. You've swum this river before and this time you will have to swim more strongly than ever against the current.

Once again Polly rationalises the situation by ascribing it to the tyranny of distance, and the need for time together to move the relationship to a different level. She sits for a while, thinking carefully about her own commitments, about when it would be possible to take a longish break to go to England. Christmas is good, assuming Stella is okay, because both Joyce and Mac will be here, Ben and Vanessa and their girls will be around too, and if she starts talking to Stella about this now she can probably also organise a carer. Someone to come in regularly, get the shopping, clean the house, take Stella out sometimes. And she writes a note to remind herself to chase this up tomorrow. Then she picks up the phone and dials Leo's number.

'Hi,' he says, 'I was just about to pop out.'

'It's early for you,' she says, 'where are you off to?'

'Following up with someone about a possible joint publication, so I don't have long.'

'Okay,' she says. 'I just want to run something past you. I feel we need to spend more time together soon . . .'

'Sure do,' he says, impatiently. 'Let's work on that.'

He sounds as though he is ready to hang up, but Polly is determined. 'I already have,' she says. 'I think I'll fly over in mid-December, we can have Christmas and New Year together. I'll probably stay for a month, perhaps a bit more depending on how Stella is at the time.'

There is a small but perceptible pause at the other end of the line.

'I see,' he says. 'The thing is, I actually have plans for Christmas. I need to spend some time in Cornwall . . .' he seems to hesitate. 'And there are other family issues I have to deal with. '

'Oh . . .' Polly pauses, disappointed, 'well, couldn't I come with you? I'd love to meet your sister and her friend and the rest of your family too.'

'Of course,' he says. 'Of course, but it seems a bit soon. I haven't told Judith about us yet, I'd like to tell her when I'm with her, so I'll do that at Christmas, then she won't . . .'

'Won't what?'

'Well . . . it won't take her by surprise.'

Polly hesitated. 'Well I don't really understand why you haven't told her already. Do you think she'll mind that you have someone in your life? Wouldn't she want you to be happy?'

'Of course, but she's a bit fragile around . . . well, around change, I suppose. I'd rather tell her in person. Look, it's all fixed now; besides, the pre-Christmas airfares will be ridiculous, and it's always freezing here at Christmas.' He gives a little laugh. 'I remember how you hated the cold in Edinburgh.'

Polly's pleasure at having decided on something positive is evaporating; she feels hurt and offended that her presence in Leo's life seems to involve embarrassment and explanation; he seems to be closing her off from his family, but she fears sounding needy and petulant.

'Didn't you say you had to go back to Paris?' he says in a much more positive tone. 'Why don't we meet up in Paris in the early spring and then come back to London together? Wouldn't that be fun? Paris, hot chocolate, marvellous food and wine, the Louvre, the Seine . . . all that, wouldn't it be lovely?'

Polly senses that her inner Stella is dying to tell her something, but she pushes it aside. 'It would,' she says. 'It would be wonderful, but that's months away.' His response has hurt her, but to pursue it would make her seem needy, and maybe he's right anyway; Christmas is often a difficult emotional time in families. Maybe meeting Judith and the rest of them in the spring is a better plan. And so the conversation drifts to its end leaving her disappointed and slightly ashamed that she hadn't managed to negotiate her own preferred solution with him.

Several hours later Polly sits at her computer and clicks Alistair's Skype icon. He answers almost immediately.

'Of course you can come for Christmas, darling,' he says, 'that would be wonderful. Stevo,' he calls, turning away from the screen, 'the mad tart from Fremantle wants to come for Christmas – okay with you?'

Steve appears behind him. 'More than okay,' he'd said. 'Do come, Polly, then I won't have to spend Christmas in solitary confinement with this old fart.'

They talk for a while and when they hang up Polly checks the flights, makes her booking then, closing the computer, she lets herself out of the front door and walks up to talk to Joyce.

*

Joyce is sitting in her study reorganising a lesson plan. Setting up a course is, it seems, a matter of trial and error. She has got off to a cautious start with seven students, all women, three of whom are mothers with children, twin sisters aged nineteen from Sri Lanka, and a woman in her late fifties who has arrived here from Somalia with her daughter and a nine-year-old granddaughter, having lost the rest of their family on the journey. It was strange at first, having so many strangers in her home, but after the first couple of classes it began to feel good. The big dining table in the kitchen is ideal; they had bought it donkey's years ago, when they had renovated, in fact almost completely rebuilt, the back of the house. She had spotted it in a second-hand shop.

'Look,' she'd said, dragging Mac over to see it. 'It's just what we need, bit knocked around but you could clean it up couldn't you?'

The table was fine old teak and Mac and Dennis together had cleaned, sanded and varnished it to perfection. Their two families had eaten at it more times than Joyce could remember, ten of them, sometimes twelve at a push if the kids had friends with them. Joyce runs her hand over the smooth weathered surface thinking how well it lends itself to this new purpose.

After two classes a week for three weeks everyone's progress is obvious, and the energy and pleasure of the shared time seems to fill the whole house. The front doorbell rings and Joyce sighs irritably and puts down her pen. How grumpy I'm getting, she thinks, I never want to be disturbed these days, and she stops dead as she crosses the kitchen, the memory of the last time she saw Helen hitting her like a bullet in the chest. She takes a deep breath and walks on out and up to the door, determined to treat whoever it is with patience and courtesy, however annoying they are.

'Oh, Polly – it's you, thank goodness,' she says. 'That's a relief, come on in. Why didn't you come through the back gardens?'

'Because I didn't want Stella to see me and decide to join us,' Polly says. 'And why is it a relief?'

'Because my tolerance for time wasters is decreasing with age, but seeing you always does me good. Is it time for a glass of wine?'

'Overdue, I think,' Polly says, holding out a chilled bottle of Semillon. 'I came prepared.'

Joyce gets glasses from the cupboard. 'How's Leo?'

'Fine, busy of course.'

Joyce raises her eyebrows and clinks her glass against Polly's. 'Cheers,' she says. 'Isn't he always?'

'I think he's frightened of not being busy,' Polly says. 'Can't or doesn't want to imagine how life could be otherwise! And scared of being displaced by a new upcoming generation of equally smart arses.'

Joyce smiles. 'Mac had to cope with that,' she says. 'He hung on for a long time because of it. And when he did go they got him back quite a few times for some projects so I suppose that helped to ease him out of it.'

'Mmm, I remember that,' Polly says. 'But I must say that this preciousness about ageing pisses me off a bit. If we're lucky enough to get old I feel we should make the most of it. But actually it was Stella I came to talk about, and this is where I'm being more than a bit precious. I've never been responsible for anyone's wellbeing before and I really don't have a clue. It seems an enormous responsibility.'

'It *is* a big thing,' Joyce agrees, 'but we'll help you. And at least now she's sold the car. Essential, really, in view of the visit to the cemetery.'

Polly raises her eyebrows. 'I don't know about that. But when we got back and she told me she'd sold the car to Dennis I was hugely relieved. So what about the cemetery?'

She listens as Joyce explains. 'Poor Stella,' she says. 'That must have been terrible for her. Thank goodness for Mac, he must have hated taking the keys away. But look, I *have* organised an appointment with her doctor. I'm taking her next week.'

Joyce nods. 'Good, I just hope that she gets to spend Christmas with us and in her own home. Will you be here or are you going to stay with Leo?'

Polly shakes her head. 'With Alistair and Steve, just over the actual holiday, and I'm thinking I'll get a carer for Stella. I'd like to get this started straight away, get her used to the idea of having someone else to help; someone who can also be a friend, take her to places, help her shop and so on.'

Joyce nods. 'That's a really good move. If you can get the right person and introduce her slowly it would be ideal.'

They pour more wine and talk on and it is after nine when Polly gets up to leave.

'I'll walk out with you,' Joyce says, and the two of them stroll back down the road, past Stella's house, where the lights are still on and music is drifting softly out into the street.

'She's listening to *South Pacific*,' Polly says. 'She plays it a lot. She was in it years ago, played the lead.'

They stand there for a moment in the shadows and Polly turns to Joyce again.

'Thanks for always being there.'

Joyce reaches out and hugs her. 'Honestly, I'm glad you came. I needed to know what was happening. We'll work things out for Stella, and you will eventually sort things out with Leo. One day at a time, that's all we can do.'

She waits on the pavement until Polly has closed her door behind her, turns then stops again outside Stella's house. She is playing something different now, and Joyce opens the gate, walks quietly up the path to the door and stands there, listening. Stella is singing along with . . . who is it? . . . Bing Crosby perhaps, or maybe Sinatra. Joyce hums softly trying to recall the song, something about being bewildered, about being like a child again, confused . . . she shakes her head in irritation unable to conjure up the lyrics. I'm getting as forgetful as Stella, she murmurs. And then she remembers, *Bewitched, Bothered and Bewildered*, that's what it's called. Tears well in her eyes, what was in Stella's mind when she chose that song? And she wanders slowly down the path and out of Stella's gate looking beyond her own house to the darkened shapes of the houses that occupy the block next door. Years ago there was always a light in Helen and Dennis's place, always a feeling that it would be fine to knock on the door or slip through the gate in the fence. But for so long now there has been no one there. So many changes, she thinks. Some creep up slowly, others hit us like a ton of bricks. How lucky we've been with our neighbours, such special memories. She pauses, remembering a day, years ago, when Helen had turned up at the back door, hammering furiously on the locked flyscreen.

'Why?' she had shouted at Joyce through the mesh. 'Why does it have to be me? Just as my kids have left home . . . just as I stop caring for the young ones, I have to start again caring for the old people.'

Joyce remembers fumbling with the latch to let her in and how Helen, her face contorted with frustration, had stormed into the kitchen, shaking her head.

'I never wanted to look after people,' she'd said. 'I wanted a career, I wanted to do something impressive, to *be someone*, and here I am, in my fifties, still spending every day feeding, cleaning, shopping, washing, being an unpaid nursemaid, driver, secretary and god knows what else for other people. When is it going to be my turn, Joyce? When will it be my turn to do something for me?' And yet she had done it conscientiously and largely with good grace, and neither her own mother nor Dennis's parents would ever have known what it cost her. And when Helen's time for herself *had* come, when she finally saw time and space stretching out in front of her, she had lacked the energy or perhaps the imagination to work out what she really wanted. 'I miss you, Helen,' Joyce whispers now. 'I really miss you. And I'm so sorry I allowed myself to forget the person you used to be.' And slowly she walks back up her own front path, through the open front door, and closes it behind her.

Chapter Twenty-four

'I really don't think this is necessary,' Stella says, getting into the front seat of Polly's car. 'Derek will think it's a waste of time.'

'Derek has been your doctor for years and as you know, Stella, he thinks everyone over sixty should have regular check-ups. When did you last have one?'

Stella snaps the seatbelt into place. She's been finding Polly very irritating lately, and not just Polly, Joyce and Mac too. They seem to think she's incapable of managing her own life. 'Well I've no idea when it was,' she says. 'But there's certainly nothing wrong with me.'

'You've been concerned about your memory for some time,' Polly says.

Stella sighs. 'No I haven't. There's nothing wrong with my memory. And frankly, Polly, I find this business of you coming with me a bit insulting. I know you mean well, but I am perfectly capable of going to the doctor alone. And I don't know why you were so insistent we go in your car, I would have preferred to drive myself.' She sees Polly take a deep breath and peer sideways out of the driver's window, waiting for a car to pass before pulling out. 'I'm not a fool, you know – I've managed to look after myself for seventy years, and I can do it now.'

'It's eighty years,' Polly says. 'You turned eighty earlier in the year, and Joyce made you that amazing Tim Tam cake.'

'I remember that cake. I didn't know it was my birthday. Someone should have told me.'

'We did,' Polly says. 'We all sang happy birthday and you blew out the candles in one go.'

'Well there can't be much wrong with me then,' Stella says, sensing that she has won this round. Polly is so argumentative these days too, she never used to be like that.

This doctor's appointment is all her idea. Stella has managed to get it postponed three times so far and now it's November, and she'd thought Polly had given up but no such luck. Oh well, better get it over and done with and then perhaps the nagging will stop.

'I expect it's that man's fault,' Stella says. 'The one who was hanging around your house recently.'

'Leo, you mean?'

'That's him. I didn't like him.'

'I know,' Polly says. 'And what do you think is his fault?'

'Um . . . well, this doctor business, this bee you've got in your bonnet.'

'Why do you think that's Leo's fault?'

'Because he didn't like me, he made that quite clear. He said, "Shut up, you old bag, or I'll punch you in the face".'

Polly laughs out loud. 'Stella, Leo did *not* say that. You're thinking of the man who was bullying the bank teller. Last year, he was shouting at the teller and you were in the queue and you went over to him and told him not to be so rude. Remember? He shook his fist at you and the security guard came over and took him out of the bank. That was *last year*, before I even *knew* Leo.'

Stella shakes her head. 'Well personally I think *you* are a bit confused. But anyway, he didn't like me and I hope he's not coming here again because I don't trust him.'

'Okay,' Polly says. 'Well let's not talk about Leo. Let's just try and get to Derek's surgery without arguing, shall we? Then when we come out we could go and have coffee and Danish pastries at Gino's if you like.'

'Splendid. I can almost smell the coffee. So why are we going to the doctor?'

Polly parks the car and Stella gets out, straightens her skirt and wraps her cardigan more closely around her. She thinks she is feeling the cold more as she gets older. But I'm seventy, she tells herself, it's bound to happen. 'I was cold on the rocks,' she says, taking Polly's arm to cross the road. 'When I was there in my nightie.'

'I'm sure you were,' Polly says. 'But Gareth told me he got you a nice warm blanket, while you were waiting for the light.'

'Bloody Gareth,' Stella says. 'It's such a long time, years, since I saw him.'

Inside the surgery they take their seats in the waiting room. Stella fidgets with the handle of her bag, trying to remember why they're here. Is it her blood pressure, or maybe it's Polly who's seeing the doctor. 'Why are we . . .' she begins, but Polly who has been flicking through a copy of *New Idea* cuts across her.

'Look, Stella, look at this picture,' she says, folding back the pages and handing it to her.

The picture shows a very old woman with wild grey hair in a white nightdress, standing against a background of rocks, with waves crashing beneath her. 'What is it? Who *is* that?' Stella says, fumbling for her glasses.

'It's you,' Polly says. 'It's an article about the new series of *Cross Currents.*'

'*Cross Currents*?' Stella says, taking the magazine from her in amazement. 'Is there a new series then?'

'You know there is,' Polly says. 'You're in it. That's why you were in Albany, on the rocks, in your nightdress. You were playing Cassandra again. Here, see!' She stabs it with her finger. 'Remember?'

Stella takes it from her, 'Ah, yes, the rocks and the water.'

'It says here that it's due to start screening in the New Year.' Polly says.

'I can't find my glasses,' Stella says, frustrated now; her bag seems to be full of annoying things, and she starts slinging them out onto the floor.

'Shh!' Polly says. 'Calm down, Stella, calm down. Here are your glasses, but anyway I'll read it to you.' And she hands her the glasses, gathers other items from the floor, slips them back into Stella's bag and starts to read.

'*Fans of Cross Currents will be happy to know that not only will Cassandra return from the dead in the new series, but she will be played once more by the stalwart Stella Lamont. Lamont has emerged once more from retirement to play the spirit of Cassandra and puts in as strong a performance as ever. Welcome back, Stella – you're an inspiration.*'

*

'She's not in good shape, is she?' Derek says later. He leans across his desk towards Polly and lowers his voice. 'You're quite right, Polly; the indications are that Stella has Alzheimer's. I'm going to refer her to a geriatrician and she'll need to be seen by the Aged Care Assessment Team. We'll organise this from here and see if we can get it all fixed up soon, and I'd be amazed if they don't tell us that she needs some sort of residential assisted living.'

Polly's heart sinks; she'd known this was coming but hearing it makes it a reality. She glances across to the door of the treatment room, where Stella is still with the nurse. After Derek had finished his physical examination, he left the nurse to take some blood samples, and then to give Stella a cup of tea.

'I should have made her come sooner,' she says. 'But it's just such a big step. And although she's been struggling with her memory, and blanking out occasionally, the rest of the time she was just the old Stella. It's all so confusing. Sometimes I feel it's me who's losing it not her, and then . . . well, you've seen how she is this morning.'

'I have,' he says, 'and I think there's a slight personality change too, isn't there?'

Polly nods. 'More than slight on occasions. She can be quite off hand, even arrogant, which is so unlike her, and she's more stubborn and critical too. That's the side you saw this morning. The old Stella never shied away from saying tough things, but she was thoughtful and sensitive about how she put it.'

Derek nods. 'Well, she is now the centre of her own world, and that world is narrow and distorted. This change may well become more pronounced. Try not to take it personally. And don't struggle to correct her misconceptions, just hang in there, keep her calm and happy if you can, and we'll get all this moving straight away. Physically she's in good shape for her age but mentally . . . well, you know all that. You could start thinking about a place for her but we need to be sure what level of care she'll need. And of course we may not be able to find a place before Christmas. Can you manage in the meantime?'

Chapter Twenty-five

'Dinner's on me,' Ben says, as he and Mac climb into the car. 'I thought we'd go to the pub that has those amazing pies.'

'The Earl of Spencer,' Mac says. 'Excellent, my favourite; and I feel a pint of Guinness coming on.'

'You've made a great job of the place,' Ben says as they head into town. 'What's next on the list?'

'Painting the main bedroom, and I'd like to renovate the bathroom, but that's a big job, so I won't be starting on that until I come back after Christmas.'

Ben frowns. 'I think, when you told me what you were planning to do this year, I may have said something patronising about it. Something about your wanting a boy's own adventure.'

'You said exactly that, and you were right, that's exactly what I *did* want, only I wanted it under the most comfortable conditions. No campfires or sleeping rough. Just wanted to get away, be on my own doing my own thing. No domestic restrictions.'

'So Dennis turning up and staying must have messed that up?'

'Not really, although I'll admit it was longer than I anticipated. But we did a lot of work together, repaired all the fences, built those new bookshelves in the lounge, and the fitted desk in the small bedroom, and he did a lot of the painting. I was a bit anxious at first, but it turned out to be pretty special, just the two of us here, talking, working together. It made me realise that what I'd been struggling with was simply the idea of getting old.'

'Were you? I didn't realise . . .'

'No, well nor did I until then. I'd been feeling a bit useless, kept telling myself that there was a time when I was a really important person, when I'd won those CSIRO research awards and people wanted to work with me, it was all pretty good for the ego. Even after I'd retired they kept getting me back in. And then I started thinking, well, it doesn't seem to matter now, so what am I supposed to be doing? Who am I supposed to be now?'

Ben laughs, shakes his head. 'Bloody hell, Dad, I never thought you'd be one to have an existential crisis.'

'Well there you go. I've been having one for several years – stretching it out, wallowing in it. Being here turned out to be a time of reckoning. You see I always liked feeling impor- tant, Ben, being in charge of things. And I really liked being deferred to, feeling as though I was up in the top ranks. But mooching about down here, on my own and then with Dennis, I began to think, well, if this is getting old I rather like it. In the end it's the people you care about that matter, that make life special and precious.' He feels quite choked up as he says it and knows that Ben must be able to detect that in his voice.

'That sounds a pretty good way to be,' Ben says. 'And what about Mum?'

'Your mum wanted something new and different. I think she had something to prove to herself. That course and then being offered this work at the language school . . . it's meant a lot to her.'

Ben pulls into the car park and switches off the engine. 'You don't seem quite the same together though,' he says. 'Nessa and I thought that when you were back home there was something going on between you. I thought it was because Mum's still very upset about Helen.'

'You're both right,' Mac says, looking away from his son out into the darkness of the car park. 'But there is other stuff too. Stuff we have to sort out between us.' He looks back at Ben and sees the concern in his face. 'It's all right, my fault of course, but nothing for you to worry about. We'll get there eventually.'

They get out of the car and saunter towards the pub where Ben orders two pints of Guinness and they browse the dinner menu.

'Thanks for coming down, Ben,' Mac says, raising his glass. 'It's great to have time with you, so long since we did anything like this.'

As they wait for their meal an old school friend of Ben's strolls over and thumps him on the back and as the two of them catch up Mac's thoughts drift back to Dennis, to the end of a marriage which had seemed rock solid, and then to Helen. There had been a time when he had thought that Dennis might never get over her death, the manner of it had haunted him for weeks, but slowly he got himself together and began to mould his life into a new and different shape: the house sitting, changing the car, and he's looking for a place of his own. He wonders how Dennis had thought about his old age before any of this happened, and how he feels now about the future. Mac knows that their time together down here is something he'll remember with a special fondness, not only for his friend, but because it helped him to get to grips with growing old.

Meeting Carol has been an important part of that too. The time he spent with her took him back in time. She showed him glimpses of himself as a young man, and in contrast to the time he spent with Dennis, it was dazzling, seductive. A slideshow of his life – who he was, who he is now – had begun to unfold for him. He'd reflected on the journey that brought him to this time and this place: the decisions, the successes and failures, the struggles and the rewards. Back home again, with Joyce and the family, as they all faced the tragedy of Helen's death, he'd realised how important it was to appreciate the present, value each day; not just to tolerate ageing, but to enjoy it.

He has met up with Carol a couple of times since he got back, tried to explain what had happened when he told Joyce, but he'd done it badly, leaving her with the impression that everything was now fine. Meanwhile this elephant is slap bang in the middle of the room between him and Joyce, something that has to be dealt with before the last pieces of the new jigsaw puzzle of life drop into place. Joyce still hasn't raised the subject so is she waiting for him? And if so what does she want him to do? It can't be as simple as apologising can it?

*

'So what did you think of Valerie?' Polly asks.

'Who?'

'Valerie, Val, she came this morning, to help you.'

'Oh is that her name?' Stella says. 'Very pleasant, she did a good job with the cleaning, and she made me some lunch, a very nice tuna and salad sandwich. Yes, I liked her, and I can see that it'll be good to have someone to do the cleaning. I can't get down in corners like I used to. She said she'll be back on Wednesday, but I told her not to bother, once a fortnight will be fine.'

'She doesn't only come to clean,' Polly says. 'She can shop for you, drive you anywhere you want to go. You can go out together for a coffee or lunch, whatever you want.'

'Oh, I don't think so. You do all those things for me. And I'd rather have lunch or coffee with you.'

'Well let's see how it goes,' Polly says.

'That man, Leo,' Stella says, 'his name is actually Leonard, I looked him up on Google. Most Leonards settle for Len, but I suppose he thinks Leo is more dashing. Anyway, I don't like him and I don't trust him. He's very self-centred, one of those men who is incapable of really caring about anyone other than himself.'

'Do you think he doesn't care about me?' Polly asks. Stella thinks she sounds angry, or perhaps hurt.

'I think he cares as long as it suits him, and that may not be for long,' she says.

'He came all the way from England to visit me.'

'Yes, well he probably likes the grand gesture. There's something he gets from you, from being with you, but it will either not be enough, or possibly it will be too much. I especially didn't like that he doesn't look you in the eye. You have to ask yourself what that's about.'

Polly laughs. 'Okay,' she says, patting Stella's hand. 'You don't have to like him.'

'No, I don't, but I do love *you*, Polly, I don't want you to get hurt,' Stella says and she feels herself on the verge of tears. 'It's a gut feeling, but I won't say any more. No one wants to hear bad things when they're in love. Now that's something I *do* remember.'

Chapter Twenty-six

Christmas

*P*olly carries a pile of plates into the kitchen, stacks them carefully into the dishwasher, and turns to the steamer to check on the pudding. A couple more minutes, just for luck, she thinks, and she stands there looking out across the terrace by the pool where Alistair and Steve and half a dozen of their friends are gathered at the table, mellowed by two courses and awaiting the third. It's early evening, the candles are barely flickering in the still air, the blossoms on the frangipani trees have aquired a pearly glow in the fading light. They had eschewed a traditional Christmas dinner and opted for local fish and seafood with salads and she and Steve had shared the work. The only concession to Christmas fare is the pudding.

Throughout the day, particularly during the late afternoon and the flow of champagne, the exchange of presents and arrival of friends, Polly has struggled to appear festive and light-hearted, but it hasn't been easy. Last night she dreamed she was carrying a big brown paper bag full of shopping, clutching it in her arms, desperate to hang on to it all until she reached her destination. But it started to rain and slowly but steadily the paper bag began to disintegrate, and bit by bit its contents slipped from her grasp. She woke to the sound of rain and, trying to shake off the dream, got out of bed and opened the blinds. The dawn light was still pale, and the rain splashed down across the terrace and into the glittering aqua glow of the pool. She stood there for a while, watching the light change, thinking about the dream, feeling that it was about both Stella and Leo, a manifestation of her anxiety about her relationships with both of them. For years now, more than two decades, her friendship with Stella has been the one that she has treasured above all others. Stella has been both sounding board and counsel, sometimes critical, never judgemental, stalwart in her love and support. But Stella is changing, and with those changes the boundaries are blurring; everything that existed unspoken between them is being swept away by the tide of dementia.

'You're going to have to let go, Polly,' Leo had said. 'You talk about her as though she's your mother or your sister; she's just a friend.'

His words had shocked her so much that she said nothing. What she had wanted to say was that Stella was in so many ways both mother and sister to her. She had been only twenty and Alistair almost twenty-four when their parents died, and for years she had thrashed around struggling to find an emotional framework for her life.

'We're orphans,' she'd said to Alistair. 'We're entirely alone in the world.'

'We have each other,' he'd said. 'And we need to cling to that, Polly, it's the rock we share.' And he was right about that. Nonetheless Polly had longed for a connection with an older woman, a connection that would sustain and nourish her as her mother had done. Years later that woman turned out to be Stella.

'We've held hands to stop each other falling for years now,' Stella had said almost a year ago when Polly set off to the Edinburgh conference. And as she feels Stella's hand slipping from hers Polly wonders whether Leo is capable of this level of loyalty and commitment; whether he even understands what his promise to always be there for her really means. His silence since a couple of days before Christmas, and particularly today, adds to the feeling that her life is falling apart.

Out on the terrace she sees Steve get to his feet, clear the rest of the plates and carry them towards the house.

'How's the pudding?' he asks, adding the plates to those already in the dishwasher.

'Almost there,' she says.

He joins her, looking out at the group on the terrace. 'So how does Al seem to you?'

'Amazing. Honestly, he looks better than he has for years, and he seems stronger.'

Steve nods. 'He is. He's been in his chair today because he knows it's a long tiring day and he needs to conserve his energy. But often, when we're on our own, he'll potter around, fetch things – well, you saw that yesterday.'

'I did,' Polly says, 'and he was doing that again this afternoon while you were out, and I thought he might fall so I tried to stop him.'

'Oh dear, did he have a hissy fit?'

She laughs. 'A minor, haughty one. He said, "Thank you, Polly, for your concern but I manage to live my life pretty effectively during your absence, so unless you have any especially testing hazards for me, you can trust my judgement on what I can manage".'

'Ha! Pompous git.'

'That's exactly what I said! And then he just laughed.'

'He's never lost that unique skill for putting people in their place,' Steve says. 'Seriously though, it's good, isn't it? He's got more energy and his balance has improved.'

'Is he on new medication?'

'No, nothing's changed except him. I don't know whether to be thrilled or terrified.'

Polly looks at him in surprise. 'Why terrified?'

'Oh well, you can't tell, can you? I mean, I know he's never going to get better but I watch him do something he hasn't been able to do for ages and I get hugely optimistic. Then I get into bed at night and think – what if this is some final sudden burst, you know, a last terrific surge of life before I wake up in the morning and find him dead?'

Polly catches her breath. 'I see, yes, I see. It's hard to imagine, looking at him now, but I do understand what you mean.'

They stand there watching as Alistair pulls a bottle of champagne from an ice bucket and hands it to the woman sitting beside him, nudging her to fill up the glasses.

'It's interesting to see how he *does* manage himself,' Steve says. 'A few months ago he couldn't have picked up an almost full bottle, now he can, but he knows he can't quite trust himself to stretch out his arm with it and fill people's glasses. So yes, he's right, he *can* be trusted to manage, to know his limitations.'

Polly turns to look at him. 'And how do *you* manage, Steve?'

Steve shrugs. 'Well, you just do what you have to,' he says. 'It becomes a way of life. We're really lucky, we have enough money, and one of the prerequisites of living here is that you have to employ a local person. And we've been so lucky to find Jasmina.'

'But the responsibility,' Polly says. 'Doesn't that sometimes feel crushing, doesn't it squeeze the life out of you?'

Steve looks at her, reaches out and puts a hand on her arm. 'You're thinking of Stella?'

She nods. 'Yes, and I know it's pathetic because I've never had to do anything until now, and whatever lies ahead it's not going to be anything like what you've done for Al for years, decades. I suppose I hadn't realised that I was – am – such a selfish person.'

'It *is* different, Poll,' Steve says. 'We had a lot of great years when he was fine. You're struggling with Stella because she's changing, she's hard to handle, sometimes she seems like a different person. Al's changed too, but fortunately he's changed into a kinder, more loving person – all those hard edges have been knocked off him. In his own way he's also learned how to care for me. So it's a mutual thing. I'm not saying it's always easy, it's just that he understands what he creates for me, and he works at trying to make that easier. We understand each other. It's very different from your situation with Stella.'

She sighs and turns to the steamer. 'Yes, I suppose it is,' she pauses briefly thinking again of what he has said. 'Okay,' she says, in an attempt to sound more positive, 'let's get this pudding on the road. Can you bring the brandy and matches, please?'

Later, when the pudding has been demolished, Polly sits back in her chair, listening to snatches of conversation, joining in the toasts, and thinking about Leo, wondering again why he hasn't called. They had last spoken on the morning of the day before Christmas Eve, she was already here in Bali, and he was about to leave to catch a train down to Cornwall. Since then there has been nothing, no Christmas greeting, no call, no noisy Skype tone.

'Email me your number so I can call you in Cornwall,' she'd asked, but he hasn't done so and her emails remain unanswered. What can he be doing that is so important that he can't call or at least send an email at Christmas? Her attempts to hide her distress are wearing thin, but she feels this abandonment as shame, as though it is she who has somehow failed. His silence builds up in her like layers of concrete forming a hard lump in her chest, a lump of hurt and shame. Questions spin through her head: what have I done to deserve this? Why is telling his sister such a big thing? Is he ashamed of me? Why is this happening?

When he was staying with her there had been times that she had felt him pulling away from her. He no longer took her hand when they walked along the street and if she took his he soon let go. And he began to turn away from her at night, avoiding her attempts to cuddle up to him. Once back on email, some of the old Leo seemed to return, but now, once again, he has retreated from her. She pushes back her chair and gets up from the table, which is still laden with fruit, cheese and chocolates.

'Where are you going, Poll?' Alistair asks.

'To make coffee,' she says. There is a rumble of appreciation around the table and, smiling, she slips away to the kitchen, puts the kettle on, gets out the coffee and goes to her room to check her mobile. She had forced herself to leave it there knowing that if she kept it with her someone, probably her brother, would notice how obsessively she checked it.

There is neither message nor email. She throws the phone on the bed and walks back to the kitchen. 'I don't need this shit,' she says softly as she reaches up to take cups down from the cupboard. 'If he loves me why doesn't he call me? Why doesn't he want to talk to me? How can this be okay?'

'It's not okay,' a voice says behind her and she turns to see that Alistair has wheeled himself into the kitchen.

She leans back against the sink and hides her face in her hands. When she looks up again Alistair is on his feet, and with the cautious movements of one who is unused to being self-supporting, he walks over to her.

'It's not okay,' he says again, putting his arms around her. 'Whatever he's doing it is not okay if it makes you feel like this.'

'Why is this happening?' she asks. 'Why doesn't he call, or email?'

'I don't know,' Alistair says, 'but I'd take a bet that this is not about you at all. It's about him, who he is, and you need to ask yourself what sort of person behaves like this to someone they profess to love.'

'Profess to . . .'

Alistair nods. 'Have you tried calling his sister's place in Cornwall?'

She shakes her head. 'I don't have the number. I asked him to send it to me and he hasn't. Perhaps he's had some sort of accident.'

'Or perhaps he's just a complete bastard,' Alistair says. 'But whichever it is, it is still not your fault. And tomorrow we'll see if we can find the phone number. It's probably sitting right there in the British Telecom directory.'

*

It's been an exceptionally hot day and Joyce is thankful for the sea breeze that came in with gusto around four o'clock to take the edge off the heat. Sitting by the pool in the fading light watching her family, along with Dennis and Nick, she allows herself to feel again the loss of Helen, which she has been holding at bay all day. She can't remember when there was last a Christmas that the two families had not spent together. Remorse over what she feels was her failure to support Helen through a difficult time still haunts her, as does the continuing tension with Mac. Maybe she should just give up and tell him to forget about the Carol business, but part of her still resists. He created the situation and he should be the one to resolve it. It would take a simple apology and admission of his stupidity. From time to time she wonders if she is being petty, but for too long she has been the one who makes the effort to put things right. How long will it take him to recognise that she really has changed? She had almost succumbed this morning when they had talked to Gemma on Skype; her delight at Gemma's news made her want to drop back into that old habit again.

Gemma was about to go to bed. 'If you've called to tell me that Santa's coming you're too late!' Gemma had said. 'The parcel arrived yesterday, such gorgeous presents, thank you so much. I'm so lucky, I especially love the wrap, the colours are perfect. But everything is lovely, it was such a treat opening that big package and then unwrapping everything.'

'We thought we might come and visit you next year,' Mac had said. 'What do you reckon?'

Gemma had grinned. 'Well actually Dad, you'd be wasting your money because I'm coming home.'

'No! How wonderful, darling,' Joyce said. 'Is it a holiday? It's been ages since you were here.'

'I'm coming home to stay, moving back,' Gemma says. 'Can I stay with you until I find somewhere?'

'Of course, of course you can.'

'But why?' Mac had asked. 'I mean, it's brilliant news for us, but is this your choice? You love that job.'

'I do,' Gemma says. 'But I've got a job with your old firm, Dad. I'm coming back mid-year, having a six-month break before I start there.'

As Mac and Gemma talked about work Joyce could see how much this meant to him. He has always been exceptionally proud of his daughter and the fact that she had wanted to follow him into a similar career and she sat back listening to them. 'And what are you going to do in your six months off, Gem?' she asked when they turned back to her.

'Well,' Gemma said with a huge grin, 'I think I'll be pretty busy! This is the really big news. I'm pregnant. Due in June.'

'But you're . . .' Joyce began.

'So old!' Gemma cut in, laughing. 'Yes, Mum, I know, I'm forty-two, but I'm very fit and really excited.'

'Bloody hell,' Mac said, 'that's a ripper, isn't it, Joyce? A new grandchild to spoil, and this time we've both got time and space to enjoy it.'

'It's the best news ever, Gem, and . . . well . . . what about the father? I mean, when can we meet him? Will he be coming with you?'

'He'll be there with me and I think you'll like him,' Gemma had said, 'but I'm not going to tell you anything. Of course you'll meet him, as soon as I get back. But I want you to meet him cold turkey, then you get to make your own decisions about him without my interference.'

'Well all we care about, Gems, is that you love each other and he's good to you, and the baby. Isn't that right, Joyce?'

'It is,' she'd managed to say. 'Although of course the waiting to meet him is going to kill me! Is he Swiss?'

'He's Australian,' Gemma said. 'And that's all I'm telling you for now.'

Joyce turns now to look at Stella, who is sitting nearby fast asleep. She's dying to share the news with her, and with Polly, but she knows that Gemma will want to tell Stella herself, they have always been close. To Joyce's relief Stella has been more like her old self in the last few days, calmer and apparently less offended by their efforts to keep an eye on her. Now she moves slightly in her chair, then sits up, rubbing her eyes and looking around.

'Someone's missing,' she says, puzzled. 'Helen, Helen's missing, where is she, Joyce?'

Joyce takes a deep breath. 'Helen died, Stella, do you remember? We all went to her funeral, back in July.'

'Died?' Stella says. 'Died? Surely not. Wasn't she here this morning in the kitchen, helping you?'

'That was Vanessa – you know, Ben's wife.'

'Really?' Stella looks puzzled. 'And you're sure she's dead? Helen's dead?'

'Quite sure,' Joyce says.

'Well that's very sad,' Stella says, shaking her head. 'I should have gone to the funeral.'

'You did,' Joyce says.

Stella looks at her with disapproval. 'I don't think so, Joyce,' she says, her tone quite stern. 'I think I'd know if I'd been to Helen's funeral, don't you? Perhaps I was working at the time. Fancy Helen dying. I never liked her much, you know, but it's sad that she's gone.'

And she gets to her feet and wanders off to the kitchen where Vanessa and Kara are making tea and coffee. Joyce smiles and shakes her head. What would Helen have made of that? She wonders. Stella had not, after all, been Helen's favourite person either.

Chapter Twenty-seven

Fowey, Cornwall

On the morning of Boxing Day Leo wakes early, pulls on his warm clothes, boots and a big parka, writes a note saying he's gone out for a long walk and may not be back until lunch time and leaves it on the kitchen table. Then he lets himself out through the back door and strides out into the newly fallen snow. It's the first white Christmas for years and its magic is not lost on him despite the blackness of his mood. It's a relief to get out of the house and he sets off, walking briskly at first light along the steep downward path to the centre of town. There is a little café down by the harbour that opens at six every morning of the year, a rough little place but with the best coffee for miles around, and he heads straight for it. Sure enough the lights are on and there are a couple of other men in there in boots and beanies escaping, like him, he thinks, from the over-bearing company of their families.

Leo orders coffee and a bacon sandwich and sits on a stool by the window, looking out over the inlet to the opposite bank where lights in the windows of a few small shops and scattered houses on the steep snow-covered slopes look like an image on a Christmas card.

'Fuck Christmas,' he says softly, only it comes out louder than he planned.

'Hear, hear,' says one of the men, who is walking out with his coffee in a beaker, 'but cheer up, it's nearly over.'

'Can't be soon enough for me,' Leo growls, and he bites into his sandwich. He hates Christmas on principle, the religious side of it, the commercialisation, the stupid rituals, everyone pretending to be warm and fuzzy in the bosom of their family. Most of all he hates having to spend Christmas with *his* family, having to pull crackers, wear a paper hat, make conversation with his weird cousins and their children, and the neighbours, and constantly being reminded of his responsibilities to Judith and Rosemary, and how consistently he neglects them. He's only been down here twice this year, as they keep reminding him. They don't seem to understand how busy he is and how many people rely on him. This year, as usual, his attempt to compensate for his absence has been to buy expensive gifts at Selfridges and have them gift-wrapped in the store. Gifts which were, he had realised as they were opened by the recipients, all slightly misjudged.

'You really are hopeless,' Judith had murmured under her breath as his godson unwrapped a copy of the *Guinness World Records*. 'You gave him one of those last year and I told you afterwards that he'd given it to the Oxfam shop, before New Year.'

Leo has always struggled with his feelings about Christmas. He loves the house in Fowey, loves Fowey itself, but he hates being there. The whole family thing: the responsibilities, the expectations that might as well be carved in stone given the weight of them, suffocate and scare him. Responsibility – so important to him in his professional life – is something that he finds crippling in his personal life. This morning all he wants is to get as far away as possible, and as he sits there wondering where he'll walk to, he remembers that the ferry to Mevagissey runs on Boxing Day, and the first one leaves in about ten minutes.

He finishes his coffee, wraps the second half of his sandwich in a paper serviette, stuffs it in his pocket and makes his way along the path to the ferry port.

Christmas is made more complicated this year by the Polly factor. She was hurt, possibly offended, maybe both, when he had told her he was coming to Cornwall for Christmas. But what does she expect? Anyway, she'd got over it and gone to visit her brother in Bali. Now, though, he has compounded a difficult situation by not calling her. She has emailed several times and is obviously upset, but he hasn't responded. He's bad like this, but he can't help himself. When he's cornered he just shuts off and waits for things to go away. Not that he wants Polly to go away, but he desperately wants Christmas to go away, to be over, and to be able to get back to London and resume normal life. It's difficult too because he deliberately put himself in this situation without any real plan about how he could make it work. What he needs, he realises, is a space in between, something he should have planned for from the start; a neutral corridor to insulate this new part of his life from the rest of it. Great distance, which had seemed like the answer, now seems hugely complicated. He has taken risks with relationships in the past but those risks were better calculated because they were not based on need. But for almost a year now his fear of irrelevance and loneliness in his old age has confused him. He's not as good at keeping the balls in the air as he used to be. And he is not even as good at sex as he used to be; in fact his body continues to let him down time after time. Not that Polly had minded; she'd said all the right things, tried to get him to talk about it, but that was impossible for him. He faces into the wind and as he descends the steps to the ferry port he feels the cold stone of fear in his stomach and wills himself to think only of this moment, to push everything and everyone else out of his mind to allow himself to breathe again.

A few people are waiting for the ferry, standing in an orderly line, stamping their feet, shoving their hands in their pockets, their breath puffing out in pale clouds on the cold air. Some speaking softly to each other to avoid being overheard in the still dawn silence. Eventually they file onto the boat, and soon they are out on the open water, the icy wind freezing Leo's nose and reddening his cheeks. He feels and sees the growing body of water between himself and the house. This distance is what he always loves about the ferry crossing. It transports him from tedious reality into literature and romance. Halfway across the open water, even in this early wintry light, you can see back to the beach and the boathouse, where Rebecca conducted trysts with her lover in Daphne du Maurier's novel, and beyond that is the wild country of *Jamaica Inn*, with its images of lusty dark-haired maidens being deflowered by dashing scoundrels behind diamond paned windows in low beamed bedrooms. It's so long since he read the book he can't remember whether that actually happens, but it just feels right. Tomorrow, when he gets back to London, he will pay serious attention to how he can manage the future. Meanwhile all he will think about is the wind in his face, and the fact that he has half a bacon sandwich in his pocket waiting to be eaten.

*

Bali

Polly swims with long, slow strokes up and down the pool, deliberately stretching her limbs to work the tension out of her body. There is something wonderfully healing and relaxing about being in the water, especially in the dark on a warm night under a sky speckled with stars. She rolls onto her back and floats there for a while gazing upward, wondering briefly if she could change her mind and actually live here. The possibility hovers enticingly: a small house, a pool, day after endless day in such glorious surroundings. Alistair is right, it is good for the soul, although right now not even this can dispel her anxiety or heal her hurt.

This morning Steve had done a search and found Leo's sister's phone number in Cornwall. At least they think it has to be the number. It's the only J. Croft in the directory, and Steve had Googled the corresponding address and brought up an image of it on street view.

'What do you think?' he had asked, homing in on number thirty-two.

'I think I should have done this myself ages ago,' Polly had said, sitting down beside him at the table. 'What a lovely place, those narrow streets and the cute little houses.'

'Yes, but what about this one?' Steve asked. 'Has he told you anything about the house, could this be it?'

Polly studied the white house with its mullioned windows and canary yellow front door. 'It's like something out of *Doc Martin*,' she'd said, 'the front door opening straight onto the pavement. It's quite big, isn't it? Can you pull back a bit so we can see the location? He said it's on a steep street and looks out across the river to a village on the opposite side.'

Steve moved the cursor and clicked it, bringing up a panoramic view.

'That's it,' Polly said. 'It must be, the river runs past the back of the house.'

'There you are then,' Alistair had said. 'You can call him, ask him what he thinks he's playing at.'

'Yes,' she'd said, 'I can.' And she had put the number into the contacts list on her mobile. But she knew then that, desperate as she was and still is to speak to Leo, to hear his voice, to demand some sort of explanation for the way he has abandoned her over Christmas, she just wasn't quite ready to call him.

Along with her anger and hurt she feels shamed by all sorts of small slights that seem to have become a part of the way he treats her. Logically she knows that it's not her fault that this is happening, but it doesn't change how it affects her.

'I'm like Spud,' she'd told Alistair, referring to a dog they'd had as children. 'Remember how, if you trod on his paw and hurt him, he'd yelp and then behave as though it was his fault and he'd do that funny apologetic face and try to lick you to death? I can't call Leo until I know that I won't somehow apologise or take responsibility for the way he's treating me. I have some thinking to do first.'

Alistair had raised his eyebrows but refrained from saying anything, which had clearly not been easy for him. And now it's evening, well night-time really, and Steve has gone to bed, Alistair is reading in his chair on the terrace, and she is floating silently in the pool wondering what to do. Eventually she swims across to the shallow end, climbs out and sits down on the sun lounger, drying her face and hair with the towel. Her mobile is lying there on the low table with her book and her glasses, and she sees that there is a little red flag indicating that she has email. Polly clicks on the icon and opens her inbox.

The email is from Leo and for a moment she stares at it in confusion. What is in this message that he couldn't say on the phone or face to face on the computer screen?

Darling Polly, he begins. *I know I am a complete bastard, and I am so sorry for my silence. The fact that I haven't been in touch doesn't mean I haven't been thinking of you all the time, wishing we were spending Christmas together. I know my behaviour is inexcusable, but I have been under such pressure because I hate being here, and want so much to be with you. I struggle to be myself when I am with my family, there are so many expectations. One day perhaps I'll be able to explain this to you. I hope you will accept this for now and forgive me.*

Tomorrow I'll be heading back to London, and I will call you as soon as I get home. I hope you've had a lovely Christmas, and that you found your brother in good health. Love always, Leo x

Polly reads the message several times, then she gets to her feet, walks back to the terrace and, without speaking, hands Alistair the phone.

'Are you sure you want me to read it?' he asks, looking up at her.

'Positive,' she says.

He reads it, glances up at her, then reads it again. 'So how do you feel now?'

She shrugs. 'I don't think I know. Flat certainly. Confused. Annoyed. I do know he hates going there and didn't want to go there for Christmas. But why could he not phone or Skype – why just an email?'

Alistair shakes his head. 'Search me. Why does he hate being with his family so much? Does he hate his sister? I mean, I know you think he had problems with his mother.'

'I don't think so, it's just that he can't handle her condition.'

'Poor darling,' Alistair says in a tone of biting sarcasm. 'I wonder how *she* feels about that.'

'Maybe she's just a really difficult person – after all, he did say that he would have to tell her about me face to face, he was going to do it over Christmas.'

'You mean he hasn't told her yet?'

'Well, maybe by now.'

'Or maybe not!'

'What are you thinking?'

Alistair sighs. 'I don't think you really want to know what I think.'

'I do,' she says, slipping down into the chair next to him. 'I know I'm not going to like it but I do want to know.'

'I think he's a prize tosser,' Alistair says. 'He's secretive, keeps sections of his life quarantined from each other; compartmentalised. I bet he hasn't told her and he won't – he'll find a way not to. Lord knows why. And I think there should be a statute of limitations on the amount of time that men can get away with pathetically blaming their bad behaviour on their mothers. So I don't trust him. I think Stella was right.'

'Stella?'

'Yes, she called me. While you and Leo were away in the southwest.'

'She called you?'

He nods. 'She did and she sounded surprisingly like her old self. But in view of what you'd told me I didn't take too much notice of what she said.'

'Which was?'

'She said she thought he was shifty. And I said, "Go on with you, you're just jealous". And she laughed and said, "Well yes, I am a bit, I don't want him taking Polly away. But what I don't like about him is that he just never looks you in the eye".' Alistair pauses for a moment. 'And then she said she'd mentioned it to Mac, who'd been there helping her with something, and he'd said exactly the same thing; no eye contact, always looking just past you.'

Polly stares at him in amazement. 'Why didn't you tell me?'

'Stella asked me not to. Said she didn't want to upset you. Maybe it was nothing to worry about but she wanted me to know in case . . .'

'In case of what?'

He shrugs. 'I don't know . . . just "in case". And she sounded okay, but because of what you'd said about dementia I thought she might be wandering a bit. So I did as she asked and just kept it to myself.'

Polly nods. 'I see. He makes eye contact with me.'

'Of course he does.'

'Is it because he's shy, do you think?'

'I don't know, Polly, I've never met the guy. Do *you* think he's shy?'

She sighs, shaking her head. 'I think he's awkward when he's not in his own environment – he's ill at ease outside that.'

'I think you should ignore this message for a couple of days at least,' Alistair says. 'Don't let him think that you're hanging out to hear from him. Make him sweat. Look, he may be, as I said, a prize tosser, or just very bad at relationships and family stuff, as you said. But he may also be a manipulative bastard who's messing you around. And right now I favour the latter.'

Polly stares out over the pool to the frangipanis beyond, and the silky darkness of the sky. 'I suppose I think he's just not coping very well,' she says. 'And the eye contact is probably a sort of shyness. And it seems a bit childish to pay him back by playing his game, making him sweat, as you say.'

Alistair gives a little snort of impatience. 'Polly darling, you are a wise and strong woman but this man has had the upper hand with you ever since you got into that long and seductive email exchange with him. The night you met you didn't go to his room for a drink, you didn't agree to breakfast and later you didn't stay on in London. But – and you're not going to like this – he sucked you in by email and since then it seems as though he's been calling all the shots over what happens while also dumping all his existential angst about his family and his work and his little crisis about getting old onto you. You need to pull back a bit, reclaim some of yourself before you lose any more ground.'

Chapter Twenty-eight

hen Stella wakes up on the second day of January she is surprised to find herself lying on the floor. As she tries to turn onto her side to sit up she is stiff and sore, and struggling to stretch her arms she realises that she is trapped inside the duvet, which is wrapped tightly around her. She fights her way out of the cocoon wondering how she got there. Her head was resting on two pillows so she can't have fallen out of bed. I must have put myself here, she thinks as she drags herself into an upright position. How ridiculous. She scrambles awkwardly onto her knees and then to her feet, and sits down abruptly on the edge of the bed contemplating the fact that she is fully dressed. 'I really must be losing my marbles,' she mumbles, kicking at the bedding on the floor, 'no wonder everyone's flapping around me as though I'm a basket case.' And she stands up, feeling like a naughty child anxious not to be caught up to some mischief. Lord knows what Polly or Joyce would think if they knew she'd put herself to bed on the floor. And she pads across to the bathroom, takes off her clothes and turns on the shower.

Polly, she murmurs, back today, now what was it I was going to tell her? And as she pours shampoo onto her hair she remembers that last night she was looking for something, something so important that she was really upset. 'But of course I can't remember it now,' she says aloud, 'isn't that just typical?' The important thing that she needs to remember hangs like a charcoal coloured cloud on the edges of her consciousness, just out of reach. It's still there when she's dressed and sitting on the verandah drinking her tea, and as she stares at it it morphs into a scornful dark grey face, taunting her, laughing at her. Bugger off, she tells it, reaching out to bat it away, but it won't go, and the laughter echoes through her head. Stella covers her eyes and gasps in recognition as the face settles into its features. 'I don't know why you're so upset, Stella,' the face says. 'It's not important, it meant nothing.' She can see him clearly now. 'Really it was nothing, you're making a fuss about nothing.' Stella's eyes fly open and she stands up quickly, knocking her cup to the floor. The garden is dazzlingly bright in the morning light and for a moment she pauses, swaying slightly, a little dizzy, trying to get her bearings again.

'Bastard,' Stella says aloud. 'It was you, wasn't it? You're why I slept on the floor. Well I remember now and I *will not* forget this.'

And kicking aside the shattered fragments of her cup she hurries back into the house and stops. There is a pen and a pad of ruled paper on the kitchen table, and a couple of sheets are covered with her own writing, writing that was once neat and precise and is now a scrawl. Of course, I was writing it, she thinks, and she sits down at the table and begins to read what she had written the previous night. *Dearest Polly,* it begins, *there is something I need to tell you and if I don't write it down now I fear I may not remember it later.* Stella stops abruptly, looking down at the wavering words and lines, unable to make sense of them, but recalling how she sat there last night, tense with the urgency of trying to get everything down. Her writing doesn't seem like real writing, just like scrawls, perhaps she needs her other glasses. Well, it doesn't matter, Polly's eyes are better than hers, she'll be able to decipher it, now she just needs to finish it.

She picks up the pen and begins to write again, covering page after page, the need to put it all down burning furiously inside her. As she writes her sense of urgency increases – she must get it all done before something happens to stop her. And the more she writes the more convinced she becomes that something *will* stop her and that she won't be able to tell Polly what she needs her to know. At last the writing is finished and with a sense of relief Stella folds the pages, puts them into an envelope, writes 'Polly' on it, and wanders between the rooms trying to decide on the best place to put it.

She feels cross now, and giddy. The effort of writing has exhausted her and her head is spinning with a mix of past and present. She opens the door to the spare room and is horrified to find it in chaos. Papers all over the place, empty shoe boxes, others full of more papers. And shoes; why is there a pile of shoes in the middle of the bed? Who put them there and whose are they? She thinks she recognises some of her own in there but then she can't be sure. She puts the letter to Polly on the bookshelf and picks up a shoe.

'These might be mine,' she says aloud, 'perhaps I should have a look for the other one.' And clutching it she sets off to her bedroom to find the other shoe. But she remembers then that she was going to make a phone call and she sits down on the side of her bed trying to remember who she needs to talk to. Alistair, yes, Alistair. She has to tell him about sleeping on the floor and all that other stuff, just in case he ever needs to know. But maybe she should take some of the papers with her. Shoe in hand she returns to the spare room and gathers a bundle of papers which slip and scatter from her grasp as she heads for the kitchen. There she dumps them on the table where they lift off in the draft from the open door. Stella stares at them, shrugs and still holding one shoe reaches for the phone.

Twenty minutes later, having explained everything to Alistair several times over, she stares in dismay at the papers scattered across the kitchen. There is an old theatre program there too and she pulls it towards her and opens it. Among the list of photographs and profiles of the cast of some play she doesn't remember she sees her own and Annie's. Me and Annie, she says, I must tell her, she'd like to see this . . .' The doorbell rings making her jump.

'Bugger off, I'm too busy,' she says, and continues staring at the images, but the bell rings again, this time for longer.

'Oh for goodness sake!' she says aloud and she gets to her feet and marches down the passage to the door. A skinny woman with long, wavy, grey hair, wearing jeans and a t-shirt is standing there holding a plastic box.

'Yes?' Stella says, and she thinks the woman looks taken aback.

'Oh! Hi, Stella,' the woman says. 'How are you?'

'What business is that of yours?' Stella says angrily. She can see that the woman is shocked, but Stella has no time for door-to-door sales people or charity collectors, which is what this person obviously is. 'What do you want?'

'Er . . . well, I just thought you might like some fish . . .'

'I don't buy at the door,' Stella says, recalling how briskly Nancy used to deal with the brush salesman. She's about to close the door when the woman steps forward as though she wants to come in; her foot is just inside the door. Stella looks down at the foot in a navy and white sports shoe.

'Oh, I don't want you to *buy* it,' the woman says. 'It's just that Bill went out with a friend on his fishing boat and they caught heaps of fish, and they cleaned it all, so I thought you might like to have some. I've kept some for Polly too. She's due back today, isn't she?'

Who *is* this woman, Stella wonders, the cheek of it, standing here with her foot in the door, with fish, talking about Polly?

'You do know who I am, don't you, Stella?' the woman says. 'I'm Jennifer, Bill's wife, remember? Bill and Jennifer up the road at number twenty-three.' She glances across to Joyce's house then gets her phone from her pocket. 'How about I give

Joyce a call, she'll vouch for me.' And she dials a number and starts talking.

Stella stands in the doorway for what feels like quite a long time staring at this intrusive stranger with the box of fish.

'Joyce is on her way,' the woman says eventually.

But Stella has had enough of this nonsense. 'Get out of here,' she says, kicking at the woman's foot. 'Take your foot and your smelly fish out of my house now, and don't come here again or I'll call the police.' And she takes a couple of steps forward and pushes her in the chest.

The woman staggers, loses her balance and falls backwards down the front step onto the path.

'Oh, Jennifer! Goodness me, are you all right?' someone cries, and Stella sees Joyce step over the low wall between their driveways and run across the lawn to the fish woman.

'She tried to come into my house with fish,' Stella calls. 'Shall I call the police?'

Chapter Twenty-nine

*T*he flight home seems endless and Polly, who has dozed, watched two movies, dozed again, eaten everything the flight attendants have offered her, drunk two glasses of wine, and tried several times to concentrate on her book without success, is thankful when they begin the descent. She's longing to get home even though she suspects she's heading for rough waters. Tomorrow she'll contact the aged care people and see if they have found a place for Stella.

'Give her my love,' Alistair had said as she left. 'And call any time about the mysterious Mr Croft. You know I love giving you pretentious, intrusive advice. We're always here for you.'

And they are; but they are also several thousand kilometres away, and the phone and the computer are poor substitutes for their reassuring physical presence.

'Could I be making a fuss about nothing?' she'd asked at one point when they'd tracked down the house in Cornwall, and both Alistair and Steve had frozen in their seats and stared at her in disbelief.

'Don't be ridiculous,' Alistair had said.

'Of course not,' Steve said. 'It's a horrible way to behave and however much you want to talk to him, Alistair is right, you should let him sweat for a while.'

Leo had called twice that evening and the second time left a message telling her he was home and asking why she wasn't answering.

'I need to hear from you, Polly,' he'd said. 'I'm worried. Why don't you call?'

Polly had played the phone message several times, listening to it with disbelief, wondering how it was that he felt able to ignore her for several days and then expect an immediate response to his call. She had turned off Skype, but turned it on again the next day and within an hour it beeped with his call.

'At last! I've been worried about you,' he'd said, sounding more irritable than relieved. 'Where were you, why didn't you call or email?'

'I guess you were as worried about me as I had been about you,' she'd said, her tone curt.

'But you knew where I was.'

'And you knew where I was.'

'But you couldn't be or you would have answered.'

'Not if I was behaving like you,' she'd said. 'You obviously thought that was okay.'

He was silent then. She thought he looked tired and unhealthy and clearly not refreshed by his Christmas break. They went back and forth a few more times and finally he apologised, grudgingly, but seemed unable or unwilling to throw any more light on why he had dropped out of contact for five days. Eventually Polly had given up. Judith must, she decided, be a difficult and demanding woman and Leo feels oppressed in her company. She wonders vaguely what this means for their future – the prospect of family upheaval and tension is not an inviting one. But in the last few days she has learned something: Spud is gone now, and she'll be damned if she'll let anyone step on her paw.

In the arrivals area the carousel shakes into life, the first bags appear, and as her own case emerges Polly pushes her way through the crowd and grabs at the handle, but slips and loses her grip.

'Shit,' she says as her bag moves on, and she pushes past a knot of people to follow it.

'I've got it,' someone shouts further up the line and a hand reaches out to grab the bag and pulls it off the carousel. As she pushes past a group of teenagers she spots Mac, pulling up the handle of her suitcase, then turning towards her.

'Mac?' she says. 'Whatever are you doing here? What's happened?'

*

London, Late December

Even in London Leo hates the holidays – Christmas, New Year, Easter, public holidays – when no one is at work. It makes him feel as though his world has stopped spinning, and everything is on hold waiting for people to return to their desks. Even if he's not expecting anyone to call or email, even if there is nothing specific he needs, he just hates the shutdown, laidback feeling. And it's worse these days because now it extends right through from Christmas to New Year, and often beyond that because so many people take extra time off so the whole holiday stupidity goes on for even longer. Even usually sensible people are still irritatingly festive, dashing off to the sales, going to parties or to weekend cottages in the country or, worse still, taking their grandchildren to pantomimes. Insufferable! And hard as Leo tries he can't seem to concentrate on anything at the moment. Judith and Rosemary are both furious with him for buggering off for most of Boxing Day and then leaving to go back to London the following day. Polly is prickly with him because he didn't call when she expected him to, but really what *does* she expect? He does have other things to cope with. He is suspended in this ridiculous seasonal stupidity and he actually has nothing to concentrate on.

When he got back from Cornwall he'd put up a new wall planner and when he went to enter things on it realised that his diary was almost empty. There are a couple of op ed pieces he's agreed to, but he is not expected anywhere until May. Months away! There are invitations, but they are just to attend the things other people are doing. They are not about him.

There have, of course, been fallow periods before, but never has he faced such a barren landscape. Worse still, he feels unable to generate anything, to pursue anything new; no developing public debate has called to him, no long-term issue on which he's been a commentator has taken an interesting turn to inspire him. He yawns at the sight of the stack of new books on his desk, balks at the prospect of filing away some of his papers, and whichever part of his brain usually generates ideas is clearly on strike. For the first time in his life he has nothing new to say, and no new way to say something old.

To help him get through this disturbing time he has filled a gap by organising one of his dinner parties for tonight. It was quite hard to track down anyone who wasn't committed elsewhere. And a few people he'd called were going to events to which Leo thought he should have been invited. So he's ended up with a retired colleague from his days in Manchester who has just married a woman half his age, and Kurt, whose recent retirement as convenor of the Euro Conference had so annoyed him, and who is now in London on holiday with his wife. And then there's Marcia, a minor celebrity journalist, known for her crushing profiles of politicians, actors and anyone else foolish enough to agree to an interview. Marcia, who comes and goes, fits in easily to any group of people; drinks too much, has rather overdone the Botox, but is always good company. The weather is appalling so it's obviously an osso bucco night, but as he jots things down on his shopping list, Leo feels it's all a lot of trouble but there's no turning back now.

He is almost out of his door on the way to Waitrose when he remembers Polly. Better give her a call now in case he forgets later. He goes to the computer and tries Skype, but there is no reply. No reply from her landline either. Finally, wondering grudgingly what the call is costing him, he calls her mobile.

'I thought you'd be home by now,' he says when she answers. 'You said you would.'

'I'm at the hospital,' Polly says. 'I had to come here straight from the airport.'

'You're not sick, are you?' Leo asks, glancing at his watch and hoping he doesn't have to do sympathy; he's not in the mood for it with osso bucco on his mind.

'I'm fine,' she says, 'but Stella's had a stroke and I'm waiting to see the doctor. Joyce and Mac are here with me.'

Leo smothers a yawn. 'Oh dear, that's a shame. Well don't wear yourself out, she'll probably be okay.' There is silence at the other end of the line. Obviously he's said the wrong thing. 'Sorry,' he says, 'I'm not very good at this. I mean, I do hope she gets better soon. I know you must be upset.'

'Very,' she says, 'especially as I wasn't here when it happened.'

'Well you can't be with her all the time,' Leo says. 'That's what you were saying before, that's why you're going to make other arrangements and . . .'

'Leo,' she cuts in, 'this is really not what I want to hear from you right now. I'll call you later.' And there is a click on the line and she has hung up.

Leo looks at the phone in surprise, shrugs, puts it back on the kitchen bench, adds another couple of items to his list, puts on his Australian coat, and runs down the three flights of stairs into the street.

*

Fremantle, Late December

'It really was awful,' Joyce says later as she and Polly sit at the big table on the verandah, waiting for Mac to come back with fish and chips. 'Jennifer went flying off the top step just as I came out,' and Stella was standing there looking really bolshie, shouting about calling the police. Anyway, I helped Jennifer up. She was pretty shaken but not hurt, and she went off home and

I went inside and there were papers everywhere, all over the spare room bed, along the passage, on the kitchen table and scattered across the floor, along with those wretched shoe boxes.'

'So how was Stella then?' Polly asks.

'Well, sort of okay. She was standing there in the middle of it making tea, and she was quite calm, but a bit defensive, like a child who knows she's done something bad but isn't sure what it was. And she said, "Look at all these papers, Joyce, where did they come from?" So we had a cup of tea and I just bundled up the papers. If they were ever in any sort of order they aren't now, so I just stuffed them in the boxes and put everything in the spare room and shut the door. And then I showed her the container with the fish and told her that Jennifer had left it for her, and she said, "Really? How kind, I must have missed her." And then she said she was tired and she thought she'd have a rest.'

'So how did it actually . . .?' Polly's voice trails off.

'The stroke? Well she got up from the table and her face looked a bit odd, sort of startled, and she lurched over as though someone had pushed her. I leapt up but couldn't get to her before she fell. And by then she looked terrible, sort of grey and twisted, her eyes looked just terrified, and she was dribbling from the side of her mouth.'

'I'm so sorry you had to cope with this, Joyce. It should have been me.'

'No, no, it could have been any of us,' she says, 'and at any time. We all know the clock's been ticking, but none of us really wanted to do anything about it.'

'But it was my responsibility . . .'

'We all thought it was fine to wait until after Christmas, even the doctor,' Joyce continues. 'I know legally it has to be you, but Stella's been our dearest friend for years too, we're in this with you, Polly, me and Mac, with you all the way.'

Mac arrives with the fish and chips and as they dig in he pours himself a glass of wine and reaches out to top up their glasses.

Joyce shakes her head, knowing she's already had enough. She's tired, exhausted, any more wine and she'll be crying.

'Well,' Mac says, tucking into his food, 'Stella is safe now, and what happens from here on is to some extent out of your hands.'

'I know,' Polly says. 'Perhaps it may make it easier for her to accept things this way.' She pauses. 'Do you think I should try to look after her at home for a while at least?'

'Absolutely not!' Mac cuts in. 'Stella's always made it clear that's not what she wants. She was adamant about it.'

'Mac's right,' Joyce says. 'I remember we were having dinner here one night last summer – when you were in Scotland, I think. We were talking about getting old, what we wanted, what we dreaded, and Stella said the worst thing for her would be for someone close to her to have to deal with all the intimate and embarrassing things. I can promise you, Polly, she would not want you to take on her day-to-day care, and she'd want you to have a life of your own, I know she would.' She can see that Polly too is exhausted and close to tears. 'We've been so lucky here, for so long,' she sighs. 'Here in Emerald Street, it was like our own little corner of the world. Always a safe, friendly place to come home to.'

'It still is,' Mac says, reaching out for more chips. 'Remember how you felt when Dennis and Helen moved? You hated it, you said things would never be the same, and of course it *was* a big change but you've found what you want to do, the course, the classes, all those amazing women.'

Joyce nods. 'I know, but just the same this feels huge, almost as though this is how it'll be from now on, losing people.'

Mac shakes his head. 'You can't think like that, Joyce. Gemma's coming home, we have a new grandchild to look forward to. Nothing, no one, can replace Helen, or Stella, but that's how life is, it's fluid. I miss Helen and I'll miss Stella even more, but she'll still be part of our lives. And we might be getting new neighbours soon.'

Joyce nods. 'I can't wait for Gemma . . .' she takes a deep breath, watching as Polly picks at the few chips left on her plate. 'Anyway, how were Alistair and Steve?' she asks, in an effort to lighten the mood. 'Did you have a good Christmas?'

Polly smiles. 'I did, really lovely, thanks. Alistair's doing amazingly well. Some days he even manages to walk around a bit.'

'And Leo?' Mac asks.

'Ah, Leo,' Polly says, 'he's something of an enigma. Wonderful one day, pain in the arse the next.'

Mac laughs. 'Aren't we all like that? Men, I mean.'

'Maybe, but Leo . . .' Polly pauses, then shrugs. 'Well let's just say that Leo seems to be a law unto himself.'

Chapter Thirty

'I like this place,' Stella says as Polly wheels her down the passage. 'I think I've been here before.'

Polly stops the wheelchair outside a door, opens it. 'You live here now, Stella,' she says. 'Look, all your things are here.'

Stella looks around, confused for a moment, and sees that Polly is right: her dressing gown is hanging on the door, the patchwork quilt that Annie made for her more than thirty years ago is on the bed. Here is her own armchair, and on the wall is the signed, framed photograph of her with Jason and Kylie on the set of *Neighbours*.

'How did that get there?' Stella asks, leaning forward to take a closer look.

'Mac framed it and hung it for you last week,' Polly says, 'and the theatre programs, he did those too.'

Stella looks across to where she's pointing and sure enough there is *South Pacific, The Importance of Being Earnest, Separate Tables, Oklahoma*, and her favourite – Ibsen's *A Doll's House*. 'I remember that,' she says, pointing to the poster, 'I got wonderful reviews.' She goes to stand up but Polly puts a hand on her arm and stops her.

'Wait please, Stella,' she says. 'I have to move the footrest,' and she bends down, folds it back and offers Stella her hand.

Stella takes it, slides herself forward in the chair, gets to her feet and takes a few steps, steadying herself with a hand on the back of the armchair. 'I got a bit confused while we were out. I thought I still lived there and I was worried how I'd manage.' She looks at Polly, who seems uncomfortable and sad, and she shuffles slowly across to where Polly is standing near the door, and slips a hand into the crook of her arm.

'I'll look after it all for you, Stella,' she says. 'Today we just went back to the house to collect some more of your things.'

'I can barely remember my own name these days,' Stella says, laughing, hoping Polly will laugh with her. 'My head is like . . . like . . . one of those things . . .' The word eludes her and she shakes her head to clear it. 'The thing with holes for vegetables . . .'

'A colander,' Polly says.

'Yes, a colander, things drain out through the holes.'

'I know. But it doesn't matter, this is your place, everyone here knows you now. They bring you tea in bed in the mornings here, so you don't have to get up and make it yourself.'

Stella nods; a sense of familiarity is returning: the bedspread, her programs, tea in bed. 'Yes, I do like it here. Do you know, there's a woman here older than me and she plays the piano beautifully, and I sing for the old people – they remember me, you see. We sing songs from *South Pacific* and the *King and I*. It's lovely here. I do like the music.'

Polly squeezes her hand again and Stella sees that although she's smiling her eyes look as though she might cry. 'Probably that man's fault,' she says, airing this random thought. 'Don't let him upset you, Polly, he's not worth it. You were happy before he turned up. Now, I wrote you a letter, where can I have put it . . . the house . . .'

'You gave it to me this morning,' Polly says, and she pulls an envelope out of her pocket.

Stella looks at it for a moment, trying to remember. 'Not that one,' she says, 'that's for . . . that's for, um . . .'

'For Jack, the solicitor,' Polly says.

'Yes, Jack. But there's another letter.'

There's a tap on the door and a woman in a dark blue uniform pops her head around it. She is wearing a badge with 'Dorothy' printed on it. 'Ah, you're back, Stella,' she says. 'Did you have a nice morning?'

'I had a wonderful time,' Stella says. 'We packed some things, and then we had . . . we had . . . something . . . in the big place on the corner . . .'

'We had lunch at the Arts Centre,' Polly tells Dorothy, 'in the courtyard.'

'Yes, the courtyard, lovely. I had a toasted sandwich.'

'Good,' says Dorothy, looking from Stella back to Polly. 'And everything went off all right?'

'Very well,' Polly says. 'Better than expected really . . .' she hesitates. 'So I might be on my way now?' she says, looking at Dorothy, who nods in agreement.

'Where are we going *now*?' Stella asks.

Polly clears her throat. 'Just me, Stella. I'm going home now, and you . . .' she stops suddenly and Stella thinks she looks quite drained and rather lost.

'You're already home,' Dorothy cuts in.

'Oh good,' Stella says, relieved that she doesn't have to go out again. 'I'm rather tired and I'm going to sit down and have a cup of tea.'

'You do that,' Dorothy says. 'I'll open the window a bit, it's such a lovely afternoon, not too hot. And then I'll fetch your tea.'

Stella thinks she sounds quite brisk, rather like Nancy. 'Brisk,' she says aloud. 'You're brisk Nancy . . .' she hesitates wondering what's wrong.

'And who's Nancy?' the woman asks, steering her towards the chair.

'My . . . my . . . you are . . .' she looks at Polly, lost for a moment.

'This is Dorothy,' Polly says. 'Nancy was your aunt, she looked after you when your mother left.'

'Yes, and she was brisk, like you, Dorothy,' Stella says, pleased that she has everyone in order now. 'I like that.'

'That's why we get on so well,' Dorothy says. 'I see you've brought some more of your things, so when you've had a rest I'll come back and help you unpack.'

'Thanks, Dorothy,' Polly says, and she bends down to kiss Stella's cheek. 'I'll be back tomorrow,' she says, 'have a good rest.' And she straightens up, turns and walks very quickly out of the door.

Stella looks back to Dorothy. 'Poor Polly,' she says, shaking her head. 'I worry about her, she feels responsible, you see . . . for me, I mean, but of course I'm fine. In fact,' she leans forward and lowers her voice, 'I like it here. I like the company and I don't know if you've noticed, but I forget a lot these days and I worry about that. I feel safe here. That's what matters, isn't it? In the end, that's what matters, knowing someone's looking after you, knowing you're safe.'

*

Outside the main entrance Polly pauses, leans against the wall, eyes closed trying to hold back tears and failing miserably.

'Are you all right, Polly?'

She looks up to see Dorothy standing beside her.

'I don't know how to do this,' she says. 'For years we've been so close . . .'

'It's very hard,' Dorothy says, 'but Stella does need to be here. And I promise you this is a good place, Polly. We care for our residents, they become like family to us. Stella will always be treated with respect and kindness. We don't infantilise or patronise.'

'I know, I know, but Stella . . . She should be at home in her own house where she can still feel a bit independent. I've let her down so badly . . .'

'No,' Dorothy insists, 'you've done the right thing, you and your friends all agreed on this when you came to discuss it with us while Stella was still in hospital. Stella is not unhappy. She's well, and comfortable and she does understand that she needs this sort of care. She knows she can't live alone, and she knows she's safe here. You've seen how much the other residents love her. Some of them have been her fans for years. They love having a star in their midst.'

'But that's not the real Stella, the Stella I know.'

Dorothy sighs. 'No, it's not. I understand that and I know it's hard for you, but it's the truth. This is who she is now. You still see the old Stella and you grasp at that but you can't make her come back and you shouldn't try. Every time you argue with her and try to set her right you put her and yourself under pressure. You can't make her remember, you can't force her to have the correct version of things.'

'But I want her to understand,' Polly says. 'She has a right to have the correct information . . . it's a basic human right, isn't it, to make your own decisions, or at least have a say?'

Dorothy grabs Polly's hands and holds them firmly in her own. 'Polly, you are trying to convince yourself that those moments of rationality mean you can force the old Stella back to life. What you have to learn is to accept who she has become, and from now on that's something of a work in progress. If you insist on correcting her, trying to make her understand where she's wrong, you'll spoil your last months or years with her. I know this because I did it with my parents, my father especially. I needed him to be rational, to be in charge as he had always been. I couldn't accept the way he had become and so I fought him over every little illusion or distortion, and all it did was hurt both of us. I spoiled our last months together with my insistence that he should accept what I told him and see that it was right. I hurt him, Polly, and I hurt myself. Each time I corrected him I diminished him – *he* felt that, very keenly I think. Every time you try to set Stella right you diminish who she is, who she has become.'

'But what can I *do*?' Polly says, her voice hoarse now. 'I want to do what's best for her, honestly I do.'

'Then learn to love and accept her as she is now, alongside the memory of how she was. Make the decisions for her wellbeing, reassure her, don't try to wring decisions from her or force her to understand. Go along with what she says, it doesn't matter that it's wrong because five minutes later she'll have forgotten it and there'll be something else on her mind.'

'It's so chaotic, Dorothy, it feels like madness . . .'

'Yes, and if you love her you enter into it with her. Let her have her way if it's not dangerous to her. Grant her some peace in her confusion and delusion. Because you can't change this, Polly, it's not going to get better, you are not going to get the old Stella back. Don't lock yourself into a battle for her rationality because it's a battle that is already lost.'

*

On a sweltering morning later that week, they sit in the solicitor's office where the air-conditioning is almost too cold.

Polly shivers slightly. 'Could you go through that again, please?' she asks.

'What Jack is saying, Polly,' Mac cuts in, 'is that because you have power of attorney and you're also both the executor and the sole beneficiary of Stella's will, you're free to do whatever you think is best.'

'Well yes, within reason,' Jack says, leaning towards them across his desk. 'You have to make proper provision for Stella of course, you'll need to manage her finances and set up arrangements for the payments to the care home, make sure she has money for extras – clothes, outings and so on – pay the medical insurance, but as you can see the money is not going to be a problem. Stella's been a solid saver, despite – or maybe because of – the fact that she was always going on about the unreliability of her profession.'

'And the house?' Mac asks.

'Again, it's up to Polly. It will become yours on Stella's death, Polly. You could sell it now and put the money into Stella's account – it will all come to you in the end – or you might want to think about renting it out until . . . well until . . .'

'Yes I see,' Polly says, nodding. She rubs her hands over her face. 'I had no idea . . .'

'You didn't know she'd left everything to you?'

She shakes her head. 'I didn't even know she had a will. I was always intending to suggest that she should make one. But she'd asked me to do the power of attorney and after that I felt uncomfortable, I didn't want to seem to be pushing her into something she might not want to do.'

'She made her will seven years ago,' Jack says. 'It went into our safe then and it's been there until I took it out this morning.'

Polly sighs. 'Clearly I misjudged her, she was way ahead of me.'

'So how did you come by this?' he asks, holding up the envelope that she had handed him half an hour earlier.

'A few days ago I took Stella back to her house to see if there was anything else she wanted for her room. She went straight to the dressing table drawer, took out that envelope addressed to you, and gave it to me. I said I'd put it in the mail and she said, "No, I want you to go and see Jack, make an appointment and take this with you. I asked her what it was about, and she said, "Jack'll give you some papers", and she wouldn't talk about it anymore. It's so weird, she's all over the place, forgets things, confuses things, sometimes she's like a completely different person, difficult, grandiose, aggressive. But in that moment she was totally focused.'

The three of them sit in silence and Polly gazes out of the office window to the park where a couple of young women are watching their toddlers playing in the shade of the Norfolk pines. She feels empty, drained of the ability to think straight.

'So what do you advise, Jack?' Mac asks. 'What do you think Polly should do next?'

Jack smiles. 'Well, obviously, this is all a bit of a surprise,' he says. 'I think you need time to think about it, Polly. Talk it over with Joyce and Mac. Then come back and see me. We can tidy up the legalities and we can set up a framework to manage Stella's money, and we'll discuss everything else then. If you feel you want to involve Stella in the decision-making we could go together and talk to her, although from what you've told me I do think that, in the end, the decisions will have to come from you. And frankly you look wiped out, so give yourself a while to think about it. As long as you are making proper provision for Stella, there's no rush to do anything.'

'Coffee?' Mac says as they walk out into the street. 'I'm sure you need one, and Joyce's students will still be there, so I'd like to stay out of the way.' They stroll up towards the cappuccino strip in silence and Mac steers Polly to the one free table on the pavement outside Gino's. 'You sit down and I'll get them. Large flat white?'

'Please,' she says. 'And could you get me a croissant? I didn't eat breakfast.'

Mac disappears inside to order and she sits there watching the mix of locals and tourists around her, the traffic crawling along South Terrace, the book hunters rummaging through the trays of books outside the second-hand bookshop. Gino's was Stella's favourite spot, the heart of Fremantle, she'd called it, and no matter how many cafés came and went, Gino's was always her first choice. The best coffee, the best risotto, the best potato skins, she insisted, but when Polly had brought Stella here last week the café had been erased from her memory.

'Is this place new?' she'd asked. 'I don't think I've seen it before.'

'It's Gino's,' Polly had said, 'your favourite. Remember your favourite – risotto marinara?'

But Stella had looked at her in amazement. 'Not me, Polly, you must be thinking of someone else.'

It spoke volumes: such an essential part of their past together, an iconic place in the history of their friendship, had disappeared, cauterised from Stella's memory, unlikely to ever return.

'Hey,' Mac says, slipping down into the seat opposite her. 'Are you crying, Poll?'

She nods, rubbing her hands across her eyes. 'Just thinking about Stella, things we've lost, how much I miss her.' She shrugs. 'I can't get my head around her not being there, next door. It's horrible.'

'I know, Joyce and I feel it too. She's been part of our lives for so long, and it's harder for you because you were so close. I'm so glad she left you the house.'

Polly grimaces. 'I'm very grateful but it makes me feel so guilty. I was so pissed off with her these last few months, so addled at the thought of being responsible for her. And I've been grumpy with her because she stopped being the Stella I loved and relied on and a lot of the time she seems like someone the old Stella wouldn't really like.'

'Don't beat yourself up about this,' Mac says. 'We're the same. Over Christmas, she was playing the famous actress thing. It was so unlike her. I remember Joyce said that she was becoming the sort of showbiz bore that Stella herself used to hate.'

Polly nods. 'She hated it when people behaved that way, but now that's . . . well, it's part of her now. It's so sad.'

'But I don't think Stella herself is sad,' Mac says, as the waiter brings their coffee and croissants to the table. 'I think she's pretty content most of the time. I was watching her last week when I went to hang her pictures. The other people there all remember her and they make a huge fuss of her. She was loving it. And anyway, she deserves it. She's always been very modest and restrained, maybe this was always a part of her that she kept hidden.'

Polly nods, breaks off a piece of croissant and dunks it in her coffee. 'She's gone, hasn't she? Our Stella's gone, devoured by this other personality that the dementia's created. But maybe it is easier for her, she does seem okay, it's just so hard to get used to someone you love changing so much.'

They drink their coffee in silence and it reminds Polly how much at ease she has always felt with Mac, and how often, when she is with Leo, she feels on edge, as though he is wanting something, expecting something from her, something she doesn't understand.

'How's Leo?' Mac asks, seeming to read her thoughts.

'He's fine.'

'When are you going to Paris?'

'It was supposed to be the end of April but he wants to bring it forward. Last night he was saying we should meet up again as soon as possible. Have some time in Paris and then I should go back to London with him.'

'Do it,' Mac says decisively. 'It's just what you need. Stella's settled and apparently pretty happy. Do what Jack said, give yourself some time. I don't think your visiting every day is necessarily a good thing, let her get into her new life, start easing off a bit.'

'You think?'

'I do.'

She hesitates. 'You didn't really like Leo, did you?'

Mac looks awkward. 'I didn't *dislike* him, Poll, I just didn't really get him – didn't get to the real person. He seemed to be trying to impress us. Perhaps it was uncomfortable coming here and being surrounded by your friends. But I'm sure we'll get through that and get to know him better next time.'

'He does take a bit of knowing. I wonder how well I know him myself, but for the last month things have seemed better between us. It'll be good to have more time together, and to see him on his own stamping ground.'

'Go then,' Mac says. 'You won't work him out at a distance.'

'Perhaps you're right,' Polly says, and as she says it she feels how good it would be to be away from here, away from the emptiness next door, from the sinking feeling that besets her whenever she walks in through the door of the nursing home, and to have time to think about Stella's future, and how to manage her own feelings about it.

'Of course I'm right,' he says with a grin. 'I'm a man, I know about these things.'

Polly splutters into her coffee. 'Oh yeah,' she says, 'I forgot about your vast experience in relationships. How many have you had exactly?'

Mac laughs. 'One. Well, only one that matters.'

She laughs. 'Maybe I'll talk to him when I get home. I certainly need to do something to move myself along.'

Half an hour later Mac turns the car into the top of Emerald Street and pulls up a little way back from their houses.

'What's up? Why have you stopped?' asks Polly, who has been silent during the short drive back from town.

Mac indicates his own house where Joyce's students are trailing out along the path and into the street. 'Class is over, just letting them get on their way.'

The women are laughing as they make their way out across the garden, a vibrant, colourfully clad group, with Charlie weaving between them giving an occasional excited bark.

'That dog is such a flirt,' Mac says. 'He adores them.'

'And you don't?'

'On the contrary, I love 'em. They're terrific, the stuff they've been through . . . amazing. See that big woman in the middle . . . fiftyish; her name's Marla, she's from Somalia. She's here with her daughter and granddaughter. Her husband and son-in-law were murdered in Somalia. She's a nurse, and she has the most wonderful singing voice, really deep and resonant. How she got her daughter and granddaughter out, and then here . . . oh well, I won't go into it now. But they are lovely women, and rather full-on. You know me, Poll, I like a quiet life. The first week they were so shy and cautious they hardly spoke at all, now they never stop. It seems as though just a little language makes a huge difference and of course they've made friends here.' He glances at his watch. 'The class should have finished almost an hour ago but they're so involved and they enjoy each other's company so the time just runs on. Joyce has made this happen, I'm so proud of her.'

'But it's taking over your home?'

He sighs. 'Oh well, they occupy the main living area of the house three mornings a week, and now Joyce wants to run an evening class for some of the men who have jobs and can't come during the day.' He takes a deep breath, straightens up in his seat. 'But I'm just being selfish; we own two houses and most of these people have lost everything, in the hope of finding a better life, safety for their children . . . It won't hurt me to concede to temporary occupation of a bit of my space, but I *am* wondering how it'll be when we have Gemma and a baby here as well.'

Polly is silent for a moment, watching him.

'There's always Stella's studio,' she says.

'The studio? Oh, the place she built for that artist who was going to move in with her?'

'Yes.'

'What about it?'

'It would make a great classroom. It needs clearing out of course, but the stuff could be moved into the garage. It's actually a lovely room, air-conditioner, heater, little sink and fridge and all that stuff. It hasn't been used for years . . . might need a coat of paint to freshen it up. It's even got its own little shower room and toilet.'

'We could get some trestle tables and chairs,' Mac cuts in. 'A kettle or an urn, perhaps, for their morning tea.'

'Exactly.'

'It'd be perfect, plenty big enough.'

'Yep.'

'D'you think Stella would be okay with that?'

Polly gives a long sigh that feels somehow comforting. 'I think that the old Stella would love it and wish she'd thought of it herself. Now . . . well hopefully she'll still think so. More to the point, what would Joyce think about it?'

Chapter Thirty-one

Early March

The spring sunshine is inviting but, as Leo discovers when he settles himself on the terrace, the air is still pretty cold. He takes the sweater he'd slung around his shoulders and pulls it over his head, thrusting his arms into the sleeves and pulling it down with a shiver. It's his favourite sweater: navy blue oiled wool, the traditional fisherman's sweater bought in northern France about ten years ago. It's one of what he thinks of as his signature garments purchased in various parts of the world and identifiable by anyone who travels and is sensitive to quality, culture and reputation: the sweater, the Drizabone, an Italian cashmere scarf, his British Warm overcoat, a Louis Vuitton overnight bag, a cream linen jacket from Milan, his Rolex watch. These things, he feels, define him to anyone who matters, they demonstrate his taste, and contribute to his sense of himself as a citizen of the world.

He gazes out across the sparkling river to the sunlit slopes and roofs of Bodinnick. Gorgeous, he thinks, if only the circumstances were different. Glancing right he sees a huge cruise ship making its way into the mouth of the river towards the harbour, scattering small boats in its approach. His heart sinks. Tourists!

They'll be swarming all over the town in the next couple of hours, looking for tat to buy, filling the pavement cafés and the pubs.

'Gee, that's a whopper,' Rosemary says, putting a mug of coffee in front of him and sitting down alongside him clutching her own. We seem to be getting more and more of them.'

Leo nods. 'Fowey's too small, they shouldn't be allowed.'

'I doubt you'd think that if you were a local trader,' she says, drily.

'What time are you leaving?' Leo asks.

'Soon as I've finished my coffee,' she says, glancing at her watch. 'I'm catching the ten-thirty to Paddington. I've left all the instructions on the worktop in the kitchen. Just make sure you read them and follow them and you'll be fine.'

He nods grudgingly. 'And how long is it again?'

'Five days, I'll be back on Friday afternoon.'

He sighs. 'Oh well, it'll be a nice break for you.'

Rosemary turns sharply in her chair. 'I'm going to a *funeral* Leo, not on holiday.'

'Oh yeah, sorry, I forgot . . . but five days for a funeral?' As soon as he's said it he knows he's in trouble.

Rosemary slams her mug onto the table sending coffee splashing in all directions.

'For fuck's sake! This is the first time when I've had to go away that you have actually deigned to look after Judith in . . . well . . . it seems like in living memory. Yes, five whole days – a day each to get there and back, a day at a funeral and a couple of extra days to catch up with friends in London.'

'Sorry,' Leo says, sighing inwardly, 'sorry, yes of course.'

'Meanwhile you are always on the move, racing off hither and thither, free tickets, posh accommodation, poncing around the EU.'

'Not so much these days,' he adds weakly. Rosemary always strikes at his vulnerabilities with the vicious accuracy of a dentist's drill. There are few points that activate his sense of guilt but Rosemary knows them as well as he does himself and she never fails to turn her rapier-like scorn upon them.

'Well you're getting old and stale,' she says now. 'People have heard it all before, Leo. If you want to maintain your privileged professional persona you'll have to buck your ideas up. Do something new, innovative and . . .' she pauses, apparently searching for another word, '. . . and cool.'

Leo opens his mouth and shuts it again. Cool? Does Rosemary even know what cool is? But she is so painfully right that he can think of nothing to say.

'And when I come back,' she continues, 'don't think you can board the train back to London the same day. We need to talk about the future. Judith's future, mine too, long term, and your part in it.'

Leo's brain is starting to hurt.

'And speaking of that, you mentioned you're off to Paris before long. Now why don't you take Judith with you? It's her sixtieth birthday and it would be wonderful for her. It's so long since she's been anywhere with anyone but me.'

Leo tries to swallow the lump that has risen in his throat, and bursts out coughing as a result. 'That's ridiculous,' he splutters eventually. 'I'll be working. What would she do all day, evenings when I have to go to dinners? It's not a holiday, you know.' How easy it is for him to lie.

'Doesn't matter, just take her with you. She's smart, highly intelligent and well-informed. Judith can fit in anywhere. Everyone who meets her thinks she's wonderful and as intellectually switched on as she ever was. You're the only person who can't cope with disability, who feels it sets her apart, and frankly it often seems that you think it makes her somehow less of a person.'

Leo feels the world closing in on him. He sits up straighter in his chair in order to feel more authoritative. 'It's not that at all,' he says, wondering if it actually is. 'But I can't take her away at the moment, absolutely not, it's just not . . . well . . . appropriate.'

And then, still weakened by Rosemary's powers of guilt activation, he makes a terrible misstep. 'Later in the year, perhaps, I'll take her somewhere later in the year, Paris, or somewhere else, Italy perhaps . . .'

And already Rosemary is on her feet. 'Excellent!' she says, clapping him on the shoulder. 'I'll just go and say goodbye and I'll let her know there's a lovely European trip in the offing . . . June, shall we say? She can think about where she'd like to go. She's such a great planner, you and she can sort it all out while I'm away. And now you seem to have more time it means I'll be able to get away a bit more too. So this week will be good practice for you. Mind you look after her properly. Read the instructions.' And thumping him harder on the shoulder this time, she disappears and he hears her calling out to Judith: 'Jude, I'm off now. Leo wants to take you to Europe, a lovely holiday to plan . . .' and her voice fades away into the recesses of the house and is gone.

'Fuck,' Leo says aloud, 'what is it with women? Why do they expect so much from me?' The week stretches ahead of him like a dark tunnel. Judith, he knows, is about as undemanding as anyone in her situation could possibly be, but at the same time he resents having to look after her, resents having to be here for a whole week when he could be doing so many other interesting and important things. Except that at the moment there are no other important things that have to be done. The bleakness of it torments him, almost as much as a week of having to cook meals, help Judith with her clothes, with getting in and out of bed, and the shower, and . . . oh all those other tedious, embarrassing, distasteful things. All the things that his work has protected him from are threatening to take over his life, to reshape it in ways he dreads. But he still can't seem to break out something new. He's worried about it a lot, eaten an awful lot of chocolate, drunk far too many bottles of red, and binged for hours on dark Nordic crime series, historical dramas and science fiction.

Leo sighs and finishes the dregs of his cooling coffee. The one good thing he's done is to get things on track with Polly. He has won her back with his brilliant emails, just as he had captivated her at the start. Since she spat the dummy at Christmas they have settled back into the way they were. It's easy enough to keep the messages moving, and they don't argue on email. She's also been under pressure looking after her friend and, thankfully, she's now been moved into a retirement village or something. So Polly's free, and she's brought forward the trip to Paris: romance, food, wine, sex – if he can get his act together in that department. Perhaps now that the pressure of work has lessened he'll get his mojo back. The prospect is cheering. Just get through this week, he tells himself, and life begins again.

*

Joyce stands alone in the middle of the studio looking around her. Three weeks ago when she, Polly and Mac had opened the door and walked in she had been daunted at the prospect of what had to be done. The place was packed with cardboard boxes, piles of old theatre curtains, unwanted pieces of furniture and even a couple of rows of old theatre seats.

'Crikey,' Mac had said, rubbing his chin. 'Theatre seats – wherever did she get those?'

'She bought them at a sale when some old cinema was being closed down,' Polly had said. 'The curtains too. As for the rest of it, I've no idea, except that I think there are some old costumes in there. But she's not touched any of it for years. In fact I don't think it's ever actually been used for anything but storage. I mean, the artist . . . what was his name . . .?'

'Gordon,' Joyce had said. 'Gordon Chase, she called him Gordie.'

'Of course, Gordie, how did you remember that?'

'I did a bit of research on him at the time,' Joyce said. 'I was worried he might be dodgy, something about him sounded dodgy.'

'Well he never turned up so you were right about that,' Mac said. 'Dodgy is exactly what he proved to be. Showed up instead in the newspaper getting married to a twenty-year-old.'

'Mmm. Well I don't think she had the heart to use it after that,' Polly had said. 'So it's a long time ago and it'll probably be a big job to clear it out.'

'Not really,' Mac said. 'We just have to move the boxes into the garage, and the other stuff too – get those theatre seats out and we can go and get some lightweight chairs from Ikea and some trestle tables. I can get Ben to help me shift it all. And then Dennis and I can give it a coat of paint. It's a really nice room.'

And that's exactly what Joyce thinks now – a really nice room, a beautiful room in fact, two big windows onto the garden, a door that opens onto the drive, great light, an air-conditioner that's apparently never been used. And Mac, Dennis and Ben have transformed it, polished the concrete floor, separated and lined up the theatre seats on either side of two long trestle tables, and put in some new light fittings.

Yesterday Polly had wheeled Stella in to see what they'd done and at first she'd seemed bewildered. 'Gordie's studio,' she said, '. . . bastard.'

Joyce and Polly had stood there holding their breath, wondering what would come next. Polly had, of course, explained what they wanted to do and Stella had agreed immediately, but they had all been anxious about how she'd feel when she saw it, or if she'd even remember that she'd agreed to it. She'd looked around, taking it all in, delighted to see the theatre seats in use but unable to remember where they'd come from.

'A classroom,' she'd said eventually, 'it makes a lovely classroom, but you need books in a classroom, shelves with books. I think there are some shelves in the house . . . you should bring them in here with the books then people can borrow them and read them if they want.'

And so Ben and Mac were at it again when she'd left, moving two bookcases and their contents from the house to the studio.

It's perfect, Joyce thinks now as she takes her final look around before everyone starts to arrive. There is no class this morning, but a morning tea to launch the conversion of the studio.

'Happy with it?' Mac asks, walking in through the open door.

'Ecstatic!' Joyce says. 'I can't tell you how wonderful this feels. Thank you so much, for putting up with us in the house for so long, and for doing all of this.' He looks awkward, she thinks, ill at ease and she feels her will about to crumble. He did something stupid and she has dug in refusing to do her usual patching up job. But has it been worth it? Maybe now is the time for her to flick the switch and just let it go. 'Really,' she begins, 'you've been so patient and never even complained so I . . .'

'I complained to myself,' he cuts in. 'But I'm glad we could do it. I'm so proud of you, Joyce.'

She moves to put her arms around him, and is surprised when he catches her hands in his and holds them tightly, moving back from her. 'Look,' he says, his face is flushed now and she can see the tension in his body. 'I've been a total moron,' he says. 'The thing with Carol, well it wasn't a thing but I behaved as though it was by not telling you. It was stupid. And for months now it's been standing between us. I don't know how to make it right, but I . . . it took me back to the past, helped me reflect on what matters now. I'm so very sorry and I don't know what to do to make it better.'

Joyce smiles. 'You've done it,' she says, 'you've just done it. You've taken the first step, to talk about it, to try to put it right. Perhaps you don't realise it but in the past it's always been me. But this last year has changed me, this time I needed you to accept responsibility and try to fix it.' She moves close to him puts her hands up to his face and kisses him. 'It took an awful long time but you did it. I love you to bits, and I'm so grateful for everything that you've done.'

He looks bewildered. 'That was it? That was all you needed?'

She nods. 'That was all. Simple really.'

Mac takes a deep breath. 'So it's okay?'

'It's okay, we're back to being us again.' She can see that he can't quite believe it yet, but his expression is beginning to soften, the tension lifting.

'I love you,' he says. 'I honestly don't know what I'd do without you . . . ah,' he nods towards the door, 'we have company.' And he squeezes her hand. 'I missed being us.'

'Me too,' she says.

Polly and Marla are elbowing their way through the door, laden with trays of tiny sandwiches, sausage rolls and cupcakes. On the other side of the street a big four-wheel drive draws up and Joyce is about to turn away to greet some more of the students when she sees Ewan Heathcote get out of it, walk around to the passenger side and open the door.

She had been back in touch with him at the start of the year to let him know that the classes were going so well that she wouldn't be taking the job at the school.

'Well, if you ever change your mind . . .' he'd said.

Last week she had emailed, inviting him to the morning tea, and she'd got an automatic reply saying he was out of the office for two weeks.

'I thought you must be on holiday,' she calls out now, crossing the street to meet him.

'I am,' Ewan says, 'but I couldn't miss this. How are you, Joyce?'

'Terrific,' she says, 'and absolutely delighted to see you. What's all this?'

There are several boxes on the front seat and Ewan leans in, lifts out a couple and hands them to her. 'If you can manage those I'll bring the rest,' he says.

'But what's in them?'

'Wait and see,' Ewan says. 'Is your husband around?'

'Reporting for duty,' Mac says, strolling over to them. 'I'm Mac, nice to meet you. Need a hand?'

They shake hands and Ewan leads Mac to the boot and opens it. 'Think you can use this?' he asks.

Mac bursts out laughing. 'Can we indeed!'

'What?' Joyce says. 'What is it?'

'Just what you put at the top of your wish list,' he says. And together he and Ewan lift out a large, freestanding whiteboard.

'Oh my god it *is* just what I wanted!' she cries, almost dropping the boxes.

'Well it's seen better days,' Ewan says, 'but it's not in bad nick. We're refitting all the classrooms and these are redundant now.'

Joyce can't believe her luck, and as they make their way across the street and into the studio she's bursting to open the boxes. Most of the students have arrived now, and are standing around talking while Marla and Polly make the tea and coffee and strip the cling film from the food. Joyce sets the boxes on the end of one of the tables, rips the tape off one of them and pulls back the cardboard flaps.

'Textbooks! Oh Ewan, how wonderful, and they're in such good condition.'

'I picked the least battered ones,' he says with a smile. 'There are three levels which should be fine for your classes. And if I haven't brought enough there are more, but they're a bit tatty. You should come in sometime and see if there's anything else you want. We're replacing heaps of stuff at the moment.'

'Thank you so much,' she says. 'I can't tell you what this means to me, to us.'

'We're so proud of you, Joyce,' Ewan says. 'I'd like to send along a photographer to get some pictures of you and the students for our new brochure. We often have pictures of graduates who go on and get terrific jobs but we've never had anyone do anything like this. It's a brilliant illustration of the value of language teaching in the community.'

Marla strolls over to them and thrusts a plate in front of Ewan. 'I'm Marla and don't know who you are,' she says, 'but you made a good thing with the books.'

Ewan takes a sandwich. 'I'm Ewan,' he says. 'And your English is very good, too good for a beginners class.'

Marla laughs. 'So you got me, I am . . .' she hesitates. 'A freed . . .'

'A fraud?' Ewan suggests.

'Yes, fraud. But without me my daughter don't come. And Joyce, she is good teacher, the wise woman. Since I come here I don't sit in the house no more. I meet people, go shopping, I can have new life here now.'

*

Two days after the morning tea Polly calls in to see Stella and finds her doing something previously unimaginable: she is in an exercise group. Half a dozen women of Stella's age and older are sitting in a circle, exercising their ankles in time to music, in front of Josie, the young physiotherapist. Polly stands in the doorway watching Stella as she follows Josie's instructions. She is totally absorbed in the exercise, and when Josie changes to something different, getting them to toss a ball between each other in the circle, Stella enters into the exercise, laughing with the woman beside her, clapping her hands together as each person catches the ball and passes it on.

Polly is transfixed; it doesn't seem all that long ago that she and Stella had visited a former neighbour here.

'I could never live in a place like that,' Stella had said then. 'It's too regimented. I mean, they're very nice, the people there, but it's too . . . well, social, communal. I've never been any good at that sort of thing, and there's nowhere like your own home, is there?'

Now as Polly watches from the doorway she can see that Stella is thoroughly at home here, at ease in proximity to her fellow residents, enjoying things from which she would previously have turned away in disdain.

'Polly,' Stella calls when the music stops. 'Polly, come and meet Agnes. This is my friend Polly, my best friend, she's like a daughter to me.'

'I've heard all about you,' Agnes says. 'Stella says you were in *Neighbours* with her.'

'Well, not exactly *in* it, I was writing . . .' Polly stops, remembering what Dorothy had said about things not having to be exactly right.

'Well I'm very happy to meet you,' Agnes says. 'And we're all looking forward to seeing Cassandra on the television again.'

'She mixes us up,' Stella whispers. 'Me and the character, but I don't mind. They all love *Cross Currents*. When will it start again, Polly, the new one?'

'Tomorrow night,' Polly tells her for at least the tenth time. 'I thought you might like to come and watch it at my place with Joyce and Mac. I'll come and pick you up.'

Stella hesitates, looks thoughtful. 'I don't think so,' she says. 'I think I'll stay with my friends here, they're all so excited about it, and the staff too. I wouldn't like to disappoint them.'

Polly musters a smile, not without some difficulty. 'Well, if you're sure . . .'

'I'm positive,' Stella says. 'It'll be lovely. We can all sit together and watch it. You can come as well, Polly, if you like. I think we're having sausage rolls, you love sausage rolls.'

*

'I couldn't believe it,' Polly says the following evening as she hands Joyce a glass of wine. 'It was such a shock that she wanted to be there with them, rather than here with us.'

'It's good,' Mac says.

Polly nods. 'I know. She has everything she needs, and she really loves being the centre of attention. She wasn't in the least disturbed when I told her I'd be away for several weeks.'

'Come on, come and sit down,' Mac says, grabbing the remote control. 'It'll be starting in a minute,' and he turns up the volume as the last strains of the news theme fade down.

They settle back in their seats waiting in anticipation through the trailer for a new documentary series, and then it begins.

Dark water swirls across the screen to the sounds of the sea, dawn light breaks in the distance turning the waves from black to deep blue, to dazzling aqua.

Good, Polly thinks, well done Gareth. Great start.

In the foreground the names of the four main actors float up in ripples from the white crests of the waves followed by 'Cross Currents' scrawled across the screen. The light increases with a few more secondary actor credits, and then against the bright white and blue of the morning sky the figure of a woman appears on the rocks high above the water. She is wearing a long white nightdress and a tattered blue dressing gown. Wisps of wild grey hair lift and tangle in the wind as she gazes out to sea, her back to the camera. Slowly the shot closes in and suddenly she turns, steely grey eyes boring into the camera lens. More white letters rise from the water forming into words *And featuring Stella Lamont as Cassandra* as the music swells. Stella tosses her head, the wind whips tendrils of hair across her face and her grey, unblinking eyes flash suddenly red as she lets out a fearsome laugh, and her image starts to spin, tornado like, and disappears into the distance.

Polly, as anxious as if she herself had written the script and directed the action, sits tense on the sofa, frozen with anticipation, while her heart pounds in her chest. Alongside her Joyce moves a little closer and reaches out a hand. Without looking Polly takes it, hanging on to it as though to a life raft.

'It is going to be wonderful,' Joyce whispers.

And Polly nods, still speechless, and leans in closer for reassurance as all three of them hold their breath, waiting for Stella to come back as the best she's ever been, to launch herself into the final steps in her own hall of fame.

Five kilometres away Stella sits in the centre of the front row of the chairs that have been set out in three neat, curving lines in front of the huge widescreen television. Everyone seems very excited about it, but for the life of her she can't remember what it is.

'We're all going to watch it together,' Dorothy had said when she had come to collect her from her room.

To Stella it all seems a bit of a chore, but Dorothy went on and on about it, and so eventually she had given in and allowed herself to be wheeled into the big communal sitting room where Agnes had saved her a place in the front row.

'I hope it's not football or rugby,' she says but no one takes any notice.

Stella loathes football, but they watch a lot of football here and get very worked up about it. 'Boring! A lot of men running around in shorts kicking a ball,' she says, more loudly this time, leaning closer to Dorothy, who is sitting beside her.

'It isn't football, Stella,' Dorothy says. 'It's your new series.'

Stella looks at her wondering what on earth she can be talking about. 'I haven't . . .' she begins, but everyone shushes her. Stella sighs and watches blackish sea water on the screen; it looks vaguely familiar, and she thinks she's heard the music somewhere before too. Words appear and disappear before she can read them. It's all gone from dark to light now and an old woman, looking like a witch, is wandering across rocks in a dressing gown. Dorothy nudges her and smiles as the camera moves in close to the back of the old woman's straggly hair. Two words come up: 'Cross something,' she reads aloud, and she jumps as the witchy woman, who looks a bit like someone she used to know, turns suddenly and stares straight at her. More words appear and a little cheer goes up from the people in the room as they read the words on the screen.

'Stella, Stella, Stella,' chants Jim, who has the room next door to hers. And he makes a fist and punches the air.

Stella thinks he must have gone completely barmy.

'Stella, Stella, Stella . . .' several of them are at it now.

'Oh shut up,' Stella says. 'Who *is* that?' she asks above the vaguely familiar music. 'I think I know her.'

'It's Cassandra,' Dorothy says, taking her hand, holding on to it tightly.

'It certainly is not,' Stella says, 'Cassandra is dead.' But the familiarity of it, the scenery, the music, that face – it's all so unsettling. '*Cross Currents*,' she says again now, 'that's what it is, *Cross Currents*.' The old woman's eyes flash red and Stella's heart jumps and she puts a hand to her chest. '*Cross Currents*,' she says again, irritably this time. 'No wonder it's familiar, that's just typical of the ABC these days, it's all repeats, repeats, repeats.'

Chapter Thirty-two

Early April

Leo wakes from a deep, red wine induced sleep and lies staring up at the hotel ceiling, his head pounding. Sunlight pours ruthlessly in between the open curtains, and he screws up his eyes, rubs both hands over his face and hair, picks up his watch and realises that at this very moment he should be waiting in the arrivals area at Charles de Gaulle airport to meet Polly. As he sits up the contents of his head crash around and seem to explode like crockery smashing on a tiled floor. The room sways and he has a horrible queasy feeling in his gut. He really should know better, he's never been able to handle too much red. Polly – what should he do? Briefly he registers that things would be easier if he had a mobile phone but the twin horrors of availability and accountability still loom: anyone can find you at any time, can ask you for things, demand answers to questions, expect to speak to you at embarrassing moments. He staggers to the bathroom, puts as much of his head as possible under the cold tap, towels it dry, drinks a glass of water and then goes back into the bedroom and stares at the hotel phone.

Sitting down on the bed again he dials Polly's number, forgets to include the international code, misdials the second time and at the third attempt it starts to ring and he gets the answering message.

'Polly, I am soooo sorry,' he says, attempting to sound contrite rather than just hungover. 'I was in a very early meeting and lost track of time. Can you grab a cab and come straight to the hotel? I'll wait for you outside the café next door. See you very soon.'

He puts down the phone, yawns and stretches. He has, he reckons, at least an hour, probably more, before she arrives: time for a shower, coffee and something to eat.

*

An hour and a half later he is sitting at a table on the pavement outside the café next door to the hotel. It's a small place, the hotel, full of character, not the five-star variety to which he's grown accustomed, but it has uniquely French décor and ambiance. He has stayed here in the past, and the location is ideal: in a narrow side-street just off the Boulevard St Michel, less than two minutes from the Seine and the Shakespeare and Company bookshop.

'Encore un café, Monsieur?' the waiter asks, indicating his empty cup.

Leo shakes his still jangly head; he's already had three, one more might have a disastrous effect on his stomach. He closes his eyes against the morning sun, cutting himself off from the steady stream of pedestrians and from the traffic cautiously nosing its way around them, and tries to get himself into the right state of mind for Polly's arrival. His emails have done the legwork, things have, he believes, returned to where they were in the earlier months of their relationship, and believes he has regained the ground lost over Christmas. It's just a shame that he bumped into a couple of acquaintances on the Eurostar yesterday. The three of them had polished off two bottles of wine on the train then repaired to their separate hotels to check in, and met up later. Then they each drank a couple of Pernods before dinner, then more wine, a lot more wine. He wonders now why he drank so much. To stop himself brooding, perhaps? He feels himself drifting towards delicious sleep until his head falls suddenly forward, jerking him awake just as a taxi draws up nearby. Fleetingly he wonders what lies beneath the interesting manhole cover on which his left foot is resting; if he could just disappear down there . . . escape into the darkness. A bit damp and smelly, but at least none of the women in his life could plague him with their expectations.

Polly steps out of the taxi and follows the driver to the boot to collect her bag. She stands there briefly, chatting with him, nodding, laughing, sharing something that has been exchanged between them enroute from the airport. She is relaxed, unhurried, Leo feels a stab of something unfamiliar – a sense of exclusion perhaps, or jealousy? He gets to his feet, straightens up, strolls towards them. Any minute now she will turn to him, he will have her attention, she will focus on him in the way she does so well, looking into him, seeing what he wants her to see, making him her priority. He stands behind her waiting for her to turn away from the driver, but she seems unaware of him. It is the driver who is facing him who indicates his presence to Polly and causes her to turn to him.

'Oh hi!' she says. 'I thought you were asleep at the table. Won't be a moment,' and she turns back to the driver and continues the conversation, which is too fast for him to follow. They shake hands, laugh, and at last the driver walks back to his seat and Polly turns to Leo.

'Hi,' she says again, and steps up to kiss him, stands back and looks at him. 'An early meeting? It looks rather more like a very late night!'

*

A couple of days into their stay in Paris they settle at a pavement table outside Polly's favourite café on Rue de la Bucherie, and order coffee and croissants. The sky is overcast, growing darker all the time.

'Not a day for a romantic trip along the river,' Polly says, 'we'll have to leave the bateaux-mouches for another day.' She tears a piece off her croissant, dunks it and leans forward to eat it over the wide brim of her coffee bowl.

'That is a disgusting way to eat a croissant,' Leo says, dusting dry crumbs from the sleeve of his black cashmere jacket. 'All soggy and messy, like baby food.'

'It is,' Polly says, leaning back in satisfaction, savouring the remains of the croissant. 'It is also traditionally French: the café au lait in the bowl, the dunking, I love it. You are such a fusspot.'

'No, I'm not,' Leo fires back, 'I just don't like people messing with their food.'

Polly rolls her eyes. 'This is not messing . . . oh forget it.' They have been together for two days now, two days in which perfect harmony and bursts of irritation and tension seem to alternate with annoying regularity. Leo, Polly thinks, is at his best and his worst, more changeable, more unreadable, more accessible and more withdrawn than ever. Earlier this morning she had called him out on this, and he had sighed and shrugged.

'Sorry, I've got a lot on my mind.'

'Okay,' she'd said, 'so do you want to talk about it, about what's on your mind?'

'No,' he'd replied. 'Let's go out for breakfast and do something nice.'

Now the first spots of rain start to fall, big fat drops splash onto the awning above their heads, and a sudden wind blows up, ripping at the white tablecloths.

'A good day for the Louvre?' Polly suggests. She knows Paris and its landmark places so well, but she likes the idea of being a tourist with Leo, the chance to see familiar places in a new light.

Half an hour later as the taxi approaches the Louvre, the rain has become a downpour.

'Bugger that,' Leo says, spotting the length of the queue of visitors by the glass pyramid. 'I don't queue for anything. We'll go somewhere else. Where do you want to go?'

'I want to go to the Louvre, and that's where *I'm* going,' Polly says. 'We won't have to queue.' She leans forward and speaks to the driver, who nods and changes direction.

'Where are we going?' Leo asks.

'I've asked him to take us as close as he can to Porte des Lions,' she says. 'You rarely have to queue at that entrance, and it leads straight through to the Italian galleries, which is where you said you wanted to go.'

Leo sits back in his seat and says nothing, and she hides her desire to smile; he hates it when she knows something that he doesn't.

They make their way up the steps between the stone lions and, once inside, are heading towards the Italian gallery when Leo stops suddenly.

'Hang on a moment,' he says, 'I've just seen someone I know.' And he strides away from her towards a short, thickset man who is pulling on a trench coat and heading for the exit.

Polly follows him slowly, looking around, picking up a couple of fliers about special exhibitions. Eventually, sitting on a bench, she watches Leo, his back turned towards her, talking intently to the man, whose eyes are wandering around the foyer. He looks at his watch and makes as if to leave, but Leo won't let him go. She gets to her feet, walking towards them as the man looks at his watch again, and smiles at her approach.

'Hi,' she says, and he smiles, his eyes moving between them, obviously uncomfortable that she is standing there unacknowledged, but Leo is in full flow about a piece he is thinking of writing about politics and art, something he'd tried out on her at dinner last night. Now, he glances sideways at her, then turns back to his friend.

'Hello,' Polly says, this time moving closer into their space, holding out her hand as Leo pauses for breath. 'Polly Griffin,' she says.

Leo turns to her looking slightly affronted.

'Ted Sparks,' the man says, shaking hands. 'Your name's familiar. Did you write the book on the erotic writers group?'

'I did,' she says, surprised.

'Congratulations, terrific book. I read it a couple of months ago and was planning to find an email address and write to you. I'm working on a history of gay men in Paris in the same period – there are some interesting intersections. I have to rush off now, do you happen to have a card?'

'I do,' she says, and she reaches into the side pocket of her bag and passes one to him.

'Great, thanks,' he says. 'Here's mine. Sorry about the rush but I'll be in touch.' And he pats Leo on the arm. 'Good to see you again, Leo, I guess we'll bump into each other again sometime.'

But Leo will not let him go. 'Look, Ted,' he says, walking beside him towards the exit, 'I'd really like to catch up with you back in London, can we make a time . . .?'

They are out of hearing now, and Polly watches as Leo walks out with him, putting up the umbrella, urging Ted underneath it, and they disappear out of sight.

*

'So where the hell did you get to?' Leo asks, several hours later. He stands in the entrance to their room, his face like thunder. 'I've been looking everywhere for you.'

Polly, who is sitting in the armchair by the window, gets to her feet. 'I went to the Louvre, to see the things we had decided to see together,' she says, seething.

'Well you could've waited,' Leo says, pulling off his jacket.

'I waited for twenty minutes in the foyer,' she says, coldly, wishing she was a woman who could scream and shout. 'How dare you treat me like that, ignore me, not even introduce me to your friend and then disappear with him. And he was trying to get away from you, Leo, couldn't you see that? Do you have any idea how overbearing you can be? Do you ever give a thought to the effect you have on other people, or is it always all about you?'

Chapter Thirty-three

*M*arla moves over to the pot on the stove and shakes it. 'Joyce,' she says. 'Come, Joyce, now you can put beans.'

Joyce steps up beside her. 'Now you can *add the* beans,' she says, automatically.

'No, no, *you* put them, because you are make the dish.'

Joyce puts her hand on Marla's arm. 'I'm correcting your sentence, not discussing who is doing the cooking,' she says.

'Okay, but when we cook we must cook, this be done quickly. Then you correct sentence, now you put the beans.'

Joyce adds the beans to the pan and starts to stir. 'You're a tough teacher,' she says.

'Just like you I am,' Marla says with a smile, and proceeds to lead her through the next steps of the recipe.

Joyce watches and listens, paying more attention to Marla than to the recipe. Her broad but somewhat shonky command of English works remarkably well and she has no fear of making mistakes. This woman, Joyce thinks, has the most indomitable spirit she has ever encountered. In the last few years murders and drownings have seared through the family's long struggle to survive and reach a place of safety, and yet she keeps going. Marla is stoic; invaluable in the class, supporting the other women, encouraging them in their language learning, and chiv-vying them to venture out of the confines of their temporary accommodation and try new things. She and Joyce have become friends, and although Marla is almost ten years younger than her Joyce feels her presence as a wise, older woman, the same sort of presence that Stella has been in her life. Perhaps that's a sign of my own ageing, she thinks, still stirring the beans. Perhaps as we get older it's younger women who start to play that role.

In recent weeks the students have progressed rapidly and the rapport in the group is a delight. Joyce knows she has done a good job but that without Marla's contribution they would not have made it this far. Last week the two of them managed to persuade several of the shyest members, whose meagre ward-robes were wearing thin, to risk a visit to some of the Fremantle op shops. They had spent a morning cautiously fingering fabric, choosing things and using their new language with the shop volunteers. Joyce had been moved by their obvious pride in what they'd learned, and their pleasure at finding bargains. She'd remembered the stack of boxes of Helen's clothes, currently stored in their garage, and the two huge trunks of clothes, costumes and fabrics that they had discovered when they cleared Stella's studio.

'Of course you can have them,' Dennis had said when asked about Helen's clothes. 'I just didn't want them to be thrown away, but I can't think of a better use for them. Helen would approve!'

Joyce thinks that when Polly gets back she'll talk to her about Stella's trunks. Maybe they can do another tour of the op shops and find a couple of sewing machines. If only Stella could be on hand with her skills at reshaping and repurposing striking combinations.

Now, as Marla orders her to add spices to the pan, she real-ises how much she's enjoying all this, how important it is to have something new and growing in her life: work, new ideas, new friends alongside the old.

'People was going in that house next door?' Marla says as Joyce tosses in the last pinch of spice.

'Really? I missed that. What sort of people?'

'I see only the big van, this morning. Some furnitures on the pavement.'

'Well it's about time,' Joyce says. 'First the sign went up, then it was taken down again and nothing happened. It's been empty for more than a year now.' The aroma of the spices stings her eyes and she pats them with a tea towel, just as her iPad starts to beep.

'It's Gemma,' Joyce says, 'she said she'd call today.' And she hands the wooden spoon to Marla, wipes her hands on a tea towel and clicks on the icon.

'Hi, Mum,' Gemma says, 'what are you up to?'

'I'm cooking with Marla.' She beckons Marla over so she can introduce her. And the three of them talk briefly before Marla returns to the cooking.

'Is everything still going well, Gem?' Joyce asks now. 'You and the baby, you're both all right?'

'We're both fine, Mum,' Gemma says, 'terrific. I've just been for a final check-up . . . I had to get a certificate from the doctor in order to fly.'

'Fly?' Joyce feels her heart jump into her mouth. 'Why are you flying, you're pregnant, do you have to . . .?'

'I'm fine to fly, Mum, and so is the baby. And I'm coming home.'

'Home? What, here?'

'Well that *is* my home,' Gemma laughs.

'But you said after the baby was born . . .'

'But I changed my mind, I want the baby to be born at home. I'll be back in Perth next Wednesday. So do you think you'll be able to find a space for me and your new grandchild in your busy new life?'

*

323

Mac draws back his arm and hurls the ball, sending it far and fast above the waterline to drop into the shallows where Charlie, thrilled by the chase, plunges to retrieve it. He stands there watching, massaging his bowling shoulder with his left hand; it's been giving him a bit of trouble recently, old age probably, and he's decided against trying to finish the painting this visit. Maybe Dennis will come down and help him with it sometime in winter. They can spend a few more days here together, breaking open a few cans, watching the footy, putting the world to rights. Dennis is doing fine, Mac reckons; he has his own place now and spends a lot of time at the wheelchair workshop. He also has a friend – just a friend, he has been at pains to assure them – who lives nearby. They go dancing twice a week. Helen, he'd reminded Mac, never wanted to go dancing but he'd won some ballroom dancing awards in his youth. Margaret, he says, has also lost her husband of thirty-six years within the last twelve months in similarly sudden and dramatic circumstances and this, above all else, has drawn them together.

The summer has raced away from Mac; they never managed the planned break down here with Ben and Vanessa. Joyce's work has taken more time than he had imagined, and now he too has been drawn into the support group in a small way, moving their meagre possessions into often grim accommodation, where his skill with a drill, a sander, a few planks of wood and some nails is appreciated. Sometimes he drives people to medical appointments or interviews, helps them to deal with the required form filling. He is humbled by their stoicism and determination.

It is just over a year since he and Joyce began their year of living dangerously, and none of it has been as he had predicted. He can admit now that he has become an old man, doing the things old men do in an old man's way – more slowly, more carefully, and often more thoughtfully than sometimes in the past. Savouring time, making hours and days matter. Even his grandchildren are old now; they have cars and boyfriends and live in shared houses with people he's never met. A few years ago he had feared all this, closed his eyes to reality, trying to hold off this stage of life. He had worked on beyond retirement age, believed he would want to go on doing that forever. But now he takes pleasure in other things, savouring this last gift of time, which he had once struggled to hold at bay.

Charlie bounds up to him, soaking Mac's legs with salty spray, smiling his joyful doggy smile as he drops the ball at his feet. 'Okay okay,' Mac says, bending to pick up the ball just as his phone begins to ring. 'Let me take this call first.'

'Mac, I need you to come home,' Joyce says. Her voice is strangely high-pitched and anxiety prickles through his veins.

'Why, what's happened? Are you okay?'

'I'm fine,' Joyce says. 'Totally fine, wonderful in fact. It's Gemma; she's coming home! She'll be here on Wednesday; she's going to have the baby here. And she's coming home to stay.'

Charlie barks impatiently, nudging the hand holding the ball with his hard, wet nose. Mac reaches up and throws it far enough for Charlie's temporary satisfaction. His daughter is coming home. His heart soars and he longs to hug Joyce, to jump up and down with excitement like a kid.

'But is that okay though?' he asks, suddenly anxious as he pictures Gemma squeezing into an airline seat. 'I mean, she's not got long to go, is it safe for her to fly?'

'Apparently it is, she's just within the restriction if she comes now,' Joyce says. 'The doctor has signed her off, she and the baby are fit as fiddles. We need to organise her old room, Mac, maybe we have time to paint it? Get some baby things and . . .'

'I'll be on my way in a couple of hours,' he says. 'And I'll call Dennis, we're a great painting team.'

And he stuffs his phone into his pocket, whistles to Charlie, and strides rapidly across the beach. Being old is fine, he thinks, and it will be even better because he will have real time to spend with this new grandchild, time he missed with the others as he struggled to hold the future at bay. Charlie jumps up onto his old rug on the front seat.

'Good man,' Mac says as he starts the engine. Charlie is smiling again, panting, eager as ever for a ride in the car.

'We're going home, mate,' Mac tells him. 'We're going home and we're having a baby.'

Chapter Thirty-four

April

Polly settles into her seat on the Eurostar to London with a cup of coffee. She's earlier than planned but their two week stay in Paris together had already been disrupted when, at the start of the second week, Leo checked his email only to discover an invitation to launch an exhibition of photo-journalism in Brighton.

'It's a bit last minute-ish, isn't it?' Polly had asked. 'If it's such an important collection why didn't they organise the launch earlier?'

'Apparently they did,' Leo had said, 'but I seem to have over-looked the invitation.'

Polly had turned away to hide her smile. The thought of Leo, currently desperate for relevance, overlooking such an opportu-nity was inconceivable. Besides which, the way he'd delivered this information – his eyes drifting from hers, the tension in his voice – was less than convincing. Doubtless someone had dropped out and they were grabbing Leo at the last minute, and as she thinks of it now Polly hates herself for not calling him out. But since the big argument following the visit to the Louvre, things had been going really well and she had not wanted to rock the boat. Leo, having apologised, seemed warmer, more relaxed. The weather improved, and so did he, to the extent that Polly felt he was at his best, just as he had been when they first met.

'Well of course you must go,' she'd said. 'You're the obvious person to do it.'

Two decades earlier he had published a small but influential book called *Eyes on the World*, on the power of photojournalism and its impact on understandings of twentieth-century history. She had now read all four of his books and many of his long form essays and op eds; *Eyes on the World* was, she thought, outstandingly original and undoubtedly his best work.

'I'll come back with you,' she suggested. 'We can go to Brighton together, then to London as we planned. Then I can stop off here and spend a few days in the archives on my way home.'

He'd seemed startled, as though her suggestion had somehow wrong-footed him; he had mumbled about schedules and complications.

'No, no, you should do it now,' he'd said, 'no need for you to change everything too. I'll go and do this and meet you back in London.'

And so he left early and Polly had sailed through her work in rather less time than she expected. She had called him to let him know she'd be arriving on Tuesday instead of Friday, and left a message when he didn't answer. She'd left the same message again yesterday.

'No need to call back, I'll see you tomorrow,' she'd said, and she added the time of her arrival at St Pancras, hoping he'd be there to meet her.

Now, as the train speeds north through the suburbs of Paris towards the coast, she rests her head on the seat back and closes her eyes, remembering how badly their time there had started, and how dramatically it had improved. He had been, once again, the Leo of the hotel and the emails, attentive, more affectionate, he had held her hand, from time to time spontaneously put his arm around her. And although they had not made love he seemed comfortable in bed, curling towards her, holding her. There were a couple of occasions when he'd seemed detached, dismissive, but they had soon passed, and she'd begun to wonder whether his life, which seems so devoid of anything except work and professional self-promotion, has simply led him to forget how to behave, how to manage more personal relations, how to live with intimacy or express affection. Perhaps she just needs to hold him to account more often, help him to learn to rebuild a part of himself that he has neglected. Hey ho! Stella whispers into her consciousness – trying to fix a man again, Polly?

Her phone rings, jerking her out of contemplation, and she rummages for it in her bag.

'Where are you now?' Alistair asks, his voice as clear as if he were in the seat alongside her. And her first thought is that she should have asked Leo to meet her in Bali, or taken him there last year, because Alistair is the one person who could understand Leo, translate him for her, help her to learn his language.

'On the Eurostar,' she says, 'about an hour into the journey.'

'And how was Paris?'

She hesitates.

'Uh-oh, what's happened?'

'It's not really a question of what happened,' she says. 'Lots of it, most of it, was really lovely. But we did have a big row early on when I spat the dummy.'

'Good, I suspect more of that is what's needed. Everything you've told me about him makes him sound like a man who always gets his own way. You have to stand up to him, Poll. Don't keep letting him get away with stuff because you think he's having a hard time getting old. Most of us do, especially men. But you're not his mother and it's not your job to try and fix things or find solutions for him. I've seen you do this before. Tough love, remember? Be tough.'

When Alistair hangs up Polly looks down at her phone again, at the list of times she has tried to call without success. Could he have gone away? To see his sister perhaps, and fallen into that weird state that sent him into silence over Christmas? Or maybe Judith is sick, or there's some other sort of crisis. Of course, that's what it is. It's a relief to have a reason for this silence. But Polly wonders about Judith. What sort of person exerts such a powerful and apparently negative impact on her brother? She thinks of the photograph of the house that she and Steve had studied on Google Earth, imagines Judith in her wheelchair, helpless but demanding, and Rosemary, the old school friend, short of funds and thankful for a live-in job as carer. Eventually, quite soon in fact, these two women will become a part of her own life; she's determined to get Leo to take her there before she leaves. His descriptions of Judith and Rosemary are some-what off-putting and she pictures them as older – quite a bit older than her; two of those rather haughty, horsey, elderly women with head scarves and raincoats who occupy the villages in *Midsomer Murders* and hold sway over book clubs, annual fetes and planning applications, terrorising lesser mortals.

It's mid-afternoon when she arrives to find that Leo is not waiting for her at St Pancras. Once again she calls his flat without success, and she contemplates turning up at the door, but what's the point? Tough love, Alistair had said. She needs to be less accommodating, stronger, more demanding, like she was after the Louvre. She wonders now whether she comes across as pathetic or needy. If she does then perhaps he tries to distance himself from her when she's like that. But Stella is in her head again. This is not you, it's him, this is who he is, get used to it or get out. But for Polly it's not as easy as that. Leo is a complex person, she tells herself, and she *does* know who he is: he is the man in the hotel, taking the soldier's other arm, strong, compassionate, a person of integrity. And I love him, she tells herself, and love is often hard work but worth it.

Polly hails a cab and tells the driver that she wants to find a hotel in or near Sussex Gardens. In the great tradition of the London cabbie he is a mine of information, and they make their way through the traffic to the one he recommends and she is soon ensconced in a spotlessly clean, comfortably furnished, second floor room with a bay window from which she can see down the street to the corner on which Leo lives. This arrangement makes her feel stronger, in control of the situation, in control of herself, and she takes a shower and then flops down on the bed and sleeps for a couple of hours, before trying Leo's number again, but there is still no response.

For a full fifteen minutes she sits on the side of her bed contemplating her next move. She would like to be able to step back from this, to treat it as though it doesn't matter, but it increasingly does matter, very much. This is not reasonable behaviour; they are lovers, partners, they are planning a future. Tough love. She takes a deep breath, picks up her mobile, and dials the number that Steve had found for the house in Fowey.

Almost immediately a woman answers by announcing the number – an old-fashioned habit now. She has a slight South African accent almost identical to Leo's and the sound of her voice seems to suck Polly's breath away.

'Oh, hello,' she says. 'Could I speak to Leo Croft please?'

'He's not here, I'm afraid,' the woman says. 'Who's speaking please?'

'Polly,' she says, 'Polly Griffin. I think Leo's told you about me, about us . . .'

The silence is freighted suddenly with tension.

'He doesn't live here, you know,' the woman says, eventually. 'In fact we don't see much of him at all.'

'Oh, I see,' Polly says, playing for time. 'Well you see I arranged to meet him in London, but he's not answering his phone. Do you know where I might get hold of him?'

'If he's not at his own place then I've no idea. He doesn't usually bother to tell us what he's up to.'

'I see . . . am I speaking to his sister?'

'That's me,' the woman says, in a more friendly tone. 'I'm Leo's sister, Rosemary.'

Polly goes blank for a moment. Has she got this wrong? No, surely not, he'd definitely said Rosemary was the carer. 'Ah . . . sorry, I actually wanted to speak to his sister Judith but if you . . .'

Polly hears her take a deep breath. 'I think you must be confused,' she says. 'Judith is Leo's wife, *I'm* his sister.'

Polly's throat is dry as sandpaper and the room sways alarmingly. 'His . . . wife?'

'Yes, Judith is his wife. I'm his sister and my name is Rosemary.'

'I'm so sorry,' Polly says, her voice faltering. 'I . . . I must have misunderstood . . .'

Another awful pause.

'Perhaps so,' Rosemary says, and her tone is different now, kindly almost. 'Or possibly you were given incorrect information.'

And as Polly struggles for words she hears a click as the receiver is returned to its place.

*

'Has she gone yet?' Stella asks as she and Joyce sit in the sunshine on the terrace outside her room. 'I hope she hasn't gone yet.'

'Polly's been gone for two weeks. She came to see you to say goodbye.'

Stella shakes her head; try as she might she can't remember this. She twists her hands together. 'I had something to give her . . . a letter.'

Joyce nods. 'You gave her the letter a few weeks ago. She took it to the solicitor, Mac went with her, and everything is organised as you wanted it.'

'The solicitor?'

'Yes . . . Jack. It's fine, Stella, Polly is looking after everything for you.'

'But the letter, she must read it before she goes . . .' she stops for a moment, trying to remember where Polly is going, 'to England,' she says, grasping it at last. 'Before she goes to England.'

'Yes, she read it, she saw Jack.'

'Not *that* letter.' Stella fidgets irritably. People can be so annoying, you have to tell them the same thing over and over again. 'I wrote her a letter about him, about . . . about . . .'

'About Leo?'

'No . . .' Stella rummages for the name; her head seems like a big cupboard where she can't find anything she wants. 'Perhaps . . . yes maybe. Who is Leo?' She feels very hot now, angry; no one seems to understand her these days. 'What's the matter with all of you?' she says aloud. 'Are you all stupid or something? Why don't you listen to what I'm saying?'

'Are you all right, Stella?' a woman in a blue uniform asks, appearing suddenly beside her.

'No,' Stella says in her grumpiest voice. 'No I am not all right, nobody listens to me.'

'We *are* listening to you, Stella,' Joyce says, resting a hand on her arm. 'Dorothy and I are here and we are listening to you.'

'Would you like some tea, Stella?' the woman in blue asks.

'Tea, yes, tea. My friend and I would like tea, and some cakes, no, some of those things I like.'

'Tim Tams?'

Joyce laughs. She looks at the blue woman. 'Stella's always been the Tim Tam queen.'

'Yes, we keep well stocked up,' Dorothy says with a smile. 'You settle down, Stella, and I'll bring you both some tea and Tim Tams,' and she hurries out of the room.

Stella leans across to Joyce. 'How many Tim Tams are there in a packet?' she asks, winking at her.

Joyce looks bewildered. 'I've no idea,' she says. 'A dozen maybe. Why?'

Stella throws her head back and laughs out loud. 'Wrong answer – no Tim Tams for you. Want to know the right answer? How many Tim Tams in a packet? Answer – never enough!'

It's as she bites into her third Tim Tam that Stella remembers the letter.

'I wrote her a letter about Neville,' she says through a mouthful of biscuit. 'Neville Sachs, it wasn't his real name, but like me he'd changed it. His real name was, was . . . Norman . . . Norman something or other, but he thought that wasn't good enough for an actor, not convincing, I suppose. Neville Sachs he'd called himself, he chose Sachs because it was Jewish and his mother was Jewish, he thought it made him exotic – typical! Exotic indeed!' She stops, wondering what she was going to say next, surprised to find herself talking about Neville because she never talks about him.

'So you wrote a letter for Polly about this Neville?'

'Of course, well he was the same, you see, like that man, her man.'

'Leo?'

'Yes, Leo. The same as him. So I had to tell her.' Suddenly she remembers that Polly is not here, she has gone away. 'Did she take it with her?'

'I don't really know,' Joyce says. 'She didn't mention it to me.'

Stella throws her hands in the air, knocking her glasses off the arm of her chair. 'We must find it,' she says, trying to get up, 'I must tell her.'

Joyce takes a firm grip on her arm. 'I'll look for it when I leave here,' she says.

'Too late,' Stella says. 'Too late.' She slumps back into her chair.

'Are you going to tell *me* about Neville Sachs?' Joyce asks.

'Bastard,' Stella says loudly, then she shouts it again. 'Bastard!' It makes her feel better. 'Do you *want* to know about Neville, Nancy?'

'I'm Joyce, and I *would* like to know about him.'

'Well I'll tell you, you might need to tell Polly.'

Chapter Thirty-five

eo, returning to his flat around midday, is wondering what exactly he and Polly are going to do for the next couple of weeks. It all feels like a bit of a chore now. He stands in the kitchen trying to imagine how it will be. Guests, in Leo's experience, are demanding, they want your time and space, their belongings creep into every room, their needs and wants and their individual, often irritating habits have to be accommodated. They expect attention to be paid to them. And it's not only about this visit, but about the future. Leo's vision of ageing alongside someone who will help him through that process, support him, encourage him and, of course, care for him is one thing. The reality of living with another person is something else entirely.

He wishes now that he had made a plan for them to stay somewhere on neutral territory and wonders whether he can solve this by suggesting a trip away somewhere, the Cotswolds perhaps, or Oxford, nice country pubs with cosy bedrooms, sloping ceilings, oak beams, country walks, a bit of history and some good food and wine. She'd like that, he'd like it, love it. That's what this whole thing should be about, he thinks, selected moments together, little cameos scattered into the calendar.

The message light on the phone is flashing, and he puts down his suitcase and presses 'play'. There is a message from

Marcia about a pair of glasses, and several from Polly, left over the course of the last few days, obviously with increasing irritation. She seems to have arrived early and is staying somewhere nearby. Leo stands in the kitchen pondering the situation, shaking his head. Same old, same old, he thinks, loving someone is such a trap. In his experience women always weight any sort of relationship with their expectations of how a man should behave, so that love, in whatever form, inevitably drags behind it a trailer load of responsibilities. Fall short on those and you're in hot water. Of course he should have told her that he was staying longer in Brighton, and again when he'd decided to go from there up to Manchester. But he just hadn't got around to it.

Staying on had been a last minute decision, taken when he bumped into Frank Watson at the exhibition launch.

'So you're still at it, then,' Frank had said. 'Haven't seen you around in a while. You're usually popping up everywhere like a rash – thought you must be dead. And anyway, I thought that bloke from *The Guardian* was opening it.'

'He was sick,' Leo said. 'I stepped in at the last minute. Good to see you, Frank, want to get something to eat after this?'

They'd been at university together decades ago, and their paths had frequently crossed at conferences or writers festivals. Frank was, Leo thought, looking quite seedy; he'd retired five years ago and his wife had died the following year. He looked like the stereotype of an unhappy, heavy drinking, ageing writer who wasn't looking after himself, and as Leo discovered over dinner, that's exactly what he was.

'I guess you're going to the media bash?' Frank had asked later, rummaging in his pocket for the invitation. 'They're holding it at our alma mater. John Snow's doing the keynote.' And he pushed the invitation across the table.

Leo had studied it, seething inwardly at not having been invited, and trying to remember which year it was that he had delivered the keynote. 'I must've overlooked it,' he'd said.

'Well come anyway,' urged Frank, pouring himself another glass of wine. 'In fact why not come back to Manchester and stay at my place. Joe Clark's coming, proper little house party it'll be. I'll ask Marcia too. Haven't had anyone to stay since Miriam died.'

Leo had been about to decline but the idea of a nostalgic trip to Manchester began to appeal to him. And the following morning he and Frank had taken the train from Brighton to London, stopped off at Leo's flat to pick up a couple of changes of clothes, and then taken another train to Manchester. It proved to be a lively weekend, despite the distressing evidence of Frank's self-neglect. The house was a mess inside and out; the sheets on Leo's bed smelled musty, dust coated the horizontal surfaces everywhere, cups and mugs were stained with tannin, and there were several piles of old clothes lying around as if in the hope that someone might turn up to wash them. And there were newspapers everywhere, small stacks, large stacks, damp and yellowing.

The sight of this had brought Leo up short. This couldn't happen to him, of course, thanks to the housekeeping service. Even so it was a picture of a life in decay in more than just physical terms; living evidence of the advantages of a relationship in later life. Must call Polly, let her know where I am, he'd told himself soon after they'd arrived. And an hour or so later he realised that when he'd gone back to his own place to get clean clothes, he'd put his laptop down on his desk and failed to pick it up again. Everything was in it – significantly, his address book with Polly's mobile number in it. Fuel, he knew, for another conversation about how he should get a mobile. He thought he'd ask Frank if he could log into his computer to send an email, but then the others started to arrive and he'd not given it another thought. Frank's motley crew of guests left early on Monday morning, back to London or elsewhere to work. Leo was planning to follow suit a little later until he thought he might just take advantage of being there to suss out possible opportunities.

Perhaps the place where he started might now start something new for him. But it had proved to be a complete waste of time. Anyway, Polly will be here on Friday and he should probably give her a ring now.

He picks up the phone and dials her number. The line is busy and, rather than leaving a message, he hangs up then replies to a couple of other messages. Ten minutes later he dials again and this time her phone rings at just the same moment that the doorbell buzzes. Phone in hand, he strolls to the door and opens it to find Polly standing there, pulling her own ringing mobile out of her bag.

*

Polly's call to Cornwall had left her frozen with confusion. It wasn't merely the shock of what she had learned, but the way she learned it. Rosemary's tone had changed from one of irritation to something akin to sympathy. Polly sat there, on the edge of the hotel bed, staring blankly at her phone. Was it her mistake: had she simply mixed the two women's names? But no, of course not, it was clear that one of the two women in Fowey was Leo's wife and the other was his sister. There was no way that her conversation with Rosemary could be reworked to any other conclusion. And what was that about Polly having been 'given the wrong information'? That was weird and it was then that Rosemary's tone had softened. Why? What did that mean? Why didn't she ask if she could help, or whether Polly still wanted to talk to Judith? Why . . . unless . . . unless . . . something like this had happened before; unless in the past some other woman had called also believing that Judith was Leo's sister. One other? Maybe more than one?

Polly's head was pounding, she lay down, got up again and a wave of dizziness and nausea hit her. Cautiously she lay back down, eyes closed, trying to make sense of it, trying to find another explanation. But of course there was none. Eventually the feeling passed and she got to her feet and paced back and forth across her room, reliving the months since they met, searching for clues that she might have missed. There were none, she thought at first, but as she channelled deeper she saw that there were many. He had lied to her from the start, from their very first conversations in Edinburgh when they were simply casual acquaintances. Why could he not have told her then about Judith, before she was drawn into friendship and then beyond that into love? Did he always live his life this way – like a single man? She felt sick with anger and hurt. Her love for him was grounded in her belief that he was a man of great integrity, a brilliant man albeit difficult and flawed, a man who could be redeemed by love.

You fool, you stupid fool, she'd told herself; redemption, how pathetic is that? Vying with the pain of his deception was the shame of recognition. The same old pattern of being seduced by a brilliant mind and, once there, of trying to please the seducer with appreciation, admiration, and selfless acts of caring that fed his ego. Yes, she had been more assertive than in previous relationships but she had still allowed him to determine the boundaries of the relationship. She had allowed to go unchallenged many things that seemed not quite right in the belief that by loving him she could fix him.

Finally, burning with anger, she had picked up the hotel phone and tried again to call him but this time the line was busy. So – he was back. And without hesitation, she pulled on her jacket, grabbed her room key, and set off down the street, elbowing aside a man emerging from the door of Leo's building in her effort to slip through to the lift.

'Hey,' the man called, stopping in the doorway, 'you're supposed to use the security bell . . .'

But Polly ignored him, stepping into the lift as the doors closed, impatient to stand face to face with Leo and scream at him like a banshee. Dignity, she tells herself now as she ascends to the third floor, dignity. But she aches for the satisfaction of punching him in the face. Dignity, she tells herself as she steps from the lift and presses the doorbell. Dignity. And now, as her mobile starts to ring and Leo stands there in the open doorway, she reminds herself, one more time: dignity.

A big smile spreads across Leo's face. 'Polly, you're here, excellent. I was just calling you. Soooo sorry, my darling, I've made a complete balls-up of everything, raced off to Manchester and forgot to call. *And* I left my laptop sitting here on the desk. Can you believe it? And you arrived early! But all's well, you're here now.' He reaches out a hand to draw her inside. 'Come on in, is it too early for a drink, or I could make some coffee, a cup of tea? And then we'll go and pick up your bags from the hotel. I thought we might head off somewhere for a few days, the Cotswolds perhaps . . .'

Chapter Thirty-six

April

'I still can't believe this is really happening,' Joyce says as they stand at the barrier outside the arrivals area. 'I'm not going to believe it until she walks through that door. Six years since she was last here, I'd started to think she'd never come home.'

Mac puts his arm around her shoulders. 'Me too. She really loved that job, and she loved Geneva. No more trips there for us now.'

Joyce sucks in her breath, shifts her weight from one foot to the other and yawns. It's almost midnight and she's exhausted. 'I hope she's okay, it's such an awful journey, she'll be . . . oh my god, there she is . . .'

Gemma has emerged from the customs area pushing a trolley bearing three large suitcases, and is standing looking around her.

For a moment Joyce feels she might faint with excitement and relief, and as she and Mac push their way through the waiting crowd and recent arrivals she has a fleeting moment of panic. What will it be like to live with one of her children again, to have a baby in the house? But in that moment Gemma turns and sees them, her face lights up, she looks . . . Joyce hesitates . . . well she looks like Gemma, and she looks well, and happy, and absolutely enormous.

'And you really are okay?' Joyce asks for the second time when they have done the essential hugging and kissing and blotting away of tears. 'You're . . . well you're really . . .'

'Huge? Yes I know,' Gemma says. 'And I'm fine, honestly. Emirates upgraded me to business class, what a relief that was. And yes, I really am super huge, because there's something I haven't told you.'

Joyce's heart seems to shoot up into her throat. 'What, what is it? What's wrong? Is it the baby . . .?'

Gemma grins and slips an arm through hers. 'Nothing's wrong, Mum, but yes, it's the baby, or rather babies. I'm having twins.'

'Twins?' Joyce gasps.

Gemma nods. 'Twins.'

The three of them stand there facing each other, Gemma with a half-smile on her face, Joyce stunned, and Mac slowly bursts into laughter.

'Twins,' he says. 'Two babies? Are you kidding?'

'No, Dad,' Gemma says, resting her hand on her large belly, 'does this look like one baby to you?'

Mac shrugs. 'I don't remember what one baby looks like,' he says, leaning over to kiss her again. 'You could have quads in there for all I know. Congratulations, why didn't you tell us?'

'Because I knew Mum would worry so much, especially about me flying.' She turns to Joyce and hugs her again. 'And you see, I'm fine, honestly, and super happy that I'm not an elephant with eighteen more months to go.'

Joyce stares at her daughter seeing, as always, the little girl inside the grown woman, struggling to understand how this child can possibly be having twins. She shakes her head in amazement, tears running down her face.

'Are you okay, Mum?'

She nods. 'Twins,' she says again. 'I think I've died and gone to heaven.'

It's much later that night, when Gemma is installed in her newly refurbished old room, and her bags – partially unpacked – are spread across two other rooms, that Joyce climbs into bed and stretches out, letting herself unwind. It's then the reality hits her: she is nearly sixty-eight, Mac is seventy-three, she has created a demanding job which is so much more than just a job and now, suddenly, everything is about to change. Babies, nappies, bottles, disturbed nights, teething, vomit. Two babies.

'Mac,' she whispers, rolling onto her side. 'Mac, are you awake?'

He shifts his position. 'Just about.'

'Two babies,' Joyce says, keeping her voice low. 'How are we going to manage? We're too old for this, how will we cope?'

'I honestly haven't a clue, darl,' he says. 'But we've always managed every upheaval and challenge, and I guess we'll manage this one too. Relax now, get some sleep, and we'll talk about it in the morning,' and he turns on his side, tugging on the duvet.

'But what about the father? Is he coming to stay here too? I asked about him and she got that big grin on her face and just said she'd tell us tomorrow when Ben and Nessa are here.'

Mac yawns and turns back towards her. 'Don't worry, Joyce, she's fine, looks really healthy and happy to be home. We'll know tomorrow, so until then let's stay cool, like Stella used to say – very modern. Gems is here, that's what matters. Now let's try to get some sleep.'

Joyce lies there motionless, listening to the soft sigh of his breath as he drifts, almost instantly, into sleep. He's always been able to do this, even at the most worrying times, while she is wound up, her head spinning. She makes a conscious effort to let go of the tension, closes her eyes, takes several deep breaths. Mac emits a small snore. And Joyce longs for Helen, remembers her freaking out when Damian and Ellie married, convinced that twins were on the way because there was a history of them in both their families. Helen, the one person who would truly have understood this complex mix of joy and terror, this feeling of extraordinary love and excitement alongside the anxiety of the unknown, the feeling that something is happening that she doesn't quite grasp, and the fear that she may be about to lose a part of her new, confident, independent self to the mother that she used to be.

*

'Where are we going?' Stella asks. 'I like it here, I don't want to go out.'

'Just to our place, Stella,' Mac says.

'I suppose that's all right,' she says, not entirely convinced. 'But I don't like going out.' She watches as Mac gets into the driving seat. 'Couldn't we have tea here?'

'Joyce and Nessa are making a special afternoon tea,' Mac says. 'Gemma came home yesterday – you remember Gemma, don't you?'

'Of course I remember Gemma,' Stella says, her anxiety about leaving making her irritable. 'She's in . . . she's somewhere . . .'

'She was in Switzerland, but she came home yesterday and we're having a little party, and we thought that if it was a *tea* party you'd come too. Ben and Vanessa and the grandchildren are coming, and Dennis.'

'Dennis stole my car. He came into my kitchen and picked up the keys and drove off in it and never brought it back.'

'You sold it to him,' Mac says. 'And I put the money into your bank account.'

'I don't *think* so,' Stella says, craning her neck to see her home disappearing as Mac heads off down the street. 'I think he just drove it away.'

Mac shakes his head but says nothing and they travel for a while in silence until suddenly there is a loud ringing noise. 'Stop. Stop it,' Stella says, clapping her hands over her ears, squeezing her eyes shut. 'Stop it.'

Mac is talking to someone. Stella opens her eyes and looks around for the other person.

'It's just my phone, Stella,' Mac says. 'Remember, you used to have one of these too?'

'I did? Where is it? Did Dennis take it?'

'No, no,' Mac says. 'It's packed away somewhere; you don't need it anymore. Just relax, we're going home for tea.'

Stella inhales sharply. They seem to be going very fast, houses and shops whizzing past at dizzying speed. She pushes herself further back into the seat, thrusting her legs out in front of her to brace herself. 'Where are we going?'

'To see Joyce,' Mac says. 'It's very close, look, here we are already, Emerald Street.'

Mac turns into the street and drives slowly down to park outside a big old house. It looks familiar but Stella can't quite work out why. She studies the front of the house, the roses in the garden, the verandah with the blue ceramic flower pots. 'Joyce,' she says, 'this is Joyce's house. And that's my house.'

'Spot on,' Mac says, opening the door to help her out. 'Would you like to walk in, Stella, or do you want your chair?'

'Of course I'll walk,' she says.

Mac takes her hand and slips it through the crook of his arm. 'Good, it's easier to make an entrance if you walk.' And he guides her down the path.

'Who lives in my house?' Stella asks, stopping to look at the limestone cottage next door.

'No one at the moment,' Mac says, opening the front door. 'But Polly lives in the one beside it. Remember?'

'Of course I remember, I'm not stupid, you know. Is Polly here?'

'No, but she'll be back soon.'

And Stella, still hanging on to Mac's arm, makes her way down the familiar passage to the big light room at the back of the house.

*

'Could you make sure Stella gets some of these, they're her favourite,' Joyce says. And she hands Marla a plate of cucumber sandwiches, and watches as Marla crosses the room, shows it to Stella, puts some sandwiches onto a plate on the low table beside her. Marla has been with her a couple of times to the nursing home and Stella obviously took to her immediately, but has never asked who she is. Perhaps, Joyce thinks, Stella sees so many people coming and going in there that she takes strangers for granted. Joyce had wondered whether she would actually agree to leave the home this afternoon – some days she simply refuses to go out – but she's here now, sitting beside Gemma, just as Joyce and Mac would find them, years ago, when Stella sat with the kids. They would come home to find Gemma curled up on the sofa next to Stella watching a movie on the television. It feels like a magical little peep into the past now, Gemma's bulk pressed against Stella, and Stella's arm around her shoulders. One of Marla's granddaughters has one hand on Gemma's knee and is pointing with the other to her huge belly.

'It's a baby,' Stella says.

'Two babies,' Gemma adds. 'Two new babies. Will you come to see them, help me look after them?' And the child nods slowly, seriously, as though considering what she might be taking on.

How much longer, Gem?, Joyce asks herself, how long 'til you tell us what we're dying to know?

In the shaft of sunlight pouring into the passage from the open front door Joyce sees the unmistakable silhouette of Dennis with his familiar rolling gait, heading towards her like an ageing cowboy, and behind him another taller, slimmer man. Joyce screws up her eyes against the sunlight but can't make him out.

'Batman has emerged from his cave,' Dennis calls out to her. 'Turned up last night. I didn't think you'd mind him coming along.'

Joyce walks around the worktop to welcome them. 'What a lovely surprise,' she says, hugging Nick. He has always been a favourite, perhaps for his similarity, in looks at least, to his mother. 'And what a lovely coincidence, you and Gemma home at the same time.'

'Great, isn't it?' he says, grinning widely. 'Perfect timing. It's so lovely to see you, Auntie Joyce.'

'Nick, you're forty-something, don't you think it's time to drop the "auntie"?'

Nick shakes his head. 'You'll always be Auntie Joyce to me,' and he puts an arm around her shoulders.

'So why are you back? Is it a holiday?'

He shakes his head. 'I've come to stay. Given up the job, got a research fellowship at the university.'

'Turned up, just like that, out of the blue, last night,' Dennis says proudly. 'Can't believe I'll have one of my boys back here at last.'

Nick crosses the room and bends to kiss Stella, laughs with her, and sits down beside Gemma.

Mac has opened champagne and he and Ben hand out glasses. He taps on the worktop with a knife handle.

'Okay, folks,' he says. 'I'll keep this short and sweet. Thank you for coming to help us welcome Gemma home. So good to have you all here.' He lifts his glass: 'Dennis and Stella, Nick. Sadly not Polly but I'm sure she's with us in spirit. Ben and Nessa of course, shame the grandchildren are both away at uni, but we're thinking of them. And of course our newest friends: Marla with Coco and Alesa. So, please raise your glasses to Gemma, and our forthcoming grandchildren – I'm still trying to get to grips with the fact that there are going to be two of them. So here's to you, darling girl, and your precious babies – welcome home.'

Joyce sips her champagne and nudges Dennis. 'Helen would have loved this.'

'Wouldn't she just,' he says, and he clinks his glass against hers.

As Joyce turns back again she sees that Gemma is struggling to get up and Nick jumps to his feet to help her. They are both laughing, sharing some joke probably, and then it happens: Nick says something to Gemma and raises his hand to brush a crumb from her cheek and fleetingly she grasps his hand and holds it. Recognition runs through Joyce like electricity, goose bumps rise on her skin and she knows what's happening, she knows the secret, and as Gemma raises her glass and says she wants to respond to the toast, Joyce knows exactly what her daughter is going to say.

*

'I can't believe I went all that time without knowing,' Joyce says later that night as Mac climbs into bed.

'You were admirably patient,' Mac says. 'We both were. But what a turn-up, eh? I would never have picked it. Batman! They're a couple of dark horses.'

'They've always been close, we should've guessed.'

Mac laughs. 'C'mon, we'd never have guessed that they were having a long distance relationship for more than two years between South Australia and Geneva. You'd need to be psychic to have picked that.'

'I wonder why they didn't tell us. Nick was here at Christmas, and he said he was going to Europe for New Year, even said he'd try to catch up with Gemma.'

'They didn't tell us because they knew that we, and Dennis, and of course Helen while she was still alive, would be constantly pestering them, asking what was happening, were they going to get married, were they going to come home. They wanted to do it their way in their own time.'

'Did one of them tell you that?'

'No, I may just be a bloke but I managed to work that out myself.'

Joyce rolls over and props herself up on one elbow. 'You know what? I love it that Nick went to Geneva to bring Gem home, and I love it that they surprised us. And we didn't even spot him at the airport. It's so romantic.'

'I know, love,' he says, turning out the light. 'Me too.'

He snaps the switch and plunges the room into darkness.

'I wish Helen was here, I wish she could know about this,' she says. 'She would have loved it, Nick and Gemma together: the way Nick has looked after her. She'd have loved everything about it.'

But Mac is already asleep.

Chapter Thrity-seven

Polly hesitates, frozen at the sight of Leo standing there in the doorway, relaxed, full of smiles. Her basic instincts seem paralysed. How can he stand there talking about the Cotswolds as though everything is normal? He talks on, not giving her time to respond, drawing her inside, and she moves forward with him into the foyer where the overhead skylight casts a shaft of sunshine that lights up his close-cropped hair like a silver halo. He is wearing a black, long-sleeved t-shirt and jeans and as he pulls her closer she inhales the familiar scent of his skin; her eyes are drawn to the hollow where his neck meets his shoulder, the place where she has, so trustingly, rested her head, feeling that at last she had reached an emotional safe haven. She swallows, bracing herself to pull away but paralysed by a fierce and sudden longing to sink into him, to be held, to pretend that nothing has happened, and that right here, right now, everything can be put right.

He talks on, explaining his absence, brushing aside his failure to stay in touch, and then filling her in on details of his visit first to Brighton for the exhibition, and then to Manchester. His voice seems to be reaching her from a distance, as though she is in a dream, a bad dream but one from which she is unable to force herself to wake. Her jaw doesn't seem to work, her tongue is dry and heavy. Has she said anything at all? He steers her towards the kitchen and somehow she is sitting opposite him across a bench top while he fills a kettle and fiddles with tea bags, talking, still talking, talking, talking.

His confidence, his total failure to detect anything amiss, paralyses her further. Can't he see the anger and hurt that she had seen etched on her own face in the mirror before she left her hotel room? She feels invisible, as though she is standing outside herself, watching all this play out but powerless to change it. Something in her does not want to speak. Some inner demon keeps silencing her, whispering to her that if she just forgets what she knows everything will be all right, they will be together, the two of them. The reality of that house in Cornwall and the two women in it will simply fade away, a figment of her imagination. She feels strangely unreal, light-headed, and gets to her feet swaying, steadying herself with a hand on the worktop.

'I don't feel too well.' The words seem to come from a long way away.

Leo talks on: 'You do look a bit pale, perhaps you need to lie down,' he says. And he walks ahead of her out of the elaborately fitted kitchen, and she follows him along a carpeted passage, steadying herself with her hand on the wall, and into a bedroom.

'Here we are, you have a good rest. I'll bring you some tea. Is there anything else you need?'

She wants to say yes, to ask for more, to ask for lots of things so that he will look after her, make a fuss of her, sweeten the sourness that is curdling her stomach, stop the pounding in her head. She longs for him to touch her, hold her, show her some small act of tenderness. Instead she lies down, gazing up at the elegant art deco light fitting.

'Have a rest. We can fetch your things from the hotel later,' he says.

She longs for him to come to her, kiss her, stroke her hair, feel her forehead for signs of fever, behave in any way like a lover. Closing her eyes she waits, aching for his touch. But all she hears is the sound of the door closing and his feet padding down the passage.

*

When she wakes it is like coming up from under water, struggling from murky depths towards light; but as she pushes towards consciousness she feels the sickening reality of why she is here. She stares at the glowing green figures of the digital clock by the bed, wondering how long she has been here. Then cautiously she sits upright, puts her feet onto the floor and waits, trying to remember anything significant that passed between them before she ended up in here, but it is all a blur. All she remembers is the familiar sound of Leo's voice, explaining things, while all the time her secret knowledge lay, like a hand grenade, between them. She looks around the bedroom, which is comfortably furnished but bland. It lacks personal touches, family photographs, interesting ornaments; just his wallet on the dresser, a pair of cufflinks, a small partially unpacked suitcase open on the floor. On one bedside table there are a couple of books, on the other a pair of glasses with purple frames.

She gets to her feet and crosses the room to look at her reflection in the mirror above the chest of drawers. Her face is drawn and grey; she looks as she feels, empty, drained of life, of love or passion, of energy or momentum. She runs her hands through her hair and stares a little longer. Then she opens the door to the passage, pausing briefly at the sound of voices, then walks towards them. Two voices, Leo's and a woman's, both of which break into sudden, noisy laughter. Leo is sitting in a large leather armchair and facing him, in a matching chair, is a heavily made-up woman in a mustard coloured suit, her dark hair, streaked with grey, pulled back in a tight, elegant bun.

'Polly, you're up,' Leo says. 'Feeling better? Come and join us. This is my friend Marcia.'

Polly hesitates, thinking he will get up, come over to her, make some sort of affectionate gesture, but he simply indicates another chair.

Marcia leans forward, extends a hand. 'Lovely to meet you. You're from Australia, aren't you? I've been there once, Sydney, years ago.'

And she and Leo continue their conversation about some change in the government ministry.

Polly has that other-world feeling again, as though she is not part of real life, sitting here on the edge of their conversation, marginalised like a well-behaved child listening to the grown-ups. She wonders what Stella would do in such a situation. Stride across the room, perhaps, slap Leo's face, order Marcia from the flat and then demand an explanation? But Polly knows that she is incapable of this. She is professionally confident, but in social situations that confidence deserts her. Here she sits in the prison of the polite convent girl who defers to others, doesn't make a fuss, and certainly doesn't air dirty linen in front of strangers. So many times in her life this powerlessness has immobilised her. Now her resentment grows as she watches Leo and Marcia exchanging political gossip, jokes and speculations about what will happen tomorrow in question time. Question time, she thinks, that's what I want: my own question time.

The doorbell rings and Leo gets up to answer it, giving her a perfunctory pat on the shoulder as he passes her chair, and she is alone, in the silence, with Marcia.

'Such a shame you weren't here for the photojournalism exhibition,' Marcia says. 'It was so interesting, and Leo was fantastic of course, so good of him to step in and save the day when Bruno had the heart attack. And so clever of him to give such a brilliant speech at the last minute.'

Polly feels a stab of life returning. So she was right, he was filling in for someone else. 'I'm sure he was,' she says, finding now that words are actually forming in her head and making their way out of her mouth. 'And the exhibition? Was it good?'

'Fabulous. And of course we met up again in Manchester at Frank's place. Do you know Frank? Frank Watson? No, well he's a real sweetie, but a bit sad these days. But it was a great weekend, so many people we both know from the old days. Rather too much champagne and brandy though.'

Leo pops his head around the door. 'I'll be five minutes, or less,' he says. 'My neighbour can't get into her apartment, I'm just going to see if I can help.' And he is gone.

'Such a good Samaritan,' Marcia says, getting to her feet, 'but I should make a move. I just popped in to pick up my glasses. I left them here the night before we went to Brighton.' And she sashays out, down to the bedroom and returns with the purple-framed spectacles in her hand. 'Thank goodness I have a second pair or I'd have been in deep shit!'

'Have you known Leo for long?' Polly asks.

'Oh years,' Marcia says, 'but only five or six in a relationship. It's casual of course, suits both of us.' She leans forward slightly as though to share a confidence. 'This is such a perfect set-up, isn't it? I mean, who needs a full-on relationship at our age? Leo is such a darling, soooo brilliant, and such a wonderful lover. Who needs more? And here we are, Judith his wife in Cornwall, I'm his London woman, you're his Aussie woman. Anyway, so nice to have met you.' She reaches out a hand which Polly pointedly ignores.

She follows Marcia to the door, which Leo has left partially open. 'Do mind how you go,' she says, watching as Marcia steps into the lift, closes the concertina door and begins her descent. Then she steps back inside, grabs the heavy brass handle on the inside of the front door, swings it back then slams it shut with all the strength she can muster, and watches with satisfaction as its elegant, engraved glass panel shatters. She looks down at the scattered shards of glass, pushes them around with the toe of her shoe, then stamps on them, over and over again, feeling the shards crack and splinter beneath her feet, grinding the crushed fragments into the pile of the cream carpet. Then she steps back, closes her eyes and inhales deeply; she feels the anger surging through her veins but knows she has control of it now. She has breached the boundaries of her habitual good behaviour and it is powerful.

Seconds later Leo's face appears in the empty space. 'Oh my god!' he says. 'What the hell's happened here?' And he opens the door, steps inside and looks at the mess of glass. 'I had this specially made,' he says, crouching down to pick up a small shard. 'It'll cost a fortune to replace it. How did it get broken?'

Polly stands for a moment, watching as he gathers together a few of the larger fragments. 'I smashed it,' she says. 'I slammed the door as hard as I could and it shattered. And then I stamped on some of the glass and ground it into the carpet.'

Leo straightens up. 'You did what? Are you crazy or some-thing, why would you do a thing like that? What's the matter with you?'

'You, Leo,' she says. 'You're what's the matter with me. You! You deceitful, lying bastard.'

'Hey,' he says, 'steady on! What's all this about?'

She stands there holding his gaze for a moment. 'Well, let's start with Marcia,' she says. 'Marcia who left her glasses on your bedside table, and with whom you've been having a relation-ship for five or six years.'

He drops his gaze. 'Well . . .' he begins, obviously startled. 'Well I wouldn't actually call it a relationship . . . I mean . . .'

'A relationship is what Marcia calls it.'

'She's a friend. Am I not allowed to have friends?'

'Do you sleep with all your friends?'

He sighs, moves closer to her and she steps back. 'Look,' he says, 'it's not important, it means nothing.'

Polly holds her hand up to stop him coming any closer. 'Bullshit,' she says. 'And it may mean nothing to you, or indeed to Marcia, but it means a hell of a lot to me.'

'But, Polly . . .' he lifts his shoulders, tilts his head to one side in a conciliatory manner. 'It really isn't important. I'm sorry if you're upset. Marcia behaved very badly telling you . . .'

'I'm not interested in Marcia's behaviour,' Polly says. 'But I'm very interested in yours. What I'm particularly interested in is that you've lied to me from the moment we had lunch in Edinburgh.'

'Now you're being ridiculous.'

'Really?' She pauses, taking her time, lowering her tone. 'Well then how would you describe the fact that the woman you told me was your sister is actually your wife, and her carer is your sister? Or is that not important either, is that not lying?'

The colour has drained from Leo's face. 'How did you . . . who told you . . . ?'

'Rosemary told me,' she says, enjoying his look of panic. 'She told me when I called and asked to speak to you or your sister, Judith. She said she felt I could have been given *incorrect information*. And you know what, Leo? From her tone I got the feeling that other people, other women, might have been given that same incorrect information before.'

'You mean you phoned them . . . ?'

'I did.'

'How dare you! You had no right.'

'And I suppose you think you had every right to lie to me all this time? To make me believe you loved me, that we had a future together. You lied through all those months of messages, all those conversations about the future, about how we would manage it. Was it just an ego trip to make you feel young again? Well you're *not* young, and neither am I. You are an old man, get used to it. You think that because you have a brilliant mind and some level of public recognition that you're different when it comes to getting old. Well you're wrong; brilliance will not save you from old age, from aching joints, incontinence pads, or senility. I fell in love with you – with your brilliant mind, your extensive knowledge. Well, more fool me, because what's the point of brilliance if it has no place for honesty, no empathy or compassion, if it can't get to grips with acceptance? What use is it without those? You are selfish, arrogant, emotionally ruthless, and a liar. What use is all that intellect and achievement if it makes you into a man who can love only himself?'

He stands there, apparently stunned, looking at her for a long moment. Then he drops the piece of glass he's holding onto a side table, and turns away.

'You really should calm down, Polly,' he says. 'You're over-reacting. There's no need to get all emotional about it.' And he walks over to the window and stands there looking out onto the street. 'I mean, really, Polly, what did you expect?'

'Expect? I expected honesty, consideration, commitment, love. And most of all, you lying bastard, I expected authenticity.'

There is a pause and he sighs. 'What exactly did you say to Rosemary?'

'That's your response, is it? What did I say to Rosemary? Well, very little really, I didn't need to, she obviously knew what was going on.' She pauses, but there is no reaction, he still stands there with his back to her. 'Next time I call I'll fill her in on the details.'

'You can't do that,' he says sharply, turning partly towards her but not looking at her. 'It's none of your business.'

'*You* made it my business and I'll do whatever I like. Maybe I'll go and visit them, tell them everything, or perhaps I'll just put it in a letter.' She has no intention of doing any of this but she can see that it's getting to him.

He turns fully now, looks her fleetingly in the eye, then beyond her. His face is expressionless, like a mask.

'This really is very silly,' he says. 'You have everything out of proportion and you've obviously upset Judith and Rosemary, and probably Marcia as well. How am I supposed to deal with this? How am I supposed to clear up the mess you've made? I'm surprised at you, Polly, surprised and, frankly, disappointed. I expected better of you.' And he turns away again, his back to her, his arms folded across his chest looking out of the window.

His words, his posture, the turning away all flick a switch in Polly's head and in that moment she sees how well he knows her, how well he can play her, how he homes right in on her fear of male disapproval, knows how to side-step her rage and make her feel small, and powerless. She wavers for a moment, then knows that she must leave now, before he does more damage to her. And she grabs her bag which is sitting on the side table, walks out of the door, slams it once again and, ignoring the lift, runs down the wide curving staircase with its claret coloured carpet and out into the street.

Chapter Thirty-eight

Bali, May

'So is that the last time you spoke to him?' Alistair asks, handing her a large gin and tonic. 'Did you speak again? Has he tried to contact you?'

Polly shakes her head and sips her drink. 'No, thank goodness, not a word. I left his place, went back to my hotel, went online and changed my flights, and left the following morning . . . yesterday, no . . . two days ago . . . I've lost track of the time.'

She stops abruptly, drained by the effort of having told them the whole story, and by a long journey during which she relived her relationship with Leo over and over again, each time discovering clues that she should have picked up from the start. She had arrived here exhausted and heartbroken, and it is only now, that she has felt able to talk about it. The empowering rage she had felt in the apartment has long gone, banished by his final cruel cut of manipulation, his attempt to put her back in her box. And she is left now adrift in a sea of shame.

'I hate myself,' she says slowly. 'I hate myself for believing his lies, for being sucked in by him, and for what reason? I still can't work out why he did it. Why me? Why didn't he pick on someone nearer home? Why not someone younger and glamorous? Isn't that what ageing men do to help them feel younger?' She takes a deep breath and then a large sip of her drink. 'And in the end, you know, it was how he behaved right at the end that was so shaming, more even than the lies and manipulation. The way he dismissed everything I said, his failure to give me one shred of acknowledgement or respect. What did I do to deserve that?'

'Nothing, darling,' Alistair says. 'You did nothing to deserve it; none of this is your fault. In fact it's probably not about you at all, this is all about Leo, don't you think, Steve? It's all down to him.'

Polly shakes her head, brushing his reassurance aside. 'I was vain enough to attribute his sexual failures to impotence or fear of it, but no, it was me obviously, because according to Marcia he's a wonderful lover.'

Alistair laughs out loud. 'Well she *would* say that, wouldn't she? It's what she wants you to think – that *you're* the problem, because it's certainly the same with her. That's why she made a point of it. I don't doubt for a moment that he can't get his rocks off with her either. It's not an uncommon problem at our age.'

'Al's right,' Steve says, 'at least about most of this. But part of it *is* about you. I think he *did* fall for you, Polly, that he loved you or thought he did, or might or could. He saw something in you that he wanted and needed. I suspect he actually saw your strength, your intelligence, and probably your ability to empathise. He saw a lovely woman who could make him feel good, solve some of his problems. But he's a typical narcissist, his overall behaviour and particularly the things he said at the end, that's classic narcissism. He was at least being honest then because those things *don't* matter to him. The marriage is only a piece of paper – an annoying responsibility. The business with Marcia is not important to him. And he treats you like this because you aren't important to him. The only thing that's important to Leo is Leo himself. He is only interested in you and Marcia and his wife, anyone else at all, for what they can do for him – how you make him feel, and how he appears to other people when you're with him. If this hadn't happened now in the way it has, it would have eventually crashed in some other way when it got too complicated for him. He is the centre of his own world – everyone, everything else is expendable. That's the narcissist for you; it's a recognised personality disorder. Oh, and it explains the refusal to get a mobile too. Narcissists are secretive, a mobile would make him far too accessible. You could go on talking to Leo about all this, questioning him, forever, Polly, and you will never get anything more, because there is nothing more to get.'

Polly sighs, shaking her head, realising that maybe someday she will find solace in that, but that seems a long way off.

'Of course, it's very similar to what happened to Stella,' Alistair says later, over dinner.

Polly stares at him. 'Stella? I don't know what you mean.'

'Well, with that actor . . . what's his name . . .?'

'Neville Sachs,' Steve says.

'That's him. Remember, Poll?'

'I haven't a clue what you're talking about,' Polly says, helping herself to more salad. 'I mean I know, or rather *did* know, Neville Sachs, but what's he got to do with Stella?'

'She didn't tell you? She told me she'd written you a letter in case she forgot.'

'Well she was going on about a letter before I left, but I don't know where it is. And how do you know about it anyway?'

'She rang me, soon after she'd written it. When was it now? Oh I remember, just after New Year, the day you left here, when you were on your way home. That's right, it was before the stroke, that same day. She rang to tell me that she'd written you a letter about Neville Sachs.'

'I'm still confused. Why did she write a letter if I was on my way home?'

'Because she thought she might forget to tell you about it. About her and Neville Sachs.'

'Are you saying she had a relationship with him? Surely not, he was an awful man, arrogant, self-obsessed, no concern for anyone but himself and . . .' she stops. 'Uh-oh, I see what you mean.'

'Yes, well she thought if you knew what happened to her you might think twice about getting any more involved with Leo. I told her that no one wants to hear horror stories that might relate to the person they're in love with. But she insisted you had to know, and then she insisted on telling me too.'

Polly laughs affectionately. 'That sounds like Stella, no beating around the bush. So what happened?'

Alistair grimaces. 'Well it was all a bit garbled and I can't remember all the details and it was before you two met, but to cut a very long rambling story short Neville Sachs was married to a woman with some sort of mental illness. He had moved her to a cottage in Tasmania, with a carer, and he lived in Melbourne and never went near her. When Stella told me that I remember thinking there were elements of *Jane Eyre* to this; you know – the mad woman in the attic, the deception, the final hideous conflagration. Anyway, Stella knew nothing about the wife and fell madly in love with Neville because although she knew he was a deeply flawed person, she believed all that crap about the love of a good woman having the power to rescue a man from his own darkness. Pause for the sound of violins! Neville sounded a right bastard actually, and there are bits of the story that I've forgotten but the relationship went on for some time and eventually Stella got pregnant and then discovered that he was also having it off with another member of the cast of whatever play they were in at the time. *And* he already had a child by someone else. So she turned up at his door demanding an explanation, and he treated her rather like Leo treated you, as though she was stupid and emotional, making a fuss about nothing. They had a big fight and she slapped him across the face, and he pushed her and knocked her over and she fell down three steps between one part of the room and the other. And he just picked her up, pushed her out of the door and locked it. Being Stella of course, she wouldn't give up, hammered on the door for hours, shouted and screamed. But she also began to feel sick and giddy, and she lay down on the doorstep and woke up hours later feeling terrible and the long and the short of it is that she miscarried the baby. Oh yes, and what made her call *me* was that she had woken up that morning, the day she called me, to find herself lying on the bedroom floor and it made her want to tell you, to warn you.'

There is silence around the table. Polly closes her eyes, thinking through the story again, her own sadness diluted now with sadness for Stella. 'She never told me,' she says quietly. 'I thought we were so close but she never told me this.'

'Don't start making this into something about your not being a good enough friend,' Alistair says as Steve refreshes their drinks. 'Stella didn't tell you because she was *ashamed*. She said that all her life she has been so ashamed that she never told *anyone* until she told me. And by that time she had already written it down for you, and I don't think that was easy for her, after all that time. She was ashamed, and she kept blaming herself for not being good enough. But that's what these bastards do, narcissists, they have no concern for anyone else, they can't love any*one* or any*thing* but themselves and they leave a trail of heartbreak wherever they go.'

'But why didn't you tell me?'

'Because I thought you would have got the letter when you got home.' He hesitates. 'I'm sorry, Poll. Would it have made any difference if you *had* known?'

Polly stares at her plate, pushing salad around it with her fork. 'I don't know. I mean, I'd have been devastated for Stella, but would it have stopped me? Probably not. You're right, no one wants to listen to cautionary tales. I deliberately avoided letting her tell me what she thought of Leo. But I think it does make a bit of a difference now. Knowing what happened to Stella . . . knowing how that sense of shame affected her. I think knowing that helps . . .'

*

Three days later Polly steps out of a taxi at five in the morning and lets herself in through the front door.

As she walks down the passage through to the kitchen she feels the house enclose her like a safety blanket. My place in the world, she whispers, and she knows that it will be some time before she is ready to leave again. As always she walks through the rooms one by one, savouring the silence, the stillness, the scent of lemons, but wishing too that she had never let Leo in here to this precious space, knowing that it will take time to exorcise the traces of him that seem to hang in the air. In the kitchen she opens the back door to the garden where the last of the roses are still in full bloom, their perfume floating up to greet her. She sits on the verandah, remembering last year, when she came back from Edinburgh and walked through the gate to Stella's garden to see her sitting there, in her big chair, the pages of her script on the decking at her feet. For a terrible moment then she had thought that Stella was dead, but she had shifted her position, and the sickening dread that had gripped Polly's stomach had lifted.

Back in the kitchen she picks up the pile of mail that Joyce has put there for her. On the top is a sealed white envelope, with 'Polly' written across it in Stella's familiar scrawl. Attached to one corner of the envelope is a yellow post-it note from Joyce: *Stella is anxious that you read this letter, she forgot where she left it but I found it in the spare bedroom.*

So this is the famous letter. Polly turns it over and carefully peels back the poorly sealed flap. There are several pages of fine lined paper. *Dearest Polly*, it begins, *there is something I need to tell you and if I don't write it down now I may not remember it later.* It stops there and there is a big gap. Then it starts again, this time written with a different pen. *I want to tell you about something that happened to me a long time ago, it's about a man, you may remember him, an actor called Neville Sachs. I loved him, I believed he was the love of my life . . .*

And that's where the letter stops. The writing goes on but only the occasional word is legible. There is just page after page of spidery scrawls, wavy lines, letters cramped together, not one complete phrase or sentence. Polly folds the pages and holds them to her face, feeling as though she is inhaling the effort that it took to fill them. Carefully, she tucks the letter back into its envelope, takes it through to the bedroom and starts to unpack, to take back the life that had seemed complete when she left Edinburgh, but which now has a Leo shaped hole in it. A hole that she knows will take a long time to heal.

Chapter Thirty-nine

Stella watches as the woman in blue, whose name she can't remember, bustles around making her bed. She smooths it out nicely, tucks the blankets tightly, just as Stella likes it, then she picks up the empty tea cup from the bedside table, takes it out to a trolley in the passage and comes back.

'Shall I wheel you down to the lounge now, Stella?' she asks. 'It'll be exercises in about half an hour.'

Stella is finding everything a bit of a burden these days. There is so much to remember, so many people she doesn't know, it's all very confusing. She wishes Nancy would hurry up, she'd promised to come again soon.

'I think I'd better stay here,' Stella says. 'I'm expecting a visitor.'

'Well we can send your visitor to find you in the lounge,' the woman says.

'I want to stay here,' she says. The trouble is you can't trust people. Nancy might turn up and not know where to find her, and then she'd go away again. 'Nancy's coming to get me,' she says. 'She's taking me home with her.'

The woman smiles. 'That's nice,' she says. 'I haven't met Nancy. You don't mean Polly, do you? Or Joyce perhaps?'

Stella shakes her head irritably. 'I *said* Nancy,' she says. 'Nancy, my aunt, she says it's time to go.' She rests her head on the back of her chair. The woman's face has changed, she looks anxious now.

'Well,' she says, 'I'll keep a look-out for her and bring her to you when she gets here. And I'm going to leave your door open just a bit, Stella, then she can see you.'

*

Joyce makes her way down the passage towards Stella's room. The door is propped ajar and she can just see Stella sitting there in her chair by the window, her head drooping, nodding slightly. She pauses. If Stella is asleep maybe she shouldn't disturb her. But then Stella jerks suddenly, shakes her head and looks around.

'Hello, Stella,' Joyce says, pulling up a chair to sit closer to her. 'I've brought you some Tim Tams, I'll just pop them in this bag.' And she slips the packet into the cotton bag attached to the arm of the wheelchair.

Stella looks at her as though trying to remember who she is. 'Joyce,' she says. 'I was expecting someone else.'

'Polly perhaps?' Joyce suggests. 'She got back very early this morning and she's coming in to see you later.'

'Polly, yes. I want to see Polly,' Stella says, and she grasps Joyce's hand. 'Tell Polly she must come soon, come today. Before . . . before . . .'

Joyce pats Stella's hand. 'Before what?'

'Before Nancy comes, she's coming soon you see, we're going home, and Annie's there, we're going to see her. Nancy came the other day, you know, and she said she'd be back today.'

Joyce's heart skips a beat. She nods, holding on to Stella's hand, while her skin prickles at the meaning of Stella's words. 'How is Nancy?' she asks.

'Oh she's fine,' Stella says. 'She loves what I've done to the house. And there's room there for Annie too, the three of us. That's nice, isn't it?' Her voice is weak, the words beginning to slur.

A lump of sadness is forming in Joyce's chest. 'It's very nice,' she says. 'I wish I'd met Nancy. I am sure I would have liked her.'

Stella turns her head to look at her, but Joyce can tell that she does not see her. There is something remote, something entirely un-Stella in her gaze.

'You can meet her if you like,' Stella says. 'Come back later and she'll be here.' And she closes her eyes and rests her head on the back of the chair.

Joyce sits beside her, holding her hand, until she feels Stella's grip slacken. Then, sighing, she gets to her feet and bends to kiss her forehead. Then she walks out of the room, out of the building to her car, and sits there for a few moments, sobbing, before she starts the engine and heads for home.

*

The first thing Polly notices when she gets to the nursing home that afternoon is that Stella looks exceptionally frail. Has she been like this for some time?, she wonders. Did I simply not notice this before I left? Although Joyce had confided her fears, the sight of Stella comes as a shock. She is sitting, motionless, in her chair by the glass door in the residents' lounge, watching two doves on a birdbath out on the terrace.

Polly puts a hand gently on her arm. 'Hello, Stella,' she says and Stella turns to her in surprise.

'Oh, Annie, how wonderful! They told me I'd never see you again, they said you were dead. But Nancy said you'd come.'

Polly thinks she looks as though the effort of speaking has worn her out.

'It's Polly, remember, Stella? I've been away.'

Stella looks puzzled for a moment. 'Yes, you're Polly. I was waiting for you and you didn't come.'

'But I'm here now. I've been to Paris and London. I thought about you a lot while I was there, the stories you told me about the times you were there.'

'Did you see Neville?'

Polly takes a deep breath. 'Neville's dead, Stella, he's been dead a long time.'

'Good! I'm glad, he deserves to be dead. Good riddance.'

'I got your letter,' Polly says. 'I read it all.'

'Did I send you a letter?'

'You did – a letter to help me, with Leo.'

'Who?'

'Leo, do you remember?'

Stella looks at her puzzled, agitated. 'Who's that?'

Polly smiles. 'Oh, just someone I knew.'

Stella makes a clucking noise with her tongue. 'I keep forgetting things.'

Polly takes her hand. 'It doesn't matter,' she says.

Stella turns to her now, face on. 'Are you all right, Polly? I was worried about you, but I don't remember why.'

Polly's first impulse is to pretend but she stops herself. Stella deserves the truth.

'I've had a bad time, Stella, a bit like your bad time, but it's getting better. I'll be better soon, and seeing you helps. How do you feel?' she asks. 'Is there anything I can get you, anything you need?'

Stella shakes her head, drops her head back against the cushion on the chair. 'Nothing. I'm waiting for Nancy now. I wonder if Annie will come too.'

Polly bites her lip.

'We were waiting for you to come home first, Polly.'

Polly nods. 'I know,' she says. She wants to grab Stella by the shoulders, beg her to stay, not to leave her alone. She takes a deep breath. 'You can stop worrying, darling,' she says. 'I'll be fine, so when Nancy comes . . .'

'I love you, Polly. You are everything to me, sister, daughter, dearest friend.'

'And you to me Stella,' Polly says, unable now to control her voice, the tears sliding down her cheeks. 'I love you so much,

Stella. The best things in my life, the finest lessons I've learned, have all come from you.'

And she sits there, holding Stella's hand, for another hour, until Dorothy suggests that Stella might need to sleep in bed rather than the chair. And slowly Polly slides her hand free, gets to her feet, leans over to kiss Stella's cheek, and walks out of the lounge and into the street where the first drops of rain are starting to fall.

Chapter Forty

Late May

'Another year, another funeral,' Mac says four weeks later as they make their way slowly out of the crematorium. 'Another beautiful friend lost.' And he draws Polly's hand through his arm, and they stroll slowly together past the bouquets and wreaths, towards the car.

Polly had watched and waited in agony during the seemingly endless days in which Stella refused food and drink, refused to speak, turned her face from anyone who spoke to her. She had sat at the bedside for hours, days, holding Stella's hand, talking quietly to her of the days when they worked on *Neighbours* and the ecstatic reviews of the new series of *Cross Currents*. Sometimes she read her the reviews from her own scrapbook of clippings. And when Polly left to go home to sleep or eat, Joyce or Gemma or Mac had replaced her.

The news of Stella's passing has travelled across the country to cities, towns and suburbs, to remote stations and tiny communities where her work brought pleasure to so many people over so many years. Her fans, both young and old, download clips from YouTube, they post pictures, messages and memories on Facebook. And for the first time ever Stella is trending on Twitter.

'She'd have liked that,' Mac says, 'she'd have felt it was very modern.'

Back at the house he makes the appropriate toasts, and watches as the women who loved Stella, and whom he loves, struggle with the weight of their loss.

Gemma sits on the sofa, pressed firmly into the corner where Stella used to sit. Joyce staves off tears by handing out food and topping up glasses, and Polly, looking grey and cold as death, struggles to make conversation with some of the mutual friends she had shared with Stella.

'Is this how it will be from now on,' Mac asks Dennis, 'losing people all the time?'

'Yes and no,' Dennis says. 'Our numbers are thinning, mate, but we've got a good few years left in us yet. And you and I are going to be grandfathers again soon. I wish Stella had been here to meet the twins, to teach them to misbehave. But that's new life, Mac. New life, that's how it goes.'

*

The days run on into June and slowly Polly feels that she is beginning to rise once again to the surface, to breathe clearer air. She has worked hard since she came back from London, forcing herself to focus on writing rather than the painful conflicts of anger, hurt and shame that she has brought home with her. As a result she has finished her book, but she is poised now, both emotionally and creatively, in that liminal state between what is done and what comes next. She struggles with the prospect of blank space – nothing captures her imagination, nothing calls to her – and she wonders whether she will ever want to write again, the passion and commitment to start something new has deserted her. Next door, Stella's house is also an empty space. Still filled with Stella's things it feels to Polly like a tomb, but she hasn't the heart to contemplate change. And so a couple of times a week she opens the windows to the sharp morning air, and wanders between the rooms remembering times they spent there together, wondering how to use it now, and what Stella would have wanted.

Somehow, since she got back, she has not been able to bring herself to tell Joyce and Mac what happened in England. She had intended to tell them straight away, but Stella's almost immediate decline and then her death have paralysed her. She feels broken, shamed; a foolish old woman duped by the prospect of love. Her friends, she thinks, all saw Leo for what he was. She alone was blind and deaf.

'How was it?' they have all asked. 'What did you do? Did you and Leo get on all right? Did you have a really great time? It must have been wonderful to be in Paris together.' And she has deceived them by saying as little as possible. It was good. Paris was great. We did all sorts of lovely things. Yes we were fine together. But she can see that they suspect something is wrong and her own deception disgusts her. She remembers how when she felt disappointed or uneasy about Leo she had reassured herself by remembering the man she had met in the hotel passage, the strong, compassionate man who came to her aid while everyone else was fighting their way out. She remembered the man with whom she walked in silence the following morning, and whose company she had so much enjoyed in the next couple of days. But now she knows that this was illusion; that she saw what she had wanted to see, and had clung to that image. Leo never was that man in the passage and she had refused to let herself see that.

One morning as she sees the students making their way home past her front window, Polly realises that Joyce will now be back in her own house, and she wanders through the back gardens and sticks her head around the door.

'May I come in?'

'Of course. I'm making coffee, want some?'

'Please.' She hauls herself onto a stool by the worktop. 'Anything happening next door? Have you seen anyone?'

Joyce shakes her head. 'No and it's not for want of trying. I had a good old stickybeak before class this morning. The furniture arrived ages ago, Marla saw it. Jennifer heard that the people who bought it were living overseas. Moving back sometime soon.' She pushes a packet of biscuits towards her. 'Could you open these and put them in the tin for me?'

Polly picks up the packet. 'Oreos? What, no Tim Tams?'

Joyce laughs. 'Between you and me I'm a tiny bit sick of Tim Tams. I think Arnotts' profits must be on the decline now.'

Polly thinks Joyce looks unusually stressed and anxious. Balancing her work with looking after Gemma and preparing for the babies is taking its toll.

'Is there anything I could do to help, Joyce? With the students, or with the preparations for the babies?'

Joyce hoists herself onto a stool and pushes a mug of coffee towards her. 'Thanks, Poll, I could do with some help in the classes. Just helping to facilitate the conversation groups. Marla's very good with that, but just half an hour now and again would be great.'

'Count me in,' Polly says. The prospect of something new and distracting is more than welcome. 'Every day if you like.'

'Really? You're sure? That would be a life-saver. I've got so many more students now and I'm finding being an expectant grand-mother quite stressful at the moment. Gemma tries to pretend she's laid-back about it all – you know – mother of twins at forty-two – but I know she's anxious. We're all a bit tense really, getting on each other's nerves. The house suddenly seems really small! Anyway, enough! How's Leo, when are you going to see him again? You haven't mentioned him much recently.'

'Ah, Leo,' Polly says, picking up the mug of coffee. 'Um . . . well . . .'

'You can tell me to mind my own business.'

'I want to tell you, Joyce, it's time.' Polly swallows some coffee and begins her story.

Joyce listens, watching her closely, reaching out at one point to take her hand across the worktop. 'But you never said anything,' she says. 'I remember asking you when you got back and you said you'd had a good time in Paris, but you've been struggling with all of this alone.'

'Not entirely alone. I told Alistair and Steve when I stayed there. But I couldn't bring myself to tell you, Joyce, because I felt so stupid and gullible. The way he treated me when I confronted him was so shaming. I felt small and worthless and it's taken me all this time . . .' And she pauses, realising that she does feel different from when she related this to Alistair and Steve. Something has shifted; she can now separate the grief for what might have been from the shame that has crushed her.

'So, there it is,' she says finally. 'I'm coming to terms with it, trying not to reproach myself, and to remember that the shame lies with him. That's hard when each time I think of him it is as he was on that last day. Trivialising me, dismissing my reactions, my questions, and failing to accept any responsibility. He reduced me so much. Shame is a limpet, it clings on contact and hangs on. It is so hard to break free from it.'

'You were in love, Polly,' Joyce says. 'You were authentic, which, as you told him so clearly, he was not. You followed your heart and that takes courage, especially at our age. I am so sorry you've been so hurt, but you have nothing to be ashamed of.'

They talk on and eventually Polly slides off her stool. 'Thanks for listening, Joyce. I'm so glad I've told you at last. Would you tell Mac and Gemma for me?'

'Of course.' Joyce puts the mugs in the sink, walks towards the door with her. 'Not long now,' she says. 'In one way it's lovely having Gem and Nick here, but we've grown accustomed to having the house to ourselves, and so it all seems a bit much. Lord knows what it'll be like when the twins arrive. Nick wanted them to rent a place, but Gem wants to be nearby. I think she's more anxious than she appears.'

Polly stops at the kitchen doorway and turns back. 'D'you think they'd like to stay in Stella's house? Or would that feel odd? I mean, it has everything they'd need, all the furniture, crockery, linen, everything still there . . .'

Joyce stares at her in silence. 'Stella's house?'

'Well yes, why not? I should have thought of it before. It would give you all some space but they'd be right next door.'

Joyce's jaw drops. 'Really? You wouldn't mind?'

'Of course not, I'd love it. I hate it being empty, have done since the day Stella went to hospital, but I haven't known what to do with it. If you think they'd like it, they could stay there for as long as they want.'

They step outside the back door and Joyce closes her eyes, takes a deep breath. 'It would be the perfect solution. Gemma's always loved that house.'

'Well then . . .' Polly begins.

'Joyce! Joyce!' Mac calls suddenly, appearing at the side-gate to Stella's garden. 'Come quickly, Joyce, Gemma's in labour.'

They run down the back steps, across the terrace and in through the gate, looking around them.

'Quick,' Mac calls from the studio doorway. 'I've called the ambulance. I was in the garage and Marla called me. She's in the classroom with Gemma, they were repairing some of the textbooks and Gemma's waters broke.'

Polly sees that the colour has drained from Joyce's face. She hesitates at the door and Polly puts her hand on her back. 'Go on, Joyce,' she says, 'you can do this.' And she pushes open the door and Joyce walks into the classroom.

Mac catches Polly's arm. 'What should I do?'

Polly stops, looks at him. 'You're asking *me*? Crikey . . . um . . . well, clean towels, I should think, lots of them. Boiling water – I'll boil the urn in there, you do the kettle and some saucepans – and loo rolls probably, lots, for mopping up the . . . well the . . .'

'The blood,' Mac says. 'I'm onto it.'

Polly takes a deep breath and pushes open the door.

Gemma is on her hands and knees, panting in unison with Marla, who is on her knees alongside her. On her other side, Joyce, also kneeling, is making comforting noises and rubbing

Gemma's back. 'Any sign of the ambulance?' she calls to Polly, who goes back out of the door across the front garden and into the street, scanning it in both directions.

'Nothing yet,' she says.

'You forget ambulance,' Marla says, 'these baby don't wait for no ambulance. They be borned in this classroom. Come now, Gemma, when I tell you push, you gotta push . . . steady now . . . wait . . . wait . . . now *push*.'

And with a scream that makes Polly's blood run cold, Gemma pushes, and pushes, then pushes some more.

*

'I see you've got new neighbours,' Dennis says. 'Met them yet?'

'Not yet,' Mac says, snapping the top off a beer and handing it to him. 'They moved in on Monday, only saw them from a distance. Youngish, they look. About time, the place has been empty for more than a year.' He raises his beer. 'So, two grand-daughters, what d'you reckon?'

'I reckon it's bloody marvellous. They're very small, though, aren't they? Do you think that's okay?'

'I think we've just forgotten how tiny ours were,' Mac says. 'These girls are fine. The hospital wouldn't have let Gemma bring them home if not. Cheers – I think this makes us grandfathers-in-law.'

'Cheers. You don't think they'll give them silly names, do you?'

'Like what?'

'Well, Beyonce or Taylor or what's that other one, comes from Cyprus. . . Oh I know, Mileage.'

'Mileage?' Mac says, shaking his head, then gives a sudden snort of laughter. 'D'you mean Miley Cyrus?'

'That's her. Fancy calling your kid Miley or Beyonce.'

'I doubt that either of those is on the cards,' Mac says.

'I'm glad we got the house ready in time for them,' Dennis says, leaning back in the big cane chair on the terrace. 'I thought they'd keep Gemma and the babies in hospital longer, it was a bit of a rush, but we're pretty good at this decoration and renovation lark now. A crash team.'

'You're not half as glad as I am,' Mac says, laughing. 'I was working out how to soundproof our bedroom. I'm too bloody old for night-time feeds and teething.'

'I wish Helen was here,' Dennis says suddenly. 'Not with me, I don't mean that. I just wish she could've seen Nick and Gemma together. She always said they'd end up together. Said they were made for each other.' He shakes his head. 'I just wish she could see them now, with the baby girls.'

*

'Estelle is such a lovely name,' Polly says as a tiny hand grasps at her finger.

'It *is* a lovely name,' Joyce says, 'but that's actually Helen.'

'I don't think so,' Polly says. '*This* one is Stella's namesake.'

Joyce shakes her head. 'Polly . . . I'm her grandmother. I can recognise my own granddaughters.'

Polly laughs. 'I know you recognise them, Joyce, but you can't tell one from the other.'

'And *you* can?' Joyce sounds a little affronted.

'I can because I am the godmother to both of them, and I've memorised Gemma's instructions on distinguishing marks. Estelle has a small mole on the back of her neck.'

'Yes, I know that,' Joyce turns the baby on her side and puts on her glasses, 'and I think you'll find that . . . uh-oh! Sorry, you're right. This is Helen.'

Marla laughs out loud. 'You two, so funny.'

'I hope you dames aren't squabbling,' Gemma says, appearing in the doorway. 'Look, I was taking the stuff out of the top of Stella's wardrobe, and on the very top shelf I found this.' She walks into the room, kneels down on the floor, and puts a large photo album, bound in faded red leather, onto the coffee table. 'It was tucked away, right up the top at the back.'

'I remember Stella looking for this album,' Joyce says.

'Me too,' Polly says. 'I think she was looking for photographs of Annie at the time, or her aunt Nancy.' She takes the album from Gemma, and opens it to a photograph of a slim, attractive woman, hair piled on top of her head, holding the hand of a small, plump girl in a smocked dress, standing outside this house. The child's head is tilted to one side, her face screwed up against the light. In one hand she holds a toy sized trowel, and her knees and socks are grubby with earth.

'Stella with Nancy,' Polly says, choking back a sob. 'Look at her, she looks so grumpy, she always hated gardening.'

'I bet she was a real handful as a kid,' Joyce says.

And they turn the pages slowly, watching as Stella grows through adolescence and teenage years to a twenty-first birthday party, as she poses with Annie on the Manly ferry, to her first leading role on stage at His Majesty's theatre, to leading roles, taking a bow, in Paris with Annie and . . .

'Oh my god!' Polly says suddenly, at a shot of a very young Stella, backstage, laughing, clutching a bouquet, and alongside her, a man. An older, debonair looking man with a fine black moustache. 'It's him, that's Neville Sachs.'

And they pore over the photograph, Polly, Joyce, Gemma and Marla.

'So what is this man?' Marla asks.

The others exchange a glance. 'A bastard,' they say in unison.

And Marla laughs. 'They everywhere,' she says. 'All over the world.'

Polly rocks back on her heels, still studying the photographs. 'She had such an extraordinary life,' she says. 'And so did Annie, who of course was better known than Stella and died in her early sixties. In fact,' she hesitates, a shiver of excitement running through her, 'I could write their stories, two friends, both actors, eccentric, talented women who made it in the theatre and on the screen. This is it, this is what I need to do next.'

*

'I can't believe that I got so caught up in Leo that I didn't even see the story in front of me,' Polly says later that evening when she and Joyce are sitting out by Joyce's pool, wrapped in big scarves, gazing up at the clear sky of a mid-winter night.

'Sometimes the most precious things are right under our noses,' Joyce says. 'Those small things that matter so much, the things you can barely put into words, a moment, a feeling, a glimpse of the past, and suddenly it all falls into place. And you see the whole picture. Sometimes what we need is right in front of us and it just takes time to recognise it.'

They sit there in silence until a sound floats out on the still air, the sound of a baby crying, softly at first but soon gathering volume and energy, and then another baby starts. A light goes on in Stella's house, and then another.

'Hmm,' Polly says, 'they've got fine pairs of lungs, your granddaughters.'

'They sure have,' Joyce says. 'But you need to remember that when they wake half the neighbourhood at night, they're *your* goddaughters. It's when they are being adorable and perfect – that's when they're my granddaughters. Time for bed, I think, and I don't feel in the least bit guilty.'

*

On a bright, cold morning a couple of weeks later, Gemma, having struggled with the seemingly endless morning routine of feeding, winding, washing and dressing the babies, perches briefly on the edge of a chair at the kitchen table and tucks into a bowl of muesli, as her daughters are falling asleep. It's ten-thirty and she's already exhausted. A shower if I'm lucky, she thinks, and maybe if they're still asleep, I might get an hour of sleep myself. But by the time she is showered and dressed, little grunts and moans from Helen, the more restless of the two, tell her that there will be no peace this morning.

'I think we'll go for a walk,' she says, picking Helen up and kissing her, just as Estelle starts waving her arms and kicking.

She wraps them warmly, puts them into the pusher, and makes her way out through the front door, down the path and turns right at the gate. Ahead of her she sees someone coming out of the house where Nick's family used to live.

'Signs of life,' she murmurs to the twins. 'Interesting.'

The woman is backing out of the front door, just as she does, manoeuvring a pusher down the steps.

'Hello,' Gemma says, stopping at the end of the path.

'Oh hi!' the woman says.

She looks younger than me, Gemma thinks, and fitter. 'I'm Gemma,' she says, 'next door but one.' And she points back to Stella's house. 'How's it going, settling in all right?'

'Sort of,' the woman says. 'But I don't think a new house and a new baby are an ideal combination. I'm Stephanie, by the way. Oh my god, you've got twins, they're gorgeous. But however do you cope?'

'Who says I'm coping?' Gemma says. 'But I'm lucky, my mum lives here, and she points to Joyce and Mac's house.'

'Lucky you. My mum lives in Barcelona with her third husband.'

They both laugh.

'You walking this way?'

Stephanie nods. 'Yep, to the bakery on South Terrace.'

'Me too.'

They walk in silence for a moment.

'I'm so glad we've met,' Stephanie says. 'I was feeling a bit bleak, not knowing anyone. My husband's away quite a lot.'

Gemma smiles. 'Then you've come to the right place,' she says. 'You'll be fine here, we're big on neighbours in Emerald Street.'

Acknowledgements

Cate Paterson you are a legend! Thank you for rescuing me when I was drowning. Special thanks too to Mathilda Imlah for coming in at a late stage with wise and thoughtful suggestions and, as always, to Jo Jarrah for applying her forensic editing skills to get me out of trouble. And to all the staff at Pan Macmillan who work so hard to turn a story into a book and get it out there on the shelves. You are simply the best.